THE KREMLIN DEVICE

To Janet and Sarah

THE KREMLIN DEVICE

by

Chris Ryan

Century · London

First published by Century in 1998

Copyright © Chris Ryan 1998

Chris Ryan has asserted his right under the Copyright, Designs and
Patents Act, 1988, to be identified as the author of this work.

First published in the United Kingdom in 1998 by
Century, 20 Vauxhall Bridge Road, London SW1V 2SA

Random House Australia (Pty) Limited
20 Alfred Street, Milsons Point, Sydney
New South Wales 2061, Australia

Random House New Zealand Limited
18 Poland Road, Glenfield
Auckland 10, New Zealand

Random House South Africa (Pty) Limited
Endulini, 11a Jubilee Road, Parktown 2193, South Africa

Random House UK Limited Reg. No. 954009

A CIP catalogue record for this book
is available from the British Library.

Papers used by Random House UK Limited are natural, recyclable
products made from wood grown in sustainable forests. The
manufacturing processes conform to the environmental regulations
of the country of origin.

ISBN 0 7126 7996 0 – Hardback
ISBN 0 7126 7989 8 – Paperback

Typeset by SX Composing DTP, Rayleigh, Essex
Printed in Great Britain by
Mackays of Chatham plc, Chatham, Kent

'For what is a man profited,
if he shall gain the whole
World, and lose his own
Soul?'

By the same author
The One That Got Away

Novels
Stand By, Stand By
Zero Option

ACKNOWLEDGEMENTS

I wish to give special thanks to someone who shall remain anonymous but without whose editorial help I would never have finished this. To all my family and friends for all their patience and understanding. Also to Mark Booth, Liz Rowlinson, Katie White and Rachael Healey at Century.

GLOSSARY

ATO	Ammunition technical officer
Bergen	Rucksack
BG	Bodyguard (noun or verb)
Blue-on-blue	Accidental strike on own forces
Casevac	Casualty evacuation
CND	Compact nuclear device
COBR	Cabinet Office Briefing Room
Comms	Communications
CQB	Close-quarter battle
CTR	Close target reconnaissance
DF	Direction finding
Dicker	Lookout
Director	Officer commanding special forces, generally a brigadier
DOP	Drop-off point
DPMs	Disruptive pattern material, camouflage garments
DZ	Drop zone
EMOE	Explosive method of entry
ERV	Emergency rendezvous
Exfil	Exfiltrate
FMB	Forward mounting base
FOB	Forward operating base
FSB	Federal Security Bureau, part of former KGB
GPS	Global positioning system, navigation aid
HALO	High altitude, low opening
Head-shed	Headquarters
Incoming	Incoming fire
Int	Intelligence
IO	Intelligence officer
Kremlin, The	SAS headquarters
LO	Liaison officer

LUP	Lying-up point
LZ	Landing zone
MAC	Military Air Command
Magellan	Brand-name of GPS
Omon	Special forces, Russian Ministry of the Interior
OP	Observation point
PJI	Parachute jump instructor
PNGs	Passive night goggles
PUP	Pick-up point
QRF	Quick-reaction force
Rat	Radio alarm trigger
RTU	Return to unit
Rupert	Officer
SAM	Surface-to-air-missile
Satcom	Satellite telephone system
SAW	Subversive Action Wing
Scalie	Signaller
SCR	Satellite Communications Responder
SEAL	Sea, Air and Land American special forces unit
SOCO	Scene-of-crimes officer
SP	Special projects
Spetznaz	Russian special forces
SSM	Squadron sergeant major
US	Unserviceable
VCP	Vehicle control point

RUSSIAN EXPRESSIONS

Babushka	Granny, little old woman
Chush!	Rubbish!
Chyort!	Damn! (literally 'devil')
Davai	Carry on
Dosvidanya	Goodbye
Huinja!	Bollocks!
Idyom	Let's go
Isvinite	Sorry, excuse me
Kak dela?	How goes it?
Kakovo khuya sidite?	Why the fucking hell don't you shift your arse?
Khorosho	Good
Khuyevo dyelo!	Shit!
Konechno	Of course
Kontraktnik	Professional soldier
Mne zhalko	I'm sorry
Nichevo	Not to worry
Orushiye k boyu	Stand by
Otlichno!	Great!
Pojaluista	Please
Polkovnik	Colonel
Poshli!	Go!
Poyekhali	Bottoms up
Prinyato	Roger, got it
Spasibo	Thank you
Starik	Old man, veteran
Starshina	Warrant officer
Tochno	Precisely
Uchodite	Get lost
Valite otsyuda	Piss off
Vas ponyal	Roger, understood
Vot beda	Pity

Vpered!	Go!
Vstali i poshli!	Shift your ass!
Vzdrognem	Cheers
Ya ne znayu	I don't know
Yefreitor	Corporal
Yestj	OK
Zdorovo	Brilliant
Zdravstvuite	Hello

ONE

With the tailgate open, the cabin depressurised and five minutes to run, we'd all gone on to individual oxygen. That knackered voice communication: for one thing, we had masks over our mouths, and for another the Herc's four turbo-props were deafening. We were wearing covert radios, with throat mikes on our necks and earpieces under our helmets, but we couldn't use them until we were in the final stages of our descent, because of the risk that they'd foul up the pilots' comms.

Our PJI – the Parachute Jump Instructor from Hereford – stepped along the line of bulky figures, giving our kit final checks. The hold was so dark he was doing most of the work with his hands, following lines and straps with his fingers, pulling on rings and clips. Then the red jump-warning lights came on, like half ping-pong balls one either side of the tailgate. Two minutes to go.

Our kit made us cumbersome: GQ-360 chutes on our backs, oxygen tanks on stomachs, 120lb bergens clipped upside-down on the backs of our legs and tucked high under our chutes, so that they rested against the backs of our thighs from knee to arse. Our weapons, 203s or Minimis, were tied with para-cord to our left legs. With that lot on I had a job to waddle to the rear of the plane.

As leader of the team, I'd be the first to jump.

Stars wheeled across the big, square opening as the pilot put in his final turn. I glanced to my left at Harry Price, known to all as Pavarotti, the hefty Welshman famous for singing in the showers and for the eyes tattooed on the cheeks of his arse. He'd had them done one night when he got pissed in Cardiff, by a

1

Chinese bloke for a fiver a side, and the eyes were a bit slitty.

Now, under his helmet, goggles and oxygen mask, not much of his face was showing, but I could see the muscles in his jaw working as he swallowed. He was thinking the same as I was: for fuck's sake, let's get out of this damned aircraft and on our way.

Anyone who says he's not nervous when about to free-fall at night wearing full equipment is bullshitting. All eight of us were crapping bricks. A night-time HALO – a high-altitude, low-opening drop – is no picnic, however many times you've done it before. After two seconds you're heading for the ground at 125 miles per hour. You roar through the first thousand feet of air in ten seconds, the next in five, and so you keep going.

A clean free-fall is one thing; a drop with full kit something else, because of the risk that your load may move and render you unstable. Tonight we were jumping at 22,000 feet and dropping to 4,000 before we popped our chutes: a free-fall of ninety-five seconds. This way, on this moonless night, we'd come out of the blue – or rather, out of the black – as far as anyone on the ground was concerned: until our chutes deployed nobody would see a thing.

Our target was a clearing among the chestnut forests of the Cevennes where, according to the exercise scenario, partisan forces would be waiting to guide us in, meet us and take us to safe houses.

The captain of the aircraft had given the wind as eight knots on 260 degrees – just south of west. We were going to jump four ks west of our target and fly ourselves in towards it. The sky was clear but the air was full of turbulence, and the Herc kept juddering and twitching so that the guys were being jostled against each other as we huddled on the ramp.

Somebody gripped my right arm. I twisted and saw it was the head loadie, asking with thumb up if I was all set. I nodded and gave him a thumb in return. He raised a single finger. One minute to go. Cushy bastard: we were going out into the black night while he was safely tethered to his aircraft by a harness and long webbing strop. By the time we hit the deck he'd be well on his way back to Lyneham and a warm night tucked up in bed . . . I caught myself up. Geordie, I told myself, stop pissing around. You're in the SAS, and this is what it's all about. If you did the crew's job you'd be bored out of your mind.

I passed the signal to Pavarotti and glanced down at my altimeters, one strapped on either forearm: both dials were registering 22,000. I felt the angle of the floor change slightly as the pilot throttled back, dropping speed for his final run-in towards the DZ. Screwing my head round, I got a glimpse of Whinger Watson, my second-in-command. All I could see was the red light glinting off his goggles, but I could imagine the oath he was muttering to himself: 'Firekin ell,' again and again. He and I were the old men of the party: at thirty-six and thirty-seven, we could almost have been some of the guys' fathers.

Time for last-minute checks: harness straight, bollocks clear of crutch straps, bergen in position, weapon secure, mask tight, gloves on. I reached round and bent the Cyalume light velcroed on to my bergen, cracking the glass phial in the middle and setting the chemical reaction going so that everyone would have a marker to steer towards when they followed me out of the plane.

Thirty seconds to go. Into my mind came a sudden vision of Moscow. For a moment I imagined we were doing a night drop into the heart of the city, heading down towards all those red-brick towers and golden onion domes. I knew that the dark land below us was France, not Russia, and that we were only on a preliminary exercise; but Moscow was our ultimate destination, and for the past few days we'd heard so much about Spetznaz, Omon, Alfa Force, the Mafia and the break-up of the KGB that I'd started seeing red in my sleep.

Then I felt the head loadie grip my arm again. I tensed myself and hunched forward.

The two little jump-warning lights were still on. Still on . . . Still on . . . Then the bottom half of each ping-pong ball sprang to life. *Green on!*

GO!

All I had to do was tumble forward, head-first into the black space outside. Lean forward – gone.

As I cleared the belly of the aircraft upside-down, the slipstream hit my front with a huge thud. Head up, chest out . . . An instant later I was horizontal and falling in a good position – face down, arms and legs spread, chest thrust out, steering with my hands turned up and out. The engine scream had been replaced by the roar of air blasting past my helmet.

So far, so good. Now I needed to get eyes on the other guys, make sure everybody was OK. Pavarotti had jumped a couple of seconds behind me, the others after him. I wanted to slow my descent so they could catch up. Bending in the middle, I de-arched myself – that is, curled my body into a banana shape to increase resistance to the air.

Staring down, I saw long streaks of haze between ourselves and the ground: a thin layer of cloud. As I hit it, drops of water stung my cheeks and forehead like fire. A second later I was through, and aware of someone coming down on my right, a black shape slanting in at an angle, monochrome, but more solid than the surrounding darkness. Another appeared, then another. There was no way of telling who was who, but I was glad they were keeping a safe distance from me, facing inwards in a wide ring.

I stuck out my chest again and straightened out to pick up speed and keep pace with them.

Below us the wooded hills were crow black, not a light in sight. Then, at three o'clock to me, I saw a brilliant spark flare up: a Firefly, our reception committee. Now I could count six other guys around me, all more or less level. Good work. But where was the seventh? Maybe behind me, out of my vision.

For a few moments I positively enjoyed myself. Hurtling through the night, keeping control, gave a feeling of terrific exhilaration. I was free as a bird, flying; everything seemed easy. Inside the thin gloves my fingers were freezing, but what the hell!

Again I thought irrationally, Moscow, here we come!

Against the illuminated faces of my altimeters the hands were unwinding fast. My mind was making continual checks: I'm

4

fine. Eighteen thousand. My position's stable. Sixteen. Keep that posture. Left hand down a bit. Now you're OK. It's fourteen. You're good. It's twelve.

Then *wham!* Some heavy object flew down from the side and slammed into the back of my right leg with a terrific blow. Jesus, I thought, a meteorite. No – a falling human body. The impact knocked me out of the posture I'd been working to hold. Worse, it knocked my bergen from its central position behind my knees and pushed it over to the outside of my left leg. In an instant I was destabilised, still face-down, but spinning.

I knew I was in the shit. A spin is the worst thing that can happen to a free-faller, the fate everybody dreads. If one starts on its own it may wind up slowly, and you stand some chance of correcting it. But after an impact of that kind, you're away. The combination of momentum and air pressure is so ferocious that you're rotating like a propellor, and that's you gone.

I struggled with hands, arms and legs to adjust my posture, to regain control. But whatever I did, I just spun faster. For the first few seconds my mind stayed clear. Maybe one of the lads will see what's happening, I thought. Maybe someone will steer in to give me a hand. Then I realised, No, they can't. This is too violent. If anyone tried to make contact I'd smash them, or they'd smash me. We'd break limbs, knock each other out. If they've got any sense, they've pulled off to a safe distance. I'm on my own.

All this went through my mind in a flash. Then I thought, I'm going to have to cut my bergen away. Pull the cord to dump it. Lose all my kit. But by the time I'd taken that decision it had become physically impossible. The centrifugal force of the spin was so great I couldn't get my hands anywhere near my body. No way could I reach my knife, still in its sheath on my right leg. My arms were locked straight out, hands and fingers throbbing with the pressure of blood forced into them. They felt as if the skin was going to burst. My head seemed to be swelling, too, the skin round my eyes bulging, vision deteriorating. Geordie Sharp, I told myself, this is it. During your career in special forces you've got out of plenty of tight corners, but this time, finally, you're fucked.

I wasn't exactly frightened; everything had happened so fast there was no time to worry. I just seemed to accept that fate had got me by the short-and-curlies, and I was going in at 125mph. Obliteration, I thought. Fair enough.

In fact I must have been losing consciousness. Then an almighty jolt brought me back to my senses. It was as if a huge hand had arrested me in mid air. The thump knocked the breath out of my lungs, and I was still spinning, but much more slowly. It took me a few seconds to realise that the auto-release had fired my main chute, and that I was descending more slowly, in a sitting position.

Instinctively I reached up and pulled on the webbing strops to test the reaction. Something wrong: a rough, grating feeling, too much resistance. Glancing up, I saw from the outline of the chute against the stars that the canopy was lopsided. Instead of being rectangular, it was all sharp angles. The rigging lines had tangled round each other in the spin. Instead of working down to a position just above my head, the spreader bar had become jammed in the twisted ropes.

Because it wasn't properly deployed, the chute started spinning as well, winding me around like a fairground ride. But by then, thank God, my mind was back to normal. I saw my options clearly. I was descending much too fast. If I couldn't free the main chute in the next few seconds I'd have to cut it away and deploy my reserve. Also I'd have to ditch my bergen, because its weight was too great for the reserve chute to support.

I held the strops and started giving violent twists, turning my body hard to the left. The third jolt did the trick. Above me there was a hefty *smack* as the chute deployed fully, then a twitch came down the lines. When I next looked up, the spreader bar had slid down to its proper place and everything was back to normal. I took a few deep breaths, thanked my lucky stars and turned my attention to the ground.

As far as I could tell, I was little the worse. My eyes felt funny and my face was glowing red hot, but nothing was broken. My breathing was OK, vision fair. There was the Firefly, away to my left. Because of the spin I'd drifted several hundred metres off my heading.

I'd just started steering back towards the DZ when I became aware of someone else flying in dangerously close to me. What the hell was he doing?

'Piss off, you stupid git!' I shouted. Still he came at me, slanting in.

Belatedly I realised that, now that we were under canopy, the others should already be on comms. I switched on my set and immediately heard guys coming up to check in: 'Seven, roger . . . Eight, roger.' Then Whinger was saying, 'Come in, One. One, are you OK?'

With a jab on my pressel switch I said sharply, 'One, roger. I'm all right. And I'd be even better if some cunt hadn't flown into me. Now get off the air.'

After that close call, the rest of the exercise seemed pretty tame. Our reception committee met us in the forest clearing. They'd seen nothing wrong, and didn't realise we'd almost had a fatality; when they heard, there were a good few *mon Dieus* flying about, but I'd recovered my composure, and we let down the tension by having a laugh. We quickly established that it was Pavarotti who'd nearly written me off. I couldn't hold it against him, because it turned out that he himself had gone unstable when clearing the aircraft, and he'd had a load of trouble of his own. The result was that he'd got separated from the rest of the group. He'd been flying back in to re-establish contact when the collision occurred, and he'd never seen me until the impact.

'Christ, Pav,' said Whinger. 'With eyes in your arse like you've got, you ought to be able to see in every fucking direction at once.'

As we gathered up our chutes, Pav and I felt our legs stiffening from the bruises we'd sustained, and knew we were going to be pretty sore in the morning. But our French colleagues spirited us past the opposing forces and put us in position to take out the power station that was doing duty as the enemy's comms centre.

No snags there – and after a wash-up next morning, we

moved into the civilian phase of our exercise, which required us to make our way back into England under assumed identities. Use of the tunnel was banned, so we had to travel by sea, using either Dover or Folkestone. The rules laid down that we had to land between midday and midnight – and we knew that the immigration authorities had been briefed by the Int Corps guys from Hereford. In other words, the bastards were poised to intercept us.

We travelled up to the Channel individually, and by the time I reached Calais at about 6.30, after two nights with no proper sleep, I was knackered.

One of the first people I saw on board the ferry was Whinger, easing his nerves with a quick pint of lager in one of the bars. It wasn't beyond the bounds of possibility that someone had put dickers on the ship, trying to eyeball us before we'd even landed; so I went past without giving any sign of recognition. With his Mexican moustache, Whinger looked every inch a veteran SAS operator, and I had myself a private bet that the watchers would pick him up. His face was deeply lined, with telltale furrows up his cheeks and across his forehead, giving it that strained, prematurely aged appearance brought on by years of pushing yourself to the limit.

If I was being honest, I'd have to say I looked much the same, with the odd grey hair appearing. Worse, my eyes were so bloodshot from the centrifugal force of the spin that I looked like Count Dracula after a satisfactory attachment to some young lady's jugular.

One thing I knew for sure was that I did *not* want to get caught in the net and have to submit to prolonged interrogation. I'd been through all that six years earlier, during my first tour with the Subversive Action Wing, the most secret unit within the SAS. That first time I'd been pulled in and put through the mill. Now, as then, everyone assigned to the SAW had to be able to maintain a cover identity for up to thirty-six hours: it was an essential part of our training, especially when a delicate task like our trip to Moscow was in prospect. It wasn't that, as commander of the team, I felt I should be exempt from such indignities: just that I was tired, and the thought of answering endless questions gave me a pain in the arse.

I'd toyed with the idea of wearing shades when I came to Immigration, but I dropped it, because all they do is attract attention. Instead, I'd gone for a white baseball cap with a long peak, green on the underside, that came well forward over my face. What with that, a blue T-shirt, jeans and trainers, and a scruffy little civilian haversack on my back, I hoped I could pass for the self-employed carpenter I was claiming to be. I'd also taken the precaution of loading up with booze, like all the genuine tourists and day-trippers around me.

I found myself a seat in the forward upper lounge and settled down. All round me people were laughing and chatting, kids screaming; but I pulled the peak of my cap down and closed my eyes, which were itching and aching, and the next thing I knew a voice on the tannoy was blaring out that we would dock in five minutes' time. I'd managed to sleep the two-hour trip away.

I had time for a wash and the hundredth run-through of my own cover identity, just in case I was pulled. According to my passport I was Malcolm Barrow, aged thirty-six, from Alnwick in Northumberland. I'd been to France to visit friends who'd bought an old pub in Normandy and wanted some restoration done. I had the name of the place in my head – L'Auberge au Vieux Puits – but, conveniently for me, it was very primitive and had no telephone, so no quick checks could be made.

Our cover stories had been created by the Firm – our name for MI6 – and were adapted from our own real backgrounds. Because I'm obviously a Geordie, by my accent, my phoney address was in the correct part of the country: Castle Row, Alnwick. The first names of my parents were Derek and Mabel. The telephone number I'd use – a real one – was that of my brother, who'd been primed to tell anyone calling that Malcolm was on a job in France. Often the lads got muddled when they gave the names of imaginary parents, and, under cross-questioning, confused them with the real ones. But for me it's easier: being an orphan brought up by my Uncle Phil, I never knew any real parents, and so had no trouble remembering Derek and Mabel.

We were off the ship in short order. Normally these days there's practically no passport control at the Channel ports; but that evening immigration staff manned all the desks, probably for their own training, and certainly as part of our exercise. But as the crowd was lining up to go past the desks I got a lucky break. Immediately ahead of me was a stunning black girl in a lime-green top and skin-tight, lemon-yellow satin pants, lugging two bags of bottles in one hand and dragging a small, coffee-coloured kid along with the other. I didn't deliberately position myself behind her, you understand: she just happened to be there. The point about her was that one of her carrier bags was splitting.

'Eh,' I went, 'watch yourself. You're about to lose a few bottles.'

I bent down, picked up the child and held it on my hip – a boy, by the look of him.

'What's the matter?' she said sharply. 'I'm OK.'

Probably she thought I was trying to pick her up. Maybe she didn't fancy my fiery eyeballs.

'No, really,' I said, 'it's no bother.'

A second later we were side-by-side in the immigration queue, looking like any other couple coming back from a holiday. She smelt of lemon, too: lemon pants, lemon scent. Nice.

She was glaring at me and I saw that she was really *very* pretty, with a wide mouth and big hazel eyes. She looked so suspicious that I couldn't help smiling.

'I've got a kid of my own,' I said. 'Older than him, but much the same. It's quite a way to carry him. Maybe you can take my passport and hand it over. How's that?'

'It's a deal.' She relented and gave a dazzlingly white smile: 'What's your name?'

'Malcolm. Mal.'

'OK. I'm Jane.'

We closed on the cubicle as a pair, and the short, sandy-haired guy in occupation was so riveted by her cleavage that he scarely got his eyes on our documents or on me. In a couple of seconds

10

we were through and waltzing through the Customs hall. Glancing back, I saw Whinger in another of the queues, still on the wrong side of the barrier.

As soon as we were clear, I said, 'Thanks. Where would you like him taken?'

'We're on the train.'

'OK. This way.'

When I sneaked another glance behind me I saw that Whinger had been rumbled: the man on the desk had stopped him, poor bugger, and called in a superior.

We started walking again and I said, 'Where are you going?'

'London. Don't tell me – you're coming as well?'

'Wish I was. No – I'm driving. But I'm not in any hurry. I'll see you on board.'

In the terminal a train was already standing at the platform, so I did as I'd promised and sat the child down and waved goodbye, not without a touch of regret. Lemon Jane could have been a lot of fun.

Then, as I stepped back on to the platform, I was jerked out of my reverie by the sight of a stocky, fair-haired young guy walking past. There was something familiar about his shape and gait – a bit of a roll in his walk – but at first I didn't recognise him. Then suddenly I saw that it was Rick Ellis, one of our team, wearing a blond wig. I almost called out to him but stopped myself just in time: it was still conceivable that someone was tailing him, and I didn't want either of us compromised.

Crafty sod! His disguise had carried him clean past Immigration, and it looked like he was away.

I knew that anyone captured would be taken to the Intelligence Corps headquarters at Ashford, which was running the exercise, so I dug my mobile phone out of my pack and called the Ops Room. After being passed around for a bit I heard a familiar Scottish voice – Jock Morrison, the Assistant Int Officer from Hereford, who was monitoring the interrogations.

'How are we doing?' I asked.

'They've got two of your guys here already, and they reckon they've just picked up a third at Folkestone.'

Whinger, I thought. But all I said was, 'OK – I'm through, and I'm coming in.'

I knew the lads would have been taken across in blacked-out vans so that they wouldn't know where they were, and although they wouldn't get physically knocked about, they would have a hard time of it all the same, being deprived of food and sleep, and repeatedly brought back for re-interrogation throughout the night.

Having hired a Golf from the Avis desk in the terminal, I shot up the M20 and reached Ashford in under half a hour.

'How did *you* get through?' Jock demanded when he saw me.

'Walked,' I told him. 'What's the crack?'

'They're questioning two of the lads now.'

The Central Control Room had a bank of TV monitors ranged high along the front wall, each connected to one of the interrogation rooms. A couple of guys in shirtsleeves were watching them and making notes, exchanging the odd remark.

On one screen was Johnny Pearce, one of our weapons specialists, twenty-eight years old, black-haired and high-complexioned, looking even darker than usual under a couple of days' stubble. His long eyelashes gave him a deceptively gentle appearance, though in fact he was as hard as they come, and an ace at martial arts. A Scouser, he'd practised kick-boxing ever since he was a kid. He always said he'd needed it to survive in school, fights taking place every day in front of appreciative audiences, and every boy having to look after himself.

Johnny was wearing an open-necked, short-sleeved blue shirt and sitting on an upright wooden chair in the middle of the cell-like room. Facing him across a bare wooden desk sat a detective in a pale grey suit. The camera was looking straight at Johnny from somewhere behind the interrogating officer, whose head and shoulders were visible at the bottom of the screen. Johnny looked tired but calm, and whenever one of the controllers turned up the sound on his channel, his answers sounded perfectly composed.

'You said you went to school in Worcester?'

'That's right.'

'How come you have a Liverpool accent, then?'

'Born there. Never lost it.'

'All right. What was the name of the school again?'

'Hadlow Comprehensive.'

'Address?'

'It's on Kidderminster Road.'

'Does it have its own sports fields?'

'Yes.'

'Where are they?'

'Right behind it.'

'Swimming pool?'

'I dunno about now, but it didn't then.'

'What dates did you say you were there?'

'Let's see.' Johnny paused. 'I must have gone there in eighty-three, left in ninety-one.'

'That's funny.' The detective's voice remained level and polite. 'We've checked the records, and they don't mention anyone called Martin Turner attending between those dates.'

'Really?' Johnny raised his eyebrows and looked coolly at the man opposite. 'You know they had a big fire the year after I left, in the spring? I think a lot of records got burnt.'

'Well, we'd better check again . . .'

Good on yer, Johnny, I was thinking. Great stuff! I knew his cover story nearly as well as he did, and I could see that he was sticking to it. The home team was probably bluffing: Johnny certainly was, and he seemed sure they were. Since this was Saturday, and in the school holidays, how could they have checked the school records?

'Good!' said one of the supervisors in the control room. 'He's doing well. I like that.'

Next door, things weren't going so well. Pete Pascoe, a Cornishman, was letting his temper get the better of him. His reddish hair and moustache hinted at his Celtic origins: he could be a fiery devil and needed to watch himself.

His interrogator seemed to have realised this. 'Your family,' he said. 'Your brother's how old?'

'Twenty-four.'

13

'And he's a mechanic?'

'That's right.'

'What's his address?'

'Twenty-eight . . . twenty-eight Northcourt Avenue, Reading.'

'That's where you said your *sister* lives.'

'It is. She does. Simon lodges with her.'

'He's not married, then?'

'No.'

'But she is?'

'Of course. I told you.'

'And her married name?'

'Jenkins.' Suddenly Pete's patience ran out. 'For Christ's sake!' he snapped. 'We've been through all this before. Have you got nothing better to ask?'

'Just checking,' said the detective smoothly. On the monitor I could see Pete's nostrils working in and out – a sure sign that he was getting steamed up. Beside me, one of the supervisors made a grimace and wrote something on his notepad.

I watched for a while longer, but then I thought, To hell with this. It was amusing to see the guys getting grilled, but I decided the time could be better spent: we still had a long way to go in preparing for our Russian trip, and not many days in which to get everything done.

I looked at my watch: 9.35. The exercise had gone on long enough. That sort of thing's OK if there's no big deal in prospect, but we had a hell of a team job to tackle. What we should all have been doing was learning Russian, not pissing about with cover stories in pissy Ashford. It was time we went back to Hereford and got stuck into our final training.

A guy from Spetznaz, the Russian special forces unit, was due in on Monday, coming to have a look at our set-up and give us advice on kit. On Thursday our advance party would fly to Balashika, the base outside Moscow, to suss out the accommodation and facilities, with the main party following within two weeks.

I slipped out of the control room and found Jock Morrison.

14

'Listen,' I said, 'do we have to go through with this?'

'What's the matter?'

'I want to stop it. For one thing, they've only caught three of our guys. I'm through, and I know Rick Ellis is too – I saw him boarding a train. I bet the other three are clear as well. And anyway, we've got more important things to do than sit around here playing games.'

'Well . . .' Jock looked doubtful. 'It's not my decision.'

'I know. It's down to me. Tell you what – we'll give it another hour and see how things are going then. I'm going to call the Feathers and find out who's made it.'

The Feathers Hotel, on the old London road, was the RV for anyone who'd passed through the screen. We'd got rooms booked, but it was a sure bet that the lads would be in the bar, so I had my call put through there.

'Have you got a Mr Terry Johnson there?' I asked, using Rick's cover name.

'One minute,' the guy replied. There was a pause, during which I could hear the buzz of conversation, then Rick came on the line.

'Mr Johnson?' I said in a phoney, genteel voice. 'I saw you, you poncified twit.'

'Who's that, for fuck's sake?'

'Geordie. I was behind you at the station.'

'Never saw you.'

'No, but I saw you. Who else is there?'

'Dusty, Mal and Pavarotti.'

'Four of you! That's everyone accounted for, then.'

'Where are you, Geordie?'

'In the torture chamber. They've got Whinger, Pete and Johnny. But listen – I'm going to call it off in a minute. Are they still doing food over there?'

'Just about.'

'Ask them to keep four dinners, then. We'll be across in an hour.'

Back in the control room, Pete Pascoe was still on the second screen, but one glance told me he'd got hold of himself and

15

settled down: he was now looking quite comfortable. As for the first screen – there was Whinger, claiming to be an undertaker called Solomon Grice, and bombarding his detective with outrageous remarks. He'd always been a bit of an actor, had Whinger, and in situations like this he could crack an extra edge on to his native Cockney accent, making himself sound almost like a caricature of what he is anyway – a true East Ender. Throw in the horrible rhyming slang, and no interviewer has a chance.

When a second interrogator took over and asked him to confirm his name, he instantly said, 'Hell of a price.' Only after a few seconds of blank silence did he come up with the second half: 'Solomon Grice.' In the next minute he said, 'Give 'em a chance' for 'South of France', then, when asked where his father lived, he replied, 'Ask some boffin.' Again he waited before completing the equation: 'In his coffin.'

'You mean he's dead?'

'Course he's fucking dead. Been dead for twenty years, ennie?'

I looked at the nearest controller, who was trying to suppress a laugh, and said, 'You'll not get anywhere with him. Not a chance. He's done this too often.'

'You could be right.'

'Let's pack it in, then. The guys are all doing OK. The rest are at the RV. We might as well join them there.'

So it was that we piled into the Feathers for big plates of lasagne and a few pints of Shepherd Neame's Spitfire ale, while we shot the shit about how we'd reached the Channel.

TWO

The moment we'd got wind of a team job in Moscow, word had spread through SAW like a charge of electricity. Russia! The very notion had put the wing on an immediate high. The Regiment had never worked there before. In the Communist era, of course, the idea would have been unthinkable. For as long as anyone could remember, Russia had been the arch-enemy, the big, ugly bear on the eastern horizon, threatening the rest of the world with nuclear destruction.

My only personal involvement in the Cold War had been during the early eighties, on stay-behind exercises in which members of the Regiment had literally gone to ground on the West German border, opposite the Soviet and East German troops on the other side of the line. We'd dug ourselves in, camouflaged the shelters, and spent three weeks at a stretch underground. Buried on top of each other, breathing the foul air, shitting into plastic bags . . . It had been a filthy experience which had almost driven several of the lads round the bend. The plan was that, if the Russians launched World War Three, their front units would roll over us, and we could come up behind them, to report troop movements, direct Western air strikes and suchlike. Everyone had known that, if it happened for real, we'd be on a one-way ticket. So, what with that and the discomfort, the whole experience hadn't been very cheerful.

Now things were entirely different. As part of the programme of co-operation between our Prime Minister and their President, the Subversive Action Wing had been tasked to go out and train Tiger Force, a special unit newly formed to fight the ever-increasing menace of the Russian Mafia. With the rupert who normally commanded the SAW away in the Far East on another assignment, it had fallen to me to lead the training team and take it out.

I'd never say it to any of them, but the seven guys under my command were a first-class lot – seasoned all-rounders who'd each done at least five or six years with the Regiment.

The oldest and best known to me was Whinger Watson, whose laid-back attitude concealed his high abilities. We'd worked together in Ulster, Colombia and other hairy places, and understood each other perfectly. His nickname was slightly misleading, in that it referred to his habit of making deliberately stupid remarks, rather than complaining about things. That was one of his best features, in fact: he never complained, but always got on with the job in hand.

The others were all in their late twenties, although Rick Ellis, our best linguist, looked younger, being fresh faced, with curly light-brown hair already receding from his forehead. He had a very good brain, and had worked closely with the Det – the intelligence-gathering unit – in Northern Ireland. Maybe it was his appearance that caused him so much trouble with women. The thing about Rick was that he could never burn his bridges: as each affair petered out, rather than simply saying goodbye he'd keep phoning the woman or sending flowers, in case he became desperate for a shag at any time in the future.

Pavarotti Price's speciality, apart from singing in the bath, was explosives. He took great delight in dropping anything, from a bridge to an obsolete cooling tower – the bigger the better. A hulking six-footer, he came from a mining family in the Rhondda valley, and was probably the strongest man in the party. Sometimes, after a few pints, he could be persuaded to perform his party trick of bending six-inch nails with his bare hands. Yet he had one failing which he tried to keep under wraps: a fear of confined spaces, which seemed to stem from his background. For generations his ancestors had worked in the mines, but his elder brother had been killed in an old shaft; they'd been playing with some other boys when part of the roof had collapsed. Pav had escaped unhurt, but the disaster had left

18

him with a horror of mine-workings and tunnels in general.

Another big fellow was Mal Garrard, a dark and rather quiet man who had originally came to the UK on a two-year secondment from the New Zealand SAS, then did Selection at Hereford, passed, and served for six years as a fully fledged member of the Regiment. For a few weeks after his arrival people had given him stick about his accent, pretending they couldn't understand what he was saying; but he'd taken it in good part, and had made himself well liked, not least because he was brilliant on computers.

The team medic was Dusty Miller, son of a Yorkshire black-smith, much addicted to horses, racing and betting particularly: a compact, dark-haired fellow with a very powerful upper body, heavily into weight-lifting. You could see him coming a mile away, because he had a peculiar walk: he moved with his toes turned out, and rose on to the balls of his feet like a duck. Doctoring was only one of his skills; apart from anything else, he was a hell of a pistol shot, and often went out on unofficial rabbit-shoots around one of the training areas, blowing the heads off his quarry with some grossly over-powered weapon like a Colt .45.

Johnny Pearce, as I said, was as tough as they come: a fearsome kick-boxer and an ace mountaineer. No doubt his physical nature, and the many hours he spent in the open air, contributed to his ruddy complexion.

Last, but of equal calibre, was Pete Pascoe, the carrot-headed Cornishman, whose special skill was signalling. He, too, was an excellent all-rounder, his one defect being his volatile temper. In his first years with the Regiment this had been a real handicap, and he'd almost been RTU'd after he rammed a civilian car in the outskirts of Hereford. He claimed his brakes had locked and he'd skidded on a wet surface, but he only just escaped prosecution. Afterwards he had admitted that the fellow he bumped had been knocking off his girlfriend while he was away on a Squadron trip. Now though, at the ripe old age of twenty-seven, he was calming down a bit and had become more reliable.

Our first action, when we heard about the Russian job, had been to put the team on an intensive language course, so that by the time we went across we'd at least be able to exchange courtesies with our opposite numbers and read Cyrillic script. Personally I found the language a pain, because so many of the characters were similar, which made words hard to read, let alone understand. But the lessons were enlivened by our Russian teacher, Valentina, a big, dark woman in her fifties, with steel-rimmed spectacles, a lot of teeth, and hair pulled back into a short pony-tail. Three times a week she swept in from London, gave us hell laced with smutty jokes, and swept out again, a whirlwind of energy. The only person who didn't like her was Pete: she teased him once too often when he forgot something basic, and although he didn't actually flare up at the time, for ever after he referred to her as BOB: the Bloody Old Bitch.

Lectures from a member of the Firm introduced us to the Russian Mafia. The main point seemed to be that it wasn't a single organisation like its namesake in Sicily, under the control of one godfather, but comprised a whole lot of criminal gangs battling each other for supremacy. Since Russia had converted to a free-market system, our informant told us, every kind of racketeering had broken out: by sheer power of money the Mafia had risen above the law and made themselves impervious to normal justice. The police couldn't control them, and corruption was spreading through every kind of business. 'Once the disease had taken a hold,' the guy from the Firm had told us, 'there was no stopping it. Now it's even eaten its way into government. Leading politicians are being bribed and pressured and threatened. If they don't play ball, they're eliminated. There's a real fear in Western capitals that the whole of Russia is soon going to be ungovernable.'

Within a week of the request for a training team, we'd set a timetable. A recce party – consisting of myself, Whinger and Rick – would fly to Moscow on 15 September and spend a day checking the facilities of the camp and training area. We'd return on the seventeenth and have three weeks in which to make final preparations. The whole team, with all our kit, would go out early in October.

Before any of that, though, the Russian course leader, Major Ivanov, was due to spend a couple of days seeing how we did things in Hereford – and as his opposite number I went to meet him off the plane at Heathrow.

I cut it a bit fine. By the time I'd put my car in the stack and walked over the bridge into the Terminal Two arrival area, Aeroflot's flight SU247 from Moscow had already landed and passengers with hand luggage only were coming through the Customs screen. By arrangement, I was carrying a white square of cardboard bearing the word ACTIVE in big black capitals, and I stood by the barrier holding it in front of my stomach.

In the end it wasn't needed, because I spotted my guest before he saw me: a big fellow, a good six feet, and broad with it, walking very upright. He had a wide forehead with mid-brown hair swept across it, a rather flat face, and a quick, alert look as his gaze swept back and forth across the waiting crowd. I also noticed a fuzzy vertical scar on his left temple. As he came towards me I had time to think that in the old days you would have expected a Russian officer to carry duelling scars, but this one was clearly the result of a burn.

The guy was wearing jeans and a black leather jacket that looked rather expensive, and was carrying a hold-all slung over one shoulder. As he drew level with me I raised my right hand to attract his attention, and said, 'Major Ivanov? *Zdravstvuite.*'

He stopped, focused on me and said, 'Sergeant Major? *Zdravstvuite.*' His face broke into a smile, revealing that his two front teeth were made of metal, and he said, '*Vui gavarete pa Russki?*'

The words slipped out so fast that I took a second to recognise them. Then I managed, '*Nemnogo.*'

'*Khorosho!*' He looked delighted. We shook hands over the barrier and I motioned him towards the exit. As he came through, he fired off something else in Russian, and my bluff was called.

'Sorry,' I went. 'When I said *nemnogo*, I meant it. Only a very little.'

21

He smiled again and said, 'Doesn't matter. I speak English OK.'

I tried to take his hold-all off him but he wouldn't let me, and we set off for the car. He walked fast, with a springy gait, and I could see straight away that he was fit.

'Good flight?'

He shrugged. 'The pilot – he landed it like a ton of shit.'

'But you survived.'

He smiled. 'It remind me of when I get these teeth. Hard landing in Siberia. Into seat before.'

He was all eyes as we walked out on to the third floor of the stack, past ranks of shiny new vehicles.

'Cars!' he exclaimed. 'Such types of cars!'

'This is ours.' I unlocked the Passat, opened the boot and put his bag inside. Automatically he made for the right-hand front door.

'This side.' I pointed.

'Excuse me!'

'Rassat,' he said as he ran a finger over the car's logo.

'It's a P,' I said. 'Passat.'

'Of course! He is English?'

'German.'

Soon I realised that, although he spoke English with fair fluency, he had trouble recognising letters, as if he'd picked up the language by ear, rather than by reading. I could see him mouthing words to himself as we passed the hoardings. I had to stop myself smiling at his accent, which was tremendously Russian. His Hs were very hot: he pronounced Os like As, and jacked Y sounds on to the front of Es – *prafyessional*. He also made 'kill' into *keell*. His L's were beautifully liquid, as if he were rolling a mouthful of vodka round the back of his tongue.

In a few minutes we were heading west on the M4.

'Your first time in the West?'

'*Da.*'

'How come you speak English so well?'

'I learn in school. Also from American attached to our unit.'

'I see. Can I call you Alexander?'

22

'Sasha, please. Sasha is small name of Alexander. The diminution. Your name is George?'

'Geordie. That's a kind of diminutive, as well.'

'*Khorosho!* And second name?'

'Sharp.'

'That is family name. I mean patronymic.'

'What's that?'

'Your father name. My father is Vassily. So I am Aleksandr Vassilyevitch Ivanov. Your father is . . . ?'

'Was. Michael, I think.'

'You think? You don't know?'

'I never knew him.'

'I am sorry. Well – anyway, you are Geordie Mikhailovitch.'

His accent made him pronounce my name 'Zheordie', but who was I to complain? His English might be fractured, but at least he could get along in it – whereas my Russian was limited to about twenty words.

Already I liked his enthusiasm, the keen interest he took in everything he saw – for instance, the surface of the motorway. 'This street!' he said. 'He is vairy good. Our streets are full of holes. Cars soon break. The suspenders – always breaking.'

Another thing that fascinated him was the smallness of the suburban houses, and their gardens.

'How many families live in such a house?' he asked, pointing at a row.

'Those are what we call semis – semi-detached, two joined together. Two front doors, you see. Probably one family in each side.'

'In Russia we have all big house. Not like this.' He saw me glance across and said, 'Apartment blocks. Fifteen, twenty pieces high. These are like *izbas*.'

'What's that?'

'*Izba* is old house in the country. Peasant house.'

'A cottage?'

'Yes, but very old. And such a house . . .' He gestured at a thirties villa standing in a large garden. 'This belongs to government?'

23

'No, no. I'm sure it's private. A private individual. I think I read somewhere that you can buy houses in Russia now.'

'Yes – it is just starting.'

'And land? Could you buy a farm, for instance?'

'By no means. No land can be sold, except for gardens.'

The afternoon traffic was light and the fast lane was often clear, but I kept my speed down to eighty and let the BMWs whip past. I explained the system of number-plates: how S indicated the current year, just started in August, that next autumn there'd be a scramble for Ts, and that freaks paid huge sums for special numbers. Just at the right moment to illustrate my point, we were overtaken by a hell-driven Peugeot 205 with the number P1NTA.

We started to compare British and Russian special forces, and I asked about the base at Balashika.

'It is home of our famous Dzerzhinsky division. That belongs to Ministry of Interior. They have many facilities at Balashika. Beeg *strelbilshze*.'

'Barracks?'

'*Nyet*. Barracks is *kazarma*. *Strelbilshze* is ranges. Beeg ranges, beeg training area. Between town and forest. Town this side, forest this side. Only thirty kilometres from Moscow, to the east. All behind concrete fences.'

'Fences?'

'Walls. Concrete walls, two metres tall. From outside you see nothing.'

When I brought up the subject of the Mafia, he instantly became indignant and twisted round in his seat to look at me. 'They keell everybody! Half the population has become what we call *vor v zakone*. That means "thief in the law". In other words, creeminals.

'They keell businessmen, bank managers, property men – anyone. Last year they even kill Larisa Nechayeva!'

'Who?'

'Nechayeva? Boss of Spartak football club. They shoot her in her *dacha*, her country house. Another woman with her. And why? Beecause she refused to pay them money. Also they kill

24

Valentin Sych, ice hockey president.'

'What's the motive?' I said. 'Why kill all these different kinds of people?'

'Marney!' Sasha held up his right hand, rubbing thumb and forefinger together. 'Marney, marney, marney! Everyone wants more. Always US dollars. Russian money no good. You know how we call it? *Deregannye dengi* or *deregannye rubli*. That means wooden money, wooden roubles. Throw it in the stove!'

'But you've just had a revaluation. Didn't they divide by a thousand?'

'*Konechno*. Of course. Before, it was seven thousand roubles to one dollar. Now it is seven. But what is the difference? Prices are still crazy. No change.'

'These murders – who's carrying them out?'

'Contract killers. Almost all. With one bullet, a man can earn half million dollars.' He looked at me and went on in a soft, menacing, ingratiating voice: 'Eemagine. You are manager of bank, big boss, yes? Somebody telephones. "Look, Meester Sharp, you should pay us some marney." You tell them, "Get to hell."

'Another call. "You know, Mr Sharp, you are in danger. You need pratyection. We do not like you to be hurt. We can pratyect you. We can look after your family. But it will cost you: two per cent. Two per cent of bank takings – a lot of money."

'Again you say, "Get lost."'

He paused, and when he went on, his voice was even more reasonable, more wheedling, more sinister.

'A week passes. Another call. "Now look, Meester Sharp. Are you not concerned for your safety, for your little children, for their lives?"

' "No," you say.

' "All right, then. Wait. Wait. Just wait."

'You think you are safe. Why? Because you have closed-circuit TV on your block. You have modern security system. You have former KGB on duty outside. But you are under terrible pressure – from your bosses to resist the threat, from the criminals to pay.

'Then one morning you go out to your car. Sunny day. Very nice. Guards are sitting there. Only twenty-five metres to walk, but that is enough. *BASH! Bang!* The contract killer fires one shot from his car – finish.'

'Nasty,' I said.

'Is very bad, and always getting worse. Now all politicians are in danger, even the President and the Prime Minister.'

'That's why we're coming over, I guess.'

'*Konechno.*'

He gave me such a long run-down on Mafia activities that we reached camp almost without noticing it. 'Here we are,' I said as we turned in towards the gate. 'Welcome to Stirling Lines.'

The police on security duty had been briefed to expect him, and I checked him through without difficulty. Then we headed for the officers' mess, where a room was booked. At that time of the afternoon the place was deserted except for Larry, the steward, who was busy cleaning the regimental silver, so I took Sasha through to show him his room, which was small but cheerful, with a shower and lavatory cubicle attached.

'Even own bathroom!' Sasha grinned. Then, pointing at the washbasin, he recited a little poem: '*Tolko pokoynik, Ne ssit v rukomoynik.*'

'What's that?'

'It is joke about Russian hotels. Usually bathroom is a kilometre away along passage. It means, "Only a dead man does not piss in the basin."'

He was delighted with the accommodation; but when we got back into the anteroom, with its sofas and armchairs and little tables, and scenes from regimental history on the walls, he became nervous.

'Zheordie,' he said. 'I am shamed.'

'What's the matter?'

'This place . . .' He gestured round the room. 'My clothes . . .' He looked down at himself, pointing to his black jacket, his faded jeans, his ancient trainers. 'Not smart.'

'Don't worry. Everyone's very relaxed round here. No formality.'

'Perhaps . . .'

Still he looked anxious, so I said, 'Tell you what. I'll run you into town and we can buy you some new stuff at Marks and Sparks.' I saw him hesitate, and explained, 'That's a chain store. Good cheap clothes. Have you got money?'

He produced his wallet, opened it and fished out some notes. 'This is enough?'

He had two fivers and two ten-dollar notes.

'Is that all you've got?'

He nodded.

Jesus! I thought.

'Zheordie, you must understand. In the army, now, we do not get paid. Five months, no marney.'

I stared at him. 'In that case, *we'll* get you something.'

'No, please. You should not pay.'

'Not me – the system. There's a fund for this sort of thing. I can square it away.'

I dived into my room in the sergeants' mess to pick up a chequebook. Thus equipped, we drove into town and got Sasha kitted out with a lightweight, dark-blue blazer, grey slacks, a pair of black moccasins, a couple of shirts and a tie. The bill came to nearly £200, but I knew I could recover the money from Bill Tadd, the quartermaster.

By 5.30 we were back in camp, and I realised that to Sasha it was already 8.30 – so I suggested that he had a shower and got his head down for an hour before I came back and collected him for supper.

The meal went fine. There were one or two young ruperts about, but we two sat in a corner of the dining-room and no one bothered us. Sasha's new gear did him proud. He couldn't help preening himself a bit, shooting the cuffs of his pale-blue shirt and brushing invisible bits of fluff off the sleeves of his blazer.

As we chatted it became apparent that he'd had quite a lot of fighting experience – more than I had. One of the pictures on the wall was of the Jebel Akhdar in Oman, where the Regiment had won a famous victory in the fifties, and it set him reminiscing about Afghanistan, where he'd been posted for a year in hellish conditions. The mountains, he said, looked very similar – but in contrast with the heat of the Gulf, the winter cold in Afghanistan had been horrendous.

Towards the end of the meal, though, our conversation became rather stilted. Several times Sasha didn't understand something I'd said, and he seemed to be preoccupied with his behaviour, eating his cheese carefully and often glancing round. So I proposed we go out for a couple of beers and his mood lightened again.

The main thing was to steer clear of other guys from the Regiment and of the local slappers, whose intelligence network is shit hot. Bush telegraph keeps all the Hereford talent fully informed about who's who and who's where – who's on the standby squadron, who's on the SP team and so on. The last thing I wanted was for those women to see a Russian walking around with me in the evening – so we drove off to the Lamb, a pub in one of the outlying villages, and Sasha put down his first pint of Theakston's Old Peculier like he hadn't had a drink in months.

With the beer came relaxation.

'Cheers!' He raised his glass for the third or fourth time. 'Tell me your family. You are married?'

'No. I was. How about you?'

'The same.'

'What happened?'

'My wife – she was killed.'

'I'm sorry. How?'

'She was shot. It was street battle. Some Mafia persons were shooting a bank manager from their car. They keeled him, but also three persons on the pavement. Olga was one.'

'An accident, then?'

'By no means!' He turned on me indignantly. 'On purpose. The Mafia keell all witnesses.'

He paused before adding, 'Olga came from Alma Ata, in Uzbekistan. That was her home.'

28

'You didn't have children?'

'She was pregnant. Six months. I think it was a boy. My son.'

'When was this?'

'Ninety-three . . . ninety-four. Four years ago.'

'Well – that makes two of us.'

'Excuse me?'

'My story's much the same.'

Keeping it short, I told him about my marriage to Kath, a Northern Irish girl, and how she'd been killed by the premature explosion of an IRA bomb outside a supermarket in Belfast. 'Our son Tim was only three then, so he went to live with Kath's parents in Belfast,' I explained – and that led on to an account of my feud with the man I held responsible for her death, the leading IRA player Declan Farrell.

Sasha listened sympathetically, then said, 'It is your own Mafia, I think, the IRA.' He pronounced the name 'Ee-ra'.

'Not really. The IRA's driven by politics and religion. Political and religious hatred, more than money. Anyway, because we couldn't get this guy on legitimate operations, I was stupid enough to go after him on my own.'

In a few minutes my reminiscences led me to describe the kidnap of Tracy and Tim.

'Tracy?' Sasha interrupted. 'She is who?'

'A girlfriend . . . Jesus!' I hadn't meant to get into all this. I pushed back my stool, looked at my companion and said, 'We need another drink.' When I stood up and went to the bar to fetch two fresh pints, Sasha came with me, pulling out his wallet.

'Put it away,' I told him. 'In England, you're our guest.'

He gave a little nod by way of saying thank you.

'Yes,' I resumed as we sat down again. 'Tracy. A great girl. At least, she *was*. A redhead. Taller than you. Good fun to be with. She worked as a receptionist at the med centre, in camp. There'd been nothing between us before, but after Kath was killed we gradually got together, and a few months later she moved in with me. It was fantastic the way she took over Tim as if she were his mother . . .

'That was great – until the IRA grabbed her and Tim.'

I described the desperate struggle we'd had to recover her. 'It took us two months – more – to get her back. And when we did, I found she'd flipped.'

'Flipped? What is this?'

'She'd gone out of her mind. The stress had made her ill. She was a different person. We tried everything: rest, a holiday in the sun, a shrink – a psychiatrist – but nothing worked. She recovered physically, but not emotionally. She blamed me for the whole episode. If I hadn't been in the SAS, it never would have happened – all that crap. As a couple we couldn't get back to where we'd been before.'

'And?'

I sat back and took a deep breath. 'She went away to her family, somewhere in the north. It's more than a year since I last heard from her.'

'And the boy?'

'He's seven now, doing well. He's living with Kath's parents in Belfast. He's growing up a little Ulsterman.'

'You see him?'

'Oh yes, from time to time. We're good buddies.'

Sasha's mind was evidently dwelling on the IRA. 'Why be so soft with such terrorists?' he asked. 'Why not eliminate all? In Chechnya we shoot many rebels, no problem.'

'Yes – but down there a lot of innocent people got killed as well.'

'Chechens vairy primitive people,' Sasha said scornfully. 'If they come to Moscow they go beggars. They make things worse.'

'And in any case,' I persisted, 'you didn't win the war.'

'And why? Because our army has such bad equipment. Many, many shortages. No guns. No ammunition. No food. But Zheordie – I tell you something . . .'

'What's that?'

'The Chechen Mafia – vairy clever at stealing gold. They have more gold than all the other Mafias collected together. Chechens are gold specialists. Drugs also. They bring drugs from

30

Central Asia and send to Europe.'

'What about the army?' I asked. 'How's morale?'

'The army? The Russian army?' He looked round wildly. 'Zheordie – if I am to speak of army, I need vodka.'

'Is it that bad?'

He nodded.

'Vodka, then. Anything with it?'

'No thank you. Just vodka.'

When I handed him a double, neat, he raised the glass in my direction, smiled, called out, '*Vzdrognem!*' and tipped it straight down. I'd got myself the same amount of water in another glass, and tipped that down with an answering 'Cheers!'

'Good vodka,' he said. 'No *samogon*.'

'What's that?'

'Vodka made at home, from potatoes, wood even. What the soldiers get. It is very dangerous.'

'Don't they drink beer?'

'Beer too expensive. And anyway, drinking in barracks is strictly forbidden. So the soldiers go out at night and buy secretly from *babushkas*, old women. Then one junior soldier stands in the passage – guarding, you say? – while the others drink themselves crazy.'

'But morale – you say it's bad?'

'Zheordie, you must understand. There are too many armies. For example, Ministry of Interior has own army, one and half million men – Kulikov's men, we say, from General Kulikov, Interior Minister. That is more than the regular army. Then Ministry of Defence has own army. Special forces for this, special forces for that. You know, there is even special force for underground?'

'You're joking.'

'*Konechno nyet!* It is called GRU. Special troops trained to live in tunnels and work in missile silos. Altogether too many armies, no money. Food is very bad. Soldiers eat shit – on starvation rations all the time.'

'Like what?'

'According to the law, it is such kind of menu. For the

31

morning, it is tea, two pieces bread – one white, one black. Fifty grams butter, but only once a day. Butter only once. And *kasha*, of course. Porridge. Always porridge.

'For dinner, they could get meat in their soup, but very small pieces. Usually young soldiers, for their first half-year, get no meat, because the *cherpaks*, the second-years, grab it. In the evening dishes, every day it is potatoes purée, with piece of so-called fish, bread black and white, tea, and three pieces of sugar.

'For celebration – on important days, state holidays – they have special menu. What does it mean? It means, two biscuits per man, and *makaroni po flotski* – macaroni naval style, with very small meats, like the ship's rat chopped up. Maybe piece of water melon, and one grape per man.

'That's what soldiers eat. That's why they are ready to rob, do anything.'

As I fetched another round of vodkas from the bar – with a double for myself this time – I wondered what the hell we'd do about our own food once we got over there. None of our cooks had high enough security clearance to come on an operation as sensitive as this one, so we'd either have to eat with our hosts or fend for ourselves.

Again Sasha knocked his spirit straight down, with another cry of '*Vzdrognem!*'

'Also,' he went on, 'there is much torture of recruits.'

'Bullying, you mean.'

'Torture also. Many beatings. If sergeant does not like junior soldier, he drags him out of bed and makes him stand on one leg half the night. You have heard of *velociped*, the bicycle? No? It is what they do to young recruit. They come to him while he is sleeping, lift up bottom of bed, and put between the fingers on the feet—'

'His toes?'

'Yes – between his toes they put paper or cotton wool, then set it on fire. When flames reach him, he does the bicycle.'

Sasha whirled his hands round in imitation, and I couldn't help but laugh.

'No laughing!' he said indignantly. 'It is very bad. Officers

32

terrorise soldiers – beat them, shoot them—'

'Not really shoot them?'

'Certainly! Many men are shot dead by own officers. Absolutely incredible.'

'Do people get fined?' I asked.

'Fined?' Sasha seemed astonished. 'How *can* they be fined? They have no so big money. And in any case, it would be very dangerous for commander to punish *kontraktnik*, a prafyessional soldier, in this way. Such persons do not like to pay. Easier just to kill officer with shooting.'

'What about special forces? They must be better.'

'Many, many special forces. Every ministry has special force. Ministry of Defence, Ministry of Interior, Ministry of Federal Security . . .'

'So who's taking on the Mafia?'

'Good question. Under whose jurisdiction is situation going? These too many bodies – in the past they have no joint policy. But now we have new initiative – result of your Prime Minister's visit to President Yeltsin last year. From this has come new agreement. Yeltsin has persuaded Ministry of Defence and Ministry of Interior to create Tiger Force, specially to combat Mafia operations.'

'So who are the guys we'll be training?'

'All *kontraktniks*. That means prafyessional soldiers with contracts – not conscripts. At least two years in the army. All officers, from junior lieutenant to captain. Good types, I hope.'

'Where do they come from?'

'From all different special forces. From Spetznaz, from Omon, from Alpha, from Vympel . . .'

I saw him stifle a yawn.

'Come on,' I told him. 'Time you got your head down. Tomorrow's a full training day. You can meet the guys and tell us what to do.'

'*Khorosho!* Zheordie – let me say thank you for very kind reception. Also for clothings.'

'It's a pleasure.'

One amusing twist that I didn't yet explain to Sasha was that

33

our own headquarters were known in the Regiment as the Kremlin. Valentina had impressed on us that the word simply means 'citadel', but we were chuffed to think that, for the first time in history, our own little Kremlin was about to join forces with its Big Brother in Moscow.

THREE

For the next few days my most important task was to keep up the momentum of our countdown to departure; but at the same time I had to show Sasha round the base and give him an idea of how we did things. Certain areas of camp were out of bounds to him, notably the SAW and the ops room, but there was plenty else for him to see, not least the Killing House, where the CT team laid on a demonstration of hostage-lifting. At first he was cautious about expressing opinions, but the more time I spent with him the more he became prepared to criticise or compare our methods with his.

For us, Killing House demos were routine, but for Sasha they were an eye-opener. The guys put him and me into the left-hand corner of a special room, corralled with two other visitors behind white tape. As usual, the live hostage-figure was sitting on a chair in the middle of the room, with his two guards, in the form of figure-targets, on either side of him. Behind the hostage stood the sergeant in charge, commentating on events.

Just as he seemed to be in the middle of his spiel, giving the principles of close-quarter battle: 'Speed, aggression, surpr—' *BANG!* Loud explosion. Door blown off. Two assaulters running in. *Ba-ba-bom! Ba-ba-bom!* Short bursts from MP5s. Targets riddled, hostage lifted and gone before anyone else could react. Nothing left but smoke and dust.

As our ears recovered, Sasha turned to me, beaming, and said, 'Vairy good! Vairy prafyessional!'

Before we went out he took a close look at the construction of the building, pulling back the metre-wide sheets of thick red rubber, which overlapped each other by nearly half their width, so that he could inspect the steel-plated wall some three inches behind them. Seeing all the crumpled bullets lying on the floor, he understood at once how the rubber caught anything which flew back off the wall, killing its energy.

'This we would like,' he said wistfully, looking round.

'You don't have it?'

He shook his head. 'Only rubber wheels.'

'Tyre houses?'

He nodded.

I knew what he meant, because I'd seen them in the States: skeleton buildings with walls made of piled-up motor-tyres filled with concrete, which, in a crude way, performed the same function as the rubber sheets.

In another room a young assaulter dressed in full black kit had his equipment spread out on two tables for Sasha to look at. The Russian carefully inspected the guy's primary weapon – an MP5 with laser marker and torch attached – and some of his EMOE devices. His close interest offered an unwelcome opening to the range warden, a retired RSM who'd been given a kind of grace-and-favour job keeping the place tidy and sweeping up empty cartridge cases. The old guy could be a pain in the arse, as he always tried to latch on to our guests, and now I had to prise Sasha away from him before we got any awkward questions about where he came from.

From Sasha I gained a more precise idea of our task. He had already explained that the personnel of the new Tiger Force were being drawn from various sources. Most were from Spetznaz, the elite military special force, controlled by the Ministry of Defence, or from Omon, the civilian militia, which came under the jurisdiction of the Ministry of the Interior. Normally, Sasha told me, Omon dealt with problems inside Russia while Spetznaz worked in foreign countries; but the point of Tiger Force was that it should be a highly trained and highly mobile unit, ready to tackle emergencies either at home or abroad. When I remarked that this made it rather like the SAS, Sasha seemed surprised: he had always supposed that we only operated overseas.

He told me that Tiger Force would be directed by the Federal Security Bureau, the FSB, the largest remaining constituent of the old KGB, which had now been broken up into several parts; the bureau was in charge of security and counter-intelligence. The person in charge of our tour, our liaison officer and interpreter, would be an FSB officer.

'And who will that be?' I asked.

He spread his hands. 'So far, no information. I find out when I am back in Moscow.'

As I guided Sasha round camp, his meetings with the CO, the ops officer and the rest of the team all went fine; but where he came into his own was in polishing up the diagrams we were preparing for the course. Technically he was way behind because we were working on computers, aiming to project three-dimensional diagrams from our laptops, whereas the Russians apparently were still using blackboards and overhead projectors – but he was very quick on the uptake.

Among the diagrams Sasha had brought with him were two of the weapons that Tiger Force personnel would be using: the Stechkin Mark 5 9mm automatic pistol, and the latest creation of the Rex Firearm Company in St Petersburg, the 9mm Gepard, a modular weapon which can be instantly adapted for use as rifle, sub-machine gun or pistol. I thanked Sasha as gently as possible for bringing them, then let him know that, as well as better diagrams, we had an actual example of the Gepard which we'd acquired via another channel. In fact I'd arranged that Johnny would give the rest of the team a lesson on stripping down and reassembling the weapon, with Sasha present.

This demo proved a big success. For one thing it gave Sasha a chance to start getting to know our guys, and for another, he hit top form during the talk, acting up and joining in Johnny's commentary.

'*Gepard* is Russian for cheetah,' he told the team. 'Very fast, very light.' He made springing, bounding movements with his hands. 'It was developed from the Ryss, which is lynx. Lynx is OK, but cheetah is faster and lighter.'

'That's right.' Johnny took him up, holding the weapon

across his knees as he sat at the front of the classroom. 'It's a beaut. It's got everything bar the spots.' He hefted it in one hand. '*Extremely* light. Under four and a half pounds without a mag. As you see, there's a strong resemblance to a sawn-off Kalashnikov AK74U: more than half the parts are inter-changeable. But it's a hell of a lot more versatile. From what we've seen on the range so far, it's accurate and nicely balanced. Handles exceptionally well. Looks like it could be a winner in CQB and law enforcement.'

He demonstrated how the tubular steel butt-stock could be flipped out to turn the weapon into a rifle, or downwards to form a grip for sub-machine-gun mode. Then he rapidly stripped it, removing the bolt and bolt-carrier, the return spring, the upper hand-guard and gas chamber. As he brought each component away, Sasha gave us the Russian names.

'Two models of magazine,' Johnny went on, having re-assembled the pieces. 'This one holds twenty-two rounds, this one forty. The selector switch here has three positions. On safe, the bolt is locked half-way back so you can just see down into the magazine. Second position, O, as you know, stands for *odin* – one. *Odinochniy* is single fire. Is that right, Sasha?'

'*Konechno.*' The Russian grinned. 'And next position, AV, is for *avtomaticheskiy* – automatic.'

So they went on, back and forth. The Gepard's greatest novelty lay in the fact that it could fire several different types of 9mm round without having to change the barrel. Sasha reeled off eight possibilities, ending with the 9 × 30 hard-alloy-core bullet called the Grom. 'You know what *grom* means?' he asked jokily. 'It means thunder! Very big impact and penetration. Will pierce body armour at three hundred metres.'

Sasha also sat in on a couple of language classes. When he and Valentina found they came from the same city – the place the Communists had called Gorki, now back to its original name of Nizhni Novgorod – they really hit it off. There was one hilarious session when somebody asked Val for a few swear-words, just to put us in the swim, and she pretended to be greatly shocked.

'Swear-words?' she said. 'In Russia, there are no such things. The Communist system was so pure that after seventy-five years of it, all obscenities were eliminated.'

Her teasing kept everyone in good spirits. Of course there was no question of her joining the team in the field, but as we broke up from one lesson, to butter her up, I said, 'Val, I wish to hell you were coming with us.'

'Get me a visa and give me a Gepard,' she quipped back, 'and I'll be there.'

One little task I set the lads was the creation of lapel badges bearing their names in English and Russian. Obviously we didn't want anything that would flap about, so I told everyone to make up a cream-coloured linen patch, with black writing on it, that could be stitched on the tunic of the Russian DPMs we would be wearing. My own name came out as ZHORDI, Mal was exactly the same – MAL – and Rick was RIK, pronounced as if he stank. Johnny became ZHONNI, Dusty DOSTI, and Pete PYOTR. Even Pavarotti could be easily transliterated. But the one name that knackered everybody was Whinger. His real name was Billy, but he'd been known as Whinger for so long that none of his mates could call him anything else. The trouble was, the Russian alphabet has no W, and the nearest we could get to it was VUINZHA.

Among the lads there was a good deal of talk about money, because this looked like being a lucrative trip. What with allowances for food, accommodation, laundry, arduous conditions and so on, our pay was going to build up to two or three times its normal level. The expenses for the whole trip had been reckoned at £6,000 per head, and four grand of this had been paid up front. Anyone prudent put most of the cash into his bank account, but Pavarotti went straight into Monmouth and put down a deposit on a thirty-five-year-old scarlet XJ120 Jag which he'd been fancying for months. I put three grand into my building society account and changed the rest of the money into dollars, insisting that the paymaster got me new notes from the bank, with no year earlier than 1997 on them and in low denominations, because I'd heard that fifties and older notes wouldn't be accepted in Russia.

When we asked Sasha about the black market for money, he said that it had collapsed. He explained that Moscow, like all Russian cities, had become so flooded with US dollars that anyone could get them, and the rate of exchange was the same everywhere – about seven roubles to the dollar, ten or eleven to a British pound. In the previous year, he told us, following rampant inflation, the rate had swollen to outrageous proportions: 7,000 roubles to the dollar, 10,000 to the pound. But then on 1 January the Russian government had divided the currency rate by a thousand in an attempt to simplify things and calm the economy down.

More briefings about the Russian Mafia came from another visiting professional from the Firm, this one a smooth, silver-haired fellow called Edgar (his surname). Again, Sasha was able to supplement his information, which had been collected from intelligence reports, with first-hand knowledge. The briefings confirmed what Sasha had already told us – that the main Mafia activity was extortion, and the worst threat was against people with big money: leading businessmen, heads of companies, bankers. We learnt that over the past few years various branches of the Mafia had risen to prominence and then faded away. The first to show had been the Solntsevo gang, named after the scruffy suburb on the south-western fringes of Moscow where its members lived. Lately, however, that lot had apparently yielded supremacy to the Ismailovskaya Mafia, also based in Moscow and led by a notorious crook called Sergei Askyonov. This group, with its strong military connections, claimed to have a private army of more than a thousand men.

Edgar, an intelligent guy, quickly appreciated Sasha's worth, and started asking for comments about what he himself was saying. 'One reason for so much crime,' he told us, 'is that there's a fantastic amount of paper money actually in circulation. One the one hand, people don't trust the banks. On the other, inflation's moving so fast that they reckon they get a better return by having dollar bills in their possession. So there's cash everywhere, and a big incentive for robbery. Is that right, Major?'

'Certainly!' Sasha gave a vigorous nod. 'More dollars in Russia now than in rest of world.'

'Outside the States,' Edgar corrected.

'Of course. But that is very much money.'

The lectures helped us all to refine the aims of our course. With kidnappings so common, hostage rescue was obviously of prime importance, and we decided to concentrate on that. EMOE – explosive method of entry, or blowing in doors and windows – was clearly going to be another key area. A third vital subject was ambush drills, and a fourth, the bodyguarding of VIPs. Strictly speaking, BG work fell outside the remit of the Subversive Action Wing, but as all the members of our team had been on specialist close-protection courses it seemed natural to include the subject in our syllabus.

Sasha's tales of the Mafia were so lurid that they acted on the team like shots of adrenalin. All right, we were going in on a training task, but soon every one of the lads was dreaming that we would somehow become directly involved in a Tiger Force hit and get some action ourselves. And it was obvious from the relish with which he described anti-Mafia operations that Sacha was a born killer.

'In Gorki, my home town, is this godfather figure,' he told us one evening. 'Real name Borzov. But he calls himself *Nepobedinyi* – Unvincible.'

'Invincible,' I suggested.

'Yes – Invincible. He thinks nobody can keell him. He is former criminal, many years in gaol. Like I told you, he is true *vor v zakone*, a criminal in the law. Now his chauffeur drives him in bullet-proof Mercedes. Always four bodyguards with him when he moves around. He lives in a palace – like the Winter Palace in St Petersburg, almost. At night, in the yard round his house, a Siberian tiger is wandering. Like a guard dog. A guard cat, you say?'

'Some cat,' said Pavarotti.

'Two hundred kilos,' Sasha said, not joking. 'We heard he

41

feeds this cat on human flesh, his enemies. This Invincible wears a Patek gold watch. His body is covered in pictures . . . tattoos. Small Mafia are not allowed such pictures. If some man gets one without authority, he can be keelled. But Invincible has on his chest a portrait of Lenin. And why? Because no one would dare to shoot at our great Communist leader. On his knees, he has pictures of stars. And why? That means he never kneels for anyone.'

Sasha broke off and gave a quick, rather nasty laugh. 'But one day soon, I think we make him kneel.'

When Sasha flew back to Moscow we missed his cheerful company, and I looked forward to seeing him again when he met our recce party at Sheremetyevo Airport.

'What's the weather going to be like?' I asked him before he went.

'In Russia, autumn is one month ahead. Days warm, nights cool. Typical September.'

His final instruction as I saw him off was, 'Breeng plugs.'

'Plugs?'

'For bath and basin. In Russian hotels, such things do not exist.'

FOUR

We had the weekend clear for our own preparation, then on Monday morning we set off for Heathrow – myself, Whinger and Rick. Obviously the commander and second in command had to go, and we selected Rick as a third partly because he was one of our signallers – he and Pete Pascoe were level when it came to radio work – but mainly because he was our best linguist. He had an incredible knack of picking up languages informally, learning wherever he went: already he spoke French and German, and Russian seemed to be giving him no problems.

In the event, our flight was delayed for nearly three hours by technical problems – one aircraft went tits-up on the runway, and another had to be brought into service – with the result that the whole day seemed to disappear, and dusk was already settling on the land by the time British Airways' flight 262 began its descent into Sheremetyevo.

In the distance and far below us on the starboard side of the plane, I saw lights glowing in the dark, and as we came closer I realised I could see the whole of Moscow enclosed within a single ring of illumination. 'Look at that,' I said to Whinger. 'Ten million people inside that circle. Can you imagine it?'

'Yeah, and a couple of well-placed nukes would finish most of the bastards.'

'Come on,' I laughed. 'They're our friends now.'

But there wasn't much sign of that when we landed. We were travelling on civilian passports made out in our own names, and so had to go through Immigration along with everyone else. The hall was hot and dimly lit. Everything looked dirty and dilapidated – walls, doors, lights, the local staff. Worst of all was the ceiling, close over our heads, which looked as if someone had nailed ten thousand copper saucepans to it, rims downward.

'Jesus!' I said quietly. 'This is worse than Africa.'

For forty minutes we sweated shoulder-to-shoulder with passengers from other flights, shuffling forward like snails in queues that stretched towards the booths manned by the immigration officials. As we inched closer, I saw that the lady we were heading for could have walked straight off the set of a James Bond movie: grey uniform with lieutenant's bars on the shoulders, a mane of long, straight streaky blonde hair and half-inch false eyelashes.

Finally reaching her booth, I summoned up my best Russian and said, '*Dobriye vecher.*'

She glared at me, glared at my passport, glared at her video monitor and punched my details into her computer terminal, then shoved my documents back across the shelf without a word. It was definitely the wrong time of the month for her.

'Friendly lot,' Whinger observed as he came through behind me. 'Roll on the fucking Customs!'

To our surprise, they gave us no trouble. We took the green channel and nobody even looked in our direction. On the far side of the screen a swarm of taxi-drivers engulfed us, all shouting and trying to snatch our luggage; but through the middle of them came Sasha, dressed in civvies and smiling as he shouldered the mob aside. I recognised his shirt as one of the pair we'd bought in Hereford.

He greeted us warmly and led us out to a battered grey saloon which he'd parked on the pavement. We put our hold-alls into the boot and climbed aboard, myself in the front, the other guys in the back. Because the hinges had worked loose, it took three slams to make my door shut securely.

'I am sorry,' Sasha said as he drove off. 'You are in Intourist Hotel.'

'What's wrong with that?'

He let go of the wheel to spread his hands. 'Not nice. We wanted the Moskva, but no rooms.'

44

'Oh, well. It's only two nights.' To change the subject I asked, 'What sort of a car is this?'

'It is Volga. Old, old. I would like to buy new one, something good. But that would be too dangerous. And why? Because the Mafia would take it. One day, in a traffic jam, my mother is driving it, she sees two gun-machines in her ears, this side and that side. "Give me the keys." Finish.'

'Can't the police do anything?'

'Police!' He shot me a hopeless look. 'They are worst. They are cowards. And anyway, half of them are paid by Mafia.'

The highway into town was wide but rough: four lanes in each direction, treacherously pitted with dips and potholes. I realised that when Sasha had described the Russian roads as diabolical he hadn't been exaggerating. We were really getting thrown around – and this on one of the main thoroughfares. We were also being overtaken on both sides simultaneously: anybody with a reasonably fast foreign car was weaving in and out of the traffic like a lunatic.

Set back on either side of the road were terrible, drab tower-blocks of flats, nine or ten storeys tall. Closer to the road, old-fashioned hoardings carried advertisements, many for Western products. When I spotted some familiar red and yellow colours and slowly picked out the Cyrillic letters for McDonald's I couldn't help grinning at my own linguistic prowess.

It took us fifty minutes to reach the city centre, the traffic thickening all the time. I noticed several good-looking older buildings, mostly pale yellow with green copper roofs, but the general run of architecture was abysmal. Then, as we were crawling downhill along another broad street, Sasha pointed ahead and announced, 'There is Kremlin.'

I peered out through the relatively clean area of the windscreen and saw in the distance a red star glowing on top of a steeply pointed tower. Only that one corner of the citadel was in sight, but even so my neck prickled. Here was the centre of Russian power, the focal point of a vast country, the power-base that had dominated world politics for all our lifetimes. If ever there was to be a breakdown of relations between Russia and the West, this was where it would start.

A moment later Sasha pulled the car over in front of a tall, faceless, modern high-rise building on the right-hand side of the road, and parked end-on to the kerb.

'Hotel Intourist,' he announced. 'I help you check in.'

Outside the entrance a few rough-looking young men were standing around, all smoking; they were hard to see clearly, but whenever the glow of a cigarette lit up a face, I didn't like the look of it. They could have been taxi-drivers, yet their presence seemed vaguely threatening.

The little glass-walled lobby was full of security men – half a dozen overweight, slovenly guys with pistols in holsters. The women staffing the reception desk were wearing bright red tunics pin-striped with white – a cheerful touch which wasn't matched by any warmth of greeting. One of them gave us forms to complete and moved off towards her office without a word, carrying our passports.

'When do we get them back?' I asked.

'Tomorrow.'

Her lack of common civility pissed me off. I can't believe *all* the women in Moscow are having their periods right now, I thought. Then I heard Sasha saying, 'Programme for tomorrow: eight-thirty, I collect you and drive to Balashika for inspection of camp. OK?'

I nodded.

'Four o'clock, visit to British Embassy. Meeting with Chargé d'Affaires. Also meet your interpreter and liaison officer. At Embassy, same time.'

'Fine.'

I thanked him for collecting us, and he was gone.

Our rooms were on the fifteenth floor – 1512, 1513 and 1514. We went up in the lift, sharing it with a couple of over-weight Yanks, a man and a woman, obviously on vacation.

'Been to the Kremlin yet?' the man asked in a southern accent.

I shook my head. 'Only just arrived.'

'One helluva monument, that place. Sure is. How long are you guys here for?'

'Couple of days.'

A quick inspection revealed that all our rooms were the same: small, hot and stuffy, without air-conditioning, and with only the small upper section of the windows openable. In the tiny bathrooms the tiles were cracked and yellowing, the grout between them black with grime. As Sasha had warned us, there were no plugs in the baths or basins . . . and suddenly – fuck it – I realised I'd left mine behind. I took a quick look round the bedroom for signs of hidden microphones, and although I couldn't see anything I felt sure they were there. We'd already agreed that there'd be no shop talk in the hotel.

'Grotsville,' exclaimed Rick as he emerged into the passage.

'You said it. Have you got your money on you? Don't leave it in there, whatever you do.'

'Got it.' He slapped his bum-bag which he had pulled round to the front, over his stomach.

'You look like that fat git we came up with.'

'*Spasibo*, mate.'

'Let's stretch our legs,' Whinger suggested. 'Eyeball the Kremlin.'

That seemed like a good plan. It was already 9.45 local time, but only 6.45 by our biological clocks, and since we'd eaten on the plane we didn't feel any need for food. Besides, I knew that the British Embassy was somewhere close by, just across the Moscow River from the Kremlin, and I reckoned we might as well suss it out, as I was going to have to report there regularly during our operation.

On our way down in the lift Rick suddenly started shitting himself with laughter.

'What's so bloody amusing?' Whinger said irritably.

'Some cunt left a menu from one of the restaurants in my room. The stuff on offer is incredible.'

'Like what?'

' "Needles in meat sauce", for one. Then there was "frog's paws in paste".'

'That's frog's legs in batter,' Whinger told him.

'I know – but think of it . . .'

47

It was a fine evening for a stroll: the sky was clear and the air cool. Out on the pavement, we elbowed through the scrum of taxi drivers and walked down the slope towards Red Square. The street was so wide and the traffic was moving so fast that the subway seemed the best way to cross. We went down some steps into a concrete tunnel, past young people busking and old women begging, and up the other side. A minute later we were walking uphill on another short, broad thoroughfare and emerging on to the huge open expanse of Red Square.

'Never realised it was cobbled,' said Whinger.

'Nor that it was so big.'

It gave me a strange feeling to be looking at buildings I'd seen a thousand times in pictures. As a young soldier, during my early years in the army, I'd spent hours in classrooms doing recognition training, staring at black-and-white slides of Soviet tanks and missiles until we could pick out T54s, T64s and T72s in our sleep and name all the main types of ICBM. The place all these weapons were photographed most often was Red Square, during big parades on the anniversary of the 1917 revolution and suchlike – so now the buildings in the background were like echoes from the past.

Rick's mind was moving on the same lines. 'Think of all the military hardware that's rolled along here,' he said.

On our right the low, squat hulk of Lenin's mausoleum sat hunched against the wall of the Kremlin. Wherever a light was shining on the wall, we could see it was made of dark red brick.

'Funny there aren't any guards on the mausoleum,' said Whinger. 'You'd expect there to be some official presence. Isn't it a national shrine?'

'Not any more,' Rick told him. 'I read on the Internet that they're arguing about what to do with the old bugger. The die-hards are all for keeping him, but a lot of people want him out.'

'Burning'd be too good for that bastard,' said Whinger bitterly, surprising me with the anger in his voice. 'If anyone sent the Russian government a bill demanding compensation for all the misery he and his bloody ideas have caused, this country'd be bankrupt for the next thousand years.'

'That's why they're not paying the Regiment anything for our job here,' I said. 'All the funds are coming from the States or the UK.'

Ahead of us in the distance rose the multi-coloured onion domes of St Basil's Cathedral, some striped horizontally, some vertically, some segmented like the skins of pineapples. Even I, ignorant as I am about church architecture, sensed that there was something wild and barbaric in those amazing shapes and colours.

'What about that German kid who landed a light plane here?' said Whinger. 'Some feat, that. I bet it made them cut about a bit. The Russkies must have been fairly shitting themselves when they found out how easily he'd got through their defences without the aircraft even being called.'

'Rust, his name was,' I said. 'Mathias Rust. He landed up the slope.' I pointed ahead. 'That means he must have come in from that direction, towards us. Didn't the cheeky bugger get a job at some travel agency in Moscow, once he'd come out of gaol? I think so. It just shows how times change.'

Soon we were walking down the gentle hill past St Basil's. At the bottom we found a bridge over the river, and decided to cross to the other side, so we'd be able to look back across the water and get a view of the Kremlin. We cleared the steps on the far bank, and had just started walking, the river on our right, when Rick said quietly, 'We've got a tail.'

'Sure?' I asked.

'Pretty much. He's been with us at least since the bottom of the square.'

'Keep walking, then. When we get to that bench, we'll sit down and see what he does.'

On the embankment a hundred yards in front, a metal bench faced out over the water. When we reached it, I sat on one end, took off a shoe and proceeded to shake out imaginary bits of grit.

Up on Red Square there had been plenty of people wandering about. Down here by the river the wide road was deserted, and our follower stood out like a spare prick.

'He's stopped,' Rick announced. 'He's leaning over the wall.'

'Let's tip the bastard in,' said Whinger.

'It could be someone Sasha's laid on to keep an eye on us,' Rick suggested.

'Hardly,' I said. 'I don't think he'd do that. More likely a common-or-garden mugger. He could have mates waiting up ahead, though. He may be trying to push us towards them. We'd better sort him.'

Whinger agreed – so we strolled forward, slower than before, then suddenly turned and began walking fast towards our pursuer. He'd started after us again, and it seemed to take him a moment to realise what was happening. Then he also turned round and began to scuttle off. By now we were running, and we were on to him in a flash.

Whinger and I each went for an arm and grabbed him, bringing him to a rapid halt. We couldn't see him too clearly in the lamplight, but he looked a swarthy lad of twenty-odd, with a bit of a ragged beard, wearing a check shirt and a thin jacket of some dark material. He was angry, but also scared.

'What the hell d'you think you're doing?' I snapped.

He let fly a stream of Russian, of which I understood not a word. Rick said something in Russian, and he spat out an answer. Then he started to struggle, and for a moment I was afraid he was going to scream to attract attention. I got my handkerchief scrumpled in a ball, to stuff in his mouth if he opened it any wider, but already Rick was frisking him, and in seconds came up with a nasty, slim-bladed knife which he held in front of the guy's face.

That made his eyeballs rotate and quietened him nicely.

'Into the river,' I said, and Rick flipped the weapon over the wall. We heard the splash as it hit the water.

'No mobile phone or radio?'

Rick shook his head. 'No wallet or money either.'

'In that case he's probably after ours.'

Suddenly I remembered one of the unofficial phrases Valentina had taught us. '*Valite otsyuda!*' told him, and indicated the direction he could go – back the way we'd come.

He got the message, no problem. As we released him, he shook himself like a dog and set off without a word. I saw that he had a bit of a limp, dipping slightly on his right leg. We watched until he had disappeared up the steps by the bridge, then we carried on along the river.

'What did he say, Rick?'

'Just that he was out for a walk.'

'Like hell he was.'

Rick was the most observant member of our party. He had a terrific knack of noticing any small object or incident that was out of line, and his memory for faces was phenomenal: even a year or more after an event he'd remember a person's appearance. Sometimes it took him a minute or two to place them, but then the setting and date would come back. I'm sure his skill derived partly from all the surveillance work he'd done in Northern Ireland, and often it stood us in good stead.

'Where did he pick us up?' I asked. 'Was he outside the hotel?'

Rick shook his head. 'I don't think so. He must have been hanging around on Red Square.'

Away to our right, across the river, the floodlit Kremlin was a magnificent sight, but we were feeling too unsettled by the incident to appreciate it fully.

'I can see three possible explanations,' I said. 'One, he was after our money. Two, Sasha detailed him to check where we went. Three, he was a Mafia dicker. I don't like any of them. If he *was* just a mugger, it goes to show how dodgy this place is. If Sasha sent him, it means we're not trusted. If he's Mafia, it means we may have been rumbled already.'

I was getting jumpy. I remembered how the Colombians had had dickers posted at all the airports, photographing people as they arrived off the planes. Someone had told me that the secret police got hold of the flight manifests, and that by using computers they were able to match up passengers with pictures, so they could keep tabs on every single visitor to the country.

We walked on, until we became aware of a handsome, old-style building set back from the road behind a courtyard on our left, and flanked by two matching outliers, evidently part of the complex. Beside the gate, in a grey pillbox, were two Russian guards in uniform, chatting, smoking, looking bored and not paying attention. Behind them, further in, was a stone gatehouse containing a guy in a red jumper who sat at a desk behind a glass screen.

'Bet that's a Brit,' I said. 'He's a bit more alert. He'll be controlling the electronic gates and the phones.'

'Look on the roof,' said Rick, 'left-hand corner. There's an infra-red light. They must have good security systems.'

We crossed the street towards the gates, where a brass plaque announced that the building was the British Embassy. The discovery made me feel a little better: at least we'd carried out one small but useful research task.

We recrossed the river by the next bridge, watching our rear all the way, and returned to base along the north side of the Kremlin, past the Tomb of the Unknown Soldier, where a perpetual gas flame burned out of a horizontal slab, and a cloak made of bronze lay folded over a plinth. We paid our respects and walked on.

Then, only a minute or two away from the hotel, we were nearly caught up in a violent incident. Fifty yards ahead, facing us, a single car was parked against the kerb. Suddenly a grey van hurtled past us from behind. Tyres screeched as it scorched to a halt inches in front of the car, blocking any take-off. From the van burst four figures in uniform – militiamen, by the look of them. They ran at the car, ripped the doors open and dragged out the driver and passengers.

In seconds the three guys from the car were spreadeagled over their own vehicle, taking heavy punishment from batons. Then one of the uniformed men stood back in the road and fired a couple of short bursts from his sub-machine gun, aiming into the air over the river. His purpose seemed to be to scare the shit out of the targets – and I wondered where the bullets were landing in this huge city. As if to emphasise what he thought of his victims, another militiaman ran in and swung his boot, delivering a fierce kick to one of the huddled bodies, catching the man in the small of the back, whereupon he sank to the ground with a groan.

My instinct was to back off as fast as possible. Whinger evidently felt the same, and hissed in my ear, 'Keep walking!' This was nothing to do with us, and we definitely didn't want to get involved. So we crossed to the far pavement and kept going. The last we saw, one of the three had been dragged into the van and driven off, leaving the others slumped in the gutter by their vehicle.

'What the fuck was that all about?' Whinger muttered. 'Were they the cops, or hooligans pretending to be cops?'

'I bet those were some of the guys we're going to have to train,' said Rick cheerfully.

The brawl had made me yet more edgy, and for the last few hundred yards to the hotel, we speeded up. The approach was thronged by hangers-around, but as far as we could see the crowd didn't include our friend who'd lost his knife. Still, I was relieved when we'd pushed through and were back inside.

By now it was nearly 11.00 p.m., and Whinger spoke for all of us when he said, 'Let's get a pint, for Christ's sake.'

We'd already spotted a bar on the third floor, so we took the lift up. Whinger stepped out first on to the landing, and he was hardly through the door before I heard him go, '*Phworrhh! Firekin ell!*'

'What is it?' I rushed out – and instantly saw: leaning against the wall was the most blatant hooker I'd ever set eyes on – fishnet stockings, black leather skirt nine inches long, white blouse open to the navel, blazing scarlet lipstick, hair a dark, coppery colour she was never born with. As we passed within a couple of feet of her she let out a long jet of cigarette smoke through pursed lips and gave us a cool, arrogant stare of appraisal.

'Jesus!' Whinger muttered as we turned along a corridor. 'How was that for an old slag? She could be quite a looker if she wasn't so plastered in make-up.'

'Rather you than me, mate,' I said. 'Wait a minute, though. You're not exactly strapped for choice.'

53

The entrance to the bar was ahead of us, at the end of the landing; in front of the doorway lurked three more women, all peroxide blondes, all smoking. We pushed past them into a dark cavern thudding with a disco beat and headed for the bar on our right.

'*Pivo, pozhaluista*,' I said, trying out two of my best words. '*Tri.*'

'Three beers?' said the barman in good-sounding English.

I nodded, and he pulled three tall glasses of Heineken, the only brand on offer. The beer was OK, but it cost the equivalent of £3 apiece.

As our eyes became accustomed to the dim light, we realised that the whole room was heaving with hookers, all dressed in minimalist kit. Two were dancing with each other under strobe lights on a small circular floor in the centre; the rest were sitting at tables or standing against the walls, gyrating in time with the beat. A quick head-count put the total at sixteen. The three other men present were paying them no attention whatsoever.

Soon it was clear that Rick had spotted someone he fancied. I saw him getting eye contact, and his gaze kept wandering off across the room.

'Bloody hell!' he muttered. 'There's going to be some crack when the rest of the lads get here.' Then he said, 'Look at that, too.'

Above my head and behind me, on a high shelf in the corner, sat a television set. I turned to look at it, and saw a guy, with his bare arse to the camera, humping a woman, going at her hammer and tongs.

When I turned back, the two girls had left the dance floor and their place had been taken by a single, pasty-faced man. The guy, who looked to be in his twenties, was pissed out of his mind. He could still just about stand upright, but he staggered whenever he tried to walk. Lurching, faltering, tripping over his own feet, he seemed oblivious to his surroundings, but at the same time hell-bent on staging a grotesque solo dance.

Only when he started a strip-tease did he become too much

for the management. Two security heavies hustled in and took him away.

We had another round of beers, watched the hookers vainly circulating, and then decided to get our heads down. At least, Whinger and I did. Rick said he was staying on for one more round.

'Watch yourself,' Whinger told him. 'This place is hopping with Aids.'

'How d'you know?'

'I can smell it.'

Out in the corridor we were accosted by yet another pair of tarts, one dark, one fair. The blonde came straight for me, stopped a foot away and said, 'We go to the bedroom.'

It was a statement, not a question. I twisted a smile into position and said, 'No thanks. I'm happy.'

'I make you more happy.' She moved even closer and ran her fingers down my chest.

'It's OK.' I gestured towards Whinger. 'I'm with a friend.'

'All four go to the bedroom.' She pointed at her companion.

The blonde was slim and quite pretty, with a good set of tits on her, but the dark girl was a nightmare, flat chested, and with a complexion like the surface of the moon. I shook my head, pushed past them and made it to the lift.

Safe inside my room – so I thought – I had a shower and stretched out on the bed to watch CNN news.

The next thing I knew, the phone was ringing. The light and the TV were still on. I looked at my watch: 1.30.

I picked up the receiver.

'Meester Sharp?' It was a woman's voice. 'I think you are lonely.'

'Am I hell!' I spluttered. 'Get lost. *Valite otsuda!*'

I slammed the phone down, switched everything off and lay down again.

Fifteen storeys below, traffic was still surging along Tverskaya. Opposite my window, huge, bright neon advertisements for Panasonic and Technics blazed on the top of another high-rise building. What a place, I thought. What a shit-heap:

overrun by commercialism, yet scruffy as hell. Nowhere else in the world had I ever known such unpleasant vibrations: nowhere had I sensed so clearly that if I got into trouble, nobody would help or protect me. When the rest of the team came out, we were going to have to take care.

Back in Hereford Valentina had told us all about *babushkas* – literally grannies – the old ladies who do menial jobs like sweeping the streets, shovelling snow and sitting at desks on the landings of big hotels. Sasha had mentioned how they also run little kiosk shops and sell illicit vodka to soldiers.

Whinger and I clocked our first specimen when we went down for breakfast: eighteen stone if she was a pound, with eyes set too close together in a huge pudding of a face, and a stack of violet-tinted grey hair piled six or eight inches above her head. On the wall behind her was a notice half in English, half Russian: CONTINENTAL ZAVTRAK: 50 ROUBLES, and the *babushka*'s function was to intercept people on their way to the dining room and take the number of their room, so that she could make sure no one sneaked in twice or let somebody else in on their ticket.

Breakfast was self-service: rolls, bread, butter, jam, cheese and so on. There were sachets of instant coffee, tea-bags and a big samovar of boiling water with a tap that spat on your fingers when you turned it. We helped ourselves and went to sit at a table in the outer room. The little packets of butter were Finnish, the redcurrant jam German; the local bread was dry and papery, and the cheese, presumably home-made too, tasted of nothing. But I wasn't in critical mood. I'd slept pretty well, it was a fine morning, and I was looking forward to seeing the camp. Whinger was also in good nick. He too had had a midnight call, but he'd sensibly seen it off.

Then in came Rick, face pale, T-shirt on back-to-front.

'Rough night? What time did you hit the pit?'

'Dunno,' he mumbled. 'Had a couple more drinks.'

'Don't try bullshitting us,' I warned. 'I know what you were hanging around for.'

He leered.

'Don't tell me you . . . Bloody hell! Which one was it?'

'That little blonde in the corner.' He blushed scarlet, then said, 'Wait a minute.'

He put two sachets of sugar into his black tea and got a couple of mouthfuls down him. Then he said, 'Natasha, she's called.'

Whinger went, 'You bastard! How much did she take you for?'

'Nothing.'

'*What?* Come on.'

'Honest. She wants help.'

'I should think she bloody well does after you've been through her a few times.'

'It's not that. It's her sister.'

Whinger and I looked at each other. Then Rick began to explain.

Natasha's home was in Rostov-on-Don, a thousand miles south of Moscow, he said. She was eighteen, a student, and supposed to be starting her autumn term at university. But like hundreds of other provincial girls she'd done a runner and come to the capital to earn some money and make a better life for herself. And along with all the rest, she'd fallen into the clutches of the Mafia.

'The point is, she's shit-scared,' Rick went on. 'They all are. They have to hand over half their earnings. If they don't pay, they're liable to have their faces carved up.'

'Is that what's happened to the sister?'

'Not yet. But she's deep in it. Irina, she's called. She went to New York on the job, with a friend, but both of them got caught up in a money-laundering racket run by the Mafia. Apparently it's got a hold on the States like a tick in a dog's arse.'

'So what was this slag doing?' Whinger asked.

'Something in a restaurant. There's drug money pouring through: she has to bank it and make out phoney bills for meals that nobody's eaten. Last week the friend got murdered, and now Irina thinks she's for it too.'

'And what is the great, all-shagging, all-conquering hero

supposed to do about it?' Whinger shot a steely look across the table.

Rick scrubbed his eyes. 'Natasha wants me to rescue her sister.'

'Fucking roll on!' Whinger cried in alarm, so loud that a Japanese couple at the next table jumped in their seats. 'Who does she think you are?'

'Part of a film company. Don't worry – I stuck to the cover. It's just that, because I'm a Brit and have dollars, she thinks I can whip across to America, sort the Mafia and bring her little sister safely home.'

'What did you tell her?' I pushed back my chair. 'How did you get rid of her?'

'I haven't yet. She's still there.'

'Where?'

'In the bed.'

'Bloody hell! For Christ's sake, Rick – she's nothing but a whore. Otherwise she wouldn't be in a dump like this.'

'No, no,' he protested. 'She's a really nice kid.'

'What did she *do* to you?' Whinger asked sarcastically. 'She emptied your head as well as your balls.'

Sasha was in the foyer at 8.30, still in civilian clothes, evidently not wanting to show any military presence in the hotel. Leaving the others, I got up, greeted him and walked him over into the area near the ground-floor bar, where a few tables and chairs were so widely scattered round the large atrium that I felt sure they couldn't be covered by microphones.

'These girls,' I began. 'The ones that hang around the hotel. What basis are they on?'

'I'm sorry?'

'I mean, are they employed by the hotel, or what?'

'No, no – Mafia. All Mafia. You have a problem?'

'Just that Rick laid one of them last night.'

'Does he not pay her? She is angry?'

'No – she's OK.'

'And he doesn't tell her who he is?'

'No, no.'

'In such case, not to worry.'

'All right, then. One other thing . . .' I described the incidents on the embankment – first our own little set-to, then the heavy hit.

Immediately Sasha was apologetic. 'This man – nothing to do with me,' he insisted. 'Nothing.' From the way he reacted, I knew he was telling the truth.

'No sweat,' I said. 'We didn't lose anything. As long as the wrong people don't know we're here.'

He shook his head. 'It was only small thief. Teepical Moscow. Zheordie, I am sorry.'

'In that case, forget it. But what about the bust?'

'Probably this was Omon. They get information of criminals in the car. Maybe they hear them on their radio.'

'Their methods aren't exactly subtle.'

He shrugged. 'Moscow is very violent place.'

'Well, we're all in one piece so far. *Idyom!*'

He smiled, like he always did when I hit a Russian word accurately, and said, 'Let's go.'

I piled into the front passenger seat of his car, the other two got in the back. As Sasha pulled into the traffic, he announced, 'One more dead.'

'Who? Where?'

'On radio news this morning. The boss of Russavto, big car import, shot dead in his Mercedes. Or maybe roasted. They found the car burning on Komsomolskaya Square.'

'Mafia?' I asked.

'Of course.'

'What did he do to annoy them?'

'Refuse to pay money – just how I told you.'

'The women in the hotel,' I said. 'How do they get in there? I mean, is the hotel supporting them?'

'I tell you, all Mafia-controlled.'

'Yes – but d'you mean the hotel or the girls?'

'Both.'

I looked round at Rick and said, 'You'd better watch

yourself, mate. You don't want to fuck this whole job just because of one hooker. You could end up floating down the Moscow River.'

We were heading out of town towards the east. The traffic going our way wasn't too bad, but the incoming stream was diabolical: crossing after crossing gridlocked, drivers hooting. When I remarked on it, Sasha said, 'Moscow traffic goes to collapse. It is impossible.'

After I'd asked about the make of a car in front of us, he was quick to point out others. 'That is big-engine Volga. This is tenth-model Lada. This is Zhigudi.' Then he added contemptuously, 'Nobody want Russian cars.' What he coveted, I could see, was a BMW or a Mercedes, a few of which nosed through the rush-hour crawl, sleek and well-polished.

As we drew away from a set of lights, he said, 'Now we are on Shosse Entusiastov.' He turned to me with a grin. 'All revolutionaries who must go to prison use this street!' He saw me looking puzzled and went on, 'Why? Because in Communist era all people sentenced to gaol passed along this highway to the gulags. They never return! Nobody return! The street goes to Siberia.'

Our journey took less than an hour, and as we drove the morning began to brighten: the air was quite warm, and as the cloud thinned we started getting glimpses of blue sky. After a scatter of new high-rise blocks on the outskirts of the city, we passed under the ring-road whose lights we'd seen from the air, and suddenly Moscow was at an end. The land here was dead flat; enormous fields stretched away on either side, apparently uncultivated, covered in rough grass, punctuated with tussocks a couple of feet high. Then, on our right, we started passing a forest which exactly matched my expectations of Russia: tall, slender silver birches with bark mottled white and grey rising among dark green pines, giving a pleasantly open texture to the wood.

I was admiring the trees when I realised that a uniformed man had walked out into the road ahead and was flagging us down with a black-and-white baton.

'What's the matter?' I asked quickly.

'It is nothing.' Sasha sounded unmoved. 'Only GAI, the traffic police, making checks.'

He pulled in to the verge, and the cop came to the window. He wore a grey uniform with a thin red stripe down the seam of the trousers. Sasha wound down his window and started to give the policeman a bollocking. Even I could understand what he was saying: that he was an army officer on an important mission and had no time to piss about. But the cop gave him as good as he got, and after a minute Sasha gave a sigh.

'*Isvinite.* He demands my documents. One minute, please.'

Muttering under his breath, Sasha leant across me to extract an envelope from the dashboard pocket, got out of the car and followed the man into the flat-topped concrete hut at the side of the highway. Waiting, we had time to take in the decrepit surroundings: the road's edge churned up, rutted mud beyond the tarmac, heaps of rusting metal lying about, broken drainpipes dumped in a heap.

'What it is,' said Whinger thoughtfully, 'is the size of this godforsaken country. At home everything's neat and tidy because we have so little space. Here there's millions and millions of fucking acres, and it doesn't matter if you scatter rubbish about.'

Five minutes later Sasha returned, sliding papers back into his folder. 'Forged documents,' he said as he started up. 'Always they are looking for forged licences. People sell them for fifty dollars.'

'Are these the regular police, then?'

'No – GAI only traffic.'

We drove on. Soon I saw a large sign which I could read easily: BALASHIKA. Behind it, set back from the road and running parallel with it, was a wall of concrete sections topped by coils of barbed wire. The solid part of the barrier was about two metres tall, so that it effectively blocked the view of everything beyond.

'Here is the camp,' Sasha announced. 'Very big.'

Certainly the wall ran for miles. On and on it went, broken

at one point by a single-track railway line, but even there baffles of concrete slabs set at angles made it impossible to see inside. At last Sasha slowed and we drew up at what was obviously the main entrance: a double gateway with sliding barriers of heavy metal bars forged in squares, and flat-roofed guardrooms on either side. The roadway was pitted, the buildings badly finished, the wall cracked where it was propped by pillars. Twisting round in my seat, I glanced at Whinger and saw that his reaction was the same as mine: the place had an instantly depressing atmosphere.

When I look back on that day, I realise that from the start I had a feeling of foreboding about our whole operation. There was no friction of any kind – indeed, our hosts were friendly and welcoming – but the squalor of the barrack blocks and the primitive nature of the training facilities made me dread spending two months in such surroundings. Get a grip, Geordie, I kept telling myself. What matters is the training. You can put up with anything for eight or nine weeks.

As soon as we were inside the camp, Sasha disappeared briefly and came back dressed in DPM fatigues, without badges of rank, but with the emblem of a tiger's head on his left lapel. On duty, we soon saw, his manner changed: he became sharper, more efficient – and that gave me confidence. He introduced us to a couple of fellow officers – who seemed good enough guys, with a positive, open approach – but they spoke hardly any English, and at this first meeting their names didn't stick.

It was Sasha who showed us round and explained the facilities. I said nothing as we toured the camp, because in the Regiment you work with whatever assets you've got, and don't start criticising others when they are doing their best. But I couldn't help noticing that most of what we saw was way out of date: again and again I was reminded of conditions when I'd joined the army nearly twenty years before.

The camp had its good points, one of which was space. Beyond the drill squares, the barrack blocks and other buildings, the land ran straight out into ranges and training areas. Several thousand acres were taken in by the surrounding wall, which struck away through the forest at the back and disappeared out of sight. You could drive or even walk to the various ranges without leaving the base's perimeter.

At the Killing House, our hosts put on a demonstration of hostage rescue – no doubt in return for the one we'd given Sasha at home.

As Sasha warned me, their building was nothing but a hollow square formed out of old lorry tyres filled with sand and cement and stacked on each other to make walls about eight feet high. Because the room had no roof and was open to the elements, we had a good view down into it from our vantage point on the observation tower. As at Hereford, the guards either side of the prisoner were represented by figure targets, much the same as our own, but the hostage between them, far from being a live human being, was only a dummy.

When the assault went down, the explosive charge failed to blow the barricaded door first time, and when the assaulters opened up with their sub-machine guns, instead of firing a couple of short bursts, they sprayed the inside of the house with dozens of rounds. The entire exercise was marked by a lack of precision. There was also a worrying lack of emphasis on safety. The assaulters had no flame-proof clothing like our black gear, only standard DPMs – and as the day warmed up I saw several guys remove the heavy Kevlar plates from the fronts and backs of their flak-jackets. Without the plates the jackets would stop secondary impacts like ricochets, but not live rounds. And whereas at home we always have a fully equipped ambulance standing by, manned by two paramedics, the Russians had nothing but an ancient meat-wagon, with jack-shit kit on board and only two squaddies in control.

Sasha seemed amazed when I told him that the SAS had only ever lost one man in the Killing House. Plenty of guys had broken arms and legs when they fell off buildings while abseiling, but in the Killing House itself only one man had died; he'd been shot in the femoral artery and had bled to death in seconds.

'Reelly!' Sasha seemed impressed. 'We lose one or two men a year.'

I almost said, 'I'm not surprised,' but bit it back and made a mental note that safety instruction was going to be at the top of our agenda when the team came out.

Another fundamental decision was about food. For lunch, we were taken to a canteen and ate with the rank and file. The menu was exactly as Sasha had described it in the pub in England: *shchi*, cabbage soup with lumps of gristle floating in it, black and white bread. The soup was OK if you avoided the gristle, but I could see Whinger's eyeballs rotating.

As soon as we were on our own outside, I said, 'We're going to get fucking hungry here.'

My spirits sank even lower when we saw what we were being offered for accommodation: the ground floor of a three-storey block which was standing empty and looked as if it hadn't been used in years. There was no shortage of space – a dozen rooms of reasonable size led off either side of a central corridor – but the building itself was in a disgusting state, with plaster coming away from the concrete-block walls, dirty cream paint flaking off, and yellowing newspapers strewn about the bare cement floors. The security was shite, as well: no locks on the doors, and several window panes broken.

Sasha saw the way my mind was working and said, 'We get it cleaned up. No bother.'

'Yes, please – and some means of securing the doors. We're going to want beds, too.'

'How many?'

'Eight – no, better make it ten.' I adjusted my estimate as I counted in the scalies.

As we left to return to the city, we took a short drive round the town of Balashika – and that depressed us even more. The road verges were sheets of dried mud, flanked by blocks of flats made from hideous yellow brick, with badly fitting windows and cracks gaping in the walls. We looked in vain for shops – and as for a pub, the idea that one might exist in such a place seemed like a bad joke.

We were driving against the tide of traffic once more, and in less than an hour we were alongside the river, passing the spot where the knife had gone over the wall and pulling up outside the gates of the British Embassy.

Sasha, who had changed back into his civvies, glanced at his watch and announced with satisfaction, 'Three hours fifty-eight.'

The security guards had been briefed to expect us. The first two – Russians – checked our documents. The inner post was manned by a Brit, as I'd predicted. He spoke a few words into his radio, then directed Sasha to drive on across the courtyard and round the left-hand side of the main building. Behind the inncr post was another open space with an attractive garden, a hard tennis court and, across the back, a low two-storey building which had obviously once been the stable block belonging to the main house. A forest-green Range Rover was parked in one corner with a small, shiny blue Fiat beside it.

By the time we arrived at the front door a man was already standing outside – a tall guy, probably in his early forties, with a shock of thick, grey hair springing forward over his forehead and a bushy moustache to match. He was wearing a white shirt and a navy tie with diagonal stripes that no doubt indicated some fancy school or regiment.

'Sergeant Major Sharp?' He came over and shook hands with a firm grip. 'Pleased to meet you. I'm David Allway, Chargé d'Affaires.'

'Hello,' I said. 'This is Major Ivanov – Sasha – who's looking after us.'

Sasha shook hands and gave a deferential nod in place of a salute. Then I introduced Whinger and Rick.

Allway swept a hand at his forelock, which instantly flopped back into its former position, smiled at everyone and said, 'Your liaison officer's here already.'

'Great,' I said. 'What's his name?'

'*Her* name . . .' he paused, smiling again, 'is Colonel Gerasimova. She's waiting in the office. Let's go in.'

'Just a second,' I said. 'A colonel . . . Is she army?'

'No – she's from the FSB, a section of the former KGB. On formal occasions they still like to use KGB ranks.'

Ah, Jesus, I thought. This is all we need.

If I don't remember much about Allway's office, it's because I was so startled by the appearance and manner of our interpreter. She was dark, with short, straight hair, and very slim – 'lithe' would be a better word, because her movements were quick and elegant. She was wearing a smart suit of cornflower-blue linen with a cream-coloured shirt underneath. After so much squalor outside, she was like a vision. When we entered the room she was sitting down, talking to a red-headed secretary, but when she stood up to greet us, I saw she was nearly as tall as me. Her face caught everyone's eyes as we came in: it was a bit too long and narrow to be classically beautiful, but there was something striking about it, especially her big, dark eyes.

'Sergeant Major Sharp? I'm Anna Nikolayevna. Welcome to Moscow!'

'Thanks.' I took her hand gently. Her English pronunciation was perfect – no trace of an accent – and it was refreshing to hear her sound British, rather than American, as most Russians do when speaking English. She smelled pretty good, too: I was getting traces of some scent that I knew but couldn't quite place.

In a few moments we were all sitting at a rectangular table and the secretary was getting a brew on. Allway sat at one end, on my left, Anna opposite me. She sat back in her chair with her arms folded, very composed, very still, as she listened.

Allway was courteous, brisk and efficient: without any faffing about, he went straight into confirming the details of our schedule.

'You arrive all together next Saturday . . . the eighth,' he said, checking a sheet of notes.

'That's right.'

'Transport is by RAF C-130, which will fly direct into the strip at Balashika. Arrival at 0030 local time.'

'Correct.'

'The aircraft will depart as soon as unloading's finished.'

'Correct. It's going to refuel in Berlin on the way here, so that it can turn straight round and be gone in the dark.'

'Good. Now – your personnel.'

He began to run through the list of names – he had them all correct – and at the end I said, 'I take it you have secure satellite comms with the UK?'

'Of course. I'll give you a list of numbers in a minute. You can call me direct from Hereford – and from Balashika, when you get there.'

I looked across the table. 'Colonel?'

'Please call me Anna.'

'Anna, then. Can you explain what our official status is going to be? I mean, what basis will we be here on?'

Her face, which had been set rather hard, softened into a smile. 'Don't worry. It's all above board. You'll be here as guests of the Ministry of Defence and the Ministry of the Interior, jointly.'

'Does anyone outside the armed forces know we're coming?'

'No. There has been no official announcement. Our aim is to protect you from possible interference by criminal elements.'

'You mean the Mafia?'

She nodded. 'They would hardly welcome the idea of foreign experts coming to train the new unit.'

'So it's important that we don't get seen or recognised coming and going, or outside the camp?'

'Precisely.'

'In that case, what about transport? One or two of us are going to have to liaise with the Embassy. I imagine we'll be coming in and out.'

'That's no problem. We'll make a couple of civilian cars available. The only thing is, you'll need driving licences. If you give me your names and details, I'll arrange that.'

'Thanks. What if we get stopped by the traffic police?'

'The GAI? There will be no difficulty, provided your documents are in order. We'll fix you up with whatever you need for each vehicle – licence, insurance and so on. And I shall give you a number to ring in case any problem arises.'

'What about your own involvement? Will you be available in the camp?'

'Of course!' She gave another brief smile. 'At your service.'

'Will you sit in on training sessions?'

'I don't know about *sitting*. I'm planning to take part pretty actively.'

'Great. We're going to need you.'

The meeting went so smoothly that it lasted only half an hour. Soon after 4.30, Allway was ushering us out into the courtyard, where a gardener was sweeping up leaves.

'Your English is fantastic,' I told Anna as she was departing. 'Where did you learn it so well?'

'I give you three guesses.'

'University?'

'Well – partly. But really in London. I worked for two years at the Intourist main office in Piccadilly.'

'Ah! When were you there?'

'Early eighties. Eighty-two to -three.'

A sudden thought came to me. 'No chance of your having supper with us tonight?'

'I'm sorry.' She gave a little shake of her head. 'I have a date already.'

'Oh well – I just thought you could fill us in on background.'

'When you're over again, maybe.'

'Definitely. I'll look forward to that.'

She made for the Fiat, shoe-horned herself neatly into the driving seat and set off.

'Well,' said Allway. 'So far, so good.'

'Yes – thanks.'

I'd been looking at the old stables at the back of the yard, and they'd given me an idea. 'There's one other thing . . .'

'Yes?'

'The security on our accommodation block is . . .' I was on the point of saying it was shite, but ended up saying, 'dodgy. What I mean is, I wonder – is there a secure room here in the Embassy that we could use for storage? A garage or something?'

Allway looked up and said, 'What would you want to store?'

'Maybe some of our comms equipment. On these team tasks we generally have some fairly sensitive kit with us.'

'Well – as it happens, we've just cleared out part of the cellar, over there.' He pointed into one corner. 'It's a bit rough – really just a garage.'

'As long as it can be locked up . . .'

'Oh yes – it's got a steel door. I'll get the key and show you.'

He disappeared into the office, came out again, and took us across to a steep ramp leading down to an up-and-over door.

'Ideal,' I said after a quick look. The cellar had no windows or other exit and, considering that it was below ground level, it felt remarkably dry. 'This'll be perfect.'

'OK then.' Allway grinned. 'I'll do my best to keep it empty for you. People and things around here have a habit of expanding to fill any space that becomes available.'

We thanked him again and set off to tab back over the bridge to the hotel.

'I give you lift,' said Sasha, pointing to his car.

'Thanks,' I told him, 'but I'd rather walk.'

'Then I say goodbye.'

'We'll see you on Sunday morning. And thanks for all you've done for us.'

'It is nothing.'

With smiles all round, he got into his car and drove off.

As soon as we were clear of the Embassy gates I said to Whinger, 'Anna. Former KGB, for sure. She must have been spying in London. Most of the Russians in England were on the KGB payroll. Certainly most of the diplomats were spies.'

Whinger didn't argue. 'Nice try, Geordie,' he said.

'What d'you mean?'

'Your eyes were all over her like a rash.'

'Piss off, mate,' I told him. But secretly I was annoyed with myself for having let my interest show.

Having scored a point, Whinger was relentless. 'On yer bike,' he said with a sneer.

'Come again?'

'She's a dyke.'

'Could be,' I agreed. 'But I don't care *what* she is. I'm keeping this on a professional basis.'

FIVE

Two days later we were on the training range at LATA, the Langwern Army Training Area just inside Wales, when my bleeper went off.

Beep, beep, beep. I immediately recognised the number that came up in the little window. It was Bill, the adjutant.

Mal might as well carry on,' I told Whinger. 'I'll be back in a minute.'

As I walked away to the range hut, short bursts rattled out behind me, so I closed the door and dialled camp.

'Hi, Geordie,' Bill said. 'Where are you at?'

'Down at LATA.'

'OK. The boss wants an immediate meeting. How soon can you be back up here?'

'Half an hour. Just me, is it?'

'No – the whole team.'

'Bill – is something wrong?'

'No, no,' he went. 'Everything's fine.'

'Has the job been pulled?'

'Not at all. It's definitely on. We'll talk when you get here.'

'Where's the meeting, then?'

'In your briefing room.'

'OK. I'll see you in half an hour.'

The lads grumbled a bit at being dragged off the range, especially Pete Pascoe, whose feelings were always near the surface. I kept thinking there was something strange about the way Bill had said, 'It's definitely on.' I got the impression that the job *was* on, but that it had changed.

Ever since our recce party landed back from Moscow, it had

71

been all singing and dancing. I'd put in a positive report, saying that everybody in Moscow was on net, and that, although conditions in the camp at Balashika were primitive, we'd been given a really good hand by the Russians and by the Embassy. Since then we'd faxed across the names and details of the team, for driving licences and other documentation. We'd also lined up a load of extra stores, and everything seemed to be under control. Thanks to Whinger, Rick's reputation as an instant Russian legover specialist had gone all round the team: he'd had a lot of stick, but he'd taken it well.

Now what?

When I saw the line-up in the wing, I knew for certain that it was something heavy. The Regiment was represented not only by the CO and the ops officer, but also by the Director – a brigadier – who must have made a special trip down from London, leaving at dawn. From the Firm came Edgar, but with him was an older and evidently senior man who was introduced as Mr Laidlaw.

The CO – a small, spare man with a bony face and receding hair – spoke first, and I could tell from the pitch of his voice that he was tensed up. Normally he talked at a deliberate pace, but now he had gone up a gear.

He began with the usual spiel about the secrecy of our operation. 'Until now, as you know, it's been classified Top Secret,' he said. 'That classification was imposed primarily for the safety of the team going into Russia. I need hardly remind you, it's essential that Mafia elements don't get wind of your presence.'

He paused and looked down at his notes. Then he said, 'The name of the operation has been changed. It is now Operation Nimrod. Further, it has become a black operation. I don't need to tell you what *that* means, but I will. It means that absolutely no further mention of it is to be made to anyone except members of the team. The reason will become obvious in a moment. Is that clearly understood?'

We were sitting facing the brass on two rows of chairs, three and five. When I glanced round, I saw everyone nod quickly.

The CO's tension had communicated itself to the team.

'Right, then.' The CO cleared his throat. 'Another element has been added to the operation. The training of Tiger Force will go down as planned, but as from today that will serve as cover for a new main task. The first priority of Operation Nimrod is now to plant two compact nuclear devices in strategic positions, where they can be detonated by satellite signal if or when such action is deemed necessary.'

Silence. For several seconds nobody moved. I felt as if I'd been skewered to my seat. When the CO continued, I seemed to be hearing him from a distance.

'We realise, of course, that this action is not in line with overt Western policy. The initiative has come from the United States Defense Department. For some time they've been looking at the concept of infiltrating nuclear devices into the former Soviet Union. Now Operation Nimrod is about to provide an opportunity. Any questions so far?'

'You mean you're expecting *us* to plant nuclear devices?' I went.

'Just that,' the CO replied.

'What – under the bloody Kremlin, I suppose?'

'Exactly. One of them, anyway.'

'Boss – you can't be serious.'

'I am, Geordie. It sounds outrageous, I know. But I am. Totally serious.'

I felt myself growing angry. 'I thought we were supposed to be helping the poor bastards.'

'We are. In the short term, we're on their side. We'll go through with the training programme as planned, and I hope we'll do them a service. The new phase of the operation is a long-term measure designed to keep the lid on things in the event of a take-over by criminal elements.'

'That's one way of putting it,' I said. 'You keep the lid on things by blowing the whole fucking place sky high.'

'Geordie!' The CO's voice sharpened. 'Get hold of yourself. The Regiment has received this request from the Pentagon, via the British Government. We've agreed to carry it out.'

Already I regarded Sasha as a friend, a comrade in arms, who needed all the help I could give him. Now I was going to have to double-cross him in everything I said or did. All my friendly actions were going to be undermined by treachery. Then there was Anna. Even though we'd only met once, I sensed that I could work with her. From day one I'd be deceiving her too.

I heard myself asking, 'Does our embassy in Moscow know about this?'

'No.' The Boss shook his head emphatically. 'Not a thing. They'll never hear of it.'

Immediately I thought, *More* people to deceive: the Chargé d'Affaires, for a start. 'Christ!' I glanced at Whinger and saw he was looking pretty sick. I looked on along the line of faces – Rick, Mal, Pavarotti, Dusty – hoping for back-up, but they all wore blank, puzzled expressions.

'These devices,' I said. 'Are you talking about suitcase bombs – the sort of things that were developed for taking out bridges or dams?'

'A modern version,' the CO conceded. 'Slightly bigger, and very much more powerful.'

'How are we supposed to handle them? I mean, are they portable, or what?'

'More or less.' The CO gestured to his left. 'Mr Laidlaw is going to give you an initial briefing.'

Laidlaw stood up to expound. Plump and rubicund, with dark hair slicked back and a big gut bulging against his double-breasted, navy pin-stripe suit, he looked a bit of a character, a man who enjoyed a glass or two. Yet his manner was anything but frivolous: 'Gentlemen,' he said in a thick, fruity Scottish accent, 'for simplicity's sake I shall refer to the devices by initials. In the trade they're known as CNDs, compact nuclear devices. Ironic that the same initials stood for the Campaign for Nuclear Disarmament, which some of you may remember. Nevertheless, those are the initials that we tend to use.

'The two CNDs you will be placing in position weigh approximately a hundred and fifty kilograms apiece. However, each one comes in two parts the size and shape of large suitcases.

One component weighs eighty kilos, the other seventy. Thus each component can be carried without much difficulty by two men. Easier with four. The device is primed by fitting the two halves together. It is then connected to a smaller unit, a radio receiver. The whole is detonated by signal from a satellite in synchronous orbit.'

He stopped, scanning our faces. 'Gentlemen, I can see you looking worried. May I emphasise that the chances of any CND ever being detonated in anger are extremely remote. The devices are being planted purely as a deterrent, which the West will use as a form of control, should the situation in Russia deteriorate to a level which threatens the international community. Think of them as an insurance policy, not as weapons of aggression.'

Seeing Johnny shift on his chair, he prompted, 'Yes?'

'These bombs. How do they get to Moscow?'

'You'll take them with you when you fly in.'

'Where are they now?'

Laidlaw looked at his watch. 'They're due into Lakenheath any time now. They should reach Hereford this evening.'

I was finding it hard to believe that this whole spiel wasn't some crazy test, sprung on us to gauge our reactions.

'How do we know where to site them, once we get there?' I asked.

'Our friends in the Pentagon have got everything worked out for you. I'll give you a quick idea from these maps. Of course, you'll have detailed diagrams which you can memorise, but these will show you the general idea.'

He bent over an open lap-top which stood on the table and punched a couple of keys. The big VDU beside him flickered into life – and even before he began to explain the coloured diagram that came up on the screen I knew where we were: on the bank of the Moscow River, opposite the Kremlin wall, practically at the spot where we'd had the showdown with the mugger.

'For security reasons,' Laidlaw was saying, 'as from now, the devices will be referred to only by code names. CND 1 is Apple,

CND 2 Orange. All right? Now – this diagram shows the site for Apple. We're right in the centre of Moscow. Here you have the Moscow River, marked blue, flowing west to east. The river at this point is a hundred and five metres wide. This, here, is the south wall of the Kremlin, running parallel with the river. The interior of the Kremlin lies to the north. Alongside the north bank of the river is a road, then there's a strip of grass. The distance from the water to the Kremlin wall is seventy-seven metres.

'Fortunately for your purpose, the ground beneath the city is honeycombed by tunnels. Not sewage tunnels like in London, because Moscow works on a system of relatively small-bore pipes, which are cleared by high-pressure water jets. Of course, there's the Metro – the underground – with tunnels on many different levels, as in London.' He stopped to clear his throat, and continued in a strange, slightly theatrical voice. 'But there are also various other tunnels, less well known. For instance, there is one major and totally secret system which was built during the seventies, in the depths of the Cold War, to give party leaders an escape route from the Kremlin in the event of invasion or nuclear attack. It's very deep, and one of them's big enough to take lorries.

'At the inner end, access is by lifts from a secret terminal under the Presidium. The tunnel runs roughly here' – he drew an imaginary line with his pointer – 'southwards under the river, and all the way out to a site near Vnukovo Airport, twenty kilometres to the south-west. There, a complete underground city still awaits its first refugees. The place has its own supplies of food, power, water, air and so on.'

He paused for effect, and saw he had us well hooked.

'More recently, in the attempted coup of ninety-three, the rebels were cornered in the White House, the parliament building. You'll all have seen TV pictures of tanks firing on it. Well, when the defenders decided to run for it, they went down tunnels – that was how they got away. The KGB were supposed to be guarding all the tunnel systems, but they just didn't have the manpower.

'Our tunnel, *your* tunnel, is much more modest, but ideal for your purpose: only six feet in diameter, but adequate for pedestrians. Again, it was built as an escape route, but during the twenties, on the orders of Lenin. This is it – the dotted line – running from beneath the Great Kremlin Palace, under the river and away towards the south. Fortunately we have been able to acquire KGB records, which show that during the Khruschev era – some time in the fifties – it was declared obsolete and the section under the Kremlin was filled in with a plug of concrete. But the next section has remained open, and appears to have been forgotten, or at any rate abandoned, by latter-day authorities.'

Once again I couldn't help making a sarcastic remark. 'I suppose it passes right beneath the British Embassy. All we have to do is open a trap-door in the floor of the ballroom and drop into it. Brilliant.'

The CO frowned at me, but Laidlaw wasn't fazed. 'You're not far wrong. In fact it passes about five hundred yards to the east of the Embassy. Here's the Embassy complex, on Sophieskaya Quay, and here's the line of the tunnel.' He drew another invisible line downwards, passing to the right of the Embassy and on towards the south-east.

'How do we get into it, then?'

'Access is via a shaft in a courtyard behind a church. I'll show you a detailed diagram in due course.'

'I know,' said Rick suddenly. 'It's that pink-and-white structure, a bit like a wedding cake. Three arches and a tall tower.'

I stared at him, amazed that he'd noticed and remembered such detail.

'Yeah,' he went on. 'We walked right past it after we'd sorted that interloper. You can look through the gateway and see a little church in the yard at the back. There was a big, wrought-iron gate at the entrance, but it looked as though it hadn't moved in years.'

'Pink and white,' Laidlaw echoed him, clearly impressed.

Laidlaw went back to his lap-top and wiped the picture. 'Let me show you something else.'

Up came a close-in photo of two heavy padlocks, their hasps passing through a pair of thick metal rings.

'These,' he said, 'are the locks on the plate sealing the access shaft.'

Pavarotti, who was good on his lock-picking, gave a low whistle. 'Fuck me!' he muttered under his breath, as though immediately sensing a challenge, then louder: 'I could go through those bastards in under a minute.'

'I didn't think they'd trouble you much,' Laidlaw said with a smile.

'So that,' he continued, 'for the moment, is Apple. Now for Orange. Some of you have already been to Balashika, I believe.'

I nodded.

'The second site is less precisely specified.'

His next coloured diagram showed mainly open country, with a few buildings and fence-lines running across it.

'This is the southern boundary of the space control complex at Shchiolkovo, next door to the training area at Balashika. It will be for you to choose the exact location, but the objective is to place Orange within a hundred metres of the perimeter, so that its blast effects will cover the entire space complex. As some of you have seen, the training area in which you'll be operating abuts the complex. It should be relatively simple to bury the device at a suitable depth.'

'Which is . . . ?'

'A minimum of six feet, a maximum of twenty.'

The guy seemed to know all the answers. Yet still I could not quite believe that what we were hearing could be for real.

'These CNDs,' I said. 'How powerful are they? What damage will they cause if they go off?'

'Apple would destroy much of the centre of Moscow, and remove the Russian high command at one stroke. Orange would take out the space complex, removing Russia's ability to launch ICBMs with any precision. In both cases, blast damage would be limited to some extent by the fact that the devices would go off underground – but it would still be extremely severe.

78

'In the city, the Kremlin would disappear. Every tunnel under Moscow would collapse. The entire Metro system would be destroyed. Escape tunnels and nuclear shelters the same. The city would come to a standstill. Within a two-kilometre radius, I would not expect anyone to survive.'

I took a deep breath. 'Between them, then, the devices would kill a few hundred thousand people. Possibly a million.'

Laidlaw said nothing, so I went on, 'This is all well and good, but we aren't trained to handle weapons of this kind. We won't have a clue about them, and unless we postpone the whole training programme there isn't time to learn.'

'No bother,' said Laidlaw. 'I gather one of your colleagues has been on a course in the United States.'

'That's right,' the boss broke in. 'In fact he's escorting the devices over. He's coming in with them this evening.'

'Who are we talking about?' Whinger asked sharply.

'Steve Lime.'

Steve Lime! The guy whose initial and surname spelt 'Slime'. Whose nickname was Toad. Jesus! This really freaked me. I glanced at Whinger. He hated the bastard as much as I did. Toad! The colleague from hell.

I heard the CO saying, 'He'll be going with you, of course. You'll need him to look after the devices, and prime them when the time for insertion comes.'

Toad had always been a pain to the lads on the squadron, but over the past few weeks, since he'd been posted to the States for a course in nuclear technology, he'd faded into the distance, as it were, and people had stopped beefing about him. It wasn't his fault that he was ugly, with oily skin and protuberant eyes; what bugged us was that he seemed to have no personality, and never got on with any of the guys. He'd go about with a smarmy smile on his face, but there was no warmth in it, and after a while you came to realise that he was wrapped up in his own affairs. At the same time, he was a real crawler, who'd lick up to anyone if he thought he could gain something from doing so.

How he had ever made it into the Regiment I could never understand. He had come from an unusual source – the Royal

Engineers – where he'd worked in bomb-disposal; he was fascinated by explosives – obsessed, almost – and he spent hours tinkering with time-fuses and remote-firing gadgets.

He'd never tell you what he was doing, or have any real crack with the lads. He'd associate with the cooks and drivers rather than with the rest of us. It was no accident that he'd ended up as an instructor on the lock-picking wing, in a dim little world of his own. I know that all SAS guys, myself included, are loners to some extent; but at the same time everyone has to muck in, and Toad never did.

The idea of having to live at close quarters with him in the camp at Balashika was a fucking wind-up. In fact I found the whole scenario a nightmare.

I'd always hated the idea of nuclear weapons because they're bound to kill thousands of innocent civilians, including any number of children – people who have no idea of what's going on. My career in the SAS has always emphasised the need for precision: what you might call 'economy of violence'. People imagine that guys in the Regiment have a cold-blooded, murderous outlook, and regard anybody as a potential target. It isn't like that. All our training is directed to making surgically accurate strikes on targets that have been properly identified.

For the moment, all I could do was grasp at straws. 'This tunnel under the river,' I said. 'How do we know it's still open?'

Laidlaw checked his notes, gave a half-smile, and replied, 'It was open on the fourth of April this year, and we have no reason to believe the situation's changed.'

'That means someone's been down it. If access is that easy, how do we know that the KGB or some other security organisation isn't sitting in there, waiting for us to arrive?'

'The suggestion is that, once you've got Apple in position, you should block the tunnel on the river side of it by dropping the roof, as if there had been a natural fall.'

'Not that easy if it's concrete.'

'I didn't say it was concrete.' A hint of irritation edged into the Scot voice. 'The tunnel is lined with brick, and it's not in the best of condition.'

I nodded in token conciliation.

'Even if you do drop the roof, it is recommended that you brick the device into the tunnel wall.'

'Hard to camouflage new mortar.'

'That'll be up to you. I imagine there may be dust or mud that you can smear around.'

Next Whinger came up with, 'How do we get the devices on site?'

The CO looked at Laidlaw, as if asking permission to intervene, and said, 'They'll travel out with you on the Herc, sealed in Lacon boxes. They can be marked the same as ammunition. The weight will be about right. At the other end it'll be up to you to devise ways of moving them to their final positions.'

'What if the Herc goes down with the devices on board?' asked Pavarotti. 'What's the chance of a premature detonation?'

'None,' said Laidlaw. 'Even when the two halves of each device are united, nothing can happen until the control box has been interrogated and primed by satellite signal. You need have no worries on that score.'

Thanks, I thought, feeling crushed with a sudden terrific weight of responsibility. The boss was going on again about the paramount need for security; but although I could hear what he was saying I was wondering how the hell I could carry out the training mission with this knowledge in my mind. Every day we'd be dealing man-to-man with our students, instructing and encouraging them, and at the same time, behind their backs, we'd be plotting to annihilate them.

As the main briefing was coming to an end, the CO drew me aside and said, 'One thing to remember, Geordie: whatever happens, don't let yourselves get involved in any live operation, like you did in Colombia.'

'That was different, Boss,' I protested. 'When Peter lifted, we had to do something about it.'

'I know. But what I'm saying is that we don't want any repetition. Even if the Russians beg you to take on a job for them, refuse.'

'Will do.'

From the briefing we went into a close-up study of the two sites. Laidlaw produced large-scale drawings with much detail on them.

'All this information is on compact discs, which you can obviously take with you,' he said. 'The discs are programmed so that if anyone tries to get into one without using the correct password, the contents are automatically destroyed. Nevertheless, you obviously want to handle the discs with the greatest care.'

As soon as the brass had dispersed, I called the team together for a Chinese parliament. We got a brew on, and sat round discussing this amazing turn of events.

Rick remembered that, a few months ago, there'd been reports of the Russians losing a whole load of such devices. 'There was something on the Internet that I downloaded on to our Russian file,' he said. 'Wait one, and I'll pull off a copy.'

While he went to make a search, Whinger and I filled in the other guys on the layout of the Kremlin and the British Embassy, which had suddenly become of critical importance. I felt instinctively that because the Orange site was out in open country, we'd be able to hack it without too much trouble: it was Apple, right under the walls of the Kremlin, that made my neck crawl.

In a few minutes Rick returned with a couple of pages printed off his lap-top. 'Listen to this,' he began, reading out his transcript. ' "A respected Russian scientist and former adviser to President Yeltsin said on Thursday that during the 1970s, under orders from the KGB, Moscow had secretly developed suitcase nuclear bombs. The devices had an explosive capacity of one kiloton – the equivalent of 1,000 tons of TNT. They could be activated by one person, and could kill 100,000 people. The bombs were designed for terrorist purposes. Since the break-up of the Soviet Union in 1991, at least 100 such devices have remained unaccounted for." '

Rick broke off, looked up and said, 'Guess what this respected Russian scientist is called.' When nobody answered, he said, 'Yablokov. We all know what that means.'

Somebody gave a groan. *Yabloko* was one of the first words we'd learnt on our Russian course. It means 'apple'.

'Either it's a fluke,' I said, 'or someone's having a laugh.'

'Maybe someone nicked a couple of suitcases from the KGB, and we're just taking them back,' Pavarotti suggested.

'There's a worse possibility than that,' said Pete. 'If we're doing this to the Russkies, who's to say they haven't done it to us already? What if there's a CND nicely placed in the wall of the Thames, under the House of Commons terrace?'

'Yeah,' Whinger agreed, 'and another under the guardroom, right here in camp.'

'It's no bloody joke,' I told him. 'Don't you remember that time in the seventies when the Finns stopped an articulated truck and found it contained the roof for a Mexi stay-behind shelter, destined for England? If the bastards were getting dug in in the UK then, why should they have stopped now?'

'Here's something else off the Net,' Rick went on, scanning his second sheet. Again he read: ' "Russia is regarded as an increasingly unreliable partner on international issues, because of the power of corrupt officials, crooked businessmen and organised crime, a US public policy research group declared on Monday. A panel of the Center for Strategic and International Studies said that the criminalisation of Russia's economy, if left unchecked, would make normal state-to-state relations with the country unviable. It will become impossible for the United States to have traditional, satisfactory dealings with an emergent Russian criminal state." '

He lowered the paper and said, 'What about that?'

'That's it, exactly,' I said. 'The stupid bastards in the Pentagon have got the wind up. They're bobbing like the shit-house fly, and want us to do their dirty work for them.'

Once in Russia, we were going to need several days for site recces. Obviously we'd have to get the training course up and running; so no matter how fast we moved there was no way we could install Apple and Orange immediately. That in turn meant that the devices would have to be stored somewhere secure for the time being.

The idea of having them with us in that decrepit barrack block at Balashika seemed impossible, and I rapidly came to the conclusion that we must get them into the cellar at the British Embassy at the first possible moment. There, apart from other considerations, Apple would be practically on-site anyway, only a few hundred yards from its ultimate destination. The trouble was, the devices would travel into Russia with us on the Herc and be off-loaded on the strip at Balashika. How could we account for the fact that we needed to transport heavy boxes into the centre of Moscow?

'Tell the Russians we've shipped in some new comms equipment, at the Embassy's request,' Whinger suggested.

'OK,' I agreed, 'but what do we say to the *Embassy*?'

'That it's some of our own stuff. The security in the Russian barracks is shite, and the equipment's so sensitive that we don't want to leave it lying around while we're out working all day. You pretty well told the Chargé that already.'

'All right,' I persisted. 'Let's think about transport, then. That's going to be a bugger. It looks to me as though we're going to have to whip in to the Embassy pretty often. We don't want to draw attention to ourselves by using a military truck or a Brit car. I hope Anna turns up trumps with those Russian vehicles she promised.'

After a delay to the MAC flight from Nevada, Toad didn't reach Hereford until late that evening. I was having supper when I got a message to say that he was in the SAW. As soon as I'd finished I went over to the wing's special armoury – and there he stood, dry-washing his hands. After a couple of months in the desert sun, anyone else would have had a really expensive tan, but all he'd managed was to turn a sickly yellow.

'Hi, Toad,' I went. 'You made it. Where are your packages?'

'Right there.' He half-turned to his right, pointing behind him, and there, sitting on a wheeled pallet by the wall, were four black steel trunks, each maybe two feet by four feet, and only a foot deep, with a couple of smaller boxes on top of them. The only markings, stencilled in white paint, said 'A-1, A-2, A-R' and 'O-1, O-2, O-R'.

'Jesus!' I said. 'So they come in kit form and have to be fitted together.'

'Oh yes. Early portable devices were in two parts. Then, as technology improved, they started making one-piece models – real suitcase bombs. Those are still around, but when something more powerful's wanted they've gone back to this modular design.'

I was horribly fascinated by the thought of what the black cases contained and what they could do. But at the same time I couldn't help being irritated by Toad's proprietorial air. There was something in his gestures, in his attitude, which said, These are mine, and you can keep your distance.

'Everything all right?' I asked.

'Sure.' He rubbed his hands some more.

'Good course?'

He nodded.

'Have you been briefed about the operation?'

'Not yet.'

'Well, we're leaving for Moscow the day after tomorrow, so there isn't much time. Better come on up, and I'll give you the bones of it now. Then maybe you can brief me and Whinger on the devices in the morning.'

We went up to the main briefing room, and I unlocked the safe in which I'd stored the site plans and the CDs. Toad hardly spoke as I went through them, but I knew that his quick mind was soaking in every detail.

'The Orange site is out in open country,' I told him. 'Part scrub-land, part forest. As far as I can see, it's just going to be a hole in the ground: either one we find and adapt or one we dig ourselves. So I don't see much of a problem there. The tricky one's going to be Apple. This access shaft, in the courtyard, is at least twenty feet deep.'

'Pulleys,' said Toad.

'Spot on. I've thought of that. Those small titanium pulleys the Mountain Troop use for hoisting heavy machine guns and mortars up steep hillsides. The thing is, how robust are the devices? Can they stand knocks, or have they got to be feather-bedded?'

'Oh no, they're pretty robust. You could probably drop one down the shaft and it wouldn't come to any harm.' Toad frowned and then added, 'Cancel that. Better not drop it.'

'But it couldn't go off, even if we did?'

'Not a chance. Until the two components are united they're inert. We'll have to take them in separately and couple them at the last minute.'

He studied the plan for a minute, then asked, 'What depth is the tunnel running at as it comes to the Kremlin wall?'

'We don't know. But it's a hell of a wall. Must be thirty or forty feet high, so the foundations have to go down some way.'

'We'll need to get the SCR within ten feet of the surface.'

'The SCR?'

'The Satellite Communications Responder. That's the unit which the satellite sends messages to and interrogates.'

'How big is it?'

'Oh – those small black boxes downstairs. Didn't you see them? Like this.' He held up his hands a foot apart.

'Can they be some way away from the device?'

'Sure. The connecting co-ax cables can be any length.'

'Maybe there'll be an old ventilation shaft. Or maybe we'll have to bore into the tunnel roof.'

'An auger, then.'

'Good thinking. What else?'

Slimy though he was, Toad had his head screwed on, and in the morning he gave the whole team a good briefing. This time he started with the SCR, and described how it needed to be positioned with its antenna coming up to within three or preferably two feet of the surface. The controlling satellite, he told us, would send it signals to check that the system was working. There was no chance of an accidental explosion, because detonation could only be achieved by a complex sequence of questions and answers, and confirmed by coded messages from the Pentagon.

'The SCR contains its own nuclear power source, which gives it an indefinite life,' Toad said. 'One snag is that the generator contains radioactive fuel and could become a health hazard if it gets crushed or broken. That's why it's so heavy: it's encased in a lead jacket.'

'What happens if the Russian security forces do an electronic sweep along the front of the Kremlin, up above?' asked Rick. 'Won't they detect it?'

'Almost impossible,' Toad replied smoothly. 'For ninety-nine per cent of the time the SCR's passive. It's just listening. Its response periods will be pre-set to times like three in the morning, when people are least likely to be about.'

Seeing Rick frown, he added in a patronising voice, 'I wouldn't worry about it. You can take it from me that it'll be OK. I could go into a more technical explanation, but I don't think you'd understand. The bottom line is that the satellite sends signals down, and the SCR only answers for a split-second every twenty-four hours.'

He looked round the row of faces, clearly enjoying his role of teacher. 'For security when the devices are being moved around,' he went on, 'there's this very useful piece of equipment.'

He crossed to the end of the small case marked A-R and applied his thumb to a shallow depression near one corner. The sprung lid of a small compartment flew open, and from it he took out an object the size of a compact mobile phone. 'This is the radio alarm trigger, generally known as the Rat. Whenever this is switched on it has to remain within thirty metres of the device. If it goes farther away than that it automatically triggers a radio alarm in the device itself. The signal can be picked up by satellite. So if you have to move the device in enemy territory, I suggest that the guy in charge keeps the Rat on his belt – like this.'

He clipped the thing on to his own belt, then returned it to its lair.

'What about having a shufti inside one of the components?' I suggested.

'Not a chance.' Toad started dry-washing his hands again. 'They're all sealed down, and I don't want to break them out until they're about to be put in position. There are quite a few checks I'll have to make then.'

We couldn't argue with him and he knew it. He wouldn't even come clean about the damage each bomb was likely to do. He pretended the information was classified and kept it to himself. We had to be content with staring at diagrams of bewildering complexity which he brought up on a lap-top from his own CD. We all knew, though, that the destructive capacity packed into the black boxes in front of us was something awesome.

'What would happen if we got the devices in position but didn't prime them properly?' I asked. 'What if you deliberately connected them up wrong?'

'The satellite would detect the fault. That's the beauty of the system. The Pentagon would know there was something wrong. They'd probably send us back to put it right.'

'Well,' said Pavarotti, as if to sum up. 'I'm not going down any fucking tunnel. That's for certain.'

'I wouldn't be so sure,' I told him.

Our 'last-minute' checks seemed endless. We were taking our own main weapons and ammunition – MP5s and G3s – so that we could give demonstrations without having to worry about handling unfamiliar kit. Stun grenades for CQB work; plastic explosive, detonators and det cord for EMOE. Also, I'd cleared it with Sasha that we could take pistols, to carry covertly when we were outside the camp. With crime running at the level it was, he'd agreed that it would be only sensible to have some means of self-defence.

Covert comms equipment was another basic item we'd need for demonstrations. Also, I foresaw that it would be indispensable when it came to recceing sites for Apple and Orange and then inserting the devices. Plenty of batteries were required, therefore, and recharging kit. For work in the tunnel we needed good head-torches, short-handled picks and jemmies, plus a wire climbing ladder for going down the access shaft, and lightweight pulleys and nets for lowering the component parts of Apple. Also sandbags for removing spoil from the insertion-point, lock-picking kit for the padlocks, shovels for possible digging on the Orange site . . . All this on top of our normal equipment and personal kit.

At one point the CO called me in for a private chat.

'Sit down, Geordie,' he began. 'I can see you're not happy. You've just got to make the best of it.'

I nodded. 'This mass-destruction – it's not like the Regiment.'

'I know. But what you've got to believe is that the devices will probably never be used.'

'Easy enough to say that. One thing I'd like to be bloody sure of is that they're not going to get used while the team's still over there.'

'Don't be stupid. There's no chance of that.'

'How do we know? What if the Resident gets assassinated and there's some kind of Mafia takeover? What if Clinton decides that Russia's going down the tubes and criminals are about to take over? The international situation might go to ratshit in a few hours.'

I stared at the boss, and he said nothing.

'What I'd like to know is, whose finger's going to be on the button? Who's really in charge? If it's the Yanks, I'm not at *all* happy. They're just as volatile as anyone else. Worse, probably.'

The boss gave a non-committal grunt, and I went on, 'It's bloody two-faced of our own government, anyway. All these overtures to the Kremlin about giving them help – and now this.'

'That's politics for you.'

There was no good counter to that, and I came away feeling pretty pissed off. Thinking ahead, I put in a call over the secure satellite link to the Chargé d'Affaires in Moscow. He sounded friendly enough, to the point of asking if there was anything he could do to help.

'Well, thanks,' I said. 'We're coming in tomorrow night, as

89

planned, but we don't start the course till Monday – so I wondered if we could bring some kit to store in the cellar on Sunday evening?'

'Ah.' He sounded a bit taken aback. 'I shan't be here. But I tell you what. I'll leave the keys with the duty officer. That's going to be . . . wait a minute . . . Richard Henshaw. I'll tell him to expect you. What time will you get here?'

I had to think fast. 'I'm not certain we'll have transport by then. But let's assume we will have. We should be there between six and seven in the evening. If there's anything different, I'll call to say so.'

'Right-oh. I'll leave a message at the gate.'

So far, so good. Then, to take my mind off immediate problems, I called Tony Lopez, late of the US SEAL special forces, but by now working in CIA headquarters at Langley, Virginia. I had come to know Tony after he'd rescued me when I got hurt in Iraq during the Gulf War and we'd been interned together for a month. Then, a couple of years later, he had come over for a tour with the Regiment, and had done brilliantly until he'd had his left arm smashed.

His wound was serious enough to finish his career in the armed forces, and when he'd recovered, he joined the CIA. He'd been too discreet to tell me exactly what areas he was working in, but it didn't take a genius to guess that he would have reponsibility for special forces projects.

Now, when I got through, he sounded his usual lively self.

'Hi, Tony,' I went. 'How are you doing?'

'Good! Good! How about you?'

'Fine. How's the arm?'

'Still improving. About seventy per cent now.'

'Great. Listen, Tony – d'you know people in the Drug Enforcement Agency?'

'Sure do. Why?'

I told him about Rick's friend Natasha, and her sister Irina who'd got sucked into the Russian Mafia operations in New York. I also gave him the name of the brasserie in Brooklyn where the girl was supposed to be working, and asked if he could do anything to help.

He said he'd put in a call to a friend in the DEA, but then in a different voice he added, 'So it's you who's been in Moscow. I might have guessed.'

'What's that supposed to mean?'

'Nothing. But this assignment could be a hot number. When you go back there, Geordie, take it easy. OK?'

'OK.' I wasn't going to ask him anything else. Clearly Tony knew about Operation Nimrod: he knew we'd been over, he knew we were going back . . . and there were obviously things about the task that he didn't like.

SIX

The runway at Balashika was pretty short, and the captain of the aircraft warned us in advance that he'd have to do a tactical landing. In practice that meant that he banged the Herc down so hard on the first impact that it bounced and flew on a bit before coming to earth a second time. Down in the back we all had a good grip of the cargo nets, and although we went weightless for a second or two, with legs and bodies flying up in the air, we were none the worse.

When the tailgate opened the night air struck surprisingly cool. Sasha was there to greet us, and as we shook hands I remarked on how cold it was.

'I told you,' he said. 'Summer is feenished.'

But the temperature was good for unloading and, in spite of numerous well-meaning offers of help from waiting Russians, we insisted on humping all our own kit ourselves.

'It's kind of you to have kept them up,' I told Sasha, 'but we can handle this. Let them go to bed.'

We had everything out on the apron within forty minutes, and as the Herc took off for home I watched its navigation lights disappearing into the sky with the same feeling I'd had when I'd looked at the head loadie before we went out on the HALO jump over France: Lucky bastards, I thought. They're off home. A nice, comfortable stop-over in Berlin, and tomorrow they'll be back. We, meanwhile, were left two thousand miles from base with fearful problems to solve.

As soon as I saw we had everything up together, I insisted that Sasha fall out. I knew he had a room in the officers' mess on the camp, but he'd told me that at weekends he went home to live

93

with his mother in her flat in Ostankino, a northern suburb of Moscow. At that time of night, he said, it was only fifteen minutes by car – so off he went, with promises to be back first thing in the morning.

The important stuff was locked inside green Lacon boxes, stencilled with white numbers – 1 to 27. We never let any of these boxes out of our sight. We lifted them on to hand-trolleys, wheeled them across to our designated block, and carried them up the steps ourselves. I was glad to find that Sasha had got strong hasps and padlocks organised on most of the doors, and I designated two rooms at the end of the corridor as stores, next to the kitchen on one side and the signal office on the other.

By 2.00 a.m. local time we had everything squared away. The cooking equipment was in the kitchen and the edible stores in the room alongside. We designated the best-protected room the armoury, putting the weapons, ammunition and CND components in there. The room next to that had the only telephone, so we made that our office and comms centre, housing (among other things) the lockable filing cabinets we'd brought to contain the classified CDs. I created an instant rule that all lap-tops were to remain in the office, unless being used for giving lessons, and that no Russian was allowed in there on any pretext.

As for sleeping, we billeted ourselves in twos. Whinger and I shared, with the rest of the team similarly paired off. Coarse sheets and blankets had been dumped on the beds, and the water in the showers was hot. A smell of fresh emulsion paint, not unpleasant, made it clear that some hasty sprucing-up had taken place. Mal nearly went ballistic when he saw a rat disappear down a hole in the corner of the corridor, but I told him to push a Lacon box over the place and we'd deal with it in the morning.

The odd man out was Toad, whom I'd detailed to sleep with his devices in the armoury. In fact I'd told him that as long as the CNDs remained in camp, he was to stay with them day and night, except when relieved by somebody approved by me. I also told him he'd got to screw the nut and knock his running on the head for the time being, even if it meant him going short

94

of exercise. In sum, he was to guard his charges with his life, until such time as we could transfer them to the safety of the Embassy cellar.

For our nefarious purposes, the block was brilliantly placed. It backed directly on to the edge of the training area, with no other buildings behind it, and nobody overlooking its rear entrance. Our people would be able to slip out that way, straight down a track and into the scrubby forest. Also behind the block was parking space for several cars, so we'd have little bother loading the CND components into vehicles for transport to the Embassy.

When I realised how well sited we were, I almost changed my mind about the need to move the devices: in such favourable circumstances I thought hard about keeping Orange with us. Then I reckoned, No: I don't fancy being out of the building all day, running the course, with those things sitting here – even if Toad *is* in charge. Better get both of them into the Embassy until we're set up to deploy them. Thus I decided that we wouldn't wait, but would follow my original plan and move them on Sunday evening. For one thing, they'd be gone before Anna came on the scene, at 8.30 on Monday morning; and for another, I already knew from our first visit that the Moscow traffic was far lighter during the weekend than on working days.

It wasn't long before I felt sure I'd made the right decision.

With the course not due to start until Monday morning, we had all Sunday to sort ourselves out; but we'd hardly got a scratch breakfast down our necks when Steve, one of the scalies, came up to me with a face of doom and asked if he could have a word. When I asked what the problem was he jerked his head up and back, meaning, Let's go outside. So we walked out the back, into the edge of the forest, and he said, 'Geordie, they've put bugs in the power points.'

'Where?'

'In the signals room, and in the kitchen.'

'Ah, shite! Are you sure?'

'Hundred per cent. I was making a routine sweep, and they

95

came up loud and clear. Have a listen for yourself.'

Back inside, I borrowed Steve's detector kit and ran the sensor pad along the wall in the signals room. As it passed the dual power-point, a loud *brrraannggg* sounded in the headphones, then died away as I moved the pad on. I said nothing, but shook my head, went through to the next room, and got the same thing.

What should I do? Report the bugs to Anna in the morning? Have a quiet word with Sasha? Say nothing?

In the open again, walking up and down, I asked Steve if he could disable the microphones without his interference being apparent.

'I suppose if I knocked one out, they might think it had just broken down. But if I did both they'd be bound to realise.'

'OK, then. Knacker the one in the signals office. Break one of the connections or whatever you have to do, but leave the other. Have you swept the signals room thoroughly?'

He nodded. 'There's only the one in there.'

'Better do all the rooms the same.'

Now I realised why our hosts had done so much re-decorating: they'd painted over any bits of replastering that had been needed.

The discovery unsettled me. 'I'm really disappointed,' I told Whinger. 'I hoped all that was a thing of the past.'

'Who are we to talk?' he said.

The truth of his remark kept me in a state of permanent unease. I confirmed to Whinger that I didn't intend to mention the bugs: we'd wait to see what happened if Steve took one out.

The day being Sunday, there were few people about on the camp, and we were left to sort ourselves out – which suited us fine. There was more than enough admin and physical work to keep us busy. Sasha was in and out, making sure we had all we wanted.

It was clear that all our lads were going to have to take turns at cooking, and in mid-morning Sasha took Dusty – our master chef – and Mal off on a conducted tour of Balashika's shops, from which they returned effing and blinding. The so-called

Supermagazin was a disaster, and the only place they found any half-decent vegetables was in an open-air market, where locals were selling produce brought in from the country. In the Supermagazin they'd bought scabby oranges, and at the other place they had got eggs, onions, carrots, cabbages and potatoes; but still it looked as though we were going to be relying heavily on tins, packets and boil-in-the-bag meals designed for use in the field.

After lunch, under Sasha's supervision, drivers delivered two battered-looking Volgas, one mid-grey, one black, with worn tyres and rust showing through the paint where the mudguards joined the body. He explained that they were a slightly later model than his own, but similar. The grey one had 88,000 ks on the clock, the black 13,000 – which obviously meant that it had been round the dial once at least

When I asked if it was OK to drive around the dirt roads inside the training area, to familiarise ourselves with the vehicles, Sasha exclaimed, 'Why not?'

'How about going into town?'

'Whatever you like. You've got your licences OK. But inside camp, no red-and-white bars, please.'

He meant that we weren't to go through any of the safety barriers that blocked off the danger areas; but there was plenty of other space, and four of us set out for a spin. Before we left, I got Steve to run his bug-hunter over both vehicles just in case, but the result was negative, and that reassured me a little. Nevertheless, we didn't propose to run unnecessary risks, so we took covert radios and kept the Volgas a few hundred metres apart, chatting to make sure we weren't being followed.

The cars were sluggish and noisy, with heavy steering; but even though driving them was a pain, at least we had wheels of our own. I hadn't expected such freedom: I'd imagined we would be more closely supervised. The entire training area was ringed by the concrete wall, so we were in fact enclosed. We soon found that a perimeter track skirted the inside of the wall, heading out north-eastwards in the direction of the space complex; and after a couple of ks we began to see, beyond the wall, amazingly large, white dish-aerials pointing skywards in serried ranks. Although I said nothing, I could immediately imagine why the Pentagon fancied taking that lot out.

The land was almost dead flat, with only a gentle rise and fall to relieve the monotony. Patches of pine and birch forest alternated with wide-open scrub and grass, criss-crossed by dirt tracks, reminding me of the training areas at Pirbright. Here and there a primitive wooden observation tower stuck up above the trees. Clearly the training area was well used, but two things about it made me feel reasonably secure. One was the sheer size of the landscape. In terrain as open as this it would be very difficult for anyone to watch us without our being aware of the surveillance. The other factor in our favour was the decrepit nature of the fixtures and fittings. On several of the wooden watch-towers the ladders had rungs missing, and the red-and-white barriers which Sasha had mentioned were bent and rusting. All this, we felt certain, reflected the cut-down in the Russian forces: clearly, they had nobody to do the maintenance and were generally short-staffed.

Three ks from base, as we were cruising gently, Rick suddenly pointed to his left. There, at the end of a glade with a shallow ditch running out along its base, was a derelict air-raid shelter or bunker – a dome of concrete protruding from a bank of higher ground, with a small rectangular opening in the side that faced us.

I felt my heartbeat speed up. At first glance this looked an incredibly promising candidate for the burial of Orange. The perimeter wall of the training area was only a few yards behind it, the nearest dish aerials a short distance farther off. We'd never get closer than this. I could scarcely believe we'd found one site already.

'Black to Grey,' I called over the radio. 'Stopping to have a pee. Hang off and watch my back.'

'Grey. Roger,' came Whinger's voice.

In the warm afternoon sun Rick and I strolled towards the bunker while Mal stayed at the wheel. Small birds were singing and the place had a peaceful atmosphere. All the same, I was nagged by a feeling that somebody was watching us.

'We won't go any closer,' I said quietly to Rick. 'Turn back.'

From fifty yards short of the structure, I could see planks and spars of wood piled up inside the opening. The shelter, whatever it was, appeared to be full of rubbish. All the better for us.

We slowly wheeled round and walked towards the car again. Facing that way, I realised that there was one watch tower in sight, but it was a long way off, and, as far as we could tell, unmanned. To complete the casual picture, I went over and had a piss against a gorse bush, after which we got back into the car.

'Mobile again,' I told Whinger. 'Nothing moving your way?'

'All clear.'

We returned to base without incident. Had I imagined the unseen eyes? Rick said he had felt nothing – and he normally picked up danger signals before anyone else. Once again I started wavering. My first reaction, as we drove away from the shelter, had been. Right, let's go for it. Let's get the damned CND straight in there and not bugger about taking it into the city centre. Then the feeling of unease returned, making me realise how hasty I was being. Obviously we needed to recce the site properly before we went crashing into it. Even though the building looked as though it had been abandoned for years, it could still be the scene of some training activity. Better keep calm, take time to settle in and get the feel of things.

'Carry on as planned,' I told Whinger. 'We'll aim to roll into town after dark.'

We had a meal – Dusty produced a great corned-beef hash with plenty of onions and fried eggs on top – and waited till it was fully dark. Then we backed both Volgas as close as we could to our block's rear entrance. I could tell that everyone was on edge, from the way they were talking in short bursts. We put dickers out to watch either end of the building, and when they confirmed that the coast was clear, we began carrying the kit out.

From measurements taken earlier, we knew that one Lacon box would effectively fill the boot of each car, and that the rear doors were too narrow to take one at all. We'd therefore opened the boxes up and brought out the CNDs in their original packing. The main components, in their black steel cases, were forty inches by thirty by twelve, and the SCR, an incredibly heavy lump, was a twenty-inch cube. The cases had built-in handles at the corners for a four-man carry.

Before we left the building, Toad opened up the small compartment in the base of each SCR and brought out its Rat. I hooked one into my belt and gave the other to Pavarotti. Now those two had to stay within a hundred feet of their devices, otherwise the pagers would go off automatically and start transmitting their alarm signal.

I was shitting bricks as we came down the steps with the first of them. Having a thing like that in your hands is no joke. No matter how often Toad had assured us that an accidental impact couldn't set the bomb off, I kept wondering what would happen if one of us lost his footing.

Gingerly we lowered the first case into one boot. That just left room for the SCR box alongside. The second big case had to go on the back seat, and the combined weight put the Volga down on its springs. With two guys up front, the rear mudguards were almost on the tyres.

Sasha had told the guardroom we'd be going out, so we had no problem there. We flashed some big smiles along with our passes, and the sentry raised the barrier, waving us through. Then, on the main road, it was just a question of turning left and heading down the big highway into town.

The traffic was incredibly light. I thought of Sunday night on the M4, with a million cars all trying to pour back into London at the same time. Here, I realised, most of the poor bastards who lived in the city centre had nowhere to go at weekends.

Whinger drove the lead car, the black one, with me beside him, map in hand. Rick kept the grey Volga four or five hundred yards behind, so that the two vehicles didn't seem to be associated. With him was Pavarotti, and, squeezed into the back seat beside half of Orange, Toad. There was really no need for him to come with us, but at the back of my mind lurked the

100

worry that while we were moving the devices around, something might happen to them. I could hardly imagine what the problem might be, but if one of them started ticking or heating up we might suddenly need Toad to deal with it.

The two cars were in radio contact, in case anyone saw trouble looming. The plan was for Rick to close up in the final stages of the trip, so that he could follow us and not have to worry about navigation. We also had pistols in underarm holsters, concealed beneath our jackets.

When we joined the thin stream of traffic, I realised what good cars the Volgas were to have. Never mind that they had zero acceleration and roared and wallowed like ten-ton trucks: they were anonymous, and scruffy enough not to arouse any-one's interest. As we kept to the right-hand lane at about sixty ks, any number of identical vehicles surged past on the outside.

That first run-in could hardly have been easier. The only threat was from the potholes which, with the huge load we had on board, could have done serious damage. Whinger often had to swerve to avoid a chasm ahead.

To help with the map-reading in the city centre, I'd made a list of the streets we needed to take. In fact, for most of the way all we had to do was follow the same highway right through, almost until we reached the Moscow River.

Once over the river it was plain sailing along the south bank. Ahead of us and to the right, the red stars on the towers of the Kremlin glowed in the sky – familiar landmarks already, giving me the comfortable feeling that I was back on ground I knew. In a few seconds we passed under the bridge we'd walked across that first night. Having glanced in the mirror to make sure there was only one car behind, I called Rick to say, 'Slowing now,' and Whinger dropped our speed to twenty ks so that we could get a look at the pink-and-white gateway and the churchyard.

The drive-past didn't yield much. As Rick had predicted, the tall, elaborate wrought-iron gates were open, and through them we caught a glimpse of a small, low church, set back maybe seventy metres from the road. The light inside the courtyard was exceedingly dim, and we couldn't see details, but I got an impression of ramshackle buildings round the sides, and even some bushes.

'Nice and dark,' commented Whinger.

'Not too tidy, either. Look out, though. Here we are.'

The security guards on the Embassy gate had been briefed to expect us, and let us through without bother. There was a short delay while the Brit guy phoned the duty officer to say we'd arrived: then a message came for us to drive round into the compound. There, an outside light had been switched on, and under it was standing a young-looking fellow with fair hair.

As I jumped out, he came forward. 'Sergeant Major Sharp? Richard Henshaw.'

We shook hands. I introduced Whinger properly, and the others more sketchily.

'Got some stuff for us, have you?' asked Henshaw.

'Well, it's for ourselves really. I'd just like to be sure it's in safe hands.'

'Of course. Well, here are your keys. You know where to go. There are two locks on the cellar door. This key's for the central lock, this one for a padlock that goes through a hasp at the bottom corner. But in any case, the compound's fully secure, so I imagine your equipment will be all right. D'you need any help to unload?'

'No, no. We'll be fine, thanks. Is this the only set of keys you have?'

'No, there's a duplicate set as well.'

'Do you mind if I have them too? I'd rather we didn't have anyone else poking around in there.'

'Oh – all right.' He looked a bit sniffy, but disappeared briefly inside and came back with another set.

'There you are. I'll leave you to it. As it happens, I'm quite busy.'

'Thanks again, then.'

As soon as he was indoors we opened the up-and-over steel door of the cellar and backed the black Volga to the head of the ramp. There was no point in taking the car down the slope, because the approach, between concrete walls, was too narrow for the rear doors to open more than a few inches and we wouldn't have got the boxes out of the back seat. That meant a short carry, and before we began it I scanned round to make certain we weren't being overlooked. No problems on that score: the high wall of the compound blanked off the view from outside. Reassured, I said, 'OK, lads. Here we go,' and we set about dumping our lethal load.

When all six cases were stacked, Toad brought out the two Rats, switched them off and slipped them back into their compartments in the SCRs. To put the final touch on our security, we replaced the padlock on the foot of the door with one of our own.

Toad was obviously impressed by the size of the Embassy buildings, and from the way he started dry-washing his hands I knew he was coming up with some new idea. 'Now we've got the devices here,' he said, 'hadn't I better stay with them? There must be a spare room I could live in.'

'Not a chance,' I told him. 'The kit'll be fine here. Nobody can touch it. You're coming back with us.'

The relief of getting the devices off my hands – even for the time being – made me feel reckless, and I almost went straight into a recce of the churchyard. 'After all,' I said before we re-boarded the cars in the embassy compound, 'we're on the spot. Why not have a look round?'

It was the ever-observant Rick who stopped me. 'When we drove in, there was a guy hanging around out there on the embankment,' he warned.

'Where?'

'About a hundred metres beyond the entrance. He looked everything like a dicker, from the FSB or somewhere.'

'In that case we'll not piss about in the area,' I agreed. 'Especially if he's still there when we pull out.'

He was – a figure in dark clothes, wearing a cap, leaning out over the river wall as if watching boats go by. 'He's moved this way a bit,' said Rick over the radio. 'But it's the same guy.'

'Right then,' I replied. 'That's it. Next stop Balashit-heap.'

★

I found it a pleasure to start the course the next morning. Our team had all slept well, and the weather was still fine. Whinger and I had gone for a four-mile run at first light, and after a shower and breakfast I felt in good shape. But above all I was chuffed to get back to our proper role of soldiering, and passing some of our skills on to others.

The sight of Anna in her DPMs was enough to put a smile even on Toad's face. I'd arranged with Sasha that all our guys would get an issue of Russian combat kit, so that we blended into the local scenery. Naturally, the garments didn't fit too well; we could disguise short or long sleeves by rolling them up, but the blouses hung away from our waists and the trousers tended to be bulky. Anna's kit, in contrast, was immaculately cut to flatter her slender figure, and looked as though it had been styled by some Western couturier. She wore elegant black boots, a black leather belt that emphasised her narrow waist, and a jaunty peaked cap. Even though she wore no insignia you felt instinctively that she was the senior officer present.

'You got your cars all right?' she asked.

'Yes, thanks. They'll do well.'

'Nothing special, I'm afraid. Not like a couple of BMWs.'

'Oh well – they're fine for getting in and out of town.'

I wasn't sure if she knew that we'd already been in to the Embassy, but I wasn't going to bring the matter up unless she did, so I said nothing on that score and switched to matters about the course.

To open proceedings we got the twenty-four students into the main lecture room and sat them down, while our team lined up across the stage, Sasha hovering at one side. Anna introduced herself to the course, and to the Brits who hadn't met her, with a brief explanation that she came from the FSB and that she had been appointed our liaison officer. I then introduced our lads one by one, using the names they'd chosen to sport on their chest badges. I felt a right prick saying, '*Vot Rik, vot Dosti . . .* This is Rick, this is Dusty,' followed by a couple of words about what each man would be teaching – weapons, unarmed combat, explosive entry, house assaults, vehicle drills and so on. When I came to Whinger – last, because he was last in the line – I asked Anna to explain that Vuinzha was not his proper name but the best approximation we could make of his nickname.

'And what's that?' she asked. When I told her, she immediately came up with, 'Well, we've got one of them too.' She looked around the benches and pointed to a tall, saturnine fellow with sticking-out ears. 'He's called Zanuda,' she said, 'and that means exactly the same thing. He's always moaning and groaning.'

Like us, the Russians were wearing name badges, but I got them to call out their first names all the same. This revealed that we had three men called Nikolai and three called Sergei, as well as two Semyons and two Igors.

'Right,' I said, moving along the ranks, 'I know that really we should call you by your patronymics, but it'll be easier for us if we give you numbers. You're Nikolai *Odin*, you're Nikolai *Dva*, you're Nikolai *Tri*.'

I did the same with the Sergeis and the two doubles. All that, coupled with the discovery of the twin Whingers, caused a good few laughs and broke the ice.

Finding that several of the students were from Spetznaz and some from Omon, I deliberately split the two groups, pairing off each man with one from the other organisation, so that they'd all have to mix and communicate. 'It's important you all know each other really well,' I told them. 'Your lives may depend on knowing how your partner's going to react in a particular situation. Learn everything you can about each other. Our team have been working together for years, and we're still finding out.'

Altogether the Russians looked a lively bunch, and fit: by the glow on them, I guessed they'd all been running that morning. They were all aged between twenty-five and thirty-five, but they were noticeably bigger than us – taller on average, and well built. There were a lot of broad, wide-cheekboned Slavic faces, and a couple of broken noses. When I asked how many had fought in Chechnya, nine hands went up, and a similar question about Afghanistan produced four.

'*Khorosho!*' I said warmly. 'Plenty of combat experience.'

When Anna translated, the remark brought out self-congratulatory smiles all round, and I could see we were going to get on.

The only two I didn't much care for were a pair who, I knew, had come from SOBR, the organisation that had once guarded the prisons and gulags. Sasha told me that, when the camps had broken up in 1992, a lot of these guys were thrown on to the market – and some bunch they were, too. They had the reputation of being the nastiest of all Russian special forces, with their own line in brutality and torture. Certainly the two we'd got, Oleg and Misha, looked pretty low-brow and unco-operative.

As I handed round the course programme, written in both languages, I said, 'OK, we'll be starting right away, with basic CQB. But first we want to take you on the ranges and make sure we're all together on our commands. We want to watch you firing, and see how you do things. This is as much for our benefit as for yours: we need to get to know your methods.'

So we began, with magazine changes, stoppage drills and zeroing. Their weapon-handling proved to be good, although, as I'd suspected, some of the safety aspects wanted watching. We delivered a few bollockings on this score, especially after Sergei Two let off an AK47 round vertically into the air after he was supposed to have cleared his rifle.

Over the next few days, with basic range-work satisfactory, we began teaching the theory of house assaults, starting small, with two-man teams, making the students work in their pairs, showing them how to go through a room and clear it. We then moved on to four-man teams, through an assault on a single room to one on a house with four rooms and a corridor, still using one team. Then we progressed to having several teams operating together: eight or a dozen men entering different rooms at the same instant. Next came multi-floor tactics, with guys bursting in through doors, windows and skylights, all their movements precisely co-ordinated by radio.

At first we worked in classrooms, using magnetic boards and coloured counters to demonstrate formations, but soon we started moving men through actual rooms, and finally took them out for live firing practice in their primitive Killing House. The Russians were full of energy and enthusiasm, and they fairly threw themselves into the work. But what they lacked was precision: several times, when left to themselves to make a plan, they managed to have one assault team come face to face with another in the stair well, and we had to drum into them the vital importance of logical thought in command and control.

All this was interesting and good fun – a challenge for both sides, and one that we all enjoyed. But the trouble was that, for me, the days began to slip away at an alarming speed. In no time at all it was Wednesday, then Thursday, then Friday. Our first week had almost gone, and we'd had no chance to recce either of our prospective nuclear sites.

The other aggravation was that on only the third night Rick did a runner. After supper he simply disappeared, and there were a few moments' panic before Mal, who was sharing a room with him, suddenly said, 'I bet I know where he's at. He's gone to screw that woman he met on the recce. I heard him on the phone to her this morning.'

'Not Natasha!' I said. Bloody hell! I knew he'd taken her address but I didn't realise he'd made contact again.

'Yeah – laid himself on a taxi, too.'

I wasn't going to sit up half the night waiting for the randy bastard to come back, and I never did hear what time he rolled in. But after breakfast I lit into him for taking off without letting me know what he was doing.

'Can't you see?' I told him. 'It's plain bloody stupid. If anything had happened to you we wouldn't have had a clue where you were. If you got picked up by the Mafia, for instance, the whole team would be in the shit.'

He saw the point of that, and apologised, but I still warned him that if he couldn't control himself, I'd have to send him home.

Friendships quickly formed between the two sides, boosted

on one occasion when Pete Pascoe, a great hunter-gatherer, returned from a run with a handful of brown mushrooms he'd collected in the forest. The sight of them brought vigorous protests from our own guys. 'For fuck's sake!' cried Whinger. 'Throw 'em out. Don't cook them, Mal, or you'll poison the lot of us.' But when the students saw them they went ballistic. '*Beliye griby!*' they shouted. 'Boletus mushrooms!' and rushed out to the spot where Pete had found them in search of more.

These were the best, most sought-after kind of fungus. Pete became a hero, and Anna confirmed that Russians are crazy about mushrooms. 'Weekends, at this time of year, thousands of Muscovites go hunting for them in the woods. They come out by train, car, everything. They're like locusts, and sweep the place clean. But the training areas are out of bounds to the public, so we're lucky.'

The week also saw an amazingly rapid proliferation of swear words far worse than any Valentina had taught us. The strangest thing was the way each nationality began to curse in the other's language: very soon the Brits had adopted *yob tvoio mat* (fuck your mother) as their basic expression of disgust, and several of the Russians were giving brilliant imitations of Whinger's 'firekin ell'. They'd started calling Dusty 'Dostoievsky', and Johnny, with his high complexion, had immediately become 'Svyokla' – Beetroot.

After supper on Friday evening, before the weekend break, the students invited us round to their block for a drink. It was a strictly private affair, as drinking in barracks was totally forbidden even to officers. But somebody had slipped out for a few bottles of vodka and some cans of beer, and camaraderie flowered in an impromptu sing-song.

'I hope to Christ this isn't home-brewed,' I said to Whinger as I downed a slug of vodka. 'Otherwise we may wake up blind.'

I turned to Sergei Dva, holding up my glass, and said, 'Not *samogon?*'

He looked outraged. '*Samogon?*' he roared. '*Nyet! Almas!* It is Diamond' – and he grabbed a bottle to show me that it had a big white diamond, flashing reflected light, on its blue label.

Somebody produced an accordion, and it turned out that a man called Yuri had a phenomenal bass voice. To look at him you'd never have suspected it, because he was slim and wiry: the voice sounded altogether too big for such a spare frame, and seemed to come right from his boots. After a few pints of Baltika No. 6 – a powerful, dark brew – he launched into the 'Volga Boatmen's Song', and his mates joined in the choruses with terrific growls of *'Ayee och-nyem, ayee och-nyem'*. When Pavarotti hit back for the visitors with an impassioned rendering of 'Drink to me Only', he won loud cheers.

As merry shouts shook the windows, I sat there sunk in the blackest thoughts. With a couple of exceptions, these Tiger Force guys were ordinary, lively fellows like ourselves. Too many people in Britain still had a Cold War image of the Russians, and thought of them as sinister, alien beings. Now, after a week in the country at grass-roots level, I saw that normal people, like us, had remained human in spite of all the horrors heaped on them. They had their strengths and weaknesses, their good and bad points, the same as us. And an attack on Britain was the last idea that any of them would have entertained.

Nevertheless, the job had to be done – and even as Sergei Three handed me another slug of Diamond I was saying to myself, 'Right: the city centre recce's going down tomorrow night . . .'

SEVEN

When we next went to the Embassy, we left camp at the same time as on our first run, but this time we took just the black Volga. I hadn't told the Chargé we were coming into town: officially, we were going out for a couple of drinks and a bit of a bar-crawl.

Whinger drove, I read the map, and in the back sat Pavarotti, alongside Toad, with his lock-picking kit and two spare padlocks for the cover of the shaft. I'd deliberately nominated Pav as my No. 2 in the tunnel: I'd told him I might well need his height and strength, and that he'd just have to overcome his phobia. We were all wearing civvies, but Pav and I carried thin, dark overalls to wear on top of our other clothes while we were underground.

The weather had turned wet, and rain glistened on the tarmac. We soon realised to our cost that the car's wiper blades were knackered, and created more smears than they removed; but once again the traffic was light and we made rapid progress. On the long, straight run in we turned off the highway a couple of times, waited in a side-road, then came back out, to make certain we didn't have a tail.

No threat presented itself, and this time my navigation was spot-on: we reached the embankment without a false turn. There was a chance that the dicker we'd seen before, or some replacement, might still be on station, so we put in one drive-past, cruising westwards along the gentle, left-hand curve of Sophieskaya Quay, past the pink-and-white gateway, then past the Embassy, both on our left. To our right, across the river, the great buildings of the Kremlin were splendidly floodlit, and faint reflections gleamed in the wet tarmac of the embankment. A couple of cars came from the opposite direction, and a man and a woman were walking away from us, but there was nobody loitering.

At the end, before the bridge approach, Whinger pulled into the kerb and stopped in a dark area between street lamps.

'Right, lads,' I said. 'Just to confirm. The time now is 2105. Drop-off will be in five minutes, at 2110, near enough. A couple of minutes to reach the stable. We'll assume Toad can manage the locks in five minutes. If he has any trouble, Pav, you have a try. That means we should be in the tunnel by 2120 at the latest. Half an hour to suss it out. Back at the ladder by 2150. Pick-up at 2155 from this street, south side, east of the gateway. OK?'

Everyone nodded.

'I don't think the radios will work underground,' I added, 'but everyone stay on listening watch. Pav and I are One, Whinger Two, Toad Three. Our ERV is over there, under the bridge. Right, then – let's go.'

Whinger swung round and drove back at a moderate pace. Now the gateway was on our side of the road. One car overtook at speed, and we watched its tail-lights draw rapidly away into the distance.

Whinger was slowing.

'Nothing behind,' I said. 'Now!'

In seconds the three of us were out and under the gateway. I heard, rather than saw Whinger pull away behind us.

I led us forward into the dark courtyard, keeping to the right-hand wall. Above our heads, lights were showing in a couple of windows; straight ahead the little church sat hunched in shadows, jutting from the left wall of the yard, and the inner road swung past its entrance at the right-hand end into a second yard at the back.

From an intensive study of the plans I had every inch of the layout in my head. Five metres past the door of the church we'd come to the end of the building on our right. Beyond it, set back farther to our right, was a run of smaller structures – old stables. The second little building from our end would be open-fronted, or at least without a door. The head of the shaft was in the back of that shed, behind a wooden partition.

Moving quickly, we came level with the door of the church, which stood slightly open with slivers of light shining through top and bottom. Women were talking inside, their voices rising and falling. We reached the corner of the tall building. There, just visible in the gloom, stood the low range, a few metres farther on. A dozen quick steps brought us to an open doorway.

The wooden lintel was sagging, and I ducked to go under it. Inside, the darkness was so intense that I had to use my pencil torch. The beam picked out an old wooden partition of horizontal planks, extending half-way out across the stable. Beyond it the earth floor was covered with rough, half-rotten hay. Raking some aside with my fingers, I felt iron: the shaft cover. Quickly I cleared debris away from two padlocks – the two we'd been shown in the photo, which were not rusty but coated in dust. Clearly it was some time since they'd been touched.

'Stay in the doorway,' I breathed at Pavarotti, and he faced outwards, on guard, as Toad went to work, opening the barrels of the locks with his levers. I held my torch-beam steady on his hands, wincing at every little click and scrape.

The first lock gave itself up easily after no more than a couple of minutes, but the second was more stubborn. As Toad fiddled and shook, Pav let out a sudden hiss over his shoulder. Instantly I doused my torch. Peering past our sentry, through the doorway, I saw two women come out of the church and walk towards the big building.

We let them get clear, then started again. At last there was a louder click, and the hasp of the second lock fell back. As I carefully lifted the cover its two hinges groaned. My torch, pointing straight down, lit up a square shaft with brick walls, and I could see at a glance that it was big enough to take the component parts of Apple. To make certain, I'd brought with me a piece of string thirty inches long – the maximum dimension we needed – and when I stretched it out from one edge it ended nearly a foot short of the other. That was one problem solved.

The disappointment was the ladder – or rather the lack of one. Instead of a succession of built-in steel rungs there were only two, a foot apart, close to the top of the shaft. From the holes and pits in the brickwork lower down, it looked as though the rest had been ripped out.

'We need the ladder,' I whispered.

I unrolled the springy bundle from my bergen and made one end fast round both hinges. Then I pulled on my overalls, and I heard Pavarotti rustling as he too kitted up.

'All set?' I asked.

'Fine.'

'Right, then, Toad. We'll see you in half an hour.'

I lowered my legs into the shaft and eased my weight down the wire rungs, feeling for them with one foot after the other. Fourteen changes of grip, and my feet touched bottom. As soon as I stepped off the ladder it went slack. I knew they'd feel the change up top, and that Pav would start down.

I heard him scraping on the brickwork as he descended, then felt him touch down beside me. The moment he let go of the ladder, the end went snaking up as Toad reeled it in. His brief was to seal us down with two spare locks he'd been carrying, then to hide up somewhere close by until the time came to release us. That way, if by any thousand-to-one chance somebody did come along to check the padlocks, he'd see nothing amiss. Toad would be in radio contact with Whinger throughout, and could call him in to lay on a diversion if anything started to go wrong.

When I heard the cover come down with a faint thud, I felt a shudder of claustrophobia run through me. If anything serious befell Toad and Whinger, we'd be sealed down here for the duration. Pav was obviously having the same panic, or worse: I could hear him breathing deeply and effing and blinding under his breath.

The air was rowsty and moist, full of a smell of damp decay. Our head-torches revealed a tunnel with a horse-shoe section, lined with bricks. The roof was just high enough for me to stand upright, but Pav, who was a couple of inches taller, had to crouch slightly to keep his head clear.

Somehow – perhaps because of the colour of the Kremlin walls – I'd expected the bricks to be red. In fact they were dirty cream, or had been: much of the surface was black with fungus or slime, and when I touched the wall beside my shoulder my fingertips slid along the wet surface leaving pale streaks. In many places individual bricks had crumbled or fallen out, so that there were frequent piles of rubble on the floor. That gave me encouragement; if the tunnel had been in immaculate condition, any tampering we did would have been that much more obvious.

I bent down and examined the floor. It was evenly covered with damp dust – paste, almost – the same dull colour as the walls. There was no sign of any disturbance – not even any traces of rats, which I'd expected to find. I saw that we wouldn't be able to help leaving footprints.

We'd measured the distances, and I had them in my head: 160 metres to the river bank, 110 metres across the river, seventy-five to the Kremlin wall: 345 metres in all to our preferred site. When I went forward I was going to count.

'Ready?' I whispered.

Pav didn't answer.

'Eh!' I went. 'Let's go.'

'*You* go!' he gasped in a peculiar voice. 'I'm staying here.'

I could tell he was having problems just from the way he sounded. When I put out a hand and touched his arm, I felt him shaking violently. I turned the beam of my head-torch on his face and saw beads of sweat trickling down his cheeks.

'Get hold of yourself!' I snapped. 'We haven't got time to piss about.' In my mind I added, A great big feller like you, too! But I knew his hang-up was getting to him.

A few seconds later he said unsteadily, 'I'm all right now.'

'Come on, then.'

I moved forward, counting. For 102 paces the floor of the tunnel remained level. Then it began to descend.

'Going down under the river,' I said.

'Aye,' Pavarotti agreed. 'I reckon.'

At the start of the slope was a big heap of debris. Such a chunk had fallen out of the upper right-hand wall and roof that the pile of bricks stretched across the tunnel floor to the base of the opposite wall, and we had to scramble over the lowest part of it. When I directed my head-lamp at the raw wall where the bricks had been, I saw that it consisted of moist grey clay.

'At least we can dig into that,' I muttered.

'Pity we can't put the bloody thing in right here. Save messing about.'

'It's too far from the proper site.'

We were still talking in whispers, partly out of habit, partly because we reckoned any sudden noise in a place that had been silent for generations might precipitate a further collapse of roof or wall.

We crept on again, but after a few more steps I stopped. My torch was picking out some difference in the texture of the floor ahead. Instead of light grey, it looked black. I stared for a minute, then said, 'Shit! It's water. The fucker's flooded.'

'Never,' said Pavarotti. 'If part of the tunnel was flooded, the whole thing would be full of water.'

I saw the logic of what he said – but he was wrong. At the point where the water started the floor was still dropping away, so that as we continued forward the flood gradually deepened. The water was cold and black and stank of decay, and we had no option but to wade into it until we were knee, then thigh, then bollock deep. Only when the surface was above our waists could we see that, a few more yards ahead, it came right to the roof.

'Jesus Christ!' said Pavarotti. 'We're knackered. We can't get through this lot.'

We pulled back and started wringing the filthy, black water out of our trousers.

'Pretty obvious, isn't it?' said Pav. 'Of course it's going to be flooded, under the bloody river.'

For a minute I sat on the deck, holding my head in my hands, trying to think constructively.

116

'There's no way we're going to get closer to the Kremlin anywhere else.'

'Why not forget this bastard?' Pav suggested. 'Get the other one in first and then see?'

'No, no,' I told him. 'This is the one they want. I'm sure of that. We've got to crack it. What we need to get through this lot is breathing gear and dry-suits.'

'Yeah. But how do we know what happens the other side of the water? If there *is* another side. If the rest of the tunnel's flooded we're buggered. Jesus, I hate this!'

'It must be quite a small leak,' I said. 'Otherwise, like you said, the whole tunnel would be full. Maybe the pressure's equalised itself somehow – or mud's filtered into the fissure.'

'Let's get the hell out, anyway.'

I'd been planning to sweep away our footprints behind us, but I realised now that, even if we went to that trouble, we'd still leave fresh marks and it would be obvious that somebody had been down here. In any case, the chances of anyone else coming down in the next few days seemed infinitesimal.

We were back under the access shaft just twelve minutes after leaving it. Eighteen minutes to wait. I tried the radio again but got no response. I wasn't going to shout, just in case some Russian was passing the old stable up top. I imagined Toad, on the lurk up there, and Whinger, on standby in the Volga somewhere along the embankment. Maybe they were chatting to each other on the radio.

'Have to wait,' I whispered. 'Let's take a stroll in the other direction.'

That didn't get us far. This time I wasn't counting the steps, but about a hundred metres to the south the tunnel was blocked by a major fall. The damage to the roof and walls was so extensive that I felt sure they'd been bulldozed in or deliberately dropped by hand. Bricks, rubble and clay were tumbled in an impenetrable mass.

Back under the shaft, we waited. We peeled off our sodden overalls, but still we were soaked to the waist and higher. Soon we were pretty cold. I went over the various levels of our fall-back plan in my mind. The first was that if Toad got accosted in the yard, he'd pretend he was drunk and had staggered in there to sleep it off. The next level was that if we three didn't reappear, Whinger would park the car out of the way and come looking for us. The final stage laid down that if all four of us weren't back in camp by 6.00 a.m., the rest of the team would come out to search. I knew that in an emergency we could seek sanctuary in the grounds of the Embassy, but that could only be a last resort because it would blow the whole Apple programme.

Spot on 2150 we heard faint metallic noises above our head – a clinking and scraping. Then came a slight change of pressure as Toad lifted the cover. A few seconds later the ladder-end flicked down beside us. I sent Pav up first, and heard him grunting with effort as he climbed. When the ladder twitched twice, I started up myself.

In the blackness of the shed I whispered, 'OK?' and Toad said, 'Fine' as he undid the ladder, closed the hatch and slipped the original padlocks back through the securing rings.

We pulled some of the rotten hay back over the cover and stood listening in the doorway.

'There's still something on in the church,' said Toad quietly. 'People keep coming back and forth. They're crossing to that doorway with the light showing.'

We were so wet and filthy we looked like a couple of drunks who'd fallen in the river, so even if we did meet someone there was a chance they'd pay no attention.

'Let's go,' I said.

We hustled along the edge of the yard, past the church door, back to the entrance gate. We'd hardly crossed the road on to the pavement beside the river when we saw a car coming in our direction.

In my earpiece Whinger's voice went, 'I have you visual,' and I knew it was him. Ten seconds later he pulled up beside us, and we were safely on board.

'All quiet up top?' I asked.

'Beautiful. But, Christ, what have you been doing?' He turned and glared at me.

'Eating caviar and drinking vodka,' I told him. 'What's the matter?'

'You stink like the arsehole of the universe.'

'Thanks, mate. That's what it's like down there. Stinking. The bastard tunnel's lined with shit and what's more, it's full of water.'

'Could you get through it?'

'Not this time. We waded as far as we could, but we need breathing kit and dry-suits. Head for base, Whinge. We're soaked to the bloody skin.'

Back at Balashika I called straight through to the duty officer in Hereford on the secure Satcom link. We'd set up our equipment in the office-cum-ops room, with the dish aerial on the roof of the building. Daily sweeps for bugs showed that the microphone in the kitchen was still live, so nobody talked any kind of shop in there; but there'd been no reaction to Steve's disabling of the bug in the office, and we reckoned that room was secure.

We were back at 10.40 Moscow time; England was three hours behind, and I knew the duty officer would be around in the ops room in Stirling Lines. Technically, the connection was perfect; if it hadn't been for the half-second lag in transmission as the message went up to the satellite and down again, I might have been in the next room rather than 2,000 miles away.

I recognised the voice at the other end as that of Bill Bravington: I'd spoken to him a couple of times already since our deployment, and had no need to fill him in on background.

'Bill,' I said, 'we've hit a problem. The Apple site. The approach is blocked by water.'

'Wait one.'

I imagined him reaching for a notepad.

'All right,' he went. 'Carry on.'

'We can't tell if the site itself is flooded. If it is, we'll need an alternative. But even to recce it we need breathing kits, dry-suits and half-hour tanks. Plus some of those Boat Troop rubber bags for the components. And two big underwater torches. Can you organise all that soonest?'

119

'No problem. How many suits?'

'Two. Correction: three suits and three tanks. Plus rubber bags.'

'Number?'

'For three pieces. You know – two big, one small. But we'd better have spare small bags as well. Say half a dozen small.'

'Got it. Fins?'

'Sorry?'

'Will you want fins?'

'No, thanks. The distance isn't great enough.'

'OK.'

'And Bill – listen. We need this stuff right away.'

'We'll get it all to London tonight, for the next Diplomatic Bag.'

People must have pulled their fingers out all along the line, because the kit reached the Embassy on Monday afternoon, less than forty-eight hours after we'd found the water. On Tuesday night Pavarotti and I were back in the tunnel, with the same back-up team on watch above. On a weekday evening there was more traffic along the quay and more pedestrians about, but we made it into the stable undetected, and down below everything was precisely as we'd left it: the marks I'd scraped in the dirt on the floor were still fresh, the surface of the water still one inch below a horizontal line I'd scratched in the slime on the wall.

The discovery of water and the sight of the various falls had led me to change our plan. I reckoned that if we managed to reach our destination on this second recce, we might as well start opening up the site for the CND. My reasons were: first, that the chances of any inspection team coming through the water within the next few days were zero, and second, that even if somebody did come snooping, a hole in the wall wouldn't in itself excite suspicion as there were plenty of other natural cavities already.

So it was that this time we had jemmies and small picks in a bergen. Having zipped each other into dry-suits over our clothes, we fitted our tanks and breathing kits and waded into the inky water. On our outward trip the water was fairly clear, and our torch beams reached a few feet ahead – enough for us to spot two submerged heaps of rubble before we blundered into them.

We'd been through all the measurements again, and I'd calculated that the fully flooded section of the tunnel couldn't be more than fifty or sixty metres long. So I wasn't surprised when, after two minutes half-walking, half-swimming, my head broke the surface again. As we continued to advance, an upward slope lifted us steadily clear of the water. Soon we were back on dry land.

The orginal distances given us by the Firm turned out to be spot-on. A total of 340 metres from the old stable, we came to a circular hole in the roof – the ventilation shaft. When I stood upright with my head in the bottom of it, my helmet lamp revealed that it did not rise vertically, but turned at an angle to my right. I could feel cool air flowing down, so I knew it was open at the top.

'Shit hot,' I told Pav. I brought out my tape and held it across. 'Twenty-eight inches. That's easily big enough to accept the SCR – and anyone making visual checks down the manhole won't be able to see round this corner. Made to measure.'

Five metres beyond it, the tunnel had been sealed with a wall of concrete blocks. Yet providentially, just on our side of the barrier was another big fall.

'Look at that,' I said to Pav. 'Made to measure again.'

'Yeah – and we won't even need to move any spoil. We can just add whatever we bring out to the heap that's here already.'

We'd prearranged with Toad that we would stay down for ninety minutes. That gave us an hour of work-time, so we stripped off our dry-suits and took turns to put in concentrated attacks on the clay subsoil. Soon we were both in a muck sweat and having problems with our breathing, perhaps because the air was so damp. None the less, before our hour ran out we had enlarged the cavity to about half the size we needed. We kept the overhanging roof and edges rough, and left a pile of rubble on the base of the hole so that, when we returned to install Apple, all we'd have to do would be to enlarge the hole, clear the bed and lift the components about two feet from the floor before pushing them sideways into their final resting place.

Our return to the surface posed no problems, and once again the pick-up went without a hitch.

'So it's a foot on the brake, is it?' Whinger asked as we drew away.

'What's that?'

'Piece of cake.'

'I wouldn't call it that. But it's possible – wouldn't you say, Pav?'

'Oh, yeah,' he agreed. 'It's definitely on.'

So we drove back, feeling quite chuffed.

But as we arrived in camp, the shit hit the fan. We hadn't even drawn up at the back of the accommodation block when Mal came running down the steps to meet us.

'Geordie,' he said, 'I need to have a word.'

'Walk this way, then.'

We went a few yards down the track into the woods, and as soon as we were out of earshot Mal said, 'Somebody's been tampering with number two lap-top.'

'How d'you know?'

'They've killed the disk with the plans on it.'

'Killed it?'

'The contents have been wiped. Somebody must have tried to get into it without using the password.'

I stopped walking and turned to stare at Mal, who was barely visible in the dark. 'Is it possible the person could have read the contents and then deliberately destroyed them?'

'Not a chance.' He sounded fairly confident. 'They tried a wrong password, and that did it.'

Jesus, I was thinking. Are we compromised, or what?

'If they'd got into the disk they wouldn't have wiped it,' Mal added. 'They'd have left it intact to cover their traces.'

'True. But who the hell was messing about in the office?'

My first instinct was to blame Toad, whose duty it was to

122

maintain security. But of course he'd been with us in the city. In his absence, the two scalies, Steve and Terry, should have been in occupation.

'When did this happen?'

'It must have been some time this evening, while everyone was out working.'

'So who was in the block?'

'Only the scalies.'

'What do they say about it?'

'I haven't asked them yet. I only just discovered it. I tried to boot up the lap-top and found the floppy was still in the slot.'

'Grip them, then.'

I was enraged. Trust those arseholes of signallers to foul up our entire enterprise.

I rushed into the building and dragged Terry off his pit. 'Dozy wanker!' I yelled. 'Get into the ops room, NOW!'

No. 2 lap-top, a Toshiba, stood open on the ops room table with its screen raised and the floppy disk still in the port on the right-hand side.

'There's been a major breach of security,' I started. 'Who used that computer last?'

I glared round, but one by one the lads shook their heads. None of them had been on the lap-top that day, they declared. They'd been out of doors, on the ranges, then on a night-movement exercise.

'Well then, how the fuck did that programme disk come to be in the port? It should be locked inside the filing cabinet. Everyone here knows that.'

Still there was silence.

Suddenly Rick said, 'Wait a minute. There was the Colonel.'

'The Colonel?'

'Anna!'

'Jesus!' I said. 'You mean she came in *here*? What did she want?'

'She said something about her phone having gone down. She asked if she could use ours.'

'And you let her in here?'

'Well, yeah – she being a colonel and everything. I didn't think I could tell her to fuck off.'

'So what happened?'

'She dialled a number and started talking in Russian.'

'What was she saying?'

'I couldn't understand a lot of it. Something about transport – cars.'

'And you stayed in the room with her?'

Rick shook his head. 'No – I let her carry on. I was working in the kitchen and I went back in there.'

'Ah, Jesus! How long for?'

'Five minutes?'

'Cunt!' I was almost on the point of whacking him, so angry did I feel.

Obviously he realised it, because he blurted out, 'I mean, with her being our OC, more or less, I thought everything was above board.'

'Rick,' I said, 'that's the second time you've dropped a bollock. And this one's serious. This is your last chance. Any more cock-ups and you're going home.'

I took a deep breath. It was too late. The damage had been done. But how the hell had Anna got her hands on the disk so fast? She must have had a duplicate set of keys for the filing cabinet. But how far had she managed to get? Had she been dictating stuff straight off the computer screen to some FSB colleague? Or was the conversation Rick had heard just cover for her attempt to get into the program?

'What happened at the end, when she left?' I demanded.

'I came back in here. I was going to offer her a cup of tea.'

'Bloody hell! What was she doing?'

'She was sat there at the table.'

'With the lap-top in front of her?'

Rick frowned. 'I never noticed. She was still talking on the phone.'

'And then?'

'She rang off, put the phone back on the hook. Then she said thanks and went out.'

124

Now what? It was the same dilemma as when we'd found the bug. Should we reveal our suspicions, or should we keep quiet? Even if I didn't accuse Anna of trying to break into our computer programs, should I drop some casual remark about her having used our phone, just to show that her visit hadn't gone unreported? Should I confide in Sasha and see what he thought?

'Wait,' was Whinger's advice. 'Let it develop. Say nothing. See what happens. If she has managed to bust into the program, the next thing we can expect is a massive search. If they suspect we've got a couple of suitcase bombs about the place, they're going to go mad trying to find them. On some pretext or other, they'll turn everything upside-down tomorrow.'

'What about Hereford?' asked Pavarotti. 'Are we going to report this to base?'

'Wait out on that one too,' I said. 'They'd shit themselves if they heard about it, and they've no means of assessing the position from that end. No point in stirring things up unnecessarily.'

Mal – our best computer buff but always a worrier – said, 'Yeah, and I for one wouldn't blame them.'

'Who?'

'The Russkies. If they made a search. It pisses me off that we're doing what we are, anyway.'

'Me too,' I agreed.

Most of the guys, Mal in particular, were confident that it was technically impossible for Anna to have accessed the program. They reckoned that her visit was nothing more sinister than a repercussion from her past – a return to her old KGB habits of snooping – and that she couldn't have discovered anything damaging. So, after a bit of a Chinese parliament, we decided to keep quiet.

Until that moment I'd had no cause to suspect the woman of duplicity. Quite the opposite: she'd seemed fully on side, and had been a terrific asset. She'd thrown herself into the training with real zip, and had never shown the slightest irritation when people kept calling on her for translations. Her physical presence

125

had been enough to give everyone a lift: she was very fit and energetic, and went up ropes or over the assault course as fast as any man, often joining in for the fun of it when there was no real need. And the students liked her as much as we did. They were slightly in awe of her, and referred to her as *Polkovnik* – the Colonel – in a way that was partly sarcastic but had an edge of respect as well. Several times she'd reinforced my impression that she was right behind us visitors by telling indiscreet stories about her days in the old-style KGB. She'd joke about how clumsy and stupid and suspicious all her Communist comrades had been – with the implication that nowadays everything was sweetness and light.

Her private life, though, had remained mysterious. Like Sasha, she had a room in the officers' mess at the other side of the camp, and she'd dropped hints about a flat somewhere in town. Beyond that I knew nothing about her. On a personal level I was still fancying her in a cool sort of way, and I was planning to ask her out to dinner one evening when the time seemed ripe, suggest a meal at a place of her choice and see what developed. So far, though, I'd been so busy and had so much on my mind that I hadn't got round to issuing an invitation.

For a long time that night I couldn't go to sleep. My mind kept returning to the tunnel, to the hollow we'd made in the brickwork, right under the wall of the Kremlin, and to the chaos that would follow if we'd been rumbled. Arrest? Gaol? Deportation? International incident? Should the whole team do a runner while the going was good?

No matter which way my thoughts turned, they were anything but soothing.

EIGHT

Through my sleep I heard a hammering on our door, and in burst Johnny, shouting, 'Geordie, get up! There's a panic on.'

For a moment I thought, Christ, the search has started already. They're turning us out of bed. But at least they can't search the Embassy – so sod them.

Across the room Whinger protested from under his pillow, and I groaned, 'For fuck's sake – what time is it?'

'Six-fifteen,' said Johnny. 'It's Sasha. He's desperate to see you.'

'Where is he?'

'Here. In the passage.'

'Bring him in. Sasha!' I shouted, rolling out of bed. 'What the hell are you doing?'

Sasha appeared in his DPMs, writhing with embarrassment at having crashed into our preserve and finding me naked.

'Zheordie, I am sorry . . .'

'Forget it. What's the problem?'

'We need your help.'

'Now?'

'Immediately.'

'Tell me, then.'

I began pulling on clothes as Sasha spilled his story: how a 'beeg Mafia feesh', self-styled Keet, the Killer Whale, who normally ruled the roost in Chechnya, had been sighted in Moscow. He and his two brothers, known as Akula (Shark) and Barrakuda, were the godfathers of the Chechen Mafia. Now Keet had been traced to an apartment which belonged to another known criminal in a new, sixteen-storey block in the

127

suburb of Lianozovo, on the northern fringes of the city. His presence in the capital, reported by a tout, offered the authorities a rare chance of getting at him on their own ground.

Senior officers in Omon were anxious to take him out, but they were nervous of the firepower he commanded. Not only did he have a team of four bodyguards armed with sub-machine guns for close-protection; the apartment block in which he'd holed up was equipped with the latest security systems, including closed-circuit television, remote-controlled locks and so on. The whole block was under Mafia control, from the team running the security on the ground floor to the janitors who passed out information about people's comings and goings. In other words, any attempt to storm the building would inevitably end in a major gun battle, probably with a load of casualties, and certainly with more publicity than anyone wanted.

All this Sasha poured out in a rush.

'So I come here,' he ended. 'And why? Because Omon ask, can the British experts of the SAS help?'

'Help? How?'

'Make the plan of attack. Give advice.'

'Well . . . it's not what we're here for.'

'Zheordie, I know. But this is special problem.'

Poor Sasha looked so anxious that I almost laughed. I turned to look at Whinger, who had come round far enough to prop himself on one elbow.

'Hear that, Whinge? They're needing assistance. What d'you reckon?'

'We could look at it. No harm taking a shufti.'

Pavarotti, who was hanging into the room round the door, raised his eyebrows. 'For fuck's sake don't get involved,' he said. 'Christ knows what it could lead to.'

'What about the course?' I said. 'It's an EMOE day, isn't it? You can sort them on that, Pav. Wait a minute, though. Sasha – are you planning to use some of the students on this?'

'*Konechno*. You have teached them well.'

'They're only half-trained at the minute . . .'

'All the same, it is best. We want to make attack quickly.'

At the back of my mind I heard the voice of the CO in Hereford, warning me that on no account should we get involved with any live operation. And I heard myself solemnly promising that we'd steer well clear. Then I thought, Ah, bollocks! Easy to say that from a distance. Still, I'd told the boss we'd keep our hands clean . . .

But I heard myself saying, 'OK, we'll come.'

With a big smile Sasha went, '*Zdorovo!* Breelliant!'

'How many guys d'you need?'

'You say.'

'Two teams of four? That means Whinger, myself and six more. You choose them.'

'I do that now. You and Vuinzha, please prepare immediately. It is important you start planning.'

'What about Anna? Does she know about this?'

'She's in control room already.'

The time was 6.40 a.m.

Pavarotti had gone off to the washroom in disgust, and was shaving when I poked my head round the door. 'Sorry, mate,' I told him, 'we're going to have a crack at it. You'll have to take charge of the course today.'

'You're nuts, Geordie.'

'I dunno. All good for international relations.'

In the kitchen the lads already had a brew on, so Whinger and I got some tea and a piece of bread down us, picked up our personal weapons and a few bits and pieces, and were ready for the off.

Sasha had come in some different car, newer and more powerful than either of ours, with a driver in DPMs. We piled in and set off at speed through the dawn, first towards the city centre, then right-handed into the northern suburbs, crossing one main thoroughfare after another. In less than quarter of an hour we were pulling up at the gate of another barracks, where the sentry took one look at Sasha's card and whipped up the barrier pole. Next stop was a briefing room full of men in black Omon uniform, grouped round a large-scale plan spread out on a table.

At first I thought the guys from the course must have moved like shit off a shovel, because they were there ahead of us. Then I realised that Sasha had probably detailed them already, before speaking to us. I recognised Sergei Tri, Volodya, and one other. As we entered there was a bit of muttering in Russian, and a few smiles were beamed in our direction.

Introductions to the top brass were perfunctory, but I cottoned on to the fact that the guy in charge, a major, was called Ivan – a heavily built, swarthy fellow of about my age, with dense black hair cut short into a kind of point, like a little roof over his head, and mean, yellow eyes that put me in mind of a bear. He spoke some English, but didn't understand much of what I said.

Anna glided in, her normal, suave self, quite at home in a room full of men. Staring at her, I kept asking silently, What the hell were you doing with our computer, woman? But when she caught me looking at her she gave a terrific smile, and entered into the business of the day with infectious enthusiasm.

It seemed that Keet, the target, had been reported arriving at the block in the early hours of the morning, and had gone up in the lift to apartment number 128 on the twelfth floor. Omon's information was that a meeting between him and other godfathers was due to take place in the flat at nine that evening. It seemed there'd been an argument over whether the security forces should go straight in, to make sure of arresting one man, or wait and hope to catch several.

To Whinger and myself, the plan for seizing Keet seemed amateurish in the extreme. The proposal was for an assault group to drive up to the ground floor, shoot their way in through the main entrance, secure the lifts and staircases, and then blast their way into the flat.

'It's a fucking shambles,' I muttered to Whinger. 'The guards on the door downstairs will raise the alarm with mobile phones or bleepers, and the villains will disappear from the flat like rats down holes before anyone gets near them. The assaulters'll end up killing half the people in the block; there'll be civilian casualties too, and a tidal wave of bad publicity.'

When Ivan the Bear asked my opinion of the plan, I said tactfully, 'I'm sure your basic idea's right, but maybe we can refine it a bit. Let's think this thing through.'

Ivan told us that his men had the block under surveillance, and that armed guys were posted in cars along the boulevard leading to it. If Keet did try to make a getaway they could always have a go at gunning him down. But his bullet-proof Mercedes might save him, and they didn't want to run any risk of losing him.

'Even so, you surely want to wait for tonight's meeting,' I suggested. 'Even if he goes out somewhere during the day, he'll come back. To catch four or five of them together would be fantastic.'

He agreed, and asked, 'So – what do you suggest?'

'Surprise is what you need,' I told him. 'The element of surprise. It would be much better to come down on the apartment from above.'

'From the roof?'

'Yes.'

He nodded and said something in Russian, which Sasha translated as, 'We land from helicopter.'

'Too noisy.' I shook my head. 'Too obvious. Everyone in the building would hear us coming. Immediately Keet and his party would know something was happening. They might go and hole up in other flats. You'd lose the advantage of surprise.'

At Ivan's shoulder was a tall, cadaverous fellow with a thin, long, rather grey face, a big mouth and unusually red lips. If Ivan was a bear, this guy was a wolf. I wasn't sure of his status, but he seemed to be the second-in-command. Although I couldn't understand many of his words I got the gist of them clearly enough: 'For Christ's sake let's go in and shoot the bastards,' he was saying. 'Let's not ponce about with these pissy British ideas . . .'

Ivan, however, ignored him and asked me to carry on. When we looked at a large-scale plan of the site we saw that it comprised not a single tower block, but two structures set at right-angles to each other in the shape of an L, only a few feet apart at the inner corner. I'd noticed several pairs of buildings with this plan as we had driven around town on other days.

Now Whinger and I had the same idea at the same moment.

'Cross from the other roof,' he said.

'Exactly.' I knew that in Hong Kong he'd practised this very technique with the fire brigade, laddering across from one high-rise block to another and coming down on the target from above. Here, with the flat on the twelfth floor, five down from the roof, it would be child's play to abseil and come in through the windows, while another party stormed the door from the internal corridor.

I looked at Ivan and asked, 'This other building. Is that Mafia as well, or is it clean?'

'No Mafia,' Sasha answered. 'No guards on door.'

I pointed at the plan. 'How wide is this gap between the buildings?'

Ivan gave an off-hand shrug and said, 'I don't know.'

'It's important.'

'Maybe ten metres.'

'No more?'

'*Nyet.*'

'That's OK, isn't it?' I asked Whinger. 'Forty feet?'

'Piece of cake.'

I felt my adrenalin levels rising rapidly, and, almost before I knew what I was doing, I was outlining a complete new action plan.

'Call them Block A and Block B,' I began. 'Block A to the west, B just east of it. Keet's on the twelfth floor of Block A, facing west, right? We maintain surveillance on that block, as you're doing already, but to avoid arousing suspicion we keep well away from the entrance. Instead of a direct approach, two assault teams go up to the roof of Block B and ladder across to the roof of Block A. There we split. One party makes its way down the emergency stairs and comes out on the twelfth-floor corridor. The other abseils down the outside of the building. When both parties are in position, we blow the internal door and the windows simultaneously, come in from both sides with stun grenades, and overpower everybody inside.'

As Anna translated, I saw Ivan following my scenario with ever-growing incredulity.

'All this is possible?' he asked.

'Of course,' I replied confidently – but even as I did so I suddenly realised what I'd done. Carried away by my own excitement I'd been saying 'we' when I should have been saying 'you'.

Ivan was under fire from Wolf-face, but he shut him up again with an irritated wave, and showed that he hadn't missed the implication of my words with his next question: 'So, you will lead the assault?'

'No, no. We can't. We're not authorised for anything like that. We're here purely on a training mission.'

Ivan's dismay was painful to witness. '*Starshina*,' he pleaded, 'Sergeant Major – we very much need your help. We do not have your experience in assaults of this kind.'

I looked at Whinger and saw that he was thinking the same as I was. If we did our hosts a good turn, it would ease our consciences. Besides, it would be a great gas to take part in an anti-Mafia hit. The idea was outrageous, of course – the Regiment would never sanction it. But would the Regiment ever *know* about it? Not until afterwards, if at all – provided we didn't say anything.

I looked at Whinger and said quietly, 'What d'you reckon?'

'All right by me.'

I turned back to Ivan and said, '*Yestj*. We'll help as much as we can. At least we can show you what to do.'

This led to knuckle-crunching handshakes and big grins all round.

But my decision shifted the initiative to myself and Whinger – and thereafter we had to make the running.

I'm bound to say that the Omon leaders pulled their fingers out: whatever we asked for they got, and fast.

The first things we needed were architectural plans of both apartment blocks. It looked as though the pair would be essentially the same, but we wanted to be sure. In particular, we needed to know the internal layout of the flat we were going to hit – the disposition of its rooms, and details like which way the doors opened. As the buildings were only three years old it should have been easy to find drawings, but when somebody phoned the construction firm who'd put the flats up the people there began making difficulties, claiming that their computers were down, and that without them they couldn't produce plans. I heard a good bollocking go down the line, and that seemed to produce results. 'Half an hour,' was the eventual answer.

'In that case,' I said, 'let's do a drive-past. We need to get a look at the blocks. Somebody bring a video camera.'

'Better not go dressed like this.' Whinger pointed at his DPMs.

'Good point, Whinge.'

A quartermaster figure produced sets of thin grey overalls which smelt of mothballs, and soon we were rolling northwards in two cars: myself, Ivan (who had a camera), Anna and the driver in one, Whinger, Sasha and the Wolf-man in the second.

'Tell him we don't want to get too close,' I warned Anna.

'What d'you call too close?'

'Nothing under a couple of hundred metres, anyway.'

By now it was fully light, and rush-hour traffic was pouring down the main arteries into the city centre. Heading outwards, we could move freely, and it was only five minutes or so before Ivan said something, pointing ahead and to the right.

'Those are the buildings,' Anna translated. 'The target's in the left-hand one, as we're looking.'

Two slender blocks rose out of a wasteland. They were made of pale-grey concrete, relieved by small square panels of sky blue ranged along the balcony-fronts on each of the sixteen floors. At ground level the entrances were imposing: on the end of each building was a grandiose porch with square pillars, under which cars could drive, and marble facings round the doors. Either side of the doorway into what we'd named Block A stood a guard in grey fatigues armed with a sub-machine gun.

Round the base of the buildings some attempt had been made to establish a garden or park: there were patches of grass and a few saplings had been planted, but further out much of the area was still bare earth, no doubt awaiting development. On the approach road leading to Block A numerous cars were parked end-on at forty-five degrees to the kerb, including a high proportion of Mercedes, BMWs and Audis.

The road to Block B came in from the far side and had far less transport sitting on it.

I glanced at Ivan and saw that he was already filming.

'Ask him to get close-up footage of the roof-line,' I said – and in response to Anna's request he tilted the camera upwards.

'Just to confirm,' I said. 'The target's in this near block.'

'Correct.'

'And the apartment's facing this way?'

'Correct again.'

'In fact we can see the windows now.'

'Yes. The fifth floor down from the top.'

I was looking for sniper vantage points, and immediately saw one: a third high-rise block of the same model, but with green panels rather than blue, maybe 200 metres away on our left.

'Can we drive back down the far side of Block B – over there, behind it?'

'Not very well.' Anna pointed. 'You see that long wall? Behind that's a railway line and marshalling yards. There's no road in that area.'

'What about those roofs just over the wall?'

'Those are railway offices.'

'OK.'

A kilometre or so beyond the site we made a U-turn and came back for a second pass. Again I concentrated, fixing details in my mind. The run confirmed my earlier impression that a direct daylight approach from ground level would have been disastrous: there was no cover close to Block A's entrance, and a gun-battle would have led to many casualties.

Back in the Omon briefing room we found architectural drawings of Blocks A and B awaiting us. As Whinger and I went into a huddle over them, mugs of sweet black tea beside us, we had no difficulty coming up with a plan.

When we were ready, I signalled to Ivan, and we began an informal presentation.

'I don't know if they want to make notes,' I said to Anna, 'but maybe you'd suggest it.'

Wolf-face let fly a few more disparaging remarks, but the others ignored him, and Ivan produced a notebook and pencil.

'Right,' I said. 'First thing, the assault should go down at night, after last light. If the Mafia meeting's due to start at 2100, I suggest 2130.'

I had to take it slowly, phrase by phrase, letting Anna translate in between. For a few exchanges the delays irritated me: then I realised that they were useful, as they gave everyone time to take in what I was saying.

'Next, there will be three assault parties, designated Red, Blue and Black. Red and Blue will enter Block B and cross on to the roof of Block A by ladder, as outlined. Red will deploy on the roof of Block A and prepare to abseil down the outside of the building. Blue will enter the building via the fire exit on the roof – here – then descend the fire stairs and position themselves to assault the apartment from the corridor.

'Black will deploy on the ground by vehicle. Their job will be to drive up to the front of Block A and secure the building by capturing or shooting the two guards we saw. Timing will be critical. They'll need to reach the door at the moment the assaults on the flat go in – not before.

'If possible, we'll position sniper/commentators in Block C – the green block. From there they'll be able to observe the windows of the target flat and report movements. When everyone's deployed, we'll use EMOE to blow the door and at least one window from both sides of the flat and simultaneously. The actions and timings of all three teams will be co-ordinated by radio.

'I'll be the leader of Red team. Whinger here will lead Blue team. Red and Blue will each consist of the leader and three men. Black team will be commanded by an officer nominated by Ivan. For comms purposes, the snipers will be designated Green.'

Ivan asked Anna a couple of questions in Russian, and she gave him answers herself. Then she said, 'He is afraid control will be difficult because of the language.'

'I've thought of that. If we can have you at the command centre, there'll be no problem. You'll be able to translate and pass things on. The only English commands your colleagues need to understand will be the two I'll use at the end: "Stand by, stand by" and "Go! Go! Go!"'

Anna immediately translated these. '"Stand by" is *Orushiye k boyu*,' she said. 'That means literally "weapons ready". Go is *poshli*. Easy!'

Ivan smiled briefly as he nodded his agreement.

I went on to emphasise that Whinger and I were not in the business of killing Russian citizens, whether Mafiosi or otherwise. All we would do was get the assault teams into position and blow the door and windows: it would be up to the Russians to clear the flat. Again, there was a murmur of agreement. I could see that Wolf-face was still ticking with irritation.

'Ask Ivan, please: what are his intentions? Is he aiming to capture Keet or kill him?'

As Anna translated, a faint smile spread over Ivan's face – but it did not extend to his eyes. The only answer he gave was, 'It depends.'

'In any case,' I went on, 'what we need immediately is a forward mounting base. Those railway sheds behind the wall – any chance of your taking one over?'

Ivan sent a colleague to make a telephone call. I began going into the nitty-gritty: ladders, ropes, explosive charges, weapons, comms. I said that Whinger and I would carry pistols only, for self-defence in an extremity, but added that the Russian members of Red and Blue teams should take Gepards with short magazines as well as their pistols. The guys in the Black team should have silenced weapons, to whack the ground-floor guards with minimum disturbance.

Within a couple of minutes an answering call came back: inside the railway complex, it said, were the offices of a company operating steam trips in a joint venture with a Swiss tourist firm. The place had modern communications, and also a large, empty engine shed in which we could assemble our kit and lay on some quick training.

Once Ivan had nominated the men for each of the teams, we had only a few hours in which to sort them out. My three – Nikolai Two, Igor and Misha – were all built like brick shithouses, and well versed in abseiling.

The railway office and shed turned out a big bonus. By midday Ivan had sent the normal staff home, taken the place over and set up a command post and control centre in the main office, with a dish aerial on the roof. The engine shed was high enough for us to put in some abseil practice: with ropes anchored to the steel girders under the roof, we had about fifteen feet clear below us. Ivan's video showed quite a few possible anchor-points on the roof of Block B – the tops of lift-shafts, ventilation pipes and so on – and I foresaw no trouble there.

From our study of the architects' plans we knew that the flat had two bedrooms and a living room ranged along the southern balcony face, down which we'd be coming. On the other side, along the internal corridor, were the kitchen, hallway, separate lavatory, a bathroom and a big storage cupboard. To us on the outside – and to the snipers positioned in Block C – the apartment's windows were the first four from the right-hand end on the twelfth floor. I named them *Okno Odin, Okno Dva* (Window One, Window Two) and so on, numbering from the right. One was the first bedroom, two the second, three was the top half of a door which opened inwards from the balcony into the sitting room, and four another window in the same room.

Ivan agreed that we should time the hit for 2130, in the hope of catching the big players in the sitting room. Therefore we decided to blow the window-door and go in that way.

Whinger, meanwhile, was sorting a route for his team to enter via the fire-escape door on the roof, and come down the emergency stairs to position themselves outside the flat entrance.

138

I tried to impress on Ivan how easy it would be to create a blue-on-blue – to have the Red and Blue teams firing at each other. But in fact the layout of the flat gave us two natural territories in which to operate. For Red, the balcony team, the obvious field of fire was the sitting room; for Blue, entering from the corridor, the hallway would be the main theatre. We made it a fundamental rule that Red team members would only engage targets remaining in the sitting room and not fire at anyone running through into the hall. Blue would be free to fire into the hall or either of the bedrooms.

Of the three guys allotted to me, I was happy enough with Nikolai and Igor. The one who worried me was Misha, one of the relics of SOBR. Sasha had put him in my team because he'd done abseiling, but our experience so far suggested that he had a low IQ, and wasn't all that co-operative either.

No good worrying about that now.

I took the team through our sequence of actions again and again. We'd abseil down to the balcony, aiming to establish ourselves on it thirty seconds before the raid was due to go in. We'd need to be extremely careful in our movements: not to clank our weapons against the metalwork of the balustrade, not to let a boot or elbow bump on a window. For the last few seconds we'd crouch against the wall of the flat, under the windows. As soon as I confirmed by radio that Whinger's team was in position, I'd call, 'Stand by, stand by . . . Go!', then crack off the door charge and follow it instantly with a stun grenade.

Seeing the blank looks on their faces, I started to flap a bit. I knew what standard they'd reached, and it wasn't as high as we needed. A fully fledged SAS assaulter is so highly trained that his reactions are instantaneous. These guys were nowhere near that level. Nevertheless, since Igor was the sharpest of our team, I detailed him to be first into the room. 'The second the grenade blows, you're through.' I told him via Anna. 'When you go in, stay on your feet and move to the left. None of this rolling-around we've been practising.

'You other two, give him covering fire through the blown-out window. Aim outwards into the corners of the room. Don't fire straight at the door into the hall, otherwise rounds may go through and hit your own guys coming from the other side.'

When Igor protested about being first in, I told him he didn't need to worry. The godfathers inside would be deafened and blinded by the stun-grenade.

Suitable ladders took a bit of finding. There were some in the Omon stores but they were too short and heavy for our purpose. It was Sasha who had the idea of borrowing better kit off the nearest branch of the fire service. They came up with an extending set of four three-metre sections, made from aluminium, well machined and snugly fitting. The overall length was eleven metres, and since the gap between the corners of the buildings showed on the architects' plans as nine metres, we would have a one-metre overlap at either end.

Once we'd held several practices at assembling the ladders and crossing gaps on them, we bound the ends with foam and masking tape to reduce the risk of making a noise, and handed them over to another team. These two guys, who appeared to be television technicians, drove to Block B and took the ladders up the fire stairs on to the roof, under the pretence of realigning the aerials.

By 4.00 everything was in hand. Omon had discovered an empty apartment on the thirteenth floor of Block C and installed a pair of snipers, armed with Dragunov 7.62mm rifles fitted with telescopic sights. Their brief was to watch for movements in the target flat with binoculars and report any change to the control room. When the assault went down, they were to engage anyone who tried to make a getaway by coming out of a window and escaping along a balcony.

At 4.30 Whinger and I got Sasha to drive us back to Balashika. Rather than handle Russian detonators and det cord of uncertain vintage, I wanted to pick up some of our own. At the base we found everything in order: the lads back from a good day in the open, and no further scares. We had time for a quick meal and a cup of tea.

As I sat down to eat I said to Whinger, 'I don't think very many Mafiosi are going to come out of this alive.'

By 5.15 we were back at the railway command centre for a final run-through of the plan. I made up my explosive charge for blowing the window – a ring of det cord taped on to a sheet of expanded polystyrene about fifteen inches square, to which I'd fitted a short broom-handle – and explained to my three how, once we reached the balcony, I'd apply the polystyrene gently – and silently – to the glass of the door, holding it out with the end of the handle, before I cracked off the charge.

I emphasised that, once we had launched the hit, we must go quickly through with it. If anyone saw us crossing between the buildings, for instance, it was possible that the alarm could be raised. Once we were established on the roof of Block B, we couldn't afford to hang about.

My big worry was the weather. All afternoon the wind had been getting up, and by 8.00 a gale was blowing and driving blasts of rain before it. In a way it was good, as the roar of the storm would cover any small noises we might make; but I also reckoned there'd be hellish turbulence around the edges of those tall buildings.

Everyone was nervous – myself and Whinger no less than the students. As before all operations, our watches seemed to stop or at least slow down to a ridiclous crawl, the hands hardly moving. The snipers came on the air with the occasional bit of news – 'Green One. Curtains being drawn in Window One . . . Light switched on in Window Two' – and by 8.05 all four windows had been curtained off. That suited us fine.

As we rehearsed the action sequences again and again, the only person who seemed unmoved was Anna.

It felt very strange to be dressing in Russian kit. Their flak-jackets were heavier and stiffer than ours, and made us pretty clumsy. My helmet fitted my head inside but still felt very big. Realising that it would be difficult to control my explosive charge on its panel while I was crossing on the ladder, I had Nikolai lash it flat to the small of my back, with the handle pointing up behind my head like a short antenna.

When I glanced across at Whinger I was amazed: he looked

every inch a member of Omon, with his features hidden under a black rapist's mask, and only his eyes and mouth showing.

For the tenth time, it seemed, I checked all weapons and magazines.

At last it was time for the off. We went out on foot into the cold, swirling wind through a gate in the railway compound wall, over the wasteland. The odd street lamp was burning in the distance, but the area we crossed was good and dark. With us we had one guy in civilian clothes, to range ahead as a scout and radio back a warning if he met anyone on the stairs. The covert comms system was working well: in my earpiece I could hear the Black team lining itself up in the van they'd arranged for transport, and the occasional remark from a sniper. With the finger and thumb of my right hand I settled the throat mike more comfortably in position.

In the underground car-park of Block B we waited while our scout started climbing. 'Red and Blue at foot of stairs,' I reported, and immediately Anna's voice answered, '*Vas ponyal. Khorosho.*'

A few moments later the scout called to tell us that all was clear as far as floor five, so both teams went scuttling up. After another pause there, we took the next eleven flights straight, and arrived at the top panting.

Out in the open, the wind was formidable. There was no point in telling people to watch themselves. They wouldn't have heard me, anyway, and anybody with the slightest sense of self-preservation wasn't going to start pissing about in a place like that.

All Moscow, it seemed, was spread out at our feet. Immediately below us the patches of wasteland were dark, but to the south blazed an immense galaxy of lights, and the main thoroughfares were like brilliantly illuminated rivers down which flowed endless streams of headlamps.

The ladders were lying where the pseudo-TV crew had left them, and we had no trouble locking the sections together. But when we tried to raise the whole length upright, the force of the gale nearly lifted two of us off our feet. Quickly I got a second rope round the top of the ladder and secured our ends to vertical standpipes. That way, we could exert enough friction to lower the whole bridge gently into position. Once it was down, we lashed the near end to a rail, in case it got blown overboard after we were across; even though the ladder was lightweight, it wouldn't have improved the health or temper of anyone it landed on after dropping sixteen storeys.

By now I was shitting bricks. 'Wish to fuck I'd never volunteered to lead,' I said in Whinger's ear.

'I'll go if you like,' he said – good old bugger that he is.

'No, no. I'm fine really.'

I was, too – once I'd started. '*Khuyevo dyelo!*' I said to myself. 'Shit, shit, shit!' – and then I was on my way.

With a safety rope round my waist and belayed on to the guy next in line, I crawled forward, each knee on one sharp-edged rung at a time, hands clutching the side-rails with a grip like a Scotsman's on a five-pound note. The ladder swayed horribly as gusts of wind hit me. I tried not to look down, but far below and away to my left I couldn't help catching glimpses of cars that looked like toys. Half-way across I decided it was better to keep my eyes shut.

Even without seeing I could tell how far I'd got from the bend in the ladder. It flexed most when I was in the middle. Russian ladder, I kept thinking. Russian aluminium. I hope to hell it doesn't break.

At last it began to stiffen again as I drew near to the far side. I opened my eyes and saw that I had only feet to go. A few more seconds and I was safe on the roof of Block B. As I scrambled on to the rough asphalt I was appalled to find that the ladder's overlap was more like a foot than a metre. The blocks were obviously slightly farther apart than the architects had prescribed. I watched, fascinated, as I saw the end of the ladder creeping in and out, and realised that the high buildings were swaying in the wind.

Igor came across next, and made it with no fuss. So did Nikolai, who hadn't even bothered with a safety rope. It was Misha who got into trouble. Exactly what happened, I'll never know. All the rest of us saw, as we crouched shoulder-to-shoulder in the gale, was that he stopped half-way across the bridge. Whinger came up in my earpiece saying, 'Blue – got a hold-up. Oh, for fuck's sake . . .' and then, 'Get on, yer twit.'

Obviously Whinger didn't shout. Even if he could have been heard it would probably have been counter-productive, because in that situation, if someone loses his nerve, yelling only intensifies the fright. But seconds were ticking away. From exchanges on the radio I knew that Black team were starting their final approach to the front of the building. We couldn't afford to lose time.

Another dark figure started crawling out on to the ladder. With a double weight on it, the aluminium sagged horribly. The second man reached the feet of the stationary Misha, who was frozen in a face-down attitude. The back-up guy began talking, first in a low voice, then louder. When bollockings had no effect, the newcomer turned physical. From the blurred movements it looked as though he had started thumping Misha with his fist on the backs of his knees.

Still there was no reaction.

The wind and rain were hitting our faces so hard that, even from close range, it was impossible to tell exactly what happened next. It looked to me as though the second guy had tried to crawl over Misha's prostrate body. He was right on top of him when there came a sudden eruption of movement. I saw a flurry of limbs, much faster than men crawling, as if the two were wrestling.

An instant later one of them was falling. Without a sound he dropped away into the dark.

Jesus! I thought. Too low for his chute. But of course he had no chute.

He went straight down, 150 feet on to concrete.

I grabbed the pressel of my radio and hissed, 'Red leader. We have a casualty. One guy's fallen.'

'Roger,' came Anna's unemotional voice. She said something else in Russian. Then, 'Can you recover him?'

'Not a chance. He's gone right to the ground.'

144

'Proceed, then.'

'Roger.'

The guy who'd survived the mid-ladder encounter reached us. Not Misha. It was Volodya from the Blue team. Misha was written off. Peering over the edge of the roof, I could just make out a little dark heap splatted on the deck. At least the controllers knew what had happened. It was up to them whether or not they made any move to help him. I was pretty certain there'd be no point. No way could he have survived that impact, especially with the weight of the weapon on his back, the ammunition in his pouches and all his other gear. All I could think, selfishly, was, I hope to hell nobody saw him go past their window.

The rest of Blue team quickly came across, Whinger last. He gave me a strained look, but never said a word about the setback – just a quick '*Idyom!*' to his guys, and they were gone, round the end of the lift-housing to the point where the emergency stairs reached the roof.

I led the two surviving members of Red team along the roof to the far end and round the corner, until we were positioned above the target windows. There we quickly laid out our ropes. We found ideal anchor-points in the form of a strong metal rail that skirted the raised top of the lift shaft, and in a couple of minutes we were ready to descend.

'Red leader,' I called. 'Can I have a sniper report on the windows? Are all curtains drawn?'

Anna instantly passed the request. I heard Green come in: '*Da, da. Vsyo,*' and in a second I got, 'Yes, all curtains closed.'

My watch said 9.24. 'Red leader,' I reported. 'Starting descent now.'

Abseiling down a building in the dark is never a picnic. Still less is it easy in a high wind. The longer your rope, the more you swing about, and the greater the danger of accidentally bumping against a window. But it was no good pissing about. I stuck my arse into space, walked backwards over the edge of the roof, and started down.

Luckily the shape of the building was kind to us. All the doors and windows were set back about a metre inside the balconies, so that as we came past each floor there was very little chance of any accidental contact with the inner wall of the building.

Inches at a time I tip-toed down the wall and dangled in space above the top half of the first balcony. On down past the metal rails. Sixteen done. Fifteen the same. Slowly on past fourteen. My two guys were doing OK, to the right and left of me. Between fourteen and thirteen a terrific gust of wind swung us so violently that all three of us bumped against each other. Luckily the windows were closed and curtains drawn all the way down, courtesy of the wild night.

My boots touched the top rail of the twelfth-floor balcony. I eased myself down gently until my backside was on the rail, then got my feet on the floor of the balcony itself. I'd landed in front of Window Two. The greenish curtains were drawn tight, but light was shining out round the edges.

The second I was out of my ropes I turned to guide Igor in.

By 9.28 all three of us were in our prearranged positions: myself crouching beside the door, Nikolai on my right, Igor on my left. Even in the relative shelter of the balcony the wind was blustering loudly, and there was no need to keep my voice down when I reported in. 'Red leader, on target. Blue, report your state.'

'Blue, preparing charge,' came Whinger's voice. 'Wait out.'

'Red, roger.' My heart was going like a hammer. I imagined Whinger deftly taping a length of det cord down the centre of the door. I glanced either way at the dark, helmeted faces beside me and gave a reassuring twitch of my head. The lads had heard Whinger in their earpieces, but naturally hadn't understood what he said, so I made taping motions round our own doorway. Both got it, grinned back and nodded.

But I was wrong. Suddenly I heard Whinger say, 'Blue. We have a problem. I can see through a glass panel in the fire-escape door. There are two guards sitting outside the apartment, in the corridor. Wait one.'

I made an instant decision. 'Red. You'll have to drop them. I'll use your shots as the signal to go.'

'OK,' said Whinger softly. 'Ready when you are.'

'Red. Roger. Control – is Black on schedule?'

'*Da, da. Chyornii gotovi*,' came Anna's voice. I could tell that the excitement was getting to her as well because for a moment she forgot to translate. Then she said, 'Yes. Black ready.'

'Red. Starting countdown now. Sixty, fifty, forty . . .' I imagined the Black team wagon speeding towards the Mafia entrance, silenced weapons at the ready. The gale was certainly going to help mask any noise they made.

'Twenty . . . ten . . .'

Jesus, I was thinking, I hope this goes our way, because we shouldn't be anywhere near here.

'Ten, nine, eight, seven, six, five . . . Stand by, stand by . . . GO!'

The hammer of rounds going down in the corridor came clearly through to us. With my charge held flat to the glassed upper half of the door, I knelt with my head tucked down, away from the blast, and squeezed my clacker.

BOOM! The blast made the inner wall shudder. I raised my head. The entire glass panel had vanished. Through the hole I lobbed a stun grenade and ducked again, eyes averted.

BANG! A sharper, louder explosion. I came upright again. Pieces of glass were tinkling down. The lights in the room had gone out.

'*Poshli!*' I shouted at Igor. 'Go!'

In he went with a wild yell, head-first through the gap. I heard a thud as he hit the floor and scrabbling noises as he scuttled sideways. Then Nikolai was at the opening, hammering long bursts into the room with his Gepard. He was screaming obscenities too.

Hardly had he opened up when there came a second explosion as Whinger blew the door from the corridor. More rounds started going down inside the flat – bursts of seven or eight. Too long to be properly selective.

Empty cases cascaded on to the floor of the balcony beside me. Nikolai threw down an empty magazine, smacked home a full one and continued to fire. For a moment I felt a bit of a prick, lying there against the safety of the wall while guys were risking their lives inside.

Then the bursts of fire died away. Single shots cracked out – one, two, three, four. I knew what they meant: the assaulters were using their pistols to pop rounds into the heads of their victims, making certain they were dead.

One more single shot, then silence – except for the wind.

'Boris!' I shouted. '*Yestj?*'

'*Da, da.*'

'*Khorosho!*'

I held in my pressel and called, 'Red to Blue – all secure at your end?'

'Blue,' came Whinger's voice. 'Affirmative. All inner rooms secure.'

'Red. Roger. This side secure also. You can come on through.'

Standing up, I walked in through the shattered window-door. The air in the living room was hot as hell and thick with cigarette smoke, shot through with the sharp reek of cordite. Something had caught fire, ignited by the stun grenade. The blaze wasn't serious – just enough to give flickering illumination and light up the gory scene. The lights had gone down and for the time being I let it burn.

The Mafiosi must have been in conference round a rectangular table. Now, overturned chairs and five bodies lay all round it. Igor, crouched in the left-hand outer corner of the room, was still covering Nikolai as he scurried round checking each one. The door into the hallway was closed, so I went straight over and called through it, 'Whinge?'

'Yeah, yeah. We're here.'

'OK. I'm opening up.' I turned the handle and pulled, to find the door was locked. Peering down, I saw the key was in the lock, spun it and pulled the door towards me. The two teams were safely reunited.

'Red leader to Control,' I called. 'Target secure.'

'*Vas ponyal,*' went Anna. 'Roger.'

'Piece of cake!' said Whinger. 'What's the Russian for that?'

148

'I don't know. How many have your guys taken out?'

'Four. The bodyguards. Two in the passage, two more watching TV in the end bedroom. We got them as they came out the door.' He flashed his torch into the bedroom doorway, and I saw two bodies lying across each other on the floor.

'No casualties on your team?'

Whinger shook his head. 'The stupid bastards never got a round off. The two outside were asleep on their chairs, and the others had left their main weapons in the hallway. There.' He shone the beam on a little stack of sub-machine guns in a corner. 'Didn't even have time to draw their pistols.'

I found myself shaking with reaction. 'Jesus!' I said. 'What happens now?'

After a hit of that kind in the UK, the assault teams would be instantly spirited away from the scene in a hostage reception van, and any prisoners would travel with them, to get the whole lot clear before any journalists or TV crew turned up. Then a quick-reaction force would move in and take over. The most important guy in the aftermath would be the SOCO, the scene-of-crimes officer, from the police. Until he arrived, the key rule was that nothing must be touched or moved.

Not so in Moscow. Satisfied that all the villains were dead, Igor got up, walked over and kicked one of the bodies contemptuously, rolling it over.

'Stop!' I called, waving my hands about to tell him to lay off. But that was the limit of my Russian, and he probably thought I was crazy.

Somebody found the electricity control panel. A trip switch had been thrown by the blasts, and once it was flipped back up enough of the lights went on for us to survey the wreckage.

It looked as though four of the sitting-room victims had been gunned down where they sat at the table. They were all flabby-looking, middle-aged men with bellies bulging out into their shirts and their sleeves rolled up. Their faces had probably never been pretty, and they certainly weren't now, because Nikolai had gone round and popped each one with a bullet through the head. One had an eye out on a stalk; another had spewed out half his teeth. Pools of blood were spreading over the pale carpet. Their jackets, still hanging over the backs of their chairs, had been riddled by bullets. The fifth guy, a younger man in a dark-blue polo shirt, had got half-way to the door before being dropped. On the right-hand wall, looking from the windows, water was dripping from the shattered remains of a glass fish-tank, and the wretched occupant was flapping its last in a puddle at the bottom. Another victim was an old tabby cat, which lay in a corner without a mark on it and seemed to have died of fright.

The table was covered with papers, evidently the subject of the meeting, and expensive-looking briefcases sat on the floor beside the chairs. The fire had started in a waste bin containing more paper, and I had no problem stamping it out. But I'd hardly finished when there was a commotion outside the door and in strode Ivan the Bear, with Sasha at his heels.

Ivan advanced towards me, grinning, and said something which Sasha translated as, 'Breelliant! He congratulates you very much.'

'Your guys did it.' I gestured round. 'They were first class. *Ochen khorosho.*'

Ivan accepted the praise with a nod and turned his attention to the bodies. Almost at once he gave an exclamation and began to talk at speed into a mobile phone.

'It is Keet – the Whale,' Sasha translated, pointing at the corpse of a huge man with close-cropped grey hair that lay on its back almost under the table. As he was speaking, Ivan bent down and unceremoniously ripped open the perforated, blood-stained shirt to reveal a foot-long tattoo of a whale's head and open jaws, tilted upwards towards the man's left shoulder. From the half-open mouth the feet of a human being were protruding. By a horrible fluke one round had gone in almost exactly through the whale's eye, leaving a bloody hole.

With a jerk on one arm Ivan rolled the body over and kicked the shirt up round its head. There, between the shoulder blades, was a tattooed portrait of Stalin.

'Old Uncle Joe didn't save that bugger, did he?' Whinger was staring at the effigy, fascinated. Then, as he surveyed the scene, he added, 'I like the delicate way they handle things round here, I must say.'

Ivan brought out a pocket knife, slipped the blade inside one leg of Whale's trousers, at the ankle, and slit the grey material open to half-way up the thigh. Then he pointed contemptuously and gave a short laugh.

'He has stars on the knees,' Sasha translated. 'Like I told you. The sign he would never kneel.'

It seemed that all the villains bar one were known to Ivan. By any standards it was a terrific coup for the security forces: five godfathers at one hit, plus four bodyguards and a haul of incriminating papers. Nor was that all. The two most fancy briefcases – crocodile leather by Gucci, no less – were closed with gold combination locks. Ivan picked one up, laid it on the table and started trying to open it. Frustrated, he called to Igor, who produced a small jemmy.

'Hey, wait!' I said, thinking of Toad and Pavarotti. 'That thing's worth a few grand. One of our guys will open it without wrecking it.'

But Ivan wasn't in a mood to wait, and in a few seconds he'd burst both locks. When he lifted the lid, everybody who could see gave a gasp, because the case was packed solid with fifty-dollar bills done up in little paper sleeves holding bunches of twenty notes: a thousand bucks a throw.

When you see cash in that kind of quantity, you realise how little space it takes up: I could have put ten grand in my hip pocket, no bother.

As if reading my thoughts Ivan plunged a hand into the case and brought out a fistful of bundles, holding them in my direction.

'Take,' said Sasha. 'He wants you to have it.'

'No, no.' I waved it away.

'Yes, please. He inseest. He thinks like Russian soldiers you not being paid well. You need more.'

Looking round under the table, Ivan spotted a far cheaper briefcase made of imitation black leather, with a flap closure and no locks. Having tipped the papers it contained on to the table, he proceeded to stuff it with handfuls of fifty-dollar bills and thrust it at me.

From this point things became more and more surreal. Somebody discovered bottles of special, high-octane vodka in the freezer compartment of the fridge, brought them out and began pouring slugs into short, squat glasses. Whinger and I declined, but as the icy spirit went down other people's throats in repeated doses, the volume of voices rose. While a minion collected up the papers from the table and stowed them away, Ivan himself carefully removed gold watches from three dead wrists and a couple of crocodile wallets from the jackets still on the chairs.

'Present to English friends!' he beamed, holding a watch out in my direction.

'No, for fuck's sake!' I exclaimed. '*Spasibo* – but keep them.'

Then some of his guys arrived with body bags, and at last bundled the corpses out of sight.

Outside, in the corridor, there was a great commotion as other inhabitants of the block argued with the guards on the door, trying to get in and find out what had happened.

'Let's get the hell out of here,' Whinger muttered. 'There's going to be a monster piss-up.'

'We'd better sign off with Ivan.'

'He's busy. Another day.'

'OK.'

I looked round for Sasha and beckoned him over. 'We need to get back to Balashika,' I told him. 'Can someone give us a lift?'

'*Konechno*. I drive you.'

'How many vodkas have you had?'

'Vodka? Nothing! Two only.'

So it was that we pushed our way past the new guards on the door, through the crowd outside and into the lift. Downstairs there was a heavy military presence on the entrance to the block, but Sasha spirited us through it, found the car he'd been driving, and set off.

I felt plagued by guilt – first by the thought that we should all have been in a formal debriefing session, recalling and recording every move of the raid; second by the knowledge that we had lost a man; and third by the fact that I was carrying a small fortune of ill-gotten gains in a Mafia briefcase.

'Misha,' I said. 'He was dead?'

Sasha nodded. 'Absolutely. We found his body. How did he fall?'

'Just lost his nerve.'

'It is a pity. But – *nichevo!*' He smiled broadly. 'We have beeg victory. Like in football – Arsenal nine, Tottenham Hotspot one!' He gave a merry laugh and drummed his hands on the steering wheel. Then he added, 'Only one problem.'

'What's that?'

'Mafia bosses will be angry. For sure, they make counter-attack.'

'On Omon?'

'No, on government. The President, the Vice-President, the Minister of the Interior. Perhaps one of them will be their next target.'

NINE

I thought I was going to have nightmares, but in fact I slept like the dead, and woke up unable to remember where I was. Until I heard Whinger snoring, that is: then everything flooded back.

'All in a day's work,' I'd said cheerily to Rick when we came in the night before – and a hell of a day we'd had. But it had been exhilarating too, and a sharpening change from the routine of training.

Naturally we'd had a wash-up with our own lads as soon as we had come in: they'd got a brew on, and we'd sat up till after midnight analysing the hit. We had also had a discussion – not quite an argument – about what had come to be known as the 'diplomatic bag'. A count had shown it to contain 110,000 dollars.

When the lads saw that amount of money tipped out on the kitchen table they uttered, 'Firekin ell!' in a kind of chorus.

If there's one thing that makes SAS lads take leave of their senses it's money. Normally they're pretty straight-up, but somehow the sight of cash sends them bananas.

'There's my Jag!' Pavarotti cried with his eyes glazing over.

'Bugger the Jag!' Pete told him. 'What about my kitchen extension?'

'Bet it's all forged,' said Dusty, ever the cynic.

'Never,' Mal told him. 'Big Mafia players wouldn't be carting fake stuff around. Whose is it, anyway? Geordie's and Whinger's, I suppose.'

'No, no,' I said. 'If it belongs to anyone, it belongs to the team.'

'Buy a team Merc,' said Pavarotti. 'Get a five-hundred or

something. Smoked-glass windows. Then we can take on the hoods at their own game. *How* much did you say they had?'

'Meellions,' I said, imitating Sasha. 'Christ knows. It was a big briefcase and it was jam-packed. This lot was only a fraction of what we saw. There could have been stuff we didn't see as well. We never looked in the other croc briefcase or in drawers or cupboards. The flat could have been full of money. Drugs too, I daresay. God knows what they were at: it looked as though they were carving up their empire.'

It was Rick who produced the idea of sending the cash back to the UK. 'Put it in the Diplomatic Bag,' he suggested. 'Then at least it'll be safe, and a nice little bonus for when we get home.'

'Bollocks to that,' said Pav. 'Split it up now. Then we can go out and start spending.'

'What on?' demanded Dusty derisively. 'Rotten onions? Crappy cabbage? You'll get fuck-all else in Balashika.'

'Funny,' said Mal. 'At Sandhurst it's the other way round. It's the students who have the money. Arabs slip their instructors gold watches to get an early look at exam papers. Here, the students are penniless and the instructors are loaded.'

Whinger, who'd been keeping quiet, butted up and said, 'They offered Geordie a gold Rolex as well.'

'You bastard!' roared Pav. 'Where is it?'

'I told him to keep it.'

'Bloody idiot,' Pav cried. 'I'd have taken it.'

'I know you would,' I told him. 'But the person who needs money is Sasha. I bet that mean bugger Ivan didn't give *him* anything. The poor sod hasn't been paid in months.'

I brought up the saga of my having to buy clothes for him in Hereford, which the lads hadn't heard, and finished with, 'I vote we slip him a couple of grand, anyway.'

Our Chinese parliament passed the suggestion unanimously – with the exception of Toad, who, as usual, was lurking at one side of the room, outside the main circle, listening, watching. He said nothing – just gave us a sly look – so I considered him over-ruled and said, 'Right then – here's a couple for Sasha,' and separated out two of the little bundles.

'What about the rest?'

In the end it was agreed that we keep it all together for the time being, and send it back to UK as Rick had suggested.

'All right, then,' I said. 'It's going in a Lacon box for now, and the next time we go in to the Embassy, it heads for home.'

Next morning Sasha was on top of the world, beaming at everyone, bringing thanks and congratulations from Omon's highest brass. He also brought a personal invitation.

'My mother,' he began, as we stood in the sunshine outside the back of our building. 'She would like so much to meet you. She asks, please come to supper one evening.'

'Sasha! You haven't told her about yesterday?'

'*Konechno nyet!* She knows nothing about yesterday. She knows nothing about my work. This invitation is from many days old.'

'Well – thanks. I'd like to meet her.'

'Good! Good!'

'When would it be?'

'She suggest Friday. And please, bring one friend.'

'Thank you. That's really nice. Now look – I've got something for you. Hang on there a minute.'

I nipped inside to fetch his dollars. It wasn't the ideal moment, because it looked slightly as if I was trying to pay in advance for a couple of dinners, but I thought it best to get the presentation over with.

'Listen,' I said. 'We want to give you this.'

When he saw the money he blushed bright red and tried to push it away. 'No, Zheordie. No, please . . .'

'Take it.' I caught his right hand with my left and pushed the notes into it. 'You know where it came from. We got more than we need. We want you to have a share. And change it quickly, before somebody decides it's fake.'

For a second or two I thought the silly bugger was going to cry, as he blinked and looked down at the notes. But he soon got hold of himself and said, 'Too much. Too much.'

'Put it in your pocket and shut up!' I grinned and gave him a clip on the shoulder. 'It's time we got the lads down to the range.'

The students were in fine form, and gave an ironic cheer when we appeared. Apparently there'd been a clip about the raid on the morning's TV news, and bush telegraph had whizzed a full account of it round more efficiently than the Internet. Nobody seemed in the least put out by the loss of Misha, least of all his former colleague in SOBR, who appeared to regard him as entirely dispensable.

I'd been intending to play the whole thing down, and I asked Anna to explain that, for political reasons, it was essential that Brit involvement in the bust remained under wraps. But the Russians were so enthusiastic about the hit that I decided to make a virtue of it and called a special seminar at which we took everyone – the students who hadn't been there, and our own guys – through all the stages of the raid: planning, equipment, preparations, execution.

It proved an inspired idea: everybody was gripped by the analysis and discussion, and learned useful lessons. Of course I said nothing about the handout of dollars, but I did deplore the lack of a formal debriefing session. 'I'm not criticising anyone,' I said. 'That isn't my business. But at home we'd have done it a different way – and in fact it's what we're doing now. It's always important to talk through what's happened. That's the way you avoid mistakes in future.'

'Misha,' somebody started. 'Why did he fall? Why no safety rope?'

'He was supposed to have one. I told everyone to rope up, but it seems he hadn't bothered. Your special forces people are like us: you don't take kindly to orders.'

I saw two of the Russians exchange glances, and added, 'That's not criticism. It's a statement of fact.' Finally I said, 'I must emphasise that our participation in the raid was completely un-official, so we can't have any mention of it leaking to the media. Otherwise we'll be in the shit with our own people. Understood?'

All through that day I felt I was blundering deeper and deeper into a moral maze.

Almost making matters worse was the fact that the course was going really well. Our relationship with the students had never been better. Maybe it was the success of the hit that fired them up; whatever, a lot of jokes were flying about and morale was great. Sasha was all over the place in his desire to be helpful.

At lunchtime Anna and I went for a walk. I'd already had some food when she appeared at the back of the building, yet I offered her lunch – God knows what we would have given her if she'd accepted. But she said she'd had an apple, and otherwise didn't intend to eat until the evening.

So it was that we strolled off down one of the tracks into the training area.

I think her intention was just to be friendly, and to thank us again for leading the raid; but gradually her talk turned to the present good relations between East and West, and the contrast with the bad old days of the Cold War, when the KGB was crazily suspicious and went to fantastic lengths to penetrate foreign embassies in Moscow.

'You know what happened in the Japanese Embassy?' she asked.

I shook my head.

'It was an old merchant's house, like your British Embassy. It still had fireplaces and chimneys. So the KGB decided that the way to penetrate it was by sending a man down a chimney to plant microphones. They found a very thin man, trained him to climb, and sent him off.'

She stopped, looking at me.

'And what happened?'

'Nothing! The man was never seen again. That was the end of him. Did he get stuck? Is he still there, perhaps? Did the Japanese catch him and feed him to their tame fish? Nobody knows. Of course the KGB couldn't ask, so they never found out.'

I laughed and said, 'When you worked in London, I suppose you were spying too?'

'Naturally! All Russians abroad were spies then. We were

running the Intourist office, of course, but every day we were sending in reports to the KGB.'

'What about?'

'Oh, prominent people who booked air tickets or tours, foreign visitors to London, economic activity in general . . . I'm sure most of the information was useless, but we thought we were tremendously important.'

'But how did you get into spying in the first place?'

'To see the world. Isn't that what you say about your navy? "Join the navy and see the world"? That was it with the KGB, exactly. In those days, the only chance you had of getting out of the Soviet Union was by joining the Ministry of Foreign Affairs or the KGB. Those were the two best careers on offer.'

Several times during our chat I almost challenged her about the business of our lap-top. But I decided on balance that it was better not to stir things up.

So, on the surface, everything was brilliant; and yet, undermining the cheerful atmosphere, was the presence of Apple and Orange, sitting there in the Embassy lock-up.

The CNDs were a lead weight on my mind, and Sasha's invitation to supper made everything worse. How could I chat up his old mother with this in the back of my brain?

All afternoon my mind kept wandering as I tried to think up ways of wriggling out of our commitment. What if we dropped both devices, unprimed, off one of the bridges into the Moscow River, and told Hereford there'd been an unfortunate accident – a crash which had flung the cases out of the back of the van and over the parapet? Even if they believed it they'd probably react by simply getting two more CNDs sent post-haste from America, and we'd be back in the shit, neck deep, with even less time to extricate ourselves.

What if we dumped the cases in the river but reported that we'd installed them correctly at the two sites? Obviously the satellite wouldn't pick up the right signals – but maybe we could attribute this to faults in the systems. I needed to consult Toad on that one.

What if I posted Anna an anonymous typewritten note about the contents of the Embassy lock-up? A quick raid by Omon, an almighty diplomatic row, Embassy staff expelled, SAS sent packing, international stand-off, countdown to World War Three . . .

When I confided my anxiety to Whinger that evening, his reaction was typical. 'For fuck's sake, Geordie,' he went. 'You're getting old. The only thing to do's to get the bastards in place and forget about them. It's a thousand to one they'll never get used. So let's bury them, have done with it – and don't get caught, 'cause life's too short.'

I stared at the deep lines in his face and the curls of grey in the light-brown fuzz of his hair. 'You always were a mean bastard,' I told him, 'but I reckon you're right. We'll go for it.'

Our next decision was to shift our early-morning run in the direction of the potential Orange site, to clear that one down. During the past few days we'd made a couple more passes along the track that went by the old air-raid shelter, but we'd still not looked inside, and now we needed to suss it out properly.

The nights were growing steadily longer, so the next morning we set off in the dark, and we'd covered the three kilometres to the site before the light was at all strong. This meant we had to hang around a while before we could see, but at least we felt confident that no one else was about.

The shelter proved to be not much more than a tunnel driven horizontally into a piece of sloping ground – a primitive structure with an arched roof of corrugated iron which was about ten feet high in the middle and dropped down to ground level on either side. From the front we could see that the tin was only the inner lining: on top of it was a layer of concrete maybe a foot thick, and then earth. In the front wall, made of concrete blocks, was a small opening at shoulder height, designed to let in light and air, and the entrance was to one side. Since the only illumination came through those two apertures, the inside was dark as a cave and we had to feel our way past the edge of the heap of old planks dumped in there.

'Should have brought a torch,' Whinger muttered.

161

'Yeah – but we can hack it enough for now.'

The shelter ran about thirty feet into the side of the hill and was all one space – no divisions. When our eyes had adjusted to the gloom we could see that the wall at the back was like the one at the front – concrete blocks – but in less good nick: damp had worked its way through, cracking the mortar and producing dark stains. Pressure from the earth behind had pushed two or three of the blocks forward so that they stood proud of their neighbours. When I ran my fingers down the wall they came away wet and smelling faintly of iron.

'What we should do is get behind the blocks and dig out a hollow,' said Whinger. 'Then put the wall back up. With the blocks loose like that, it's a piece of cake.'

'It would be if we didn't have to dispose of the spoil.' I bent down and scuffed my hand over the floor. 'Feels like bare earth. But the stuff coming out of the bank's bound to be a different colour.'

'Yeah – but who's coming in here to see it?'

'A hundred to one, nobody. But if somebody did we'd be buggered. Better to get rid of it. Let's recce a dump site outside.'

Back in the open, we found an ideal place within thirty metres of the entrance: pushing through scrub, well away from the track, we nearly fell into a deep pit with gorse bushes growing over it. Sand or earth dumped through the branches would vanish into the hole, which would have taken tons and was far bigger than we needed.

'That's it, then,' I said. 'When we come, it's going to be all hands to the pumps. We've got to do the whole job in one night: drop the wall, dig the recess, place the device, rebuild the wall, skim it with mud to mask the new joints, and away.'

The simplicity of the task seemed to steel my resolve. As we trotted back towards the camp I realised that for the past few days I'd been postponing the insertion of Apple on the grounds that there was no hurry. Now I'd swung round to Whinger's point of view: the sooner we got both devices squared away, the better.

'You're right,' I panted. 'There's no reason to hang about. We'll go for the Kremlin tomorrow night.'

162

TEN

We planned everything in as much detail as we could, but the timings inevitably remained untidy. I arranged with the Chargé d'Affaires that we'd remove some of our stuff from the lock-up during the evening. We'd be bound to arouse suspicion if we swept into the compound at midnight; equally, it was quite possible that watchers in the Kremlin had the Embassy's entrance under continuous video surveillance from across the river – if anyone saw a car emerge from the gates and vanish straight into the churchyard down the road, the forces of law and order would be on the scene within minutes. The same would apply if we attempted to move the Apple components on foot. We couldn't trudge out of the Embassy gates lugging heavy containers and struggle with them along to the churchyard: video cameras or not, somebody would be bound to notice. The only safe way of shifting the device to the old stable was to load it up, drive off, disappear for a while and then return from the opposite direction, cruising in through the gateway arch and straight past the church door.

Our earlier visits had shown that there were people about until quite late in the evening, and we reckoned that 10.00 p.m. would be a safer time to kick off than 9.00. That meant we'd have nearly an hour to kill.

For the tunnel team I'd nominated Toad, Pavarotti and myself. Rick would man the head of the shaft: with his reasonable Russian, he might be able to bluff his way through if anyone accosted him while we were down. During our recce Whinger had stood off in the car, and this time I wanted him in command on the surface once again; but we were going to need

163

two vehicles, because we would never fit five guys and the Apple components into one of the Volgas. That meant I had to detail Mal as our second driver, leaving only Dusty, Johnny and Pete in barracks.

I was worried by the knowledge that the guys back on the base had no vehicle in which they could come out and recover us if anything went wrong. In fact I was worried by a hell of a lot of niggling possibilities – which all seemed to become probabilities as the day ground on. We'd get a puncture driving out of the Embassy gates, with Apple on board (we'd had three punctures already). We'd meet hostile natives in the churchyard. We'd drop one of the heavy components down the access shaft and wreck it. We'd crack the casing of the SCR and absorb fatal doses of radiation. We'd find the tunnel booby-trapped. We'd find the tunnel flooded along its whole length. We'd run out of oxygen while making final excavations at the site. We wouldn't be able to lift the device into its resting place. It would turn out that the two components were incompatible. The satellite wouldn't pick up signals from the SCR . . .

Before we left I put through a call to Hereford and confirmed that we were under starter's orders. Until then I'd been economical with information about our progress. I'd reported our successful recce of the Apple site but I hadn't told anyone what we'd done with the devices. Now I simply said that it should be possible for Washington to make contact with Apple from 0200 next morning.

At last 8.00 came, and it was too late to agonise any more. I rode passenger in the black wagon, with Mal driving and Toad in the back. Whinger drove the grey car, with Rick and Pavarotti as passengers.

Unfortunately it was a still evening. The noisy gale that had blown up during the Mafia hit would have suited us fine, but tonight we had to make do without.

As we headed into town we passed one GAI team who'd set up a temporary check-point on the other side of the road: they'd got three of their little blue-and-white Gaz jeeps set out to form a funnel, and were pulling in about one driver in three. Sasha had told us that by the end of each month these traffic police were frantic for money, and imposed instant fines for any offence they could dream up – as he put it: '*for* documents, *for* speed, *for* lights, *for* breaking rules, *for* not having seat-belts done up.'

We had our documents, we had roubles, we had dollars . . . but luckily tonight there was no purge on vehicles going in our direction.

The route was familiar by now. Over the bridge, swing down on to the embankment, head west. We made one precautionary drive-past in the black car while the grey one stood off out of sight; then we came back round the block, joined forces, and both turned into the Embassy compound at 8.55.

So far, so good. But from that moment things persistently went a little bit wrong. The first shock came when, as we pulled up in the Embassy's rear yard, the Chargé himself came out to greet us. I'd assumed he'd be off duty by now.

In fact Allway was harmless enough – he'd obviously had a couple of drinks, and was braying in a loud, hearty voice that he'd only emerged to wish us well. But his mere presence outside the lock-up was a pain.

'How are you doing?' he boomed. 'All tickety-boo?'

'Yes, thanks.'

'Getting enough to eat out there? Hope they're not starving you.'

'No, no. We're fine. Just come in to pick up a couple of items of kit.'

'Ah! Some of those ammunition boxes, what?'

'Those are the ones.'

'Want a hand?'

'No thanks. We'll manage fine.'

'Well – any problems, just let me know.'

'Thanks.'

I thought the bastard was going back indoors, but he turned and said, 'Oh, by the way, the security forces had a big success against the Mafia the other day.'

165

'Is that right?'

'Caught several of the godfathers in a flat, right here in the middle of town. Killed four or five of them. It was on the news next day. Surprised you haven't heard about it.'

'No . . .' I shook my head. 'We've been pretty busy – don't have much time for watching TV.'

'Maybe the Russians are getting better at Mafia-hunting, what? Maybe they don't need you fellows so much after all. Or maybe you've taught them something already? Well – ta ta!'

I took several deep breaths, forcing myself not to utter a sound until the door had closed behind him. Then I just whispered, 'Jeeesus Christ! Let's get moving.'

Unless you were colour-blind there was no way of muddling the components, because Apple's three pieces were all marked with a light green circle, Orange's with orange. We backed the black Volga as close as we could to the cellar door and carried the three green-marked cases out, four men on each of the heavy ones. Once again they pushed the car right down on its springs. Toad removed the Rat from its lair and clipped it on his belt.

As soon as we'd secured the up-and-over door of the cellar, we drove off. I'd felt as if my exchanges with the Chargé lasted for ever, but still we had fifty minutes to kill; so, rather than hang about in the area, we followed our plan and drove up to the terrace in front of the univerity, on the edge of the Sparrow Hills. Sasha had taken us there during our first visit, and I remembered it as a favourite view-point, popular with tourists and sightseers, where strangers hanging around wouldn't attract attention.

If you ever want to get your adrenalin going, try driving through Moscow at night with a nuclear bomb in the boot of a rickety, underpowered car. Every traffic light spelt possible disaster, every vehicle that overtook seemed certain to be full of Mafia gunmen bent on a hijack.

'What we do *not* want,' I said grimly, 'is to be stopped by the fucking GAI with this lot on board.'

'Nah,' said Pavarotti. 'They don't seem to operate much in

the centre – more out on the highways.'

Luck favoured us. With me map-reading we managed to avoid the cops and find the way, and soon came out on to the huge, level esplanade, where one can park and walk forward to look out over the city. Whinger, following at a distance, pulled up some fifty yards to our right, and a couple got out of each car to take in the sights.

The prospect was spectacular, I had to admit. Behind us, the monstrous skyscraper of the main university building towered into the sky, topped by a slender spire that gleamed golden in its spotlights. On either side of it the lower towers sprouted pinnacles, and hundreds of lighted windows made the campus look like a city on its own.

In front of us, immediately over the wall was a steep drop, with a couple of rickety-looking ski-jumps – not yet in use – poised over it. Below them, the centre of Moscow was laid out in a million more lights. It reminded me of the view from the top of Block B – except that here the illumination was far more varied and concentrated. Close in the foreground was a large stadium; farther out, the floodlit buildings of the Kremlin glowed magnificently. We could also see the White House. I remembered Sasha telling us of how it had been rebuilt after the coup: apparently the workers had stayed in the nearby Kiev Hotel, and their demand for whores was so phenomenal that busloads of extra women had had to be imported from out of town.

I glanced around. There were a few other people up here, but nobody close to us. Away to our right I could see Whinger and Rick, also looking over the wall, but correctly keeping their distance.

'I feel that hepped up, I reckon if I jumped off here I'd fly,' I told Pavarotti quietly.

'Don't try it, mate. You might just keep going, never come down.'

We admired the view for a few more minutes, then returned to the car and hung around some more. As usual at such moments, our watches seemed to have gone on strike.

But at last it was 9.45, time to head down.

'Moving off now,' I told Whinger over the radio.

'Roger. I'll let you get clear.'

Mal turned the car and started to back-track our route – but we were hardly under way before Whinger came through again with, 'Watch yourselves. I think you've got a tail.'

Mal said, 'Shit,' studied his mirror and said, 'Is it that buff Lada?'

'Roger. It pulled out when you did.'

'I'll watch it for a minute.'

'Roger.'

Turning in the passenger seat to face Mal, I saw the car they were talking about. Now what? Our options were severely limited by our lack of speed and the great weight we were carrying. Shooting red lights was no good: hundreds of drivers did that anyway; the Lada would simply follow us through any crossing. And in any case we didn't want to risk a brush with the GAI. We certainly couldn't outrun a pursuer. Nor could we afford to tangle with one. We all had Sigsauer 9mm pistols, and if things turned nasty we could use them – but only as a very last resort. A collision might shunt the nuclear components clean out of the car, taking the boot lid or rear door with them, and damage the devices beyond repair . . .

'How many on board?' I asked.

'Three,' came Whinger's voice.

Mal said, 'I'm going to head away from our target area.'

'Roger.'

Before we started down through the bends of the hillside, he took a left, heading south. Then another left. The Lada followed. When a light turned red way ahead, he changed down to decelerate without using the brakes. The Lada slowed as well, keeping its distance.

'Definite tail,' I told Whinger. 'Can you sort them for us?'

'I'll try.'

'Do they realise we're a pair?'

'Don't think so. I'm driving on sidelights and keeping well back.'

168

Whinger was – and is – a hell of a guy behind the wheel. He'd done a stint as instructor in special driving techniques at Llangwern, the training area in Wales, and what he didn't know about J-turns, ramming and breaking up illegal VCPs wasn't worth knowing. The trouble was that in England or Northern Ireland he'd probably have been driving one of the Regiment's souped-up intercept cars, which have extra power, armour, strengthened suspension and belly plates, and can whack any-thing else off the road with one flick of the rear end. Whereas here he had a lumbering, lightweight Volga with little power and no protection. I knew what he was thinking: that although it would be no trouble to knock our tail into the gutter, the last thing he wanted was to end up immobilising his own vehicle.

Somehow we'd got on to a big boulevard which my wrist-compass told me was heading south-west, out of town. At a crossroads I got a glimpse of a sign and deciphered it as Leninskii Prospekt.

The Lada was still behind us.

Shit! I was thinking. We should never have come up into this area. I've dropped a bollock here. We should just have made a loop and risked going into the churchyard early.

Then I remembered a friend of mine – Andy, a Tornado pilot – saying that a key element in training to fly fast jets was that pilots must have the ability to dump bad decisions behind them. In the air, especially at low level, events happen so fast that the pilot has to take dozens of decisions every minute, and the essential skill is to dump whatever's just happened, so that your mind's free to look ahead.

OK, I told myself. Forget that one. Now what?

'Take that right,' I told Mal suddenly.

He hauled the wheel round. Our tyres squealed under the load. Sixty yards behind us the Lada copied our every move, turning through the crossing just as the lights changed.

'Whinger's got through as well,' Mal said tersely. 'Must have shot the red.'

'I've a mind to stop suddenly and sort the bastards ourselves,' I said, reaching down to draw my Sig. At the back of my mind I

169

knew that the very idea of opening up on unidentified strangers in the middle of the city was outrageous. In London I'd never have dreamt of it. But here in Moscow the level of lawlessness was so high that any form of self-defence seemed in order.

We appeared to be driving in orbit round the university; the colossal tower was still quite close on our right. If we stayed near it, at least we'd know where we were.

'Right again,' I said.

Now we were on another wide boulevard, heading back towards the esplanade. The big road stretched ahead, empty of traffic. Suddenly I heard Whinger say, 'Slow down, Mal. Come down to fifty ks.'

'Roger,' went Mal, and eased off the accelerator. He'd been doing about sixty-five, and let the needle fall back. With one eye on the mirror he said, 'Stand by. The Lada's closing. No – cancel that. They've eased off again.'

The next thing we heard was Whinger calling, 'Stand by for contact. I'm going in.'

I knew what he'd done: on the long straight he'd built up speed and was coming in at the opposition on one fast run. I twisted round in my seat just in time to see a wild flare of headlights sweeping sideways, then the black silhouette of a vehicle momentarily on end, standing on its nose for an instant before hurtling off the near side of the road. Seconds later there was a brilliant flash, and flames leapt from the wreck.

I braked and pulled in to the kerb.

'Nice one, Whinge,' I called. 'You OK?'

'More or less.' He sounded well hyped up. 'Sustained a bit of damage, but we're still mobile. *Davai, davai!*'

We carried on for a couple of blocks. Then Mal said, 'No – he's dropping back.'

'Whinge,' I called. 'You got a problem?'

'Yeah – front tyre's going down.'

'Next right, then. Get off this fucking great road.'

We turned into a tree-lined side-street and came to a halt a hundred yards from the junction. Behind us the grey Volga crawled round the corner and crept under a tree.

'Turn and park on the other side,' I told Mal. 'Face this way, so you can cover us.'

I jumped out and ran across to Whinger's car. The air was full of the stink of burning rubber. Smoke was rising from the off-side front wheel. Rick and Pavarotti were already grappling with spare and jack, with Whinger standing back on the alert against the trunk of a tree.

'Tyre's knackered,' said Rick. 'The bumper got pushed into it by the impact. The bastard's almost on fire. It's worn right through.'

'Steering OK?'

'Should be when we get this wheel on.'

I went over to Whinger. 'What was all that about?'

'Ask me another. There were three young guys in it. At least one of them had a pistol, too.'

'You up-ended them, anyway.'

'Yeah. I got up to eighty ks and came at them without lights. Took their back end away.'

'*Zdorovo!* That party won't be doing any more driving tonight.'

We could have done without that little episode. It broke our concentration and meant that, as we finally approached the churchyard, we had to go through our mental preparation all over again.

This time Whinger made the drive-past, dropping Rick and Pav off on the embankment to walk in and recce the stable on foot. Only when they reported all clear did we prepare to move in.

Never in my life had I felt more nervous. I kept thinking, Once we get underground I'll be OK. What I do *not* want is any confrontation with all this hardware on our hands. We had no plausible explanation to offer if we were caught. We were prepared to shoot our way out of trouble if we had to, above or below ground, and we hoped that if the police found bodies, they would chalk them up as victims of some Mafia feud. But as for being grabbed in possession of the bomb – to that we had no answer. If we were forced to run for it, we might not even get back to the barracks at Balashika. I had visions of a gigantic escape and evasion scenario.

Mal remained perfectly cool, and that helped steady me. He hadn't seen the yard before but I'd briefed him on the layout, and now I talked him in, yard by yard. 'Here's the gateway, coming up. There's the church ahead. Keep round to the right. Stop opposite the doorway. Here we are – GO!'

Rick materialised from the stable, opened the rear door of the Volga and dragged section one of Apple half-way out. 'Pav's done the locks,' he whispered.

'Great.'

Mal remained in the driving seat with his engine ticking over in case he needed to take off suddenly. Toad grabbed the handles on the other end of section one. Together with Rick he carried it into the stable. I seized the SCR canister from the boot and staggered in with that. A moment later Toad and Rick brought in section two. Last out of the car was my bergen, containing lightweight hoist, ladder, nets, rubber bags, dry-suits, digging tools, head-torches, spare batteries, overalls and other essential paraphernalia. The pack alone was one hell of a weight.

'That's it,' I hissed at Mal through his open window. 'See you later.'

He eased the Volga gently forward, through the bend into the rear yard, swung round and came back past us. We saw his brake lights glow for an instant before he nosed out on to the main road. Then he was gone.

In the ink-black stable we stood and listened. I found I was hyperventilating, but I knew that now the most immediate danger – of having the hardware discovered in the car – was over. Now, in an emergency, we could do a runner or shoot our way out, leaving the stuff behind, and, if challenged, deny all knowledge of it.

The yard was very still, the church dark. We waited a couple of minutes. Nobody moved or spoke. Then I whispered, 'OK.'

Our individual tasks were carefully pre-planned. Toad kept watch on the doorway. Pav, the tallest, slung a loop over the

172

main roof beam to take the top hook of the hoist. I broke out the nets, which were made of thick green nylon with a three-inch mesh, and manoeuvred the steel cases into them.

We'd just got the first one trussed when Toad let out a hiss. Torches snapped off. Everyone kept still. But it was only the usual problem – women crossing the yard from the church – and in a moment we moved again.

With all three cases netted, I pulled on my dry-suit, got Rick to zip up the back, and took over from Toad at the door while he got his suit on.

Pavarotti had the hoist well secured, the pulleys running smoothly. 'Looks good,' I whispered, running my torch beam over his ropes. 'Rick?'

'Hello.'

'I'm going down. We'll aim to be back at the base of the shaft at midnight. Lift the lid and have a listen then, anyway. If we're not back, try again every half-hour.'

'Roger. Happy landings.'

Feet into the top of the shaft. Ease down the ladder. Once my feet touched, I took a careful look round the floor in my immediate area. No signs of disturbance other than our own. The same damp, muddy smell of decay.

I switched off my head-torch to save the battery, jerked the ladder and felt it rise past me as somebody lifted it clear. Then I heard scuffling noises as the first of the loaded nets – the SCR – started down. I was tempted to peer up the shaft and watch it coming, but didn't fancy being under it if a rope should break or anything went wrong with the hoist; so I stood to one side and waited until the heavy bundle sank gently to the floor, then released the shackle.

Before the second net came down there was quite a pause. I imagined the guys struggling to manoeuvre the heavy case into position, on end above the mouth of the shaft, without letting it bump or scrape. Then more scuffling, scratching noises started, and I switched my torch on again in time to see the bulging net appear. Once more I released the shackle and twitched the rope, then walked the case out of the way on its corners and laid it gently on its back. Its weight was formidable, and I knew that the third component, section two, was ten kilos heavier still.

The pause was longer this time. The guys were obviously having more problems. Then came a thump, and some strangled curses. At last the scraping noise began again, and I stood clear in anticipation.

Suddenly a loud, sharp *crack* ripped down the shaft. A patter of particles landed by my feet, as if there'd been rapid movement above. Jesus, I thought. Somebody's fired a shot.

I stood frozen. All movement in the shaft had ceased. Some bastard's stumbled on them, I thought. They've dropped him. But they can't close the cover with the pulley ropes in the way. Why the hell don't they get on and lower away? Maybe there are more guys in the yard.

In the silence of the tunnel I could hear my heart beating. Not a sound came from above. Irrationally, I felt that if I moved or spoke I might precipitate disaster. All I could do was keep still.

For many long seconds I waited motionless in the dark. My heartbeat seemed to grow louder and louder. Then at last I heard more noises above. They sounded different from the earlier scrapings, but at least something was happening. More bumps and thuds. I shone my torch quickly up the shaft and saw that the whole of its section was filled by the third and last net. Yet, in spite of the noises, the thing wasn't moving. Had it jammed?

I tried my radio and got no response. My instinct was to yell up the shaft and find out what in hell was going on. But I realised that they couldn't shout back for fear of being heard, so I steeled myself to wait.

In the end movement resumed and the big case came on down, Toad and Pav close behind it.

'What the fuck were you doing?'

'Didn't you hear that?' Pav asked.

'I sure did. Did somebody fire a shot?'

'No, no. That was the main beam in the stable going.'

'Jesus!'

'Yeah. The whole roof dropped several inches. Shit rained down all round. We thought the place was falling in on us.'

'Nobody else heard it?'

'Don't think so.'

'What did you do?'

'Found an old timber lying at the back and managed to get it under as a prop so the beam couldn't drop any lower. Then we carried on.'

We'd lost quite a bit of time already, so we made haste to catch up. First we had the laborious task of getting the cases out of the nets, loading them into the rubber bags, then bundling them into the nets again. Experiments with nets full of sandbags, filled to the equivalent weight, had shown us that the best way of shifting our loads in the confined space of the tunnel would be by fitting slings of wide webbing to the nets, fore and aft, and advancing as a pair in line-ahead, one leaning forward and the other back, to levitate the burden between us. It wasn't easy or comfortable – because the laden net tended to crash into the heels of the person leading and drag the back marker off his feet – but it was better than hauling a huge weight along the floor.

It was obvious that three journeys would be needed, so we set out on the first with me leading, Pavarotti behind, Apple's section one between us, and Toad carrying his own bergen full of tricks. My plan was that, once we reached the site, we'd leave him there with the first half of the device so that he could start preparing it while we went back for the second.

All went well until we were on the downward slope, leading to the river. Then, as the beam of light from my head-torch danced around in front of me, I sensed that something had changed.

'Stopping,' I said.

I slackened off my end of the net and stood still.

'The water,' said Pav. 'It's gone.'

'Exactly. I'm sure my marker was just here somewhere. Look – there it is.' I pointed to the horizontal scratch-mark on the wall.

'Some bastard's been in here draining it,' said Pav incredulously.

'Can't have been.'

'Where's it gone, then?'

'You tell me.'

In fact only some of the water had gone. A lot remained. Soon after we'd moved forward again we saw its surface lying still and black ahead of us. As we advanced to the edge of it I realised that even at its deepest point it no longer reached the roof: there was a gap of about a foot under the arched yellow bricks, and I could see right through to the other side.

'Well, damn!' Pavarotti sounded very Welsh in his indignation. 'The tide's gone out.'

'Tide be buggered!' I snapped. 'We're a thousand bloody miles from the sea.'

'Only joking. We don't need our masks now, that's for sure. Hardly need the suits, even. We can walk straight through with our heads above water.'

'All the better,' I told him. 'But . . . hey, what's this?'

On the right-hand wall ahead of us, just above the water line, the top of an arched recess was showing – clearly the opening to a side-tunnel. It was bricked in, but some of the cement had washed out and I could see water welling in and out through the gaps.

'That's where it's gone,' I said. 'Or where it came in from. Part of the system.'

'So what?'

'So nothing. We carry on.'

And through the flood we went, moving slowly to create as little disturbance as possible. Once in the water the steel case, with air trapped round it inside the rubber bag, was almost floating, and towed along easily.

Very soon we were out of the water and at the site itself. We laid the case down a few feet short of the end of the tunnel, to make sure no debris fell on it when we started digging.

'There you are,' I told Toad. 'It's going in that recess. And there's the shaft for the SCR. You get cracking, and we'll be back.'

One of Toad's unnerving features was his silence, the fact that

176

he spoke so little. You felt that his brain was turning over smoothly like a well-oiled mechanism, but you hadn't a clue what he was thinking. Now, as we left him, he stood there dry-washing his hands without a word.

'I wouldn't mind sealing the bugger down here,' I said as we started out with our second load. 'That'd stop him annoying me.'

By the time we returned, Toad had the lid off the case, and for the first time we got a glimpse of its contents: a terrifying maze of bright blue and white wires snaking round compartments of different shapes. He was wearing latex gloves and a pair of headphones, listening carefully as he touched a probe on one point after another. He had small socket spanners, Allen keys and battery-driven screwdrivers laid out on a mat beside him, occasionally picking one up to tighten or loosen a connection. But as soon as we delivered the SCR, he turned his attention to that, because he was anxious to have it up and working first.

Rather him than me, I thought as Pavarotti and I peeled off our dry-suits and got stuck into the digging. Secretly, though, I felt a bit like a navvy labouring in the presence of a technician who understood things that would always be beyond me.

We were already sweating when we started to dig, and soon we were positively pouring. The ground was neither clay nor rock but something in between – a hard, shaly, grey-brown compound that sometimes broke away in lumps and sometimes split up into flakes with sharp edges. To save batteries we worked with minimum light, using only one torch at a time, whacking our short-handled picks into the face, levering out whatever the blades had got hold of, and shovelling loose spoil away with our hands. From past experience I already knew that Pav stank like a badger when he got hot – Pavagrotti, he was sometimes called – and now, at close quarters and in the confines of the tunnel, he was overpowering. But I realised I was smelling probably as bad to him, and said nothing.

Toad, as always, worked in silence, but after twenty minutes or so he stood up and said, 'This one's ready.'

Out of its cover, the SCR reminded me of the head of a

robot, with twin aluminium antennae, linked by a cross bar near the base and rigged on the top like a pair of miniature rugby goal posts. I knew that Toad wanted it installed as high up the ventilation shaft as we could get it, and we'd worked out a means of fixing it in position. From behind our block at Balashika we'd scavenged three pieces of angle-iron and had cut them into twenty-four-inch lengths so that they'd jam across the shaft at an angle beneath it, and lock in position when its weight came down on them.

Standing with my head up the duct, I chopped at the brickwork above me with hammer and chisel to make three notches that would take the lower ends of the struts. Chips of brick kept flying into my eyes, but the grooves didn't need to be very deep, and after one trial with a length of angle-iron, to make sure it would seat itself properly, we were ready to lift the SCR into place.

As a temporary support, we'd brought an aluminium pole made of short sections that slotted into one another. It was part of another satellite aerial system, and we'd worked out that we could stand it upright, with a circular pad on top, to take the receiver's weight between lifts.

When Pavarotti and I raised the box to waist height, Toad slipped the first section of pole in vertically beneath it.

'OK,' he said, 'rest there.'

Another lift, to chest height, and he got another section in.

The pole, longer now, started to wobble and flex as it took the weight. 'Keep it steady,' said Toad.

A third section propped the receiver at head height. The final hoist, into the shaft, could only be done by one person, pushing up with both arms above his head. I delegated the job to Pavarotti, as he's taller and stronger than me.

'I'll give you what lift I can on the pole,' I told him, gripping it with both hands. 'Ready?'

'Right.'

'Three, two, one – *lift!*'

Up went the black box, scraping against the sides of the shaft. Toad snapped one more length on to the bottom of the stalk and said, 'OK – steady again.' While I held the pole in the middle, Pav bent his knees, lowering the box on to the pad.

'Angle-irons next,' I said – but when I went to slot them into position, I found we still hadn't got the box high enough. We needed another three or four inches to give us the necessary clearance. While Pav and I both grabbed the pole and lifted, Toad slipped his steel tool-box under the bottom and wedged it there. That gave us the space we needed; I got the struts into position, arranged some bubble-wrap padding on top of them, and called to the others to lower gently.

All that had taken a lot of effort and concentration. When I checked my watch I was amazed at how much time had gone by. Our torch batteries were faltering and needed changing.

'Got to keep moving,' I said as we took a quick break for a drink of water. Our next task was to chip out a gully for the co-ax cables that would connect the SCR to the device – another aggravating job at which only one person could work. Again we took it in turns, going all out for a few minutes, then resting. As soon as we had a channel clear Toad moved in to connect the cables, and we went back to our main excavation.

I'd realised that our best plan was to form the spoil from our cavity into a ramp, so that we'd be able to slide the Apple components up it and into position. The trouble with this was, the ramp itself began to get in our way. Digging became progressively more awkward as we had to lean over our own heap to reach the back of the recess. By the time we had a hole of the right dimensions, we were both knackered.

All this time, when he wasn't tinkering with the cables, Toad remained bent over his charges, tightening, adjusting, listening through his headphones. Then, as we paused, I noticed he was into his hand-washing routine again, a curious look on his face.

'What's the matter?'

'Just trying to imagine it all white in here.'

'White?'

'When the device is detonated, everything in here will be vaporised in blinding white light.'

'Charming. I hope we're not here to see it.'

179

'You wouldn't see anything,' he said. 'You wouldn't *feel* anything. You'd be obliterated, just like that.' He snapped his fingers – and suddenly, as if he'd conjured up a genie, we became aware of a noise.

'What the . . . ?' Pav was crouching beside me on our ramp of spoil. He raised a hand. 'Listen!'

At first we could feel it rather than hear it: a deep vibration more than a sound, a shudder so low that it seemed to come through our boots. But in seconds it built into an audible flutter, then into a rumble, then into a roar which filled the tunnel and made it shake. The water behind us had long since settled back into stillness after our passage through it. Now I saw a ripple on the black surface, and I was convinced that the roof was about to cave in.

I looked round at the concrete blocks behind us. We were trapped between the wall and the water in a section of tunnel about fifteen yards long.

The pulsating roar built up still louder until it seemed to come from right over our heads. Particles of brick dust started to fall from the roof. I looked up at the brickwork right above us, fearful that I'd see water break through the joins, expecting to be swamped any minute. I made a grab for my mask and breathing kit.

Into the din Pav yelled, 'Fucking Metro!'

'Bollocks!' I shouted. 'No Metro line anywhere near. I checked it on the street plan.'

'Gotta be a boat, then.'

'A boat?'

'On the river.'

'Some boat.'

We were bellowing at the tops of our voices. Toad stood there looking vacant, but I think he was just as scared as we were. Then I realised that the racket was diminishing, and I felt sure Pav was right: a boat had gone up or down the river, close over our heads.

After that scare, it took Toad only a few more minutes to complete his preparations.

'OK,' he announced, 'we're ready to go.'

Anywhere else, the idea of taking orders from Toad would have made me see red, but here we were entirely in his hands and it didn't bug me at all to follow his instructions. With him directing and helping, we raised the base section of Apple – the heavier of the two – and eased it sideways on to the rough shelf we'd created. That was relatively simple. The harder part was to lift the top section, turn it over in mid-air, then manoeuvre it into position above its mate without letting the two touch or knock together until they were perfectly aligned. The second part weighed just on 150lbs, and even for two fit guys, holding that amount out at arm's length was no picnic.

Toad had had the simple but brilliant notion of bringing three slender spars of wood, an inch thick, to act as temporary buffers, and he laid these across the top of the base unit so that we could lower the top on to them without letting it touch the metal beneath until we were ready. Then, while Pavarotti and I held up one end of the top component, he withdrew the bars one at a time and we lowered away the last inch. As we stood back, he quickly went to work inserting six stainless-steel bolts – one at each corner, one half-way up each long side – and carefully screwed them down with a ratchet-handled socket spanner. Then he plugged one of the two black co-ax cables into the lower half of the package and locked it in position, using an Allen key to turn the sunken nut.

As he took hold of the second wire, I said, 'Listen, Toad. Are you quite certain this fucking thing isn't going to go?'

'Don't worry,' he replied, not even looking up. 'My instinct for self-preservation's as good as yours.'

In went the end of the wire. Again he tightened a nut down.

'OK to cover up?' I asked.

'Hold on. I need to check.'

Once more he put on his headphones, lifted a small flap at the bottom corner of the device and plugged in the lead from a control box slung across his stomach. For a minute or two Pav and I waited, running with sweat, itching with the grit that had worked its way down the necks of our shirts. My anxiety about possible premature detonation wouldn't die down. I could only hope to hell Toad knew what he was doing. Glancing sideways at Pavarotti, I could see him thinking the same.

At last that sly, secret smile stole back on to Toad's face.

'What's happening?'

'I can hear it.'

'What?'

'It's talking to us.'

'What is, for fuck's sake?'

'The satellite.'

'Jesus! What's it saying?'

'I don't know. I just recognise the signal they gave me. Listen.'

He pulled off the headphones and handed them to me. All I got was a distant chirruping and beeping that rose and fell.

'How far up is the satellite?'

'Twenty-two thousand five hundred miles.'

I handed the set back and said, 'OK to cover up, then?'

Toad nodded and began to pack up his tools.

I'd decided in advance that we weren't going to ponce about mortaring over cracks in the brickwork. The chances of somebody else reaching the site were remote − and anyway, new mortar wouldn't pass a close inspection. Now that Apple was live, I wanted to get the hell out of the tunnel as soon as possible. So we simply covered the casing with a loose mound of bricks and spoil, as though the heap had fallen from the roof, and pushed some lumps into the conduit that we'd cut for the connection, to hold the cables in the duct. Then we collected up our kit and prepared to withdraw.

'Toad,' I said, 'what happens if the water level comes right up and the thing gets flooded?'

'It shouldn't make any difference. Now the units are sealed together they're waterproof. There'd be problems if the level got as high as the SCR, but I don't reckon that's possible.'

There was one last precaution I'd decided was worthwhile. Back at the edge of the water, we used one of the empty rubber bags as a water carrier, filled it, and dragged it to the base of the blocking wall. There we tipped the lot out at once, retreating backwards before a little tide that pursued us down the tunnel. By doing that four times, we washed away every sign of disturbance and left the silt on the floor in a smooth, unbroken carpet.

Then we waded away through the flood.

We were back under the shaft by 0020. We'd missed the midnight rendezvous, but in only ten minutes Rick was due to make his next inspection. Our last batteries were all but spent. As we waited in pitch blackness, my mind wouldn't leave the twinned cases, buried under the mound across the river. I thought of the device as a time-bomb, ticking away towards detonation. I knew that wasn't how it worked, but the idea wouldn't fade. How could we be sure that some idiot in the Pentagon wouldn't set it off by mistake? We had only Toad's word to give us hope that accidents were impossible.

We waited, sweat congealing, grit itching inside our shirts. I found myself thinking of the occasion, years before, when we'd buried an old aunt in the churchyard of my village, in the north of England, how the clods of earth had rained down on her coffin as the grave-diggers started to fill the hole above her. There was something uncomfortably similar about the way we'd heaped the spoil back on top of Apple's black and green casing.

On the dot of 0030 we heard a creak of hinges above us, and a beam of light flickered down the shaft.

'Anyone for the up?' Rick called softly.

'Three,' I told him. 'Can't wait to get out. Everything OK on top?'

'Fine.'

'Let's have a rope for the bergens, then the ladder.'

So we came back to ground level. The moment we were clear of the shaft and the cover was closed, Rick slipped the original padlocks into place and scattered hay over the top.

'Where's our transport?' I whispered.

'Dunno exactly. Somewhere close. We've been talking to them. Give 'em a call.'

I switched on my radio and said, 'Green One to Black, do you read me? Over.'

'Black,' came Whinger's voice immediately. 'Standing by for pick-up.'

'Roger,' I went. 'We'll come out two and two, as planned. First pair one minute from now. Second thirty seconds later.'

By then all the nuns – or whoever they were – seemed to have gone to bed. Only a single light was burning at the back of the inner yard; everything else was dark. All the same, we stuck to our plan of coming out in separate pairs.

'Away you go,' I said, and Rick and Toad vanished towards the gate. I counted thirty, then set off with Pavarotti.

Through the gate we turned right and started walking along the pavement. The asphalt gleamed wet after recent rain, and across the river the Kremlin buildings were still floodlit. There was nobody walking on the embankment. The first pair had disappeared – picked up already.

About a hundred yards ahead of us I saw some object lying half on the pavement, half in the road. As we approached, I saw it was a man, or maybe a body, legs out in the carriageway, head in the gutter. From the horrible angle of his feet I could tell that his legs had been run over, maybe several times. One hand was clutching the neck and shattered remains of a bottle, and round it a dark puddle had spread, more like blood than vodka.

'The poor bastard's snuffed it,' said Pavarotti as we passed. But no: at that moment the figure let out a gurgling groan and shifted slightly. On any other night, anywhere else in the world, I'd have pulled him to safety on the pavement. But here, so close to the scene of our infiltration, I didn't want to know.

The contrast between the splendid buildings opposite and the sordid brutality of life in the gutter said everything about the way in which seventy-five years of Communism had brought a vast country to its knees.

We walked on. A second later we heard an engine and saw lights coming up behind us. I tightened my right hand on the butt of my Sig, just in case; but then the lights flicked up and down in recognition. Whinger called, 'I have you visual,' the vehicle slowed, and a second later we were safe on board his Volga.

'Good on yer, Whinge,' I said as we pulled away. 'No problems?'

'The whole place is lifting with drunks – but apart from them, nothing. How about you?'

'We managed it, just about. The bastard's in place. Toad said he could hear the satellite talking to it, so we presume it's all set up. But I tell you – even if it isn't, I'm not going back down that fucking tunnel in a million years.'

'You couldn't smell any worse if you did,' Whinger observed.

'Thanks. And by the way – what made that fearsome racket?'

'When?'

'About an hour ago. It sounded as though an aircraft carrier went up the river.'

'Oh, that. It was just a barge with a load of sand on board.'

'Christ – it scared the shit out of us. We thought the tunnel was coming in.'

'Oh, well.' Whinger sounded unimpressed. 'It didn't. So that's it for tonight, is it? One down and one to go.'

ELEVEN

In the morning we felt, and looked, pretty shattered. When our students noticed some pale faces and started asking questions, we pretended we'd once again been on the piss. In fact we were rapidly gaining a reputation – quite unjustified – as leading piss-artists, and we claimed to have been so smashed that we couldn't remember the names of any of the bars we'd allegedly visited.

In fact we'd got back to barracks by 1.30 a.m., and I'd sent Hereford a coded message through the patrol radio to report the insertion of Apple. Late as it was, the lads were far too hyped up by the success of the operation to feel sleepy. As we had sat round the kitchen table with a brew, Pavarotti had croaked, 'What the fuck have we done?' perhaps partly in amazement because we'd managed it, partly in alarm at the possible consequences. 'That's put the frighteners on the bastards, anyway.'

'Not yet it hasn't,' I'd corrected. 'It may do at some time in the future, but they don't know about it yet.'

'If that thing went off now,' Johnny had said, 'what effect would it have on us here?'

'Ask Toad.'

Toad, as usual, was hovering at a distance from the rest of us.

'Eh, Toad!' Pav had shouted. 'Would Apple do for us here, now, if it went off?'

'Not immediately,' he'd replied. 'We'd hear it, of course. We'd feel the shockwave. But the big danger would be the radiation.'

'How long would that take to get here?'

'Depends on the wind. An hour?'

187

'Would we feel anything from it?'

'Not until it was too late.'

'Firekin ell!' went Whinger.

'Duty, old boy. Must do your duty.' Rick could take off the CO to perfection.

We'd gone on shooting the shit till nearly 3.00, so it wasn't surprising that morning found us a bit jaded.

What brought me to my senses was an encrypted message that came in while we were having breakfast. Decoded, it read simply: WEST END CONFIRMS APPLE PIE ORDER. West End was Washington, and the rest was obvious. The Pentagon must have put out a test transmission and made contact with the SCR.

'Can you believe it?' I said to Rick. 'They're talking to the fucking thing, as if we'd buried a person there.'

'I hope they're being polite to it,' he said.

The fact that Apple was up and running gave me a jolt. I suppose I'd been subconsciously hoping that somewhere along the line the system would fail, and that, through no fault of our own, the satellite would be unable to make contact with the bomb. In that happy event we'd be absolved from responsibility.

Speculation was cut off when Anna appeared at our back door proffering a small package.

'I brought you a present,' she began.

'Great! Come in. Have a cup of coffee. We've got a few minutes.'

Perching neatly on a chair in our mess-room, she said, 'This is by way of saying thank you for your help the other day.'

'Oh, come on. We got a big thank you anyway.'

'I know. But this is more important. Your security people in London may like to have it. MI5? Yes – MI5.'

'What is it, then?'

'Only a computer disk. But it contains full details of the Mafia organisation in London.'

'In *London*?'

'Yes. They've made rapid progress there lately. Drugs, banking, prostitution – all the usual things. The London network is spreading fast: links into Paris, Brussels, Amsterdam,

Rome and other cities. This is a copy of a disk we picked up in the apartment after the raid. It's in Chechen, I'm afraid, but I'm sure your specialists will manage to translate it.'

'Is Chechen different from Russian, then?'

'Absolutely.' She saw me looking blank, and added, 'All educated Chechens speak Russian, of course. But the languages are entirely different.'

As she talked, my mind was moving at speed. Another computer disk. Had this presentation got something to do with our own disk that had been destroyed? Was this supposed to be an apology for that accident?

'Well,' I said. 'As you know, that kind of crime isn't really our field. But I'm sure the guys in London will be grateful. Thank you.'

'You're welcome. Please send it with the compliments of the FSB.'

'Sure. I'll get it off today. The guys can take it when they go into town on the post run.'

A couple of the other lads were present at this informal meeting, but as Anna and I walked out and down the steps of the building she and I were alone for a few moments. Suddenly she said, 'I'd like to offer you a more personal thank you as well.' She gave me a sideways, come-on look. 'Will you come and have supper?'

The invitation took me by surprise. Until now she'd been so formal and so correct – so impersonal, although always friendly – that the idea of trying to take her out had almost faded from my mind. Still less had I imagined that she'd ever invite me. Apart from that brief walk we'd taken one lunchtime we'd never been alone. Now, for a moment, I was stuck for an answer.

'You don't *have* to come. That wasn't an order!' She gave me that sidelong glance again and burst out laughing. She also started to raise her right hand, and I thought she was going to take me by the arm; but luckily at that moment Mal came running round the corner with a cry of, 'Forgot my flaming notes.'

Once he'd passed, I looked back at her and said, 'Terrific. I'd like that. When were you thinking of?'

'One day next week, maybe? Friday?'

'Fine.'

'I'll come and pick you up at seven-thirty. I suggest that to avoid gossip, we say we've been summoned to see the Minister.'

In the mean time I was glad to keep our rendezvous with Sasha and his mother. Since he'd asked two of us, Whinger was my obvious choice as No. 2 – but that afternoon he had developed a filthy sore throat, and by the evening he was more or less speechless. So in his place I nominated Rick, first because of his Russian, second because, if he was with us, I'd know for sure that he wasn't shagging Mafia women.

Sasha came and collected us at 7.00, and for this excursion no subterfuge was necessary, so we went off openly, casually dressed in jeans and sweaters.

At first, Sasha was on a high. He had more information about the victims of the raid on the apartment, and it had emerged that one of the five at the table had been Ruslan Beno, another big player in the Chechen mafia.

'You don't mean Keet?' I asked.

'By no means,' Sasha replied quickly. 'This Whale, Keet – I showed you, he was one. His name was Gaidar, one of three brothers, very notoriotous. Beno is also from Grozny, but younger man.'

'I know which he was,' I said. 'That dark young fellow who got dropped half-way to the door of the living room.'

'Yes. That man.' Sasha turned to me with a big grin. 'Fantastic creeminals, Chechens. They make fabulous amounts of money. For example the Lazanskaya gang, based on Lazania restaurant, here in Moscow – they got enormous riches from stolen cars. They operate very much in Brussels, stealing big cars from diplomats. Then, you know *avizo* system?'

I shook my head.

'A*vizo* is promise note. A bank signs it, to say they will pay so much money. The criminal makes forged promise note in one city, gets it signed, takes it to another city and cashes it. Simple! By such means Chechen *avizovshchiki* made meellions. No – not meellions. Beellions! In early nineties, such kind of Chechen gang got sixty billion roubles.'

The idea of Mafiosi making fortunes obviously excited Sasha as much as did the idea of knocking off big-time players, and he talked enthusiastically for most of our short journey. But then, as we drew near his flat, he fell silent. After a couple of minutes he said, 'Zheordie – you must know. My mother – she is very simple woman. Not very educated. Peasant woman.'

'That's OK,' I said. 'I expect mine was too.'

'You don't remember her?'

'I thought I told you. I never knew my parents. I was brought up by my uncle and aunt.'

That seemed to ease his mind, and his cheerfulness returned.

'Here is my house,' he announced as he pulled up outside a tower block. 'Please, this way.'

We walked down an asphalt path between patches of grass, with a few young trees scattered about. Other tall blocks rose all round, at a reasonable distance. In the dark, with only a few lamps glowing here and there, it was difficult to judge the state of the area, but it looked run-down, with litter blown up against the walls of the buildings.

We entered a cavernous lobby with bare concrete walls, and took the lift to the eighth floor. As we went up slowly, juddering and jerking, I sent Rick a glance that said, 'Might try the stairs on the way down.'

Sasha stepped out first, sifting through a bunch of keys, and ushered us towards a door – one of four on a small, dingy landing. Turning the lock, he led us in. 'Please,' he said, 'welcome to my house.'

His apartment was very small. That was my first impression as we stepped straight into the living room, which was cluttered with furniture and lined with shelves. Some held books and magazines, some vinyl albums. In one area Sasha's hi-fi equipment was stacked – Teac amplifier and turntable, dating (by the look of them) from the seventies. At the right-hand end of the room a table was laid for supper: blue-and-white check tablecloth, glasses, knives and forks, but only three place-settings. Beyond it a doorway gave on to a tiny cubicle of a kitchen, and in the opening stood a little old woman, rather bent, with her silver hair swept back into a bun, and wearing a shapeless dress of dark-blue covered in white polka-dots.

'Here is my mother,' said Sasha, following up with a few words of Russian.

Rick, in the lead, did brilliantly, cracking off a '*Dobriye vecher*' (Good evening) and a couple more Russian phrases.

The broad old face – startlingly like Sasha's – creased into a smile, and the woman gave a little bob, inclining towards us. As we shook hands, I asked Sasha her name and he said, 'She is Lyudmila.'

The first few minutes were pretty difficult. Sasha insisted that we sat down, so I perched in an armchair and Rick on a sofa.

Because the flat was extremely warm, I asked what powered the heating. The answer was that all apartment blocks in Moscow are centrally heated – that is, not from boiler rooms in individual buildings, but directly from power stations via underground pipes. Sasha said there was always plenty of heat in winter, even when the outside temperature was twenty below zero, but I noticed that there were no controls or thermostats on the old-fashioned radiators.

'How many rooms d'you have?' Rick asked.

'Living room, here. My mother's bedroom. Bathroom. Kitchen. And balcony.'

'Where d'you sleep, then?'

'There – where you are!' Sasha laughed and pointed at the sofa Rick was occupying. 'I make bed.' He obviously sensed that we found the place rather small, because he added, 'For Moscow, this is *good* apartment. Besides, I am not very much here: always I have been away in army – in Africa, in Afghanistan, in Chechnya. Not much time in Moscow.'

In spite of his protestations, I felt a pang of guilt at having accepted hospitality in surroundings as humble as these. The idea of living in such cramped quarters eight floors up also brought on a surge of claustrophobia.

Looking round, I realised that there was a huge ginger cat asleep on a shelf above a radiator – a welcome diversion.

'What's he called?' I asked.

Back came the answer, 'Tigr.'

Tiger the cat, Tiger Force. Of course. What other name could he have?

'Isn't it awkward for a cat; living high up like this? I mean – how does he go about his business?'

'No problem,' Sasha answered airily. 'He has box on balcony. But two times every day, my mother takes him down in the lift for walk in the park. Also, he is very good hunter.'

'What – mice?'

'Birds. Here on the balcony. He can go for three flats along. He is very quick' – a swiping motion with one hand – 'he catch many birds.'

I had a fleeting, uncomfortable vision of Tigr missing his grip and toppling eight floors to the ground – only half the distance that wretched Igor had fallen. Even a cat with nine lives would hardly survive such a drop.

When I turned my head to look farther round, I realised that one wall was dominated by a large sepia portrait photograph, framed in a border of carved wood. I was startled, because the subject looked so familiar.

'Surely that's our old king, George V?' I asked.

'Not English king. Russian king! It is Tsar Nicholas.'

'But it looks exactly like George.'

'*Konechno*. These men were cousins. My mother, she is beeg fan of royal family.'

'But the Russian royal family's long gone—'

'English royals she likes. Prince Charles she likes very much. When Princess Diana was killed she felt *vairy* sad.'

During our conversation Lyudmila had been bringing dishes of food out of the kitchen and setting them on the table. Now she murmured something to Sasha, who jumped up announcing, 'Please! Dinner is ready.'

He went to the head of the table, and indicated that we should sit either side of him. But his mother continued to hover in the doorway, and it soon became clear that she didn't intend to join us.

'Isn't your mother going to eat?' I asked

'Later. She prefers to serve us. Now, please, we have teepical Russian meal. First, *zakuski*.' He gestured lavishly over the spread of dishes. 'Such kinds of smoked fish, fish eggs, smoked meats, cheeses, cucumbers – help yourselves.'

I would have felt bad had I not known about the Mafia dollars which had obviously financed this banquet. As it was, I started eating fast, to provide some bedding for the vodka which Sasha kept pouring freely from a litre bottle. The food was delicious, and the vodka made a perfect foil for the sharp, salty, smoky tastes, especially of red fish roe. Whenever one of us paused for breath Sasha exclaimed, 'Please, eat! Dreenk!' and waved us on.

'Take it easy,' I muttered to Rick. 'I'm sure this is only the start.'

Sure enough, the next course was *bortsch* – thick soup, not full of beetroot as it usually is in England, but more subtle, with a meaty stock for background, small slices of various vegetables floating in it, and a good, peppery overall taste. Next came *bitochki* – meat balls in a rich tomato sauce, with mashed potatoes – and after that a special cake full of nuts, made by our hostess, with which Sasha served sweet Georgian champagne.

Throughout the feast his mother waited on us with embarrassing anxiety to please, bringing new dishes, removing empty ones, watching us, fussing around, gently urging us: '*Yest! Yest!* Eat! Eat!' Sasha, though clearly devoted to her, did nothing to help, but ate and drank to keep up with Rick and me.

By the later stages of the meal, the vodka had got to all three of us. Sasha was gabbling away about how his brother, a taxi driver, had made millions of roubles from illegal sales of booze in the period when Gorbachev tried to bring alcoholism under control. 'It was a kind of *prahibeetion*,' he kept saying. 'Everyone was crazy for vodka.'

'You mean booze was banned altogether?' said Rick incredulously.

194

'Not absolutely. But rationed. One half-litre of vodka a week – that was all.'

'Why, though?'

'Russian people were drinking all day, all night. They were falling down in street, running over by cars. They couldn't work. Very many died. Alcohol was our national disease.'

'And did the prohibition have any effect?'

'*Konechno nyet!* Black market was immense.'

Rick began to converse freely with Lyudmila in Russian. I sat listening, smiling genially at everyone, but my spirits were sinking. Once again guilt was clawing at me.

After many entreaties, we finally persuaded Lyudmila to join us for tea, and she sat at the other end of the table, obviously pleased that we had enjoyed ourselves, but still watching anxiously for any possible deficiency in her arrangements.

Suddenly Sasha raised his glass and shouted, 'Your Queen!'

'The Queen!' we echoed, slurping champagne.

'My mother, she say your Queen is beautiful woman.'

'Thank you!'

'My mother is big monarchic.'

'Monarchist.'

'Yes – big *monarknik*. She make beautiful book of royal peoples.' He switched into Russian, asking Lyudmila to fetch her prize tome. With a show of simulated reluctance she got up, opened a drawer and produced a large, cheap scrapbook carefully jacketed in tissue paper, which she laid on the table for our inspection. The pages contained dozens of photographs cut from newspapers and magazines, almost all to do with England, but including a few of Tsar Nicholas II and his family, taken in the last few months of their lives before they were executed by the Bolsheviks in 1918. Towards the end, the cuttings went fast-forwards, and pride of place inevitably was accorded to Diana, Princess of Wales.

'Such kind of tragedy,' Sasha kept saying, repeatedly translating a remark of his mother's.

'I know,' I said. 'But she'd become a bit of a loose cannon.'

'Excuse me?'

I explained that the phrase was used about people whose actions tended to be unpredictable.

'Yes, yes,' said Sasha impatiently. 'But British people loved her. When she died, they came in millions.'

Lyudmila had gone off on another tack. 'Something about the Second World War,' Rick said. 'Can't quite get it.'

'Heetler!' cried Sasha. 'My mother would like to say thank you to British and American soldiers for help in beating Nazis. She thanks you and your fathers. Her father was killed at Stalingrad, famous battle. She does not like Germans. British and American armies very brave.'

'I'm glad to hear that,' I told them. 'I've read in Communist history books that it was the heroic Soviet army who defeated Fascism single-handed.'

'*Kommunizm!*' shouted Sasha derisively. '*Kommunizm* is shit. My mother does not say that, of course, but it is what she believes. *Kommunizm* all lies and rubbish.' He turned and in Russian loudly sought confirmation from Lyudmila, who nodded and went, '*Da, da.*'

The next thing we knew, Sasha had brought out a bottle of Georgian brandy and was pouring huge slugs. His mother did not touch the spirit.

The conversation became ever wilder, with stories of army brutality.

'You know how they treat prisoners in Russian army? This soldier in Murmansk . . .'

'Murmansk?' yelled Rick. 'Where the f—' He stopped himself just in time and and finished up, 'Where's that?'

'In Russian Arctic. Far north from Moscow. Terrible place. This man is soldier in garrison. Very poor, like I told you – no money. But he is also musician, used to moonlight. He played accordion in restaurant in the evenings to earn roubles. He went *maskarad* - in disguise – with glasses and some beard. But an officer went to the restaurant and recognised him.

'So, to punish him, they put him in a cell, with acid on the floor, deeper every day. No shoes. They wanted to leave him for a week, but after three days his hair had gone grey, so they took him out. Such tortures they make in army.'

It was midnight before we reeled out. We tried to say we'd walk or get a taxi, but Sasha wouldn't hear of it and insisted on driving us back. When we went down in the lift, Lyudmila came with us to give Tigr an extra run, and as we said goodbye she kissed our hands, holding the cat against her. Rick did his best to thank her gracefully, but I felt too choked to say anything except '*Spasibo! Bolshoi spasibo!*'

Morning brought shock after shock to exacerbate our hang-overs. The first came on the news, when somebody heard that the Russian Foreign Minister, had been assassinated. There'd been a shoot-out on Leningradski Prospekt, the main thoroughfare running out towards the north-west. The Minister had been on his way to Sheremetyevo airport, en route for Washington, when a car had come up alongside his Zyl limo – in spite of the police escort – and gunmen had riddled it with bullets. The Zyl had run off the road at speed and crashed head-on into a concrete wall, and the bulletin didn't make clear whether he'd been killed by gunshots or by the impact. In any event, he was dead. So were the driver, two of the bodyguards and one policeman. The gunmen had got clean away, but blame had immediately been placed on 'criminal elements' – in other words, the Mafia.

'Chechens, for sure,' said Sasha, the moment he arrived in camp. 'And why? They make retaliation for losing their Beno. I told you.'

'It's a war, going on in the middle of Moscow,' I said.

'Zheordie, this war will last fifty years.'

Like us, Sasha was feeling rough, and we gave him a cup of strong black coffee before starting for the ranges.

Then Toad appeared, washing his hands like crazy.

'Heard the news?' he went.

'The hit on the Foreign Minister?'

'Yeah – but the stand-off it's creating.'

'What are you on about?'

'It's just been on the BBC World Service. The American

197

Ambassador was in that same car.'

'Jesus!' I sat up. 'Did they kill him as well?'

'Not quite. He's in intensive care. But the United States is threatening to break off relations with Russia. Clinton's been on the hotline to the President, giving him a bollocking. He reckons the whole country's going to ratshit.'

'He's not far wrong,' I said. I felt my gut contracting. Now we're really in it, I thought – and as if to confirm my misgivings, in came another unexpected punch from a different direction.

We were on the point of leaving the building when in burst Rick, looking chuffed to bollocks. 'You'll never believe it!' he yelled. 'Irina's back!'

'Take it easy,' I told him. 'Who's Irina?'

'Natasha's sister. The one who went to the States.'

'What about her?'

'They've got her back!'

'Who have? For Christ's sake, explain.'

'The FBI turned up at her apartment in the Bronx. They grabbed her and a few of her friends and deported them – put them on a plane for Moscow.'

'Ah,' I said. 'This is starting to make sense. You've Tony Lopez to thank for that. He must have got his finger out.'

Then suddenly I thought, Wait a minute. How does Rick know about this? He must have been talking to Natasha. Hadn't I told the prick to lay off?

I felt my face colour up and I said quietly to Sasha, 'If you don't mind, we'll meet you in a couple of minutes outside the armoury.'

He got the message and took himself off. The moment he'd gone, I turned on Rick.

'You stupid bastard! You realise what you've done?'

'No. What's the matter?'

'There's a very good chance you've compromised the entire operation. Listen. How did that woman get hold of you?'

'She phoned.'

'Exactly. And how did she know your number?'

'I'd given it to her.'

'Exactly. Jesus Christ! Are you out of your mind? Who d'you think she's busy giving your number to now?'

'What do you mean?'

'THINK, cunt! Her sister's been in the grip of the Mafia in New York. The FBI have kicked her out, along with a bunch of other slags. They snatched the whole lot and sent them home. But now she's in Mafia territory again, worse than New York. The wide boys here have access to the airlines' passenger lists. They know she's come back to Moscow. They've got her address from before. She's probably got a Russian pimp here anyway.

'In other words, they know precisely where she is. And now, because you can't stop following your prick around, they know precisely where *you* are. The next thing'll be a group of four charming young men with Gepards up their jumpers coming to the gate to ask for a fucking interview!'

I wasn't exactly shouting, but I was talking a lot faster and louder than usual. From the stricken look on Rick's face, I might as well have been hitting him.

'They don't know what I'm doing here,' he said defensively. 'All I told Natasha was that we were making a film.'

'To hell with that. Listen, Rick. You know the score. We're on a military telephone exchange, for fuck's sake. One look at the number must have told them where we are.'

To ease my feelings I started walking up and down. 'Things aren't looking good for you,' I said. 'This is the third time you've screwed up. I told you before – and that was a last warning. I've got a feeling you're on your way home. And if this doesn't end in your getting RTU'd I'll be bloody amazed.'

He started to say something, but I cut him short. 'Don't bloody well argue! There'll be time for that back in the UK. Get down to the armoury and tell Sasha I'm not coming out with the team this morning. I'm going to have to stay here and sort this mess out. In fact, you can ask Sasha to put an hour's delay on the start today. If any of our lads are down there already, bring them back. Tell them I'm holding a meeting immediately.'

He'd hardly disappeared before I made up my mind. Yes –

he'd have to go. He'd already done serious damage, and was too great a liability.

I called the Embassy, asked for the Chargé, and got put through to Kate, the red-headed secretary.

'Is David there?' I asked.

'Not yet. He had to pick something up on his way in.'

'Could you do us a favour, then?'

'I can try.'

'Thanks. It's just that we need to get someone back to UK soonest. I want him on a plane today. Could you be an angel and book a ticket?'

'Return?'

'No – one way.'

'What's the passenger's name?'

'Ellis. Richard Ellis.'

'What flight shall I go for?'

'Any flight – the earliest he can catch. He'll have to get from here to the airport, that's all.'

'All right, then. I'll call you back.'

I urgently needed to speak to the CO in Hereford, but the time there was still only 6.30 a.m., so I decided to wait until he came into his office.

When Kate rang back, she gave me another jolt. 'I'm sorry,' she said, 'I can't get through to any of the airlines. The reservation lines are all jammed.'

'Is that normal?'

'Certainly not. I phoned a friend in the Lufthansa cargo department, and she says there's some sort of a panic on. People are trying to get out of Moscow in a hurry. There are no seats available before next Thursday.'

'Jesus! It must be this thing about the American Ambassador.'

'That's right. There's a lot of really nervous talk coming out of the FCO.'

'Like what?'

'The international situation deteriorating, that sort of thing.'

'Well, listen. I really need this guy on a plane as soon as possible. Can you keep trying?'

'Of course.'

Ten minutes later she rang again and said, 'I got through in the end, but no luck. I tried BA, Aeroflot and Lufthansa, and they're all fully booked. There are no seats available before next week. The only chance is to send him first class. Lufthansa may have a seat at 1520 this afternoon, but it's via Berlin, I'm afraid.'

'That'll do,' I said. 'Take it.' Privately I was thinking, I don't care if he goes via Timbucfuckingtoo, as long as I get him off my hands. The idea of Rick sipping champagne in a first-class seat gave me a royal pain in the arse. But then I consoled myself by thinking, If he's getting binned, back to the Green Army, it's the last time he'll be travelling like *that* for a while.

'I'll charge it to the Embassy for now,' Kate was saying. 'Then we'll send the bill to Hereford. He'll have to collect the ticket from the Lufthansa desk at the airport. He needs to be there by 1400 at the latest.'

'No bother. I'm very grateful to you. Has David appeared yet?'

'Just this moment. D'you want a word?'

'Yes please.'

I hung on, then heard Allway say, 'Good morning.'

'Good morning,' I went. 'Can you fill me in on what's happening?'

'The situation's pretty confused at the moment.'

'What's causing the panic?'

'Clinton said something about Russia being on the point of becoming ungovernable.'

'Don't you feel that's exaggerated?'

'Personally, yes.'

'So what line's London taking?'

'No special line yet. But Washington is advising Americans to leave unless they have urgent business here. Are you people all right out at Balashika?'

'For the time being. Everything's been going fine. I don't know how this will affect things, though.'

'No,' Allway said cryptically. 'I get the impression that your team may be off home fairly soon.'

201

'Oh, really?' I went. 'We'll have to wait and see.'

I rang off, and called Hereford on the secure satellite link. By good luck the CO was already at his desk, and sounding cheerful.

'Hi, Geordie,' he went. 'How are things?'

'Rough. You've heard the news?'

'Yes. It sounds a bit dicey. How does it feel at that end?'

'Can't tell yet. But listen, Boss. That's not what I'm calling about. It's Rick Ellis. I'm sending him home.'

'Oh God!' he said. 'What's happened?'

I told him in short, sharp sentences. He didn't query my decision, and I was glad of that. He saw my point. I summed up by saying, 'He's dropped us right in it. At the very least, the Mafia know there's a Brit presence in the barracks here. That means there's a threat to our lads, quite apart from the potential disruption of Operation Nimrod.'

'Are you going to need a replacement?'

'Not worth it. We can manage as we are.'

'OK, then. I'll see Rick as soon as he gets back.'

'Do you need a report immediately?'

'It can wait. I'm sure you've got plenty on your hands. You can give me a full statement when you get back.'

'Will do.'

'What's the state of play with the operation?'

'Apple's in place, as you know. We've got a site for Orange, and we're just waiting for a chance to do the insertion.'

'Sooner the better,' said the CO sharply. 'If the situation gets much worse we may have to pull you out.'

'Roger. But – Boss?'

'Yes?'

'There's no chance the Yanks are going to start playing funny buggers and press the button on Apple?'

'Don't be silly, Geordie. Things aren't *that* bad.' Then suddenly he switched mode and made what seemed to me a lousy joke. 'But if they were, you'd be the last people to know anything about it.'

'Ha ha,' I said.

'Sorry, Geordie.' He realised he'd pissed me off. 'Seriously, things look OK from this end.'

'They don't from here, I can tell you. People are pouring out of Moscow like fucking lemmings.'

'Is that right?'

I told him about the airlines, then said, 'What I'm saying is this. Isn't that exactly what these bloody devices are for – to use as blackmail if things get tense, to bring the buggers to their senses in an emergency?'

'Precisely. But we're nowhere near the stage of using them yet.'

'I hope to hell you're right. Once Orange is underground we're going to be in the killing zone ourselves, never mind any radiation that might drift this way from Apple.'

'Take it easy, Geordie. Your imagination's running away with you.'

'I hope you're bloody well right.'

The lads reassembled, looking rather surprised. Having sent Rick away to his own room, I got everyone sat down and went straight into it.

'I'm sorry to say that there's a high probability Operation Nimrod's been compromised.'

Everyone sat very still. Several seconds passed before Whinger said, 'For Christ's sake, what's happened? Have they found the bomb?'

'I hope not. But next worst: Rick's sent the Mafia a message saying the SAS is in town.'

'Don't be stupid!' went Whinger.

'I'm not,' I told him. 'I exaggerated slightly, but only a little.'

I explained what had happened. Mal – careful, steady Mal – surprised me by starting to stand up for Rick. 'If he stuck to the cover story about the film, we don't need to worry.'

'We bloody do! That woman's obviously in the hands of some pimp or other. It'll take the guy about ten seconds to recognise the number Rick gave her. I bet you the Mafia have got us pinpointed already.'

'Eh!' said Johnny. 'Let's fuck off out of here while the going's good.'

'That's what Rick's going to do,' I said. 'I'm sending him home right away. The lucky bastard's flying first class because there are no other seats. And Toad – I want you to take him to the airport. OK?'

Nobody put up any good reason for keeping Rick on the team. Mal saw the point of what I was saying and finally agreed that Rick should go. The only argument was about his share of the Mafia dollars – and in the end we voted that he should still get it, provided he kept his mouth shut about the whole episode when he reached home.

So the day's training got under way an hour late. I stayed in barracks, fighting to catch up with paperwork – mainly the course reports on the students, which we were supposed to be continuously updating.

All morning I kept remembering how, at the climax of the siege of the Libyan Embassy in London, the police negotiators had kept the terrorists in play by telling them direct lies: that the Libyan Ambassador was on his way, that a coach was coming to take them to Heathrow, and so on. Even Trevor Lock, the policeman trapped inside the building, couldn't get any straight answers from the police. Several times he asked for an assurance that the building wasn't going to be assaulted – and at the very moment when the SAS men were laying out their abseil ropes on the roof, the cops promised him blind that all they were trying to arrange was the villains' getaway.

Now we seemed to be in an unpleasantly similar situation. The boss would go on saying, 'No, no, Geordie, everything's fine,' until the very moment when Clinton or some other jerk in Washington pressed the button. The CO was bound to toe the line. But for us poor sods at the sharp end it was different. Maybe we'd see a brilliant white flash. Maybe we wouldn't.

At midday I called the Chargé again and heard that the American Ambassador had died from his wounds. All US flights into Moscow had been suspended, and American citizens advised not to travel to Russia by any means. More and more I

204

was needled by apprehension that this whole train of events had been set off by us – by our participation in the hit on the apartment. Then I told myself that if we hadn't gone along with it the result of the shoot-out might have been much the same, with a few more casualties to the forces of law and order – but still the feelings of guilt were building up.

Before Toad left I took him aside and asked, 'Is there any way you can disable Apple?'

'Not unless we go back down the tunnel,' he replied. 'Now it's live, it's live.'

TWELVE

We seemed to have two options. One was to call in an RAF aircraft and lift the whole team out, taking Orange with us, on the grounds that the situation was too dangerous to stay. That definitely went against the grain: it would be unprofessional and would smell of panic. If we quit, we'd have failed in one of our main objectives.

The second option was to carry out our task and get Orange into place as soon as possible – after which we could assess the position again, and decide whether to carry on with the training course or leave immediately.

To reach a decision we held a Chinese parliament out in the open, in the middle of the assault course, well away from any bugs. Toad, as usual, remained silent, but the rest of the lads were emphatically for Option Two. The only disagreement was about what we should do once we'd buried Orange in the old air-raid shelter.

Whinger, croaking through his laryngitis, was all for playing it straight. 'We might as well see the course through. Nobody's going to push any button. They wouldn't fucking well dare.'

Johnny and Pavarotti agreed with him. But Mal, who'd done a two-year tour attached to the US Marines, had a low opinion of American decision-taking in general, and reckoned somebody in a key position in Washington might easily lose his cool under pressure. Dusty and Pete tended to go along with that, and so did I. That meant that three of us were for remaining on the team task, and four for opting out: the narrowest possible majority. In the end we agreed to debate the matter again once Orange had gone down.

Our plan for the second device was perfectly simple. Whinger and I had already decided we couldn't start digging on the site before we were ready to insert: otherwise somebody might see the spoil. Therefore, we'd fetch the components from the Embassy that evening, bring them to the camp, stash them temporarily, and take them out to the shelter the next night, starting and finishing the insertion in one shift.

Or so we thought.

For this next run we adopted the same tactics as before: using both cars and keeping well apart, in radio contact. We left Balashika at 8.00 p.m., and reached the Embassy at 8.55. Taking our normal precautions, Whinger put in a drive-past with the grey Volga; he had Johnny riding passenger with him, and when they reported all clear, Pavarotti, Toad and I went in with the black vehicle to load the components. We'd done what we could to make the Volgas more roadworthy, getting them both a service and replacing three of the worst tyres.

As we drove along the embankment and over the line of the tunnel, I got a peculiar fizzing sensation in my stomach.

I'd already sent word to the Chargé that we were coming in. My spiel had been that, because of the international tension, we wanted to recover the last of our bits and pieces so that we'd have everything in one place if the Regiment decided on a quick evacuation. Allway had said that was OK by him: there'd be no one to meet us, but he'd leave word with security, and we could hand them the keys of the garage on our way out.

That suited us fine. We loaded up at leisure, locked the door and handed in the keys. In the car, before I drove off, I got Toad to hand me Orange's Rat, and clipped the device to my belt.

We were rolling again less than ten minutes after we'd arrived. Pav was beside me in front, Toad in the back.

'Clearing now,' I called to Whinger.

'Roger,' he answered. 'I'll fall in behind.'

On our way out through the city centre I couldn't distinguish his lights from all the others behind us; but I knew he was there, because we kept exchanging messages. The traffic began to thin out, and on the highway the vehicles were well spaced. Fine rain had set in, reducing visibility. The black Volga wallowed on the wet road like a boat under its heavy load, and I kept our speed down to sixty-five ks to give myself time to avoid potholes. That meant we were one of the slowest cars on the road, and we kept getting overtaken, but I felt in no particular hurry.

So we cruised on until we were within about five ks of base. Out in the country the rain was heavier, the air murkier. We'd just gone under the outer ring-road when everything went ballistic.

'Look out,' said Pav. 'There's a flashing blue light up ahead.'

At the same moment Whinger came on the radio with, 'I think we've got a tail.'

I glanced in my mirror and exclaimed, 'Jesus! I think we have one too. There's a police block up ahead as well. Listen, Whinge. We're being pulled in by the GAI. Get off the road and wait out.'

In the road ahead, beside the vehicle with the flashing blue lamp, a man was waving us down with one of those white-ended batons. As I braked, I saw in the mirror that the car behind us had swung in close on our tail.

'Shit, Pav,' I said. 'Looks like the GAI are having a purge. What do we do?'

'Bluff our way. Stop — if he tells us to — for Christ's sake. Don't piss him off — otherwise we'll be in the nick for resisting arrest.'

A man in grey GAI uniform, with the red stripe down the side of his pants, was guiding us in towards the verge. As I pulled up, another man appeared beside the window and said, '*Dokumenti.*'

I reached down under my seat for the package Anna had made up for each car and handed it to him. He took it, but motioned for me to go with him to a hut at the edge of the highway. Then he started saying, '*Klioucha, klioucha,*' and making twisting movements with his hand.

'Keys,' said Toad. 'He's after the keys.'

209

'Suspicious bastard,' I said. 'He thinks we're going to try and drive off.'

'Ah, fuck it!' exclaimed Pavarotti. 'Shall I deal with him?'

'It's all right,' I said. 'I'll go. You two sit tight.'

I took out the ignition key and handed it through the window. I was on the point of getting out when I remembered the Rat. Better leave it in the car, I thought. Then, measuring the distance to the hut by eye, I thought, No – that isn't a hundred feet. It'll be OK.

As I stepped out of the car I glanced into the back, and was reassured to see that the component beside Toad was covered by an old blanket.

I started to follow the GAI officer. He pointed towards the hut, gesturing to me to carry on. Then he turned back to the Volga.

The hut was set just off the tarmac, down a bit of a bank and on the edge of the wood. At first my main concern was that I wouldn't understand what the cops were asking, and I wished to hell my Russian was better. Then, second by second, step by step, I began to get the feeling that something was wrong. The hut didn't look like one of the regular GAI stations, which were lit up like little guardrooms. This thing was only a roadsmen's cabin, and dark. Besides, the other cars parked by it weren't GAI vehicles, but ordinary saloons. Worst of all, there were at least five men standing in the shadows, not in GAI uniform, but wearing leather jackets that gleamed when the headlights of a vehicle went by on the road. There was something odd about their body language; their postures unnaturally rigid and alert.

At that instant I suddenly heard, through my earpiece, Pavarotti call, 'CONTACT!' Before I could react, the guys in front of me started to move in my direction. I glanced over my shoulder at the Volga and saw two men with sub-machine guns closing in from either side.

I jabbed my pressel switch and said sharply, 'Contact! Contact! Whinger, in here! Get in! Get in!'

'Negative,' came his answer. 'We can't. We're in a contact too.'

210

Over the radio I heard a rattle of shots. An instant later the shots came live, through the air.

The five men on the edge of the forest were in a ragged group only ten feet from me. They started moving towards me. Instinctively I pulled out my pistol and dropped the nearest one with a single shot to the forehead, which jerked his head violently backwards.

I looked back at the Volga. Rounds cracked past my head. As I went down on one knee. I could see that the pseudo-policeman was at the driver's door. A second guy was trying to force his way into the back seat. Another burst ripped past me. I felt a sharp tug and a stab of pain in my left shoulder. The impact spun me round, only to find one of the others almost on top of me. Automatically I fired a double tap into his chest, and he went down, but he was so close that his impetus carried him past me, and he narrowly missed me as he fell. I then emptied my magazine into the area where his three remaining mates had suddenly taken cover, and sprinted the last few yards for the safety of the woods.

The trees were pines, fairly well spaced. By luck I went between the first few, then ran smack into spiky dead branches, ripping my face. I backed off, skirted left and kept going.

Behind me, pandemonium erupted. Men began yelling like lunatics. Engines started up and revved furiously. Tyres scrabbled and squealed as cars pulled away. Somebody cracked off a few more bursts from a sub-machine gun, and rounds came snapping through the trees, but by then I was a hundred metres into the woods, and relatively safe.

For a few seconds I lay prone, head-on to the road in line with a thick trunk, gasping for breath, more from shock than from exertion. 'Jesus!' I went. 'What the fuck happened?'

Out on the highway everything had gone quiet. I jabbed the pressel of my radio and called, 'Black to Grey. Can you hear me?'

'Grey,' went Whinger. 'We've broken the contact. We're mobile.'

'Where are you?' I gasped.

'Heading on in your direction. Where are *you*?'

'In the forest behind the hut. Give me one minute. I'll come back to the roadside a hundred metres past the hut.'

'Roger.'

I tore through the trees, parallel with the road, with my left arm raised in front of my face to ward off branches. I had a stinging sensation on the outside of my left shoulder, and I could feel blood running down my side. But the arm was working, and the wound didn't feel bad. Already my night-vision was establishing itself, and I could see enough to make rapid progress.

I counted a hundred and fifty steps, then turned left, running back towards the road. I burst out of the trees and looked back, to the left. I was about the right distance from the hut. Through the rain I saw one car coming fast towards me. In my earpiece Whinger said, 'OK, we have eyes on you.' I stepped farther out into the road, and the car swung in towards me. As it pulled up, I saw that windscreen and rear window had been shot out.

'Get in! Get in!' shouted Whinger. 'Where's the other Volga?'

'They've got it.'

'Jesus! The bastards went that way. Back into town.'

'After them!'

I dived into the back and slammed the door.

'Watch your hands on the glass,' yelled Johnny. 'It's all over.'

With a howl of tyres Whinger spun the car and screamed up to high revs in each gear. Wind came whistling through the cabin, fore to aft.

Johnny was trying to tell me something, but with the internal slipstream roaring it was hard to hear. Also, after the gunshots, I was slightly deaf.

In a few seconds we passed a car burning on the other side of the road.

'Who's that?' I shouted.

'That was the lot that came for us,' went Whinger. 'What happened to *you*?'

'Ran straight into an illegal VCP. They had a man out in GAI

212

uniform, waving us down. He demanded documents and keys. Made me go with him towards the hut. Then I saw all these other guys on the lurk. That was the moment you called "Contact". What about you?'

'This car came up behind. Somebody put a burst through the rear window. The rounds must have gone right between me and Johnny, on out the front . . .'

'Slow down!' I shouted.

We'd come round a bend. Through the murky dark we could see nearly half a mile up a long straight ahead. There wasn't a car in sight.

'Either they've got right away or they've pulled off into the forest. Look for side-roads. There! Just ahead. Stop!'

Whinger slid to a halt across the mouth of a dirt track that ran into the trees at a right angle to the highway. Johnny and I leapt out, flashing torches over the surface in search of fresh tyre marks.

'Nothing doing,' I called.

We jumped back in and set off again.

'OH this fucking car!' Whinger groaned, exasperated by the lack of acceleration.

'Keep talking,' I told them.

'The car that was harassing us,' went Johnny. 'I dropped the driver with my Sig. That fucked them. They were struggling to get him out of the driving seat, so I cracked a couple more rounds off into the front of the car. Bit of luck – the thing blew up. Bullet must have severed a fuel pipe. The whole thing went *woof*—'

'THERE!' I yelled.

Another small road had loomed up. Whinger hauled on the wheel and we squealed round. This track was surfaced and quite smooth – no point in looking for tyre marks. We followed it for a minute, scanning frantically for any spur or layby among the trees where the villains could have pulled in. Then I shouted, 'This is fucking useless. We've lost them. You're sure they turned back?'

'Yeah, yeah!' Whinger was emphatic. 'Just after you'd called

213

for the pick-up, a whole shower of cars went flying back towards Moscow. A dozen at least, going like the clappers.'

'Was the Volga in among them?'

'Couldn't tell. There was a Merc at the front. The rest were in a bunch. Really motoring.'

My mind was churning. Blood had reached my waist and was sogging round my belt.

'Back to base?' Even Whinger sounded temporarily defeated.

'I guess so.'

'What happened to Pav and Toad?'

'I couldn't tell. The last I saw of them they were both still in the vehicle, with an armed guy on either side of them. I tried to get back to them but I was taking fire from the car behind ours. I got a nick in the shoulder, as it was.'

'Not serious?'

'I don't think so. More of a burn, really. It's bleeding, though.'

As we drove the short distance back to camp, the scene ran through my mind again and again like a closed loop of film. Already I was blaming myself for making mistakes. Maybe I should never have got out of the car. Maybe I should have just driven off. But then, if I had, our lumbering vehicle would certainly have been cut out by one or more of the faster cars I'd seen lined up. But again, once I *had* got out – once I realised things weren't right – maybe I should have made a greater effort to get back to the Volga. But if I'd done that, I'd almost certainly have ended up getting shot dead. The guy in the back-up car couldn't have gone on missing for ever.

'Where's the Rat?' Whinger asked suddenly.

'Christ!' I felt for it, on my belt. 'I've still got it. It must have activated the bomb's alarm signal. The thing will be transmitting by now. I hope to hell the Yanks can track it.'

Before the lift my moral confusion had been bad enough: now it was acute. What the hell was I to tell Anna and Sasha? Obviously we couldn't conceal the fact that we'd lost two guys, or that they were probably in Mafia hands. Apart from anything else, we needed the Russians to launch a search.

★

214

The lads we'd left in camp were appalled by the news. As we compiled a coded message for Hereford, they got a brew on and we brought them up to speed on what had happened.

My shoulder wound turned out to be little more than a groove cut through the skin. Dusty got out his medical pack, swabbed it thoroughly, bombed it with disinfectant and smacked a wound-dressing over the top.

'You'll live,' he pronounced. 'But you were lucky. A couple of inches lower and your shoulder would have been a mess.'

'If it *was* Rick's whoring about that put them on to us,' I said, 'he wants to be well away from Hereford before we get back. If I see him I'll bloody murder him.'

'Maybe the Mafia have been doing better surveillance than we thought,' Mal suggested. 'Maybe they'd got us marked down anyway. D'you think somebody slipped a hundred dollars to one of the guys on the gate, to shop us?'

'It was that fucking hit on the flat that did it,' said Whinger savagely. 'Somehow the bastards got wind of the fact that we were involved.'

'What if we got followed to the church?' said Dusty. 'Maybe there was a dicker out, somebody who saw us going in and out of the Embassy.'

'Possible,' I agreed. 'Jesus – now I suppose we'd better get our arses back there and check the padlocks on the shaft.'

I thought for a moment and changed my mind. 'Cancel that,' I said. 'There's no way the Mafia could have known about Apple or Orange. Our security on that front's been one hundred per cent. Even if they got eyes on the cars going to and from the Embassy they couldn't have known what we were doing.'

'Extortion,' said Pete. 'That's what we were up against. They're after money. They've scented a chance of making a quick fortune. And now, in handing them Orange, we've given them the biggest fucking lever in the world. God alone knows what ransom demand they'll make: ten million? A hundred million?'

I said, 'The question is, will they go public, or will they do it under cover?'

'If they go public we're buggered,' said Dusty. 'If they start honking about how they're holding two SAS guys, the whole operation's blown.'

'Will they realise what the components are?' asked Mal. 'After all, they're not nuclear specialists.'

'No,' said Dusty, 'but I bet they'll have access to someone who is. It won't be long before they find out. And anyway, they've got Pav and Toad to tell them.'

There was a moment's silence. Although nobody spoke, I know we were all thinking the same thing: that our guys were going to get badly knocked about. They were in for a hard time, whatever happened. And if they refused to talk, there was a high risk they'd be topped. We needed to find them fast.

We had local maps out on the table, but they were precious little use.

'Let's think where they're likely to put the thing,' said Johnny.

'Lock-up garage, probably,' Whinger suggested. 'Leave it in the car, drive in. Easy.'

'What about its alarm signal?' Mal asked. 'Will that still reach the satellite if the device is inside a building?'

'I don't know. Toad could tell us. Listen, I'm going to call Anna. She can get a search going.'

'What are we going to tell her?' Mal, ever careful, had been making notes with pencil and pad.

'That two guys have been lifted.'

'What about the bomb?'

'Not a whisper.'

I had to use the local line, which I knew was insecure. But that now seemed the least of our worries. I tried the emergency number she'd given us, and got some Russian-speaking female.

'Anna,' I said several times. 'Anna Gerasimova.'

A torrent of Russian came back.

'*Ya Anglichani*,' I went. '*Ni ponemayo*.'

Another incomprehensible rush of words. For a moment I half-wished Rick was with us. At last the woman stopped and said, '*Moment*.' A second later a man came on, speaking slow, heavily accented English.

'Anna no here.'

'Can you give her a message, please?'

'A message? Yes. It is what?'

'Telephone Zheordie immediately.'

'Zheordie?'

It was beyond me to spell the name in Russian letters, so I repeated it several times, gave the number slowly, and rang off.

'Jesus!' I gasped. In the state I was, any small delay seemed a massive aggravation.

'What about Sasha?' asked Pete.

'Good idea.'

As the number rang, I thought of old Lyudmila and her bloody great cat, tucked up there on the eighth floor.

'*Da?*'

'Sasha, it's Geordie. Sorry to bother you, but we're in big trouble.'

I told him what had happened. As soon as he got the gist of it, he said, 'No, it is impossible. Not real.'

'It's real enough,' I told him. 'They've gone.'

'I come in.'

'Well, if you can.'

'No problem. Twenty minutes.'

'Thanks.' I rang off and said to the lads, 'Sasha's on his way. Watch yourselves when you're speaking to him. This is where we need to start juggling the story.'

'The Embassy,' said Whinger. 'What about them?'

'Christ, yes. Better inform them.'

'What about the bomb?' Mal asked in his voice of doom.

'Same thing. Not a whisper.'

'They know you went in to collect kit,' Mal persisted.

'OK, we collected it.'

'So where is it now?'

'It was in the car that got through.'

Even as I dialled the Embassy number on the secure link, I felt amazed at how easy it seemed to be to invent plausible falsehoods. They were fairly whipping off my tongue. At the

217

same time, I was aware of how easy it would be to make one fatal mistake and bring the whole edifice of lies crashing down.

'British Embassy,' said an unfamiliar voice.

'Geordie Sharp,' I said. 'I need to speak to the Chargé.'

'I'm sorry. He's not here. It's the duty officer speaking. Can I help you?'

'I need to talk to him urgently.'

'I'm afraid he's not available on this system.'

'Can you ask him to come in, then?'

'Is it that urgent? Can't it wait till the morning?'

'No.'

There was a pause. Then the guy said, 'All right. In that case, I'll pass the message. Has he got your number?'

'He'll have it there in the office, yes.'

I rang off, thinking of Hereford. Where the hell was the boss? He was taking his time to come through. Maybe he was out at a party. By now it was midnight – 9.00 p.m. in the UK. Not late.

Mal looked up from his notes and asked, 'Who's controlling the tracker satellite?'

'The Americans,' I told him. But his question prompted a sudden idea.

'Jesus!' I exclaimed. 'That's a thought, Mal. I'm going to call Tony Lopez right away.'

'Who's he?'

'American, ex-SEAL. He was seconded to the Regiment before you joined. Now he's working for the CIA. It was him who put the ferrets in after Rick's girlfriend's sister. But he's a hundred per cent on side. He'll help. What time is it in Washington?'

'Five o'clock,' somebody said. 'Correction. Four.'

'He'll still be in the office.'

I jumped up, dug out his number and punched it in. Two rings, and an American voice answered.

'Tony!'

'I'm sorry, sir. Major Lopez is in a meeting.'

'Break in on him, please. This is an emergency.'

218

'May I ask who's calling?'

'Just say Geordie.'

'One moment, sir.' The guy had that ultra-polite, deferential American manner that gives me a pain in the arse.

I put my hand over the mouthpiece and said, 'He's coming.'

A second later Tony was on the line – but he didn't sound himself. His voice was quick and sharp.

'Tony,' I began, 'we're in the shit.'

'OK, I know what it is.'

'You *know*?'

'Sure. Hereford have been in touch. That's what we're discussing right now. The satellite tracker system's up and running.'

'Thank God. Can you let us know if you get a line on where they've taken the thing?'

'Sure can.'

'OK. I'll speak to you later.'

As I replaced the receiver, the phone rang.

'Geordie?' It was the night comms clerk in Hereford. 'I've got the CO for you.'

'Put him on.'

The first thing the boss wanted to know was which two guys we'd lost.

'Pavarotti and Toad,' I told him.

'Toad!' he said. 'Jesus!'

'Exactly. The next thing's going to be a ransom demand. We've got to recover Orange, and fast.'

'The Americans are tracking it already.'

'I know. I just spoke to Tony Lopez in Washington. He seems to be on the tracking team. Boss – what do you advise?'

'Very difficult. You'd better stand by to come out. The political situation's extremely volatile. The Director's coming here for eight tomorrow morning. We're going to take a decision then on whether or not we pull you.'

'We can't come out with two guys missing.'

'I don't know. We might take the view that it's better to lose two rather than risk losing nine. The shit's hit the fan in London as well.'

'Why's that?'

'The computer disk you got. The information on it has sent the police ballistic, in London and New York. They've made fifteen arrests in London alone.'

'Russian Mafia?'

'Leading players.'

I took a deep breath. Then I said, 'How does that affect us?'

'Too early to say. Your kidnap could be a reprisal for the arrests in Europe. But losing Orange complicates the issue still more. We've got a QRF on standby. We may establish an FMB in Berlin in any case. That would put them within three hours of you.'

I told him I'd be through again if there was any news, and hung up. Seconds later Sasha appeared, and we started going through everything again. He was upset about the disappearance of our guys, and kept apologising.

'Come on, Sasha,' I said, forcing myself to smile. 'They're not dead yet. We'll get them back.'

Before he could answer, the satellite phone beeped again. It was Tony.

'We got it!' he announced triumphantly. 'Your hardware's still with you.'

'Wait one.' I looked up and saw Sasha watching me eagerly.

'Sasha,' I said. 'It's our base in Hereford. This may take a few minutes. Could you get on the local line and set up a police search?'

'*Konechno!* Immediately!' He sprang to his feet and headed for the other phone. I felt a turd, lying to his face – but what else could I do?

'Tony,' I said. 'Carry on. Where is it?'

'In the south-western sector of the city. We can give you the location within a couple of hundred metres.'

'Fantastic! Can you give me the co-ordinates?'

'Sure. Ready?'

'Fire away.'

He read out a series of figures, which I took down and checked back. 'Brilliant,' I said. 'Let me know if it moves.'

'Roger – and good luck.'

'Miracles of modern science,' I told the lads. 'Correlate these on to a street plan and we can go right in and get them.'

'Wait a minute,' said Mal. 'How do we know this? I mean, what are you going to tell Sasha?'

Once again a plausible lie rose effortlessly to the surface of my mind. 'Pav has a tracking device fitted into his jacket,' I said. 'Some of our guys always do, in case this very thing happens.'

'Yeah, but if we organise a hit, with the Russians, they're going to find Orange at the end of it.'

'We'll play that one when we get to it . . .' I broke off because Sasha reappeared.

'General police alert,' he announced. 'All Moscow forces to search. I give car number. And Zheordie, I make suggestion.'

'What's that?'

'We can stop training course, freeze everything. Instead of lessons, we make students rescue your hostages.'

'Great idea!' I went. Privately I thought, Christ!

Luckily I was distracted by yet another beep from the secure phone.

This time it was the Chargé. Hell, I thought when I heard his voice. I can't send Sasha out again. Then suddenly I realised I didn't need to: the Embassy knew nothing about Orange.

I started into the whole spiel again. I said that Sasha had got a search under way, that I'd been through to Hereford, and that we were expecting a decision about a possible pull-out in the morning.

'Yes,' said Allway. 'Your people were talking to us earlier in the day.'

He nattered on for a minute about the general situation, which he described as 'jittery'. As he spoke, I was thinking, Do I tell him we've traced the signal? No, I decided. If we get our guys back, yes, of course, we tell him, but there's nothing definite enough yet.

It was just as well I didn't bother, because within five minutes of that call Tony had come through again to say, 'It's moving.'

'Ah Jesus!'

'Yep. I've got it on a computerised map screen. Heading south-west. It's already five miles out from the location I gave you. You want to stay on the air till we see what's happening?'

'Sure. I've got the map in front of me.'

'OK. It's coming up to a place called Vnukovo. Hey – wait a minute. That's marked as an airfield.'

'Vnukovo,' I said to Sasha. 'What is it?'

'Main airport for southern departures.'

'Tony,' I said. 'It's Moscow's airport for the south.'

'Then I guess they're putting it on a plane. Target now stationary. Can you organise an intercept?'

'What – in the air?'

'No, on the ground.'

'I'll ask.'

I put the question to Sasha. He frowned at the size of the problem, but headed back to the local phone.

'How far are you from that field?' Tony was asking.

'At least an hour. Our Russian contact's phoning the police down there.'

'Target still stationary. If it is Mafia, they'll have a big armed escort round it.'

'Precisely.'

'There's a major highway heading out of the city due south-west. Which side of that is the airfield?'

'Immediately to the north.'

'That's it, then. They're on the field.'

He went quiet for a few moments, then added sharply, 'Signal lost. Wait a minute . . . no. Confirm signal lost.'

'What does that mean?'

'Most likely they've loaded Orange into a plane. That would mask the transmission. Yep. It's gone dead. I'll come back if we get it again.'

'Thanks, Tony.'

I found Sasha glued to the other phone, talking hard, as if he was having to galvanise the police into action against their inclination. I left him at it, returned to the mess room and called

Hereford again.

'Boss,' I said. 'It looks like they're being taken south.'

He already knew that the moving signal had given out at Vnukovo, and had come to the same conclusion.

'What destinations does that place serve?'

'Rostov-on-Don, Sochi, other Black Sea resorts.' I reeled off names that Sasha had told me, and added, 'Word here is that the villains could be Chechens.'

'Who says that?'

'I don't know . . .' I hesitated, suddenly aware that I was on the point of dropping myself in the shit by revealing our participation in the bust on the flat. 'The idea came from Sasha, our main contact here.'

'Chechnya!' went the CO. 'Bloody hell. If that's where they're heading, we'd better scrub Berlin and start looking for jumping-off points further south.'

Sasha reappeared, scratching his head.

'Private jet has just made take-off from Vnukovo,' he said. 'Unofficial departure. No clearance from tower − no lights, nothing. This can only be Mafia.'

'Can the air force track it?'

He raised both hands in a gesture of helplessness. 'I have passed message. But you know, little co-operation between police and armed forces . . .'

'These criminals,' I said. 'D'you think they're Chechens? Is this a reprisal for our raid on the apartment?'

He nodded vigorously. 'I think so. Yes. These Chechens will demand big money for ransom.'

'When would you expect them to start?'

'Tomorrow morning.' He looked at his watch. '*This* morning − later.'

'Sasha,' I said. 'I'm afraid a couple of guys got killed in the contact on the highway.'

'Only Mafia!' he said, as if they'd been rabbits. 'No problem.'

I saw him yawn and said, 'Listen − you've been great. Thanks for coming in.'

'It is nothing. Zheordie, I am sorry.'

223

'Don't start all that again. It's not your fault. Off you go now.'

I ushered him out in a friendly way, and said to the lads, 'Better get your heads down. There's nothing to be done for the time being.'

'You too, Geordie,' said Whinger. 'You look knackered.'

'I feel it. What I'm going to do is bring a bed in here, in case Tony comes back on the blower.'

Two of us dragged my bed into the room. I took off my boots, but stretched out otherwise fully dressed. Gradually the place quietened down, but I couldn't sleep. Would the kidnappers try to use the bomb themselves? Would they have the technical capability to detonate it?

But my worst worries now were about our two missing men. I shrank from thinking what they might be going through. Much as I disliked Toad, I didn't want him hurt. I had to admit that on this task, so far, he'd pulled his weight and caused no trouble. As for Pav – still less did I want him to get beaten up. I clung to one small straw of hope. Neither of them had been involved in the bust on the apartment, so they could deny all knowledge of that.

But what were they to say about the bomb?

So far as we'd worked it out, our cover story – in the event of getting bumped – was that the device belonged to the Russians, and that we'd been moving it on their behalf. Toad had repeatedly assured me that every part of the device was anonymous and deniable: nowhere on the casing or any of the contents was there a single letter of Western writing. If he and Pav claimed to be ordinary squaddies, and professed complete ignorance about how the thing functioned, they might get away with it for a few hours. As always when someone is captured, their policy would be one of controlled release – letting out as little information as possible, as slowly as possible. The best I could hope was that they'd be able to hold out until we discovered their destination and got after them.

THIRTEEN

It was the telephone that roused me.

Tony's voice sounded incredibly close. Half asleep, I thought he'd flown into Moscow. Then I came round fully and realised he was calling again from New York.

'I think I woke you,' he said. 'Sorry.'

'No sweat. What time is it?'

'Here, we've got a quarter of nine. I don't know about you.'

'Still dark. Wait a minute. Quarter to five. What's happening?'

'We've found your missing Orange.'

'Fantastic. Where is it?'

'A nice quiet place called Grozny.'

'Ah, Jesus! Chechnya. Just what we thought.'

'That's where it is. It came back on the air ten minutes ago, and it's now proceeding westwards into the mountains.'

'OK. Can you continue monitoring it?'

'Sure. How about we update you every quarter-hour?'

'That'd be brilliant. I'm going to get right on to Hereford, ask them to establish a forward mounting base.'

'Eastern Turkey's where you want to be looking. Kars – somewhere like that.'

'I bet they're on to that already.'

They were. It was just before 2.00 a.m. GMT when I got through to the ops room, but the place was up and running. The ops officer and the CO were both there, planning to launch the QRF.

'Orange has turned up in Grozny,' the boss told me. 'We'd been talking to the Firm, and we were expecting it. We've also

225

been in touch with the Turks about using an airforce base in the east of the country.'

'Kars?'

'Probably. That looks like being our FMB. We should have that confirmed by eleven ths morning.'

'When are you launching?'

'If all goes well, later tonight. The stand-by squadron's squaring everything away right now.'

At the risk of stating the obvious, I said, 'We're not certain where the target's going to end up. The last I heard, Orange was still moving.'

'Yes. But we can only assume it's the Chechens who lifted our guys, and that the hostages are with the device. There's no point in hanging about. We're going to stage through Cyprus, so we'll get the squadron on its way. If the Turks play ball about Kars, the Herc can change crews at Akrotiri, refuel and fly straight on.'

From that moment the Satcom phone was in continual use. At 5.30 Tony came back on to say that Orange had stopped at a point just north of a village called Samashki, fifty kilometres west of Grozny.

'There's a river running east and west,' he said. 'The terrain is hilly – looks like the foothills of the main Caucasus range. The site's one kilometre north of the river.'

'Samashki,' I said. Somewhere, sometime, I'd seen that name before. 'Thanks, Tony. Tell me if the target moves again.'

An idea had developed rapidly in my mind. The site was going to need recceing. The Russians were stipulating that Sasha should co-ordinate the hostage recovery. He'd told me earlier in the night that they didn't want foreigners crashing around unsupervised in their territory, and I reckoned the same would apply, although more so, in Chechnya. What better plan than that I and he should drop in together? A HALO descent.

He was a trained parachutist, but had never done free-falling. Therefore we'd have to go in tandem, strapped together under one canopy. As it happened, at that time I was one of only three tandem masters in the Regiment. Where the other two were, I didn't know, but I decided to try it on the head-shed, anyway.

They remembered Samashki in Hereford, all right. 'Jesus!' said Dick Trafford, the ops officer. 'That's where the Russian army murdered more than a hundred people. Burnt the houses. It was tactically pointless – just a show of strength. It became one of the most notorious incidents in the war.'

'Listen,' I said. 'I've had an idea about the recce . . .' I explained what I'd been thinking, and added, 'I want to volunteer for the job. We can get down to it much quicker from here than you can from there. Why don't we do it?'

'OK,' said Dick cautiously, 'but who's Sasha?'

'Major Ivanov, commander of Tiger Force, big operational experience in this region.'

'It's possible,' Dick agreed. 'I'll check it out and let you know.' Then he added, 'We've made one bit of progress. The Turks have cleared us to use Kars as our FMB.'

'Brilliant.'

I went into the kitchen and put the kettle on, then went back on the Satcom to Hereford. This time I got the CO, and outlined my scheme. 'The recce party needs to include a Russian,' I emphasised. 'If we bump into anyone on the ground and can't communicate, we're buggered. The ideal guy's Sasha Ivanov, our contact here. He's a hundred per cent on side, and I've got to know him pretty well.'

The CO must have already been discussing my idea with Dick, because he agreed at once. 'Don't get carried away, though,' he warned.

'Has the squadron left yet?'

'No – they're going in about an hour. You'd better have a word with Pat Newman. He's right here.'

Pat Newman, leader of the HALO team, was an old mate. 'Hi, Geordie!' he said. 'Stirring it up again, I hear.'

'Just a bit. Great to hear you, Pat. Listen. I've been looking at the map. The best way to hack this is for me and my Russian colleague Sasha to meet you at Kars. I'm going to need a full patrol kit and a tandem rig. Can you make sure it's all brought out?'

'Don't worry,' he said. 'I know the score. I've been fully briefed. Your kit'll be on board. Just tell the SQMS what you want.'

'OK, then. Put me over, please.'

The squadron quartermaster sergeant was Larry Tompkins, another good friend. 'Listen, Larry,' I said, 'can you get your finger out?'

'Might be able to. Why?'

I ran through a list of what we needed: tandem rig chute, two free-fall suits, two oxygen sets working off one cylinder, harness and clips for attaching Sasha to me, GPS, Satcom phone, camcorder and lap-top computer for videoing the site, kite-sight, binos . . . 'And Larry,' I ended, 'those suits. Medium will do for me, but the guy I'm taking in's a big lad. Six one at least, and broad with it. We need a large for him.'

'Got it,' said Larry. 'We're pulling the stuff out already.'

'Thanks.'

I went back to Pat and asked, 'How about timings?'

'Depart Lyneham 0530 . . .' I could tell he was doing calculations on a sheet of paper – a habit of his. 'Six hours thirty to Cyprus. Akrotiri at 1200 – that's 1500 local. Ninety minutes to change crews and refuel. Take off for Kars 1630 local. Two hours twenty, approx. Into Kars by 1900 local.'

'So if Sasha can get me and him to Kars by then, the recce can go down tonight?'

'Yes – it'll have to.'

'And the squadron assault the night after.'

'Exactly.'

Back in the kitchen, I found the kettle had boiled dry and heated up to a fearsome degree over the gas burner. When I wrapped a cloth round the handle it gave off a smell of singeing, and the first gush of fresh water exploded into steam when it hit the base.

One or two of the other lads were starting to come round. Whinger blundered into the kitchen, scrubbing at his eyes and muttering, 'Fucking phone – it's never stopped all night.'

As if to back up his complaint the local line rang. It was Anna, spitting with rage. She'd only just got the message I'd left the night before. Her people were useless, she said, idle and stupid. Now – how could she help me?

The older you get, the more cynical you become. I couldn't help wondering if she was really that furious – or was she acting up a bit? Had she got my message hours earlier and deliberately done nothing about it?

Whatever the truth, she caught up fast. I'd barely finished outlining events when she said, 'If it's Samashki, it's certainly one of the Gaidar brothers you're dealing with. You know the big man who was shot in the apartment?'

'Of course.'

'That was Aslan, so-called Keet, the Whale. His second brother, Usman, calls himself Akula, the Shark. He's been building a big house for himself down there near Grozny, a kind of fortified palace, in the mountains. That's the Gaidars' home territory. The three of them *are* the Chechen Mafia.'

'Who's the third?'

'The young one, Supyan, calls himself Barrakuda. That hardly needs translating.'

'Are there pictures of this place at Samashki? Any air shots?'

'The FSB have some, but they're poor quality. The Chechens tend to shoot at any aircraft that comes over. And anyway, the pictures are out of date.'

'You mean the house is still being built?'

'The house is complete, but there's still work in progress on the perimeter fences and some of the outbuildings.'

'Listen,' I said. 'We're going to hit that place – provided we can confirm the hostages have been taken there. Can you bring over any information you've got about it – the pictures, exact location?'

'With pleasure. But I can tell you the location anyway. It's one kilometre north of the River Sunzha, half-way between Samashki and the next village, Sernovodsk.'

'Say those names again.'

As she spelled them out, I scribbled them down in the notebook tied to the phone for message-taking.

229

'Thanks, Anna. How soon can you get here?'

'In an hour?'

'Terrific. Do you have any photos of this fellow Shark?'

'Certainly. There were some on the disk I gave you. But I can bring you prints as well.'

Already the Satcom was ringing again.

'Geordie,' went Tony. 'It's still there. Hasn't moved.'

'Can you give me the co-ordinates?'

'Sure. Coming up.'

I took down his figures.

'I know where that is,' I said. Parroting Anna I added, 'One kilometre north of the River Sunzha, half-way between Samashki and Sernovodsk.'

'I'll be damned!' Tony exclaimed. 'How in hell did you know that?'

'A little bird called Anna told me. Seriously, any chance of satellite imagery on the site?'

'I knew you'd want that. I started to check out orbits. It's looking good. We'll have a satellite in the right place two hours from now. Also I got a met report for the Caucasus area, and the weather's fine: frost in the night, clear sky, no wind – gonna be a beautiful day. We should get some great pictures for you. I'll fax them just as soon as I can.'

The last person I had to convince was Sasha. 'Very big search, just for two persons,' he said doubtfully when he came into camp.

'Typical of the Regiment,' I told him. 'They don't like losing people. They'll go to any lengths to get them back.'

As to my suggestion of his own involvement in the recce, he didn't hesitate: as soon as he knew I was going with him, he was delighted to come.

'The point is,' I said, 'can you get us down there for insertion tonight? What I want to do is join up with the squadron at Kars – here.' I put my finger on the map.

'Hars!' he exclaimed, aspirating the initial letter. 'But that is in Turoktsiya.'

'Turkey.'

'Yes, Turkey.'

'We need to be there by five tonight. Earlier if we can.'

'Timing no problem,' Sasha said confidently. 'It is three-hour flight, not more. Plane also no problem. We get small military jet. The difficulty is diplomats. Do they give permission to enter Turkish airspace?' He spread his hands and stuck out his lower lip.

'Maybe Anna can help on that.'

'No!' He bridled. 'I arrange it through my own bosses.'

'Think you can manage it?'

'Zheordie – for you I arrange *anything*: even to become beautiful!'

When Anna swept in at 7.30 she brought good mug-shots of Usman Gaidar, aka Akula, the Shark – a mean-looking fellow, in his forties, with short, dark hair, heavy eyebrows, lean, hollow cheeks and a prominent jaw. In the photos his teeth and gums seemed to protrude, pushing his lips out – hence his name, maybe? Anna said the man was obsessive about protecting himself, and kept a private army of at least a hundred men to guard him.

She'd also brought telephoto pictures of the house he'd been building – a tall, pale building with a steeply pointed roof, set into the side of a hill.

'It looks Scandinavian,' I said.

'You're right.' Anna turned the picture round on the table so that it faced her way. 'It was designed by Finnish architects. No expense spared. Marble floors at ground level. Fitness room and sauna lined with birch wood in the basement. Whole building air-conditioned. Bullet-proof windows. It's not confirmed, but we have heard that he's building a nuclear shelter in the grounds by drilling into rock in the side of the mountain and lining the cavity with concrete and steel.'

I came within a micro-second of making some stupid joke about getting a nuclear device for his nuclear shelter, but pulled myself up just in time and said instead, 'The satellite imagery should show that, if the site's still fairly raw.'

231

When the pictures came over from the States, through the Satcom and our secure computer, they proved brilliantly sharp, and a perfect supplement to the telephoto shots. What the satellite revealed most clearly was the layout of the house and its defences. The building stood on a forested hillside inside a perimeter fence, roughly square, with sides some 400 metres long. The line of the fence showed as a pale gash through the trees, as did the single road running up to the house from a cluster of other buildings on the bottom edge of the compound. The villa was slightly off-centre – closer to the top fence than the bottom – and above it, towards the north-western corner, was a circular helipad. There was also another cleared area, nearer the house, which we assumed was the site of the shelter. A wider shot, of a bigger area, showed the river passing to the south of the site and, away to the right of it, the outskirts of Samashki village.

What caught my eye was an oblong open space in the forest, about two ks to the north-west. From its regular shape, it looked like a man-made field. 'Here!' I said to Sasha. 'This looks ideal as a place to drop into. A good opening in the trees, and far enough from the target.'

'We land there?'

'That's right – and walk in.'

So much was visible on the satellite shots. The telephoto picture showed that the pine-covered hillside was steep, with outcrops of rock among the trees.

When I invited Whinger to make an independent assessment, he came up with the same plan as I had.

'Bugger the fence,' he said. 'They'd have a job to electrify something that long – and where's the power coming from, anyway? It doesn't even look as if it's finished. You could cut throught that, or climb it, no bother. Drop on this football field, or whatever it is, and tab it in. Piece of cake. There may be a patrol on the fence, but I doubt it. The defenders are going to be here, at the bottom, guarding the approach road. There's no other way any vehicle can get near the house.'

'I reckon you're right,' I agreed. 'And when the time comes,

232

the same drill for the QRF: drop on the field, walk in, surround the house and cut it off from its defence force. A couple of guys with gympis and a 66 should be enough to suppress anyone trying to come up the road. Look at these bends in the track – it's quite some climb.'

With the basic plan in place, I was naturally on fire to get going. Whinger and the rest of the lads went off to run the course. Sasha had disappeared to organise our flight, so Anna went with the guys, to interpret, and I was left manning the phones with Terry, the signaller. The sensible thing would have been to get a couple of hours' kip, but although I lay on the bed, my adrenalin was pumping too fast for me to drop off.

At 11.00 a.m. Allway came through from the Embassy, asking if there was anything he could do. I thanked him but said that we were fine, and I gave him an outline of the plan, keeping details of places and timings deliberately vague. When I asked about the international situation, he described it as 'stabilising'.

The next time he called, half an hour later, it was a different story. He said that the Chechens had surfaced, through their representative in London. They claimed they were holding two SAS men hostage, and in return for handing them over, they were demanding not only a ransom of ten million dollars, but also the release of the Mafia players arrested in Britain.

The news made my stomach churn. In making their demand, had the Chechens said anything about Orange? I couldn't ask directly, but had to fence round the subject.

'What did they say about releasing our guys? Where's the exchange supposed to take place?'

'We have no information on that.'

'Who did they make the offer to?'

'The FCO.'

'Who's their representative in Britain?'

'He calls himself the Consul.'

My questions brought me no nearer the subject of the bomb. But surely, if the ransom demand had mentioned it, Allway would have told me.

Once again I had to contain my impatience and anxiety.

Around 11.30 I suddenly realised I was starving. I'd been up most of the night and had no breakfast, so I routed out some onions, fried them up, threw in a load of garam masala and turned a tin of beef stew into a power curry. We still had plenty of the rice we'd brought out from UK, so I boiled up some of that, and gave myself a solid meal.

I was in the middle of eating it when Sasha reappeared, all smiles.

'Mmmmmm!' He gave an exaggerated sniff. 'Smells good!'

'Have some.'

'No – you need it. We have long journey to make.'

The Turks had come on side, he said, and we had permission to fly. Better still, he'd fixed an aircraft – a P33, a ten-seat executive jet used by senior military commanders. Take-off would be from the military side of Vnukovo airport at 2.30 Moscow time. We couldn't fly direct, but were to stage through Krasnodar, in the north of the Caucasus, so that the plane could refuel before the final hop of the flight and not have to take on Turkish fuel at the far end.

That meant leaving Balashika at 1.00 – and suddenly time for planning, which had seemed endless, had almost run out.

At 12.30 I put in one last call to Tony, even though I knew it was 4.30 a.m. in the States. He was asleep, but his stand-in, Cyrus, was fully briefed. He confirmed that Orange was stationary on the same site, and that the weather in the region was likely to remain unchanged for the next thirty-six hours.

'You got a big high centred over the west coast of the Caspian, extending all the way to the Black Sea,' he said. 'Predicted wind speeds, three to five knots on 260 degrees. Moon's three-quarter full. Moonrise 1900 local, moonset 0600. Looks like you'll have God's own view of the Caucasus range as you drop in there.'

'Thanks for your help,' I went. 'Tell Tony I'll call him from Kars.'

'OK. And take some warm clothes with you. That place is six thousand feet above sea level.'

234

FOURTEEN

The P33 was noisy and cramped, with little headroom and hard, uncomfortable seats, but it did the job. There were two regular army officers on board, hitching a lift to Krasnodar, but otherwise Sasha and I had the cabin to ourselves. The seats were arranged in pairs facing each other, and for much of the flight we kept a map of the Grozny area open on our knees, discussing the terrain.

When Sasha started talking about the war he grew animated, cursing the brutality and incompetence of the whole operation. He'd been in charge of one of the Omon special units, and had done what he could to keep his own men under control, but Kulikov, the overall commander of Russian troops in the south, had gone round inciting officers and men to kill every Chechen they could get their hands on.

'Not only Chechen people,' he told me. 'One Omon unit attacked farm. They shoot fifty cows, kill them all. They set fire to cows' food – hay – burn down barns, destroy machines. It was all crazy, mad. What had the cows done to annoy them?'

'Did you get to hate Chechens?' I asked.

'Not hate them. Chechens ordinary people. Not like Afghanis. Afghanis fanaticals. Some Chechens good, some bad.'

As we flew down over the Ukraine there wasn't a great deal to see. The rolling wheatlands had been harvested and most of the stubble had already gone under the plough, so that vast tracts of black earth were showing.

The second leg was a different matter, however. 'We go on the left side,' said Sasha as we re-boarded. 'Then we see mountains.'

As we lifted out of Krasnodar, lying beside a lake in the plain, the pilot climbed slowly on a southerly heading, and soon the Black Sea came in sight, away to our right. Over the coast the plane made a slight left turn and started following the shoreline down, just inland of the water. 'Famous health resorts,' Sasha said, pointing at spots on the map. 'Sochi, Sukhumi, Batumi – many sanatoriums.'

By then the sun was setting over the sea, and on the other side of the aircraft – our left – it threw fantastic light over the forested hills which piled ever higher into the distance until we began to see snow on the peaks.

'Soon we see Elbrus!' called Sasha excitedly. 'Highest mountain in Caucasus. Highest mountain in Europe.'

Screwing round my head to look, I spotted two rounded, snow-covered humps, so high above everything else that they were still catching the last of the sun.

'They're pink!' I exclaimed. 'Like a pair of bloody great tits.'

'Precisely!' Sashsa beamed. 'This is what we would say – *kak dve siski*, like twin tits.' Then he pointed left ahead: 'Grozny over there, behind.' He started in about the war again – how the Russians hadn't been able to make headway against the guerrillas, and had no proper military objectives, so that the soldiers took it out on anyone who got in their way.

He was still talking as the sun's rays at last left Elbrus. The smooth boobs quickly turned a dirty white, stars began to show in the clear sky, and night settled over the Caucasus range.

On our descent into Kars I wondered how the pilots would communicate with the tower. Did someone down there speak Russian, or did both sides talk in English? I never discovered – but we landed safely, to find that the Herc from Cyprus was already in.

Tony's stand-in had been right about the temperature too. As we stepped out of our little aircraft, the cold bit. On that high plateau our breath condensed in the air, and frozen mud crunched under foot. All round the horizon frosty-looking mountains showed faintly in the starlight. Great was my delight when I found mates from the squadron, settling themselves into an empty warehouse with big blower heaters blasting from the corners.

There was no time to socialise or piss about. I said hello to a few of the guys, then quickly sought out the OC of the stand-by squadron, Bill Chandler, who'd got himself an office of sorts in a cabin at one end of the big shed. A scalie had already got his Satcom set up, and Bill was talking to Hereford.

As I approached, he looked up at me, gave a grin and said into the phone, 'Yes. He's here. He's made it.'

When he came off the air, my first question was, 'How do we stand on security inside the squadron? I mean, how many of the lads know about Orange?'

'Nobody yet,' was his answer. 'It's on a need-to-know basis. Obviously the HALO team are going to have to know. It's them and the Chinook crews who'll have to exfil the damn thing. I'm going to tell them at their final briefing. As far as everyone else is concerned, it's purely a hostage rescue mission.'

'That's fine.' I nodded. 'Just remember that Sasha, my Russian partner, doesn't know about Orange either.'

'Christ! This is getting complicated. He's going to find out sooner or later.'

'Not necessarily. If he does, I'll square him. But I'm doing my best to keep him in the dark.'

'That's your problem,' said Bill. 'Meanwhile, can you tell *me* what Orange looks like? You're the only person here who's seen it.'

'Three components,' I told him. 'Two identical black steel cases, roughly three foot by two foot by one. One box about eighteen inches cubed.'

'Weight?'

'The big components eighty kilos each, the small one forty.'

'OK, thanks.' Bill made some notes.

'Tell you what,' I said. 'When Sasha and I go in, if I get eyes on Orange and have to refer to it over the Satcom, I'll call it "three heavy cases". All right?'

'Three heavy cases,' Bill confirmed. 'The latest satellite

imagery suggests that they, or it, are in some outlying building to the east of the house.'

'Then that'll be the summerhouse.'

'The summerhouse,' he repeated, scribbling again. 'We're still waiting for confirmation of exfil by Chinook. As soon as we get it we'll pass it through.' Then he said, 'You and your pal had better brief the air crew. The captain wants to be on his way by ten.'

The RAF had set up a temporary base in what was obviously a training wing – a classroom of sorts, with a blackboard, tables and chairs of tubular metal, and garish, incomprehensible Turkish posters round the walls. The only member of the crew I'd met was Alec, the co-pilot, who introduced me to his captain, a solid, fair-haired Scot called Dan. They had maps spread out over two of the tables pushed together, and were using rulers and compasses to mark them up, punching figures into a lap-top.

'OK,' said Dan, inviting me into the discussion. 'There's not much civilian air traffic over this godforsaken area, but there is the occasional night flight coming up over Grozny from Baku, down here on the Caspian. Therefore our aim is to fly a normal civilian track. Your target's Samashki, right?'

'Yeah – we're aiming for an opening in the forest three ks north-west of the village.'

'Roger. The wind's about five ks on two-four-zero, so if we tip you out ten ks west, you should be able to fly yourselves in.'

I nodded. 'That'd be fine.'

'Good. That'll keep us well clear of Grozny. So . . .' He stood up and stretched before running through a quick recap. 'We go out on zero-eight-four and hold that heading till we cross the civilian track from Baku. Then we turn left on to two-eight-eight and head up between Grozny and Ordzhonikidze. Our marker point for the turn is this peak here, Dyltydag. It's over four thousand metres and fairly isolated, so we should pick it out all right – but if we can't, the computer will hack it.'

'What height will we be flying at?'

'Twenty-eight thousand. You'll want plenty of clothes on.'

I nodded again, wondering at the sight of all those peaks on the map – a range running for two or three hundred miles, north-west to south-east, with numerous 15,000-footers among them . . . We were going to fly right over the whole lot. All I asked was, 'How long will it take to get there?'

Alec did a few more calculations and came up with, 'One hour five to the turn, then twenty-five minutes to the DZ overhead. It should be no problem to get you there. It's not you that's bugging us, though.'

'What is it, then?'

'The exfil. Two Chinooks are on their way from Cyprus, and we're trying to work out a way of getting them through this bloody range of mountains. It's a hell of a proposition, I can tell you. Even if we put extra fuel forward, right on the border, it's still a fearsome distance to anyone going in low level.'

'What about coming from the other side?' I suggested.

'From Russia?'

'Yeah. Wouldn't that be a better proposition? The intervening terrain doesn't look nearly so high.'

'We're working on it. But we don't have clearance from the Russians yet – from any direction.'

'Call Anna.'

'Anna?'

'The woman who's been doing our liaison in Moscow. She's shit-hot. She'll fix anything. Colonel Anna Gerasimova, FSB.'

'Sorry, mate – what's that?'

'The Federal Security Bureau, part of the old KGB, hived off.'

I saw the guy giving me an odd look, so I said sharply, 'Write her name down, and the number. She may not be in the barracks now, but she'll be there first thing in the morning. You'll get her on our Satcom link.'

'It's bloody horrible being the passenger,' I warned Sasha, looking down at the tandem rig laid out on the floor, 'because you've got no control.'

'You tell me,' he said cheerfully. 'I do it.'

We'd already had some practices during the morning, back at Balashika, but this was a full-scale dress rehearsal with all our kit on. The two PJIs who were coming with us fitted Sasha into his webbing harness, with hooks at the shoulders and at the waist, linked him to my own harness and pulled him in tight against my front, with both our full bergens strapped to the front of his legs and a single oxygen cylinder on the outside of my left thigh. Trussed together like this, carrying a lot of weight, we found it almost impossible to walk.

'Let's go through the motions again,' I said. 'As the plane approaches the DZ, we move to the edge of the deck. Let's say it's that line on the floor. Go on, then.'

Slowly, awkwardly, moving our legs in unison, we shuffled the short distance to the line.

'OK. Now we're waiting for the two green lights on either side of the opening.' I pointed outwards at head level, right and left. 'When we get them, and a signal from the head loadie, we just lean forward together and topple out. After that, you don't need to do anything except hold the same position. Keep your hands crossed over your chest, like you've got them now. All right?'

Sasha nodded.

'Once we're under canopy, we can take off our masks and let them hang. Then I'll slacken off the straps so that you slide down, about this much.' I held my hands a foot apart. 'That means your feet will be lower than mine, so they'll touch the ground first. Just as we're coming in to land, I'll tell you to start walking. At first you'll be walking in the air, then on the deck. OK?'

He nodded.

Without changing my voice I went on, 'There are two other things you need to know. First, if our chute fails to open, cross your legs and keep them there.'

'And why?'

'So they can unscrew you from the ground.'

He stared at me, and I went on relentlessly, 'The other thing is, keep your right hand up.'

'Why that?'

240

'So you don't break your watch when you go in.'

At last he smiled and aimed a gentle punch at me. Outwardly he seemed pretty calm, but perhaps not, because he kept sliding off for sessions in the bog.

Meanwhile, I was sorting the kit they'd brought us and repacking it into my bergen. They'd given us plenty of warm clothes, including two free-fall Goretex suits with Thinsulate linings: when zipped together, the jackets and trousers gave us a perfectly windproof outer layer. There were also a couple of sweaters apiece, thermal silk long johns and long-armed vests, and any amount of boil-in-the-bag meals, which we could eat cold if necessary. If all went well, we'd be on the ground for less than thirty-six hours, so I cut down our load as far as I dared, as the combined weight of our essential kit was already formidable.

I had a 203, with eight spare thirty-round mags and two grenades, plus Sig, spare mags, knife, Satcom, GPS, covert radio, kite-sight, binoculars, fireflies, waterbottles, sleeping bag, bivvy bag and cam nets. A lot of the heaviest stuff, like the magazines, went into the pouches on my webbing, but there was still enough to fill a bergen. Sasha had his Gepard and spare mags, plus a pistol and ammunition.

At 9.30 p.m. I went for a final briefing with Bill Chandler. The met forecasts were unchanged. Orange hadn't moved: the satellite was still getting its signal. 'As far as they can tell, it's not in the main house,' Bill told me. 'If it was inside a big structure, they probably wouldn't hear it. It seems to be about a hundred metres east of the building.'

'OK,' I said. 'As soon as we're on site I'll call you and let you know what we can see.'

After a sandwich and a cup of tea we were ready to go. At the last minute I bumped into Pat, who looked in rollicking form, his bright brown eyes shining, cheeks ruddy, and his teeth flashing white as ever.

'Taking on Chechnya single-handed, are you, Geordie?' he enquired with a big grin on his face.

'Just the two of us. Pat, this is Sasha, a very good colleague from Moscow. Sasha – Pat Newman.'

241

'Hi, Sasha!' Pat shook hands quickly. 'You want to watch this fellow – he's a dangerous bastard to be with.'

Rising to the banter, Sasha took hold of my webbing and said, 'I keep him tied to me.'

'Quite right! Otherwise he might dump you in it.'

'You look out,' I told Pat. 'The Chechens are pretty handy with their guns. Move a bit faster this time or you'll end up a Figure Eleven again.'

'We'll see!' Pat grinned and gave me a smack on my sore shoulder.

'Eh,' he went, seeing me wince. 'What's the matter?'

'I got nicked there in a bit of a shoot-out.'

'Really! We live in dangerous times. Happy landings, anyway.'

'Same to you, Pat. We'll see you tomorrow.'

As we moved off, Sasha asked, 'What is Figure Eleven?'

'One of the targets we shoot at on the range.' With both hands I drew the silhouette of a man's torso in the air.

For us, down in the back of the Herc, the flight was routine and relatively short. After take-off the pilot climbed hard, under full power, to clear the mountains, and the vibration was enough to loosen your teeth. Then we levelled off, and I went up on the flight deck for a look at the terrain.

Beneath us a sea of snow peaks lay glittering in bright moonlight, with jagged ridges of rock running down from the summits in incredibly complex patterns. I plugged the end of my helmet lead into an intercom socket and said to the pilot, 'Glad we're not going out right here.'

'Aye,' he went. 'You wouldna have much of a chance. Here's our marker summit coming up already. See it?'

Dead on the nose of the aircraft a single snow-clad peak was rising from the horizon, slender and pointed. We seemed to be approaching it at a snail's pace, then all at once loomed closer. While I was staring at it the plane tilted steeply to the left as the auto-pilot made our programmed turn.

Back in the hold, the head loadie signalled us to start getting our tandem rig on, and the two PJIs helped do up the straps, clips and buckles to the correct tension.

So, for the final few minutes, we stood strapped tight together, unable to sit down, barely able to walk. My pulse rate had shot up and my heart was pounding. I'd peed into the Elsan just a few minutes before, but already I had the feeling I wanted to go again. I tried to concentrate on controlling my breathing so that I didn't hyperventilate.

On our own oxygen now, with masks in place, it was impossible to communicate any longer. In spite of the discomfort, there was time – too much time – for my mind to zip back to the fuck-up over France. The big difference now was that Pavarotti, poor bugger, was on the deck, in the hands of the Mafia, and had no chance of flying into me on the way down.

Either side of the tailgate the red warning lights flicked on. The head loadie gave me two fingers. I acknowledged them, and saw him hitch his own harness to a strop hanging from the wall. The tail opened, letting in a blast of searingly cold air. As the ramp settled into its horizontal position the guy motioned us forward, and with another well-anchored loadie steadying us from behind, we waddled to the edge of the abyss, a few inches at each step, stiff-legged as ducks.

One finger from the head loadie. One minute to go. Sixty seconds of sheer terror.

Sasha seemed totally cool, not trembling or shifting about. I could only think, He must have nerves of fucking steel. I found it impossible to think rationally. All I could do was try to keep my breathing rate down and will the seconds to pass faster.

Then suddenly both red lights turned to green.

'Green on!' I yelled. 'GO!'

I gave Sasha a tap on the right arm and as one we leant forward and toppled into a blasting, icy hurricane.

Immediately we were in a face-down attitude, Sasha beneath me. Freezing air ripped past my cheeks, scouring like crystals of ice. Far below and away to our right the snow-peaks shimmered and glinted. I felt the drogue-chute tug at the centre of my back as it deployed behind us, slowing our descent slightly and keeping us stable.

243

Then, steering with hands and feet, I turned us round until our heads were pointing north. I was still aware of the moonlit snow summits, now out on our left, but there was no time to enjoy the view. Our urgent need was to pinpoint the LZ. It should be showing up as a lighter patch in the black of the forests.

At first I couldn't pick it out and panic threatened. Every second I kept glancing back at the altimeters on my forearms. The hands were unwinding like clocks gone berserk.

At last I got it: a little grey oblong, father to our right than I'd expected, but well within reach. By dropping my right arm and raising my left, I tilted us in that direction. At the change of attitude I found myself dreading the possibility of going into another spin; but Sasha played his role perfectly, remaining passive beneath me, not trying to influence our flight-path, relying on me to steer.

Down, down, down we went. Sixteen thousand, fourteen, twelve . . . The forested hills were gloriously black below us. Far off to our right, beyond the LZ, was a small cluster of lights, which I reckoned was Samashki, too far off for anyone there to spot one little dot falling from the sky. Otherwise the wooded hills were magnificently dark, denoting a total absence of houses. No bright windows, no roads, no moving vehicles.

Ten, eight, six . . .

Our target was growing rapidy into a fair-sized field.

Five . . .

I tugged the release toggle. Away went the drogue with a snap, pulling out the big chute, and with a heavy snatch we were jerked upright, swinging beneath the main canopy. Immediately I unhooked one side of my mask so I could talk again, and released the tension on the harness buckles, so that Sasha sank down until the top of his helmet was level with my chest, giving me a better view of where we were heading.

The pale opening in the forest was well within reach, ahead and slightly to our right. 'See it down there?' I said quietly, pointing.

'Fantastic!' Sasha breathed, on a high. Now I could hear *him* hyperventilating. 'Breelliant!' he went. '*Otlichno!*'

'OK,' I said, 'take it easy, and don't make too much noise.'

I steered for the open patch, glad of the bright moonlight for the view it gave us, but feeling altogether too conspicuous. At least the LZ looked fairly level.

The black trees came up rapidly to meet us. We were over the southern edge of the clearing, sliding towards the centre. As we came in I pulled on both risers, stalling our descent.

'Get ready,' I told Sasha. 'Start walking now.'

Then I flared again: the chute came up and stalled, and a moment later we landed softly on short, frosty grass.

For a few seconds we crouched, motionless, listening. Not a murmur. The breeze carried a thin, clean scent of pines. The opening we'd landed in looked to be about two hundred metres by one hundred, with trees on all sides. Then it was out of the harness, weapons out of their ties and at the ready, and down in a defensive position, facing outwards. Sasha needed no instruction: he moved fast and instinctively.

My hands were lumps of ice. My fingers started to throb and burn as I worked them furiously, open and shut, to get the circulation going while I waited for my GPS to get a fix and confirm we were on the correct location.

As soon as the figures came up, and I saw they were right, we rolled our jumping kit into a bundle, shouldered our bergens and set off towards the edge of the field in search of a place to hide or bury the evidence.

'Big experience for me,' Sasha panted, still breathless with excitement as we hurried forward.

A sudden outburst of noise made me drop flat again. The commotion came from a distance, higher up the mountain to our left: an explosion of high wailing and howling in which several distinct voices rose and fell.

Sasha gave a chuckle. '*Volki,*' he said. 'Wolves. We hear them often during the war. They sing to moon.'

'Jesus!' I gasped. 'They gave me a fright. Do they attack humans?'

Sasha laughed again. 'Never! Wolf very shy animal – keep away.'

245

The chorus rose and fell for nearly a minute, then stopped as suddenly as it had begun.

By now the moon was on its way down, but still so bright that I hardly needed the kite-sight: the binos did just as good a job. I swept them round, hoping to see some of the ghostly howlers, but they must have been half a mile away.

At the far end of the field, in the direction we wanted to go, there was some object in a corner. The kite-sight revealed it as an old wooden farm wagon, with a primitive hay-rake beside it.

'That thing must have come up a track through the forest to reach where it is,' I whispered. 'Let's take a shufti.'

We moved into the deep shadow at the edge of the trees, then advanced slowly to the corner. There was no fence round the edge of the grass, so I reckoned that herdsmen or boys must look after any animals that came to graze there. As there were wolves about, that made sense.

The wagon had wooden wheels, the back pair twice the size of the front, which were mounted on a swivelling yoke, and it took me straight back thirty years to my boyhood in the north of England.

'Vairy preemitive people, Chechens,' Sasha whispered.

'Yes,' I said, 'but look at this.'

Beyond the cart was a drinking trough for cattle, carved out of a single tree-trunk. I reached down and felt a skim of ice in the bottom. Beside it was a broken-down hand pump for raising water from a well. Staring at it, I reckoned this was a summer pasture, on which some farmer made hay, but that now it had been abandoned for the winter. A moment later I'd found the well cover, made of planks, and lifted it. In went the para bundle, and that was one problem solved.

A rutted track led away through the wood, twisting downhill towards the east. For twenty minutes we followed it, but then the path turned right into the valley, no doubt heading down towards the village, and we had to continue as best we could through the trees, holding our height along the contour.

Our navigation proved spot-on. Seventy minutes out from the LZ, we saw something light-coloured through the screen of tree-trunks ahead, and with the kite-sight made out the perimeter fence of the compound: weldmesh on steel posts, all glowing coldly in the moonlight.

We came to the edge of the trees and stopped. I whispered to Sasha, 'We'll give it an hour,' and we settled ourselves on the top of a bank which commanded a close view of the barrier at a point where it turned a corner and ran away down the slope. Lying on our stomachs on a bed of old pine-needles, we looked straight on the fence, which was two metres high and topped by four strands of razor wire on overhang arms canted outwards.

Scanning past it with the kite-sight, I saw that the trees cut down to make way for the barrier hadn't yet been cleared. The trunks had been sawn into lengths, but the tops had simply been dragged out of the way and left in heaps. Perfect, I thought. Ideal for an OP. We can just burrow into one of them and become invisible. No digging or nets needed. We can pick the best spots for observing the villa and checking on patrols.

The more I scanned, the more evidence I saw that the fence was still being worked on. Lengths of metal and odd pieces of wire lay scattered on either side of it, and further up the hill, on the outside, was what looked like a small trailer which I assumed the builders had been using to bring up material. I'd been planning to cut our way through the bottom of the weldmesh, but with this amount of construction still in progress that seemed a dangerous idea. Instead, I decided to take a look at the stretch near the trailer, in the hope that it wasn't yet complete.

For the time being we were out of the wind, in deep shadow, on dry ground, and as comfortable as could be – so I wasn't surprised when Sasha began to snore gently beside me. I turned to look at him, and saw that his head was resting on one arm. Let him sleep, I thought. One pair of eyes is enough here.

Forty minutes later, I gripped him by the arm. He came to silently and was immediately alert. I pointed downhill, along the wire, where I'd seen the glow of a cigarette being drawn on. Then it came again, closer. A patrol was on its way round the perimeter.

I got the kite-sight aligned and saw the smoker immediately:

a single man with a weapon slung on his shoulder. At his heel a German Shepherd was ambling, apparently loose.

'Get ready!' I whispered. 'He's got a bloody dog.'

I felt for my knife, down my right leg. I hate guard dogs. You never know whether to shoot them and give away your presence by making a noise, or risk serious injury by trying to get a knife into the bastards.

We lay on the bank like logs. I felt we were going to be all right, because the drift of the wind was from the fence to us, and we hadn't put any scent on the ground by going to the wire itself. Besides, the sentry was an idle sod: he was ambling along, not looking to right and left, but humming to himself between drags. As he passed beneath us, within fifteen feet of our heads, the smell of cheap tobacco smoke filled the air around us. It wasn't surprising that the dog never deviated from its track.

We gave the pair a couple of minutes to get clear, then went for the fence. Close inspection revealed that none of the wire was insulated, and that there was no alarm system that I could see. We moved cautiously uphill towards the trailer, and found it contained drums of more razor wire. Fifty metres beyond it we found what I'd been hoping for: a section of fence not yet fitted with the overhang. In twenty seconds we'd both climbed the weldmesh and gained the cover of the heaped tree-tops.

I reckoned that by the time the sentry came round again – if he made it at all – our scent would have left the frosty surface. With the ground so soundly frozen, our boots hadn't left any traces on the fence itself.

We slipped out from our heap of pine-tops, back into the standing trees, and crept left-handed round the outcrops of rock, following the contour, the hill falling to our right. According to the map, which I'd tried to imprint on my brain from the satellite data, the villa would be below us.

From his station a pace behind me Sasha put a hand on my arm. I stopped to listen. He was pointing downhill. When I turned my head in that direction I heard what he'd detected: a faint hum, something like an air-conditioning unit. We moved on a few yards, looked over a rocky ridge, and saw the house rising tall from a levelled-out plateau below.

'Hell of a place,' I whispered.

From Anna's photographs I recognised the steep roof and high walls, glowing pale in the moonlight, but the whole place looked more formidable than I'd reckoned. There were three main floors above ground level, a fourth with dormer-windows sticking out of the roof, and some kind of a basement. At the front, on our right, five cars were parked, and on the side facing us a ramp led down to a sunken garage.

'Jesus!' I whispered. 'It's just like the cellar at the Embassy.'

'The Embassy?' I heard Sasha turn his head to look at me.

Suddenly I realised what I was saying. 'You know – in the courtyard . . .' Christ! 'Oh no. Sorry. I was thinking you'd been with us. We stored some kit at the back of the British Embassy in Moscow. There was a garage entrance a bit like this.'

Thank God, he didn't show the least curiosity.

'Beeg house,' was all he said. 'Where are your men?'

He meant that it might be one hell of a job to locate them – and he was right. For the moment I concentrated on the layout of the place.

Akula had good comms, obviously: we could see a couple of dish aerials bolted on to the wall beneath the eaves. There were video cameras mounted on the corners of the building, and what looked like an infra-red device covering the driveway. But half an hour's observation convinced me that there was no patrol immediately round the house: Akula was relying on the fence to keep intruders at a distance.

From where we lay we could see the approach road snaking off down the mountainside to our right, and once I was confident that nobody was moving inside the compound, I decided to recce the track, right down to the barrack huts, or whatever they were, at the bottom entrance.

'Stay here and watch the house,' I whispered. 'I'm going to recce the road. Back in an hour. If there's any development, call me on the radio. If there's a big drama, rendezvous back on the bank outside the wire. OK?'

Sasha nodded, and I slipped away down the slope, keeping off the road but following its line in and out through half a dozen hairpin bends. There'd be no problem about blocking it: in at least three places it came through narrow defiles where the rock had been blasted away; a single vehicle brought to a halt would stop everything coming up. A couple of guys with gympis on the high ground nearby would be able to sort any number of defenders.

At the bottom I came across the guardroom and barrack block that the satellite had seen: low, solid-looking, single-storey structures either side of the weldmesh entrance gates, with several cars and small trucks parked outside. As I watched from above, I saw the guy who'd come past us along the fence return to base, shut his dog into a kennel beside the guardroom and disappear into the building. I checked the time: 4.20. That looked like the end of the night patrol. As I watched, I began to suspect that the reports we'd heard about Akula's private army being a couple of hundred strong must be grossly exaggerated. I reckoned the accommodation below me might house a couple of dozen men at most – so, unless more were billeted somewhere off-site, we were up against a pretty small force.

I climbed back a bit, crossed the road and made my way up the eastern side of the compound. There was nothing of interest until, through the trees, I saw the line of a roof above me. This had to be the separate structure identified from satellite imagery, the building in which the trackers reckoned Orange had been housed, maybe a hundred metres east of the villa.

I circled out to the right and came in above it: a rectangular storage shed with no windows and a corrugated roof of what looked like asbestos. I felt my heart speed up. Radio signals would pass straight through that roof. Without any real evidence, I became convinced that the bomb was there. 'The Mafiosi are nervous of the device,' I told myself. 'They don't want it inside the house, so they've put it here.'

Behind the shed was a big heap of what looked like freshly excavated rock. Maybe that was spoil from the nuclear shelter they were digging out of the mountainside. Maybe the shed covered the entrance to the bunker.

To complete my anti-clockwise circuit I had to cross the mountainside above the villa, and it was up there, a couple of hundred feet higher than the house, that I came across the helicopter pad – a circle of concrete in the middle of a shallow natural bowl, from which the trees had been cleared. I could see at once that it was big enough to accommodate a Chinook, but not until I was moving away from the centre did I realise what was positioned on one side. From a distance the object looked like a crumpled garden hut. Creeping up to it, I saw that a tarpaulin was lashed down to rings set in the ground. Close inspection revealed a .50 machine gun, set up on a heavy tripod so it could engage targets in the air as well as on the ground. I felt under the cover and ran a hand down the barrel, thinking that the bastards probably had hand-held SAM systems as well.

Sasha had no action to report, so together we pulled off to a safe distance from the villa and settled in a hollow surrounded by rocks from which I could transmit without fear of anyone hearing.

By now the moon was down, and the night had become much darker. As I assembled the Satcom aerial I said, 'Sasha – I'm working on the plan for tomorrow. I'm going to call for the HALO troop to drop in as soon as it's dark. But during the day I reckon we'll want to watch both the house and another building I've seen on the far side, over there. That means we need to man two separate OPs. You all right on that one?'

'No problem. Many times I do such observation.'

'Good. We'll have radio comms with each other, anyway. Now – let's get this thing working.'

I had the Satcom set up on a flat rock, and now turned it a couple of times until I got a strong satellite signal. Then I draped my sleeping bag over my head to muffle the sound of my voice, and seconds later I was through to the squadron base in Kars.

'Blue,' said a voice I didn't recognise.

'Red here,' I went. 'Can I speak to Bill Chandler?'

'Roger. Wait one.'

I waited, imagining the hangar, guys in sleeping bags around the perimeter, and the squadron CO with his head down in some reasonably secluded corner.

'Geordie?' He sounded lively enough. 'How goes it?'

'Fine. No problems.'

'Where are you?'

'Inside the compound. We've got eyes on the villa. We're maybe a hundred and fifty metres above it.'

'Any sign of our guys?'

'Not yet.'

'Or of the three heavy cases?'

'No, but I think I know where they are.'

'Can you identify the site?'

'Not now.'

'In the summerhouse?'

'Yes. Listen, the drop was spot-on. We've recced as much as we can in the dark. As soon as it's light I'll shoot some footage with the video, get pictures back to you. But basically the plan holds.'

'So . . .' He paused, evidently looking at his notes. 'The same DZ?'

'Yep. It's an ideal place. Looks like a summer pasture. Nobody within miles. I'll get myself up there with a Firefly to guide the lads in.'

'OK, then. We're aiming to drop at 1900 your time. That's half an hour after full dark.'

'Can you make that 1930? I'll need time to get up to the DZ, and I don't want to move in daylight.'

'OK. 1930 it is. That's confirmed.'

'Great. Obviously Pat will want to work out his own plan. But as I see it there are three objectives: first is to cut the road coming up from the barracks at the bottom; second is to secure the summerhouse, third to hit the villa.'

'Roger. How many in the garrison?'

'Very few. Could be twenty. Nothing like the rumours. But they've got a fucking great machine gun set up beside the helipad, and I'm sure there are guys we haven't seen yet inside the house.'

'OK. How's the rest of the garrison deployed?'

'By the time we got here they were all in their pits, bar one.'
I told Bill about the sentry patrolling the perimeter, but said we
hadn't seen anyone inside the wire.

'Is the helipad big enough for a Chinook to land?'

'Definitely. But we'll have to take out that five-oh first.
What's the position on the exfil?'

'I think it's going to be possible from the north. Your Russian
friends are playing ball. It looks as though we'll be able to get
the choppers up to a place called Nalchik. Then they can hop
over the mountain when they're needed, and come back out the
same way. They'll be in and out of Chechnya air-space in a few
minutes. The only thing is, the met looks a bit dodgy. There's
a depression moving up from the south.'

FIFTEEN

It was at 11.30 the next morning that things suddenly started to move. Sasha and I had both made secure OPs, buried under piles of pine boughs about 400 metres apart. Once I'd left him with a good view down to the front of the villa, I moved on round and found a site that commanded not only the summerhouse but also the exit road. There, lulled by an intoxicating smell of fresh resin, I'd crawled into my sleeping bag for warmth, and dozed off for the last hour before dawn.

We'd put our covert radios on listening watch, and agreed that from 0700 we'd come up on the air to compare notes on the hour and half-hour – unless we wanted to alert each other at any other time, in which case we'd give a double jab on the pressel.

At first we hadn't much to report. Sasha told me that a couple more cars drove up to the villa, and one went down. Work started on the fence. I couldn't see the site, but when I heard an old tractor spluttering up and down and men chatting quite close behind me, to my right, I thanked my stars that we hadn't cut the wire.

Once again the weather was fine, but I sensed a change coming. Soon after dawn the sky began to haze over and the air moistened, as if snow was on the way. My priority task was to get video footage of the villa and send it back to Kars, so that the guys would have extra information to back up the satellite imagery and could start working out their assault plan. Now I reckoned I'd better go pretty soon, before the landscape got blotted out.

Breakfast consisted of slimy, cold lasagne which came out of its foil bag tasting of mud, and cold water that tasted of plastic. With that feast down my neck I slipped out of my hide, taking my 203 with spare mags in my pouches, but leaving my bergen, to give myself greater mobility.

The mountainside was so broken by gullies, rocky outcrops and stands of trees that I found it easy to keep in dead ground, hidden from the wire above me on one side, and the villa below on the other. Not that I didn't keep a sharp lookout: before I crossed any open space I scanned repeatedly with my binos in case sentries were posted on vantage points.

I filmed the helipad on my way past, hoping that shots of the .50 mounted on its tripod would give an idea of scale, and came out on a high point above Sasha's LUP. Lying face-down on a rock under some trees, I got good footage of the house, first the front, then the western side with its underground door – making sure I kept each take long enough for members of the QRF to spot detail. I zoomed in for close-up shots of the security cameras and IR devices, then filmed the road going down towards the barracks and the gate. I contemplated going down and taking in the barracks as well, but decided that any extra information I might gain wouldn't be worth the risks involved. My gut feeling told me it was the villa and the summerhouse that we were going to assault. With any luck we wouldn't need to go near the barracks: we'd just block the road to anyone trying to come uphill.

By 9.00 a.m. I was back in my own OP, having filmed the summerhouse as well. My scramble around the mountainside had got me well warmed up and my fingers were nimble when it came to down-loading information from the camera into my lap-top and sending it up via the Satcom to the squadron at Kars.

Within five minutes Bill Chandler came on air to say that the quality of the pictures was excellent. He also confirmed that Orange was still transmitting from the same site, and that we had definite permission to exfil via the Russian Caucasus.

It wasn't until 11.20 that things started to happen. I got a sudden *tsch, tsch* in my earpiece, and there was Sasha, fired up.

'Beeg development!' he went. 'I have seen your men.'

'Our lads?'

'Yes. They came from lower house into upper house.'

'Out of the basement entrance?'

'Yes. Four guards bring them.'

'How did they look?'

'Bad. Zheordie, I am afraid they are smashed up.'

'What did you see?'

'The big man, Pavarotti – his eyes are black. The small one has clothes on his hands.'

'Clothes? Bandages?'

'Bandages. Yes.'

'Where did the guards take them, Sasha?'

'Inside the house. Upstairs.'

'The ground-floor entrance – main door?'

'Yes.'

'OK. Thanks. Keep watching.'

I went straight through to Kars and relayed Sasha's information. Anger ran through me as I lay under my heap of pine branches. My first thought was to take the pressure off our guys by creating a diversion. A 203 grenade into one of the villa's windows would stir things up, all right. Sasha and I could drop quite a few of the home team if they came running out of the house. But a premature attack by just the two of us could well panic the Chechens and make them top their prisoners.

I spoke to Bill again and suggested what I'd been thinking.

'No go, Geordie,' he replied. 'For Christ's sake take it easy. It's great to know the guys are there, but until we've got the bomb secure, the plan must hold. They have to stick it out, and so have you.'

Fuck them all, I thought savagely as I switched off. When it comes to the crunch, all senior ruperts are unfeeling bastards who don't give a stuff about losing guys.

I lay there feeling furious, but not for long.

The next development was almost worse. Shortly before 12.00 I became aware of a drone, faint at first but rapidly growing louder. Chopper, I thought. Then I caught the fluttering beat of a rotor, and a few moments later the thing came swishing and roaring so low overhead that its downdraught made the roof of my OP thrash about, and I had to seize hold of some branches to stop them being blown away.

For perhaps a minute the roar persisted, as the pilot came in to land on the helipad. Then he shut his engine down and the noise fell away to a dying whine.

Sasha was already on the air. 'Zheordie – helicopter in.'

'Yeah. Did you see what sort?'

'Small civilian, passenger aircraft. Three to four persons.'

I knew Sasha couldn't see the pad from where he was, but he would get a look at the incoming party if the people walked the few yards down to the villa.

'They'll probably come down to the house,' I told him. 'Stay on the air and let me know.'

'*Prinyato.*'

A couple of minutes later he said, 'Now they are coming. Three men. I think one is Akula. I recognise . . . Yes, definitely this is Shark.'

'What are they doing?'

'They are coming to the door. Door opens in front. Inside house now. Zheordie?'

'Yes?'

'I notice something. When they were five metres distant, door open *avtomaticheskii*. And why? Some persons inside are watching with cameras.'

'That's right. They've got closed-circuit TV. I filmed the cameras.'

My mind was racing. Had the prisoners been taken upstairs for another session of interrogation, this time by Shark himself? Had he brought some ace torturer with him, or maybe a nuclear expert, to find out the truth about the bomb?

I reported the arrival of the chopper to Bill Chandler. 'It could be set to lift our guys out,' I warned him. 'Or the bomb. Is there any way the Yanks can track a helicopter if it takes off from here?'

'I'll ask,' he said. 'I'll pass the message through. You'll tell us if it does move.'

'Of course. What about binning the HALO and bringing the QRF in earlier by chopper?'

'Not a chance.' Bill was adamant. 'We still don't have clearance to fly in Russian airspace. Besides, we need the element of surprise. Our information from Colonel Gerasimova in Moscow is that the defence force is bigger than you think. There's a bigger barracks down the valley with a hundred or more in it. Plus any local guys they can muster.'

'Is that right?'

'Yep. And listen, Geordie, the colonel's done us another favour. She got on to Kelsen, the firm of Finnish architects who built the villa, and faxed us the plans.'

'Oh, great!' I said.

'There's a basement floor,' Bill went on. 'That's got gym, games room, sauna, showers and so on. Then, below that, there's another floor, a kind of sub-basement, marked "Storage". That tallies well with the pictures you sent.'

'*Tochno*,' I went, thinking of Sasha with his eyes on the building and unconsciously slipping into Russian. 'Exactly. That's where they brought our guys out of, that lower door. I reckon that's where they're being kept. When the assault goes in, we're going to need to hit that door first. Wait a minute, though. There must be some internal access from the store area to the upper floor. Isn't anything marked on the plan – a staircase or a lift?'

'There's a lift-shaft, yes.'

'Maybe the lift's knackered. Or maybe it hasn't been installed yet. Plan round taking out that lower door, anyway.'

Shortly before 12.30 Sasha buzzed me up again. Toad and Pavarotti had been taken back underground, looking even worse than before. Pav was walking with a limp, and there was blood showing through the bandages on Toad's hands.

Bastards! I said to myself. Just wait till we get in among them. Bill Chandler had already told me, 'No hostages.' Now, after what Sasha had seen, I was going to feel no compunction about taking out everyone in the villa.

★

259

The sun never came out that day. The haze of cloud thickened steadily, and early in the afternoon snow began to fall. My problem was exhaustion. I fought it as hard as I could, but I know that I nodded off several times – and when I suddenly came to, just before 3.00 p.m., I couldn't remember where I was. Then, as I moved, snow slid off the flap of my sleeping bag and on to my face. I rolled over on to my front and looked out. Snow was falling hard – a real blizzard, fine flakes slanting in towards me from my right front. The weather was coming from the south-west, from the high mountains.

When I scanned the summerhouse through my binoculars, I saw that a white blanket of snow lay unmarked all round it. Nothing doing there.

I knew that the helicopter hadn't taken off: for one thing, I'd have heard it go; for another, it would never fly in this weather. So Shark must still be in residence. Little did he realise that his time was rapidly running out.

Or was it? A new fear began to needle me. If this weather kept up, with its heavy cloud cover, the HALO jump might have to be postponed. Snow on the ground wouldn't matter – in fact it would make the DZ show up all the better, white in the middle of the black wood – but snow clouds in the air were another matter. I'd better report the conditions to the FMB.

When I tried to go through to Kars, my anxiety rose a notch. No response. I suspected the blizzard was to blame, and that the snow was blocking contact with the satellite. Comms are notoriously fickle. They go up and down, and often there seems no reason. I fiddled with the dish aerial, turning it this way and that, and then moved out of my lair on to a more prominent site. Still no contact. I tried again and again, to no avail.

Lying on my front, I realised how the snow was blotting out every sound. Work on the fence, which had been proceeding intermittently, seemed to have stopped completely, and a heavy silence lay over the compound.

Then I heard a noise of an engine, labouring up the hill from the barrack area. Presently it came into view – a mid-grey, square-bodied truck with big snow tyres, weaving slightly as it slithered over the snow. The driver swung up on to the flat area outside the summerhouse, crunched into reverse and backed to within two or three yards of the doors.

He and another man jumped out, and one of them opened the truck's rear door to release a third. All were wearing dark green overalls and brown fur caps with ear-flaps tied up over the crowns. The driver produced some keys, unlocked the doors of the shed and slid them back. A minute later, out came all three, lugging, between them, one of the components of Orange.

Snow or no snow, there was no chance of me making a mistake – the men were only sixty metres from me, and through the glasses I could see those orange markings perfectly. The sight set my adrenalin racing. Again I had to fight down my instinct to make a direct intervention. A 203 grenade into the front of the van would rearrange Akula's plans pretty swiftly. But, again, that might mean the end for Pav and Toad.

The three men went back in and brought out the second half. I snatched up the Satcom receiver and switched on. Nothing. Again – nothing.

Shit! The bomb was about to disappear, and I couldn't report it.

The men locked the shed, slammed the doors of their truck and climbed aboard. I watched helplessly as the driver started up and drove off downhill, nosing his way carefully through the bends. By now the snow was falling so fast that, even as I watched, the vehicle's tracks were becoming blurred. In a few minutes they'd be obliterated altogether.

In spite of my anxiety, I realised that what had happened carried one small advantage: now, if the HALO drop did come in as planned, Sasha wouldn't see the bomb, and wouldn't know anything about it.

The next hour was one of the most miserable I'd ever known. I spent it shitting bricks that the head-shed might call off the free-fall. They might decide to leave Sasha and me to try and spring the prisoners. I could just hear Bill saying, 'Make your own way out as best you can.' Fucking thanks, I thought. I kept reasoning, No, they can't do that – they'd be four guys down

261

rather than two. But for all my wishful thinking I couldn't be sure.

As the snow kept floating down in a dense pall, I speculated about where the bomb might be heading. Back to Moscow, I felt certain. What if the Chechens used it to threaten the Russian government, just as the Americans had been planning to do? What an irony that would be.

I convinced myself that the blizzard was going to continue all day and all night, and that Akula's men had come up to move the bomb while they still could, before everyone got snowed in.

At last the snowflakes began to thin, and the sky lightened as the storm moved on towards the north-east. I waited till I could see a patch of blue sky among the clouds, then tried the Satcom again.

This time, thank God, the call went straight through.

'Bill,' I exclaimed. 'They've moved the fucker!'

'I know. Where the hell have you been?'

'Nowhere,' I told him. 'The comms went down in a snow-storm.'

'I see. Well, the device has been on the move.'

'I was trying to tell you that. Some guys came and carried off the components in a truck. Bill – how far's Grozny from here?'

'Fifty ks. That's where it's gone. The Yanks have tracked it that far.'

'The damned thing'll be airborne by now,' I said. 'If it's gone off the air again it means it's inside a plane. What do we do?'

'Wait one.'

I held on, hearing nothing but a roar of static. Then Bill came back and said, 'We're going ahead with the drop, weather permitting. We're just waiting for the latest forecast.'

'The sky's clearing here,' I told him. 'It's bloody cold, too.'

'OK, Geordie. I'll come back to you in a minute.'

I waited tensely, longing for the hit to be over and done with. 'Let's just grab our guys,' I said to myself, 'and get out of this arsehole of a place.'

Then Bill came through again. The forecast was good: clear skies behind the storm, and a hard frost. The plan remained on.

What was more, they'd decided to advance the drop by half an hour, moving it to the original time of 1900. The two Chinooks were on their way to Nalchik, and would sit there waiting to hop over the mountain as soon as they were summoned.

'We passed all your data to the RAF,' Bill said. 'They've done an appreciation and decided to approach you from the north, down the slope. They don't fancy coming up the valley and over the compound entrance.'

At 5.30 I gave my pressel a double jab and said, 'OK, Sasha. I'm on the move. We're off to the DZ. I'll come round and pick you up. Stay still till I reach you.'

'I wait.'

Stars blazed overhead, and even though the moon hadn't risen yet the night was alarmingly bright, the snow reflecting all the remaining light from the frosty sky. This white blanket was something we hadn't planned for: the patterns on my DPMs were clearly visible, and I could have done with a snow overall.

Moving cautiously, and keeping to bare rock ridges as much as possible so that I didn't leave a continous trail, I worked my way round to the helipad. Sure enough, the chopper was still on the ground – an Alouette, painted some light colour, its rotor blades drooping under a three-inch load of snow. If it remained in position there'd be nowhere for a Chinook to land. No matter – the hostage recovery team could fast-rope down while the aircraft hovered. Then, if we couldn't shift the Alouette, we might have to exfil from the DZ in the forest.

I found Sasha ready to move. Instead of heading out to the left, in the direction of the DZ, we put in a bit of a detour and made our way straight up to the top fence, which was still unfinished. After watching for a couple of minutes we climbed the wire at a point where the wind had blown the snow off a rocky spine, leaving no tracks on the inside. The outside was a different matter. We landed in what turned out to be a gully, filled with snow to a depth of a couple of feet, and we couldn't help churning up the surface as we floundered out of the drift. I snatched up a pine branch and frisked it back and forth behind us, levelling the surface as best I could; but the moonlight was so bright that a trail still showed.

There was no time to mess about. Clear of the fence, we turned left, to the west, through the forest, and again followed the contour. Navigation was simple: I knew that if we held our height, we'd come out on the farm track that led up from the valley to the high hayfield.

Except when we brushed into tree branches, our progress was utterly silent: the dry snow lay like six inches of the softest powder, and our boots made not the slightest sound as they pushed through it.

We reached the track at 6.40 and stopped to listen. Twenty minutes in hand. Suddenly, into the silence, floated a wolf chorus, coming from much farther off than the howling the night before. Turning to look behind me, I saw that the moon had appeared over the eastern horizon, enormous and pale. For maybe a minute the distant, eerie wailing rose and fell. Then it died away.

We moved downhill until we came to the junction and the path that led to the hayfield. It crossed my mind that perhaps, for maximum security, we should continue to push our way through the trees, rather than use the track. But then I thought, To hell with it. There's nobody about. Let's just get there.

By 6.50 we were on the edge of the field, which glowed brilliant white in the moonlight.

'They'll see this, all right, when they jump,' I whispered.

Sasha nodded. I saw him swallow, and sensed that he was just as hepped up as I was.

'I've told them this is the forming-up point, by the old wagon,' I said quietly. 'You stay here, just in case anyone's been following us up. Keep back against that tree-trunk, in the shadow. As soon as I've collected everyone I'll bring them over. OK?'

'*Da, da.*' Sasha nodded vigorously, then said, 'Good luck!'

I punched him on the arm and moved away, skirting the edge of the field to keep in shadow. At 6.55 I stopped to wait, half-way up the long side, and stared to the south-east, way out among those millions of stars. I knew the Herc would be coming on the same path we'd used, flying at 28,000 feet. I also knew that I'd never see it or even hear it. All the same, I couldn't help searching for it in that phenomenal sky. I imagined the tailgate descending, the red warning lights, the guys lined up, three abreast, packed tightly together and laden with all their gear, toddling towards the lip at the back of the cabin floor with good old Pat Newman overseeing.

A minute to go. Maybe the plane was late. No – the SF air crews could hack it to the second. In that case, the Herc must be almost overhead.

I walked out a few metres into the field and stood in the open, feeling very exposed. Twenty seconds to run . . . ten . . . five, four, three, two, one. P Hour.

Now – where were they?

I found I was holding my breath, and had to make a conscious effort to relax. Were the lads on their way? It was almost impossible to believe that twenty bodies were hurtling down towards me at terminal velocity, a thousand feet every five seconds. Twenty-four thousand feet in two minutes. Then the chutes would deploy at 4,000 feet . . .

I counted the seconds, staring upwards, with the Firefly in my right hand. Then at last I heard the magic sound I'd been waiting for: the sudden, rattling, snapping flutter of a chute breaking out. It came from high in front of me, and was quickly followed by another, and another, four, five . . . then several all at once. Holding the Firefly above my head, I punched the rubber button on the base and saw a brilliant flash bounce off the snow.

In the enormous silence of the mountains the thin electronic whine of the unit building up to its next discharge sounded like a jet engine. *Flash* went the light again – and then suddenly in my earpiece there was Pat Newman's voice saying, 'OK, Geordie, I've got you. Close it down. I'm coming in.'

A moment later I saw the angular black shapes of the parachutes gliding across the stars like a formation of giant bats. In the last few seconds I heard the rush of air spilling from the canopies: then suddenly men in pairs were touching down all round me.

Brilliant! I thought – but at that instant, away to my left, a dog began to bark hysterically. The noise was coming from inside the trees, just beyond the old hay cart. I jabbed my pressel switch twice and listened for Sasha to come up on the air.

Nothing.

I jabbed again. The dog was still barking. One of the incoming figures had disengaged from its partner and was coming towards me. I recognised Pat from his rolling walk.

'Get in! Get in!' I hissed. 'That bloody dog.'

Even as I was talking the barking ceased.

The lads didn't need telling. Pat had briefed them already, and in any case their instincts and training made them head straight for the dark edge of the pines, dragging their chutes behind them.

In the shadows, Pat had a quick head count.

'We're OK,' he said. 'We're on. What's the crack?'

'Not sure. See that old wagon on the edge of the field? I left Sasha there. That's our forming-up area. It sounded as though he had a contact. Wait one.'

Two more jabs on the pressel. Still no answer. All round me there was a general scrabbling and scrunching as people rolled up their chutes, and a rattle of working parts as they readied their weapons.

'Whatever's happened, we've got to go that way,' I told Pat.

'OK,' he said quickly. 'Us two'll move up and check it out.'

In the lead, I advanced with my 203 at the ready, every sense on full alert, with Pat ten metres behind me. Our boots, cushioned by the snow, were making no sound, but I knew we'd show up as black silhouettes every time we passed an open area.

At the corner of the field I stopped to scan with the kite-sight. Nothing moved, and I'd just started again when my earpiece hissed twice.

'Sasha?'

'*Da.*'

266

'Where are you?'

'Same place.'

'What happened?'

'One man came after.'

'Where's he gone?'

'I keell him.'

'What about the dog?'

'I keell dog also.'

'OK. We're closing on you now.'

'*Prinyato.*'

'The guys can come up,' I told Pat. 'There's a cache here for the chutes.'

While the rest of the lads came up I moved on, and was right beside Sasha before I saw him, standing against the trunk of a big pine. The snow on the track beside him was spattered with black-looking stains, which I realised must be blood.

'You OK?'

'Sure.'

'What happened?'

'I am waiting here. The man comes past. I shoot him with knife gun.'

'Where's the body?'

'Here.' Sasha pointed behind him at a dark heap beside the tree.

'And the dog?'

'Same place. Knife also.'

'Was it that German Shepherd that came along the perimeter wire last night?'

'I think.'

I turned to Pat and said, 'No point in trying to hide the bodies. We need to get in and out fast before anyone comes looking. But there's a well here we can dump the chutes in.'

'OK,' said Pat. 'Let's go.'

We bundled the chutes down the old water tank, threw snow over the cover and hustled on.

I went as fast as I dared, trying to combine speed of advance with maximum alertness. The snow helped by deadening our

267

footsteps, but all the way I was thinking that the surface of the field behind us must look as though a football match had taken place.

We came to the wire at the point where Sasha and I had lain to observe the barrier.

'This is it,' I told Pat. 'Once we're over, we'll be on target in less than a minute.'

'We need to tell base we're on our objective,' he whispered. 'They'll get the Chinooks airborne right away.'

'OK.'

I waited as he quickly set up his Satcom and reported his position.

How long would it have taken for the sentry to make a normal circuit of the fence? How soon would his failure to return be noticed? We had a few minutes yet.

With the set back in Pat's bergen, we went up to climb the wire. Over the fence and hidden in the trees again, we held a quick O-group.

'Now that the device has gone,' Pat began, 'that's knocked out one of our objectives. The summerhouse is no longer relevant. Forget that.

'I've designated three parties. Party A to block the road, Party B to assault the villa, Party C to watch the helipad and prevent any take-off.

'Our objective is to rescue the hostages. But no one else gets out of that building alive. OK?'

He got a few grunts for answer, and went on, 'I've briefed the parties already, Geordie. But for your benefit, Party C consists of two men – these two.' He pointed, but in the dark I couldn't recognise faces. 'Party A, the road, is these three. Two gympis and a sixty-six. That leaves fifteen, counting Sasha. I want to leave two back somewhere to act as sniper-observers. That makes thirteen for the house assault . . .'

Pat had got everything well worked out. I knew he'd laid out plans of the villa, using mine tape, on the floor of the hangar in Kars, and that the team had walked through each phase of the assault. His plan was to keep away from the front of the house

268

altogether, so that we didn't trigger the alarm systems. A basement group would approach from the side and tape a demolition charge to the cellar door. The rear party would do the same to three ground-floor windows at the back.

Split-second timing was essential: the assault had to crack off from both sides simultaneously, and in that first instant one of the snipers would put a 203 grenade through the front door to increase the confusion.

As our ERV, Pat designated the helipad.

We moved out in single file, again at tactical spacing, in an anti-clockwise circle round the target. First stop was the helipad, where we dropped off Party C in good positions among rock bluffs that commanded the pad only thirty metres below them. Next we worked down until we could see the back of the house. Lights were on in most of the windows, but curtains or blinds had been drawn. Some fifty metres above the building we left the main assault group (which included Pat) crouching in the trees.

Round at the side I dropped off the basement group, to wait while I took Party A down to the point I had earmarked on the road. Then I hustled back up, glancing at my watch. The time was just before 8.30.

On the covert radio link I reported to Pat: 'All groups in position.'

'Roger,' he went. 'The assault will go down in figures three minutes. Move on to target at one minute before zero.'

By now the moon was well up, its light filtering through the fir branches. Beside me was Paul Anderson, an EMOE specialist, who was going to blow the door. As we crouched there, waiting, I realised that our breath was steaming in the air. For the past couple of hours I'd been so absorbed that I hadn't noticed the cold.

'Two minutes,' came Pat's voice.

I was hoping to hell the raid would give us some clue about where the bomb had been taken. Maybe we'd find messages, papers, tapes . . .

Suddenly Jim Taylor, leader of Party A, came on the air.

'Stand by,' he said. 'There's a vehicle coming up the road at high revs. What do we do? Hit it?'

'Roger,' Pat answered instantly. 'Take it out. Other groups, close on target *now*!'

We burst out of the trees and ran towards the basement door. In seconds Paul had taped a line of det cord straight down the middle. We stood back, flattening ourselves against the wall.

'Thirty seconds,' came Pat's voice. But before he could carry on the countdown the howl of an electronic alarm broke out from the front of the villa and wound up to a scream. At almost the same instant a brilliant flash split the night, and the thump of a 66 rocket exploding thundered up the mountainside, followed by the rattle of machine guns as Party A engaged the car.

'Go! Go! Go!' Pat screamed.

I turned my head away as Paul closed his clacker.

BOOM!

The door split in half and we pushed through the gap. As I went in I heard more rounds going down in the road-block.

The space inside was full of smoke or dust. Clouds of the stuff caught our torch beams and made it hard to see what there was in the room. Answer – nothing. Bare concrete block walls, bare cement floor, the room empty.

Another door at the back, steel, locked. It took Paul only seconds to make up another charge. Again we stood to one side. *BANG!* In the confined space, the shock buffeted us.

The second door swung open. Dust problems again. But this time through the haze I saw tubular steel storage shelves along one wall. On the floor at the foot of them was a long, dark heap. As my torch beam came on to it, part of the heap moved.

'Pav!' I yelled. 'Keep still! You're OK.'

In a flash I was kneeling in front of him. He and Toad were lying on their sides, head to head, their hands, behind backs, cuffed to the feet of the metal shelving. At first glance I thought Toad was dead – his eyes were shut and his face was white as chalk. When I put a hand on his cheek he felt as cold as a corpse. But at the touch his eyelids flickered.

One of the lads had bolt-cutters in his belt kit. 'Give us a light

270

while I cut these fucking chains!' I shouted. I needn't have yelled, because a torch came on right beside me – but my adrenalin was up and running.

'OK,' Paul said calmly, holding the light.

Leaning over, I saw that Toad's hands were covered with filthy bandages, and that blood had seeped out of them and on to the floor. A couple of crunching snips cut though the chain and released him. Another severed the link between his cuffs. As his hands came free he gave a groan and tried to straighten his arms, but otherwise made no movement.

Pav wasn't in quite such a bad way. He, too, felt cold as death, and his face was a mess, but when I released his hands he brought his arms to the front of his body and curled up like a child.

I hit my pressel switch and called, 'Pat?'

There was a moment's pause. Then, as he answered, his voice was almost drowned by a burst of small-arms fire.

'We've found the hostages,' I went. 'In the basement. We're going to evacuate them into the trees.'

'Roger,' he answered. 'Carry on, and call in the choppers. We're clearing the upper floors.'

'Hypothermia,' Paul was saying. 'Both of them are in a bad way.'

Mentally, I was torn in two. One half of me wanted to stay with my injured mates and see them to safety. The other was burning to get up into the villa in search of Shark and grill him about where he'd sent the bomb.

I glanced round. Apart from me, there were five guys in the group: four to carry each casualty and one to cover them.

'Get them out under the trees to start with,' I said. 'I'm going upstairs. See you in a minute.'

In the far corner of the store-room was a wooden door. A burst from the 203 shot hell out of the lock, and I ran up a bare concrete staircase; knowing that I should wait for back-up but driven on by pure aggression.

Another locked door, another burst.

I erupted into a large and brilliantly lit open area – the

271

recreation floor, with a sauna room, exercise machines and a fair-sized pool, a small swimming pool or a king-size jacuzzi. There was pale wood everywhere, on the floor, the walls and the doors of the sauna and the cubicles. The change in temperature was phenomenal: in one step I'd gone from zero to tropical.

Somebody had been in the pool until a few seconds before. The water was still moving, and a trail of wet footmarks led to one of the cubicles. The door was closed, but beneath it I could see a pair of feet.

Rounds were still going down on the upper floors. Then a heavy explosion crashed off.

'Come out!' I yelled. 'Get out of there!'

I stood off a few feet with my weapon levelled. 'Come out or I shoot.'

The door opened. Out came a man in a white towelling bath robe. From his long, narrow face I knew instantly that this was Akula. His black hair was slicked down with water and his eyes were wide open with fright or surprise. His movements were quite slow and perfectly controlled.

He said something in Russian, or possibly in Chechnyan. I didn't understand it and barked back, 'Speak English, you bastard. I know you can.'

'Who are you?' he demanded.

'Never mind that. I want to know where you've sent the bomb.'

'The bomb? What bomb? I don't understand.'

His right hand was moving up towards a pocket at waist height on the front of his robe.

'Keep still!' I shouted. 'Hands up.'

He raised them reluctantly.

I went forward and jabbed the muzzle of the 203 into his breastbone so hard that he crashed down on his arse.

'Get your hands above your head!' I shouted.

He lay on his back, arms up, while I felt in the pockets of his robe. My fingers closed on a small pistol. I brought it out, glanced briefly at it, and saw that it was covered in gold engraving. I slipped it in my pocket and repeated my question, standing over him with the 203 pointing down at his chest.

'Listen,' I said. 'I know who you are. You are Akula, the Shark. What have you done with the device?'

'I tell you, I have no device.'

'Don't fucking lie to me!' I shouted. 'Or I'll blow your bloody head off.'

That seemed to change his mind. 'You are too late,' he said. 'The device is not here.'

'I know. I'm asking where you've sent it.'

'You are American, yes?' There was a hint of mockery in his voice, of condescension.

'It doesn't matter what I am.'

'Well – you should send message to British Government.'

'Yes?'

'Tell them, release the Chechen men they have arrested.'

'What Chechen men?'

'Twelve persons.'

'What have they done?'

'Nothing. But the police arrested them. Unless they are free, London will be sorry.'

'What are you saying?'

'Only that. London will regret.'

'You mean you've sent the bomb to London?'

I was so hyped up by the thought that Orange was going to be used against us that, without any conscious decision, I fired a burst into the floor beside the Shark's right leg, then another that hit him in the thigh. As the rounds struck, he gave a convulsive jerk, then began to writhe around on his side, blood flowing out fast over the birch floor.

All at once there was a commotion at the far end of the room. A door flew open. As I looked in that direction, Akula tried to take advantage of the diversion and began dragging himself away along the edge of the pool. In a split-second I took in the fact that the newcomer was Sasha, who dashed in with his Gepard levelled. Before I could move or speak he'd opened up with three short bursts. The first missed, but the second caught the Shark full in the flank. As he rocked on his hands and knees, the third raked him again and toppled him sideways into the pool.

Behind me, from the changing cubicle he'd been in, came a sudden noise and movement and the door flew open. Out burst a young blonde woman, stark naked, holding a pistol in her right hand.

Before she could pull the trigger, Sasha cut her down with a burst into her back from point-blank range.

He was on a total high, uncontrollably violent, half mad. He fired two more bursts into the ceiling, splintering the planks, and rushed up to me with a triumphant roar of 'ZHEORDIE! WE KEELL THEM ALL!'

With a couple of bounds he reached the edge of the pool. The man's body was half-floating, face-down in the water, feet on the bottom. Blood had flooded out all round it, staining the water, dark red close in, paler farther out.

'Akula in the water!' Sasha shouted. 'Breelliant! We make him kneel! We make him swim!' Again he let drive a burst into the body, causing it to bob violently up and down.

Men came pounding into the room. Our guys. One, two, three.

'Out!' yelled one of them. 'The place is on fire. Gotta go downwards.'

'Here!' I pointed towards the door.

All five of us flew down the concrete stairs and through the wooden door. The inner store-room was empty. The hostages had gone.

Outside, the impact of frosty air cooled all of us down. I realised I'd been on just as vicious a high as Sasha.

As we drew away from the building and up the hill, we could see flames raging inside the ground-floor windows. Then a great tongue of fire burst out of the roof. Out of breath, I got down on one knee, jabbed my pressel and called, 'Pat?'

'Yes?'

'Geordie here. I'm east of the building. Where are you?'

'Straight above the villa. The Chinooks are coming in.'

274

'Great. Is there a medic on board?'

'Should be. I asked for one.'

'The hostages are in a bad way.'

'OK. RV on the helipad, soonest.'

'Roger.'

We started through the trees, but we'd only gone a few yards when another explosion burst out above us. I heard later that the guys in Party C saw somebody sneak up into the cockpit of the Alouette, so they put a 66 rocket into its fuel tank.

The fireball lit up the trees all around. By the time we reached the scene the chopper was blazing from end to end. There was no chance of shifting the wreck quickly.

Over the radio I heard Pat call the Chinook captain and re-direct him to the LZ in the forest.

By now some of our guys had wrapped Pav and Toad in space blankets and sleeping bags and lashed them into nylon stretchers. There followed a desperate struggle, as relays of us carried them along the rough mountainside, bundled them over the wire and lugged them away through the forest.

Towards the end we could hear the Chinooks circling. Then rounds began to go down behind us and bullets came cracking through the trees.

By the time we reached the edge of the field we were sweating like pigs. One man, in the lead, ran out and shone a torch to bring the first Chinook in. At the same moment I heard Pat calling the second to put down an airstrike.

'Into the trees!' he was shouting. 'One hundred metres west of the LZ. One hundred metres and farther.'

The air was full of the heavy, thudding beat of big rotors. Through that came the violent racket of a chain-gun, putting down rounds at an incredible speed, making a noise almost like a chainsaw.

The next thing I knew, one chopper was coming in. The pilot put his nose down right on the torch. A storm of snow was thrashed into the air by the downdraught. We ran through it with our burdens, straight up the lowered ramp. Within seconds everyone was on board and counted, and we were lifting away.

Kneeling between the casualties, I got my back to Toad and shouted, 'Pav. It's me – Geordie.'

When he answered, 'Where've you fucking well been, you old bastard?' I knew he was well switched on.

'Pav,' I said. 'What did they do to Toad?'

'Bolt cutters,' he replied. 'One finger at a time.'

'Ah, Jesus! How many's he lost?'

'Dunno. Four maybe.'

'Bloody hell. Listen, what did he tell them about the device?'

'Nothing.'

'Is that right?'

'Absolutely nothing. Toad was bloody brilliant.'

'So they don't know about Apple?'

'Not a whisper.'

'Thank God for that.'

SIXTEEN

We landed back at Lyneham to find a premier-league flap in progress. The Firm had been shitting themselves so badly that they couldn't wait till we reached Hereford before they started grilling me. Two men had been waiting in the airport arrival hall, and within five minutes of touchdown I was speeding westwards in a chauffeur-driven Rover.

The fact that the British Government was in a panic came as no surprise. When the Chinooks had put us down at Krasnodar in the northern Caucasus, we were amazed to find an RAF Tristar sitting on the airfield, waiting to fly us home. So desperate had the situation become that our normal means of transport, a Herc, had been deemed too slow, and the big jet had been diverted from Cyprus to get us back at twice the speed. The result was one of those disorientating flights which end at practically the same time as they start. We'd taken off at 2200, and three and a quarter hours later we'd landed at 2215 local.

During our brief stopover at Krasnodar I'd spoken to Whinger on the Satcom. Naturally he was frantic to know what had happened, and I brought him up to speed. At his end, he said, the team job was staggering on.

'I was hoping to come straight back and rejoin you,' I told him, 'but I'm off to the UK for a debrief first. Nobody's sure where the Chechens have taken Orange. London looks the most likely. As soon as the dust settles, I'll get my arse back to Balashika as fast as I can.'

'Speak to you soon,' replied Whinger laconically.

Back in England, scene after scene played through my mind

as we headed westwards through the night: the chutes of the free-fallers coming in like bats out of the starry sky; the Chechens humping away the components of Orange during the snowstorm; Akula floating face-down in his own pool; the blaze from the villa lighting up the snow on the mountainside with a huge, ruddy glow.

My trouble in the debrief was that I'd already exhausted my small store of information. Talking to the CO in Hereford via Satcom from the Tristar, I'd already given all the details I could, and now, repeating my conversation with Shark for the benefit of the guys from the Firm, I felt as if the record had got stuck in the same groove.

I sat in the back of the car with one man beside me; the other, in the front, kept screwing round to talk. I could only suppose that the driver had full security clearance.

'Go through it again,' said the guy next to me.

'The whole meeting only lasted a couple of minutes,' I said. 'Akula just said, "You'd better send a message to the British Government."'

'And?'

'That if we didn't release the Chechens who'd been arrested, London would be sorry.'

'Was that all?'

'"London will regret." Those were his words exactly.'

'From which you assumed he was sending Orange to London and planning to detonate it there.'

'That's right,' I agreed. 'Couldn't the Yanks track the plane?'

'By the time they knew what was happening it was too late. There were several planes airborne over the Caucasus. Any of them could have been the one they wanted. The most likely candidate was a privately owned Gulfstream that went to Malta, which is one of the Mafia's overseas strongholds. We think the device may have been transferred to another aircraft there.'

'What about at this end?'

'We've got a watch on all major airports. The difficulty is, a small jet could put down in dozens of different places – on a private strip, anywhere.'

'So you think the bomb may be here already?'

'We've got to assume that.'

'And you can't search the whole of London.'

The man next to me made a wry grimace. Once more I thought of the guys in furry caps, carrying the components out through the snow.

'I should have whacked them while I had the chance,' I said.

'What's that?' The man in front twisted himself yet farther round, and I had to explain all over again.

Then I asked, 'But do they know how to detonate the damned thing? *Can* the device be set off without the SCR?'

'Probably, yes. The Americans say it could be, if somebody's had the right training.'

'Bloody hell!'

'Exactly.'

'This Shark – he didn't give any other clue?'

'He never had a chance. He might have, but Sasha rushed in and dropped him.'

I described how the naked woman had come storming out of the changing cubicle, and how Sasha had drilled her through the back. My companions seemed quite unmoved by the saga: their only reaction was that the front-seat guy opened a briefcase and switched on the interior light to show me some mug shots.

'These are what we got off the disk from Moscow,' he told me. 'Allegedly the Chechen Mafia's first eleven.'

'Well,' I said. 'That's Shark, for a start.' The long face, hollow cheeks and heavy eyebrow were unmistakable.

'That *was* Shark,' I corrected. 'You can eliminate him from your inquiries.'

'What about this one?'

He showed me a photo of an even more cadaverous-looking man, but younger. 'That's the brother, Supyan Gaidar. He calls himself Barrakuda. Anna showed me that photo in Balashika.'

'What about this one?'

The third villain bore a strong resemblance to Sasha, but his face was broader and shorter. I shook my head.

'Any of these guys could have been in the villa,' I said. 'If they

279

were, I doubt if they came out alive. The only one I saw was Shark.'

'But this one,' my neighbour persisted. 'You're sure about him?'

'Definitely Barrakuda. He's pretty much like his elder brother.'

'We believe he's in the UK by now,' said the man in front. 'He was last heard of heading for London.'

In camp the atmosphere was no less frenetic. Everybody from the CO down came at me saying, 'Where have they put it? How do we find Barrakuda?' They seemed to think that because I'd been in Moscow, I must be an expert on the Chechen Mafia. They couldn't take in the fact that I knew nothing about the organisation's London dispositions.

Also, people were naturally worried about the safety of our guys still at Balashika, and kept asking questions about the situation there. All I could say was that, if they stayed inside the camp, they'd be OK.

After an hour's further debrief the boss at last realised that I was out on my feet, and told me to get my head down. He saw that there was nothing further we could do until we got some definite leads. So it was that at 0030 British time, 0330 Moscow time, 0430 Grozny time, and the end of the world by my biological clock, I eventually had a hot shower, lay down in my room in the sergeants' mess and passed out.

The next I knew, someone was shaking my shoulder. 'Get up, Geordie,' a voice was saying. 'On your feet. They've seen him.'

'Who?'

'Barrakuda.'

'Ah, Jesus! Where?'

'Central London. A police surveillance team saw him go into one of the flats they've had staked out.'

I blinked and stared at my watch: 6.15. 'What happened?' I croaked.

'He came in a taxi, carrying a small hold-all.'

280

'OK,' I said. 'I'm with you.'

Tired as I was, I knew I had to go, because I was the only person in England who'd set eyes on Orange.

Half an hour later I was heading back towards the capital, a member of the SP team, kitted out to take part in yet another hit. I knew all the other guys well enough to fit in, and as I'd recently finished commanding an SP team for nine months, we all spoke the same language.

As usual, our orders were unwritten but absolutely clear: our primary task was to recover Orange, but our scarcely less important aim was to silence Barrakuda and anyone found with him. If we got the bomb back and took out the immediate Mafia cell, the whole saga would become deniable. Anything the Chechens might say could be discredited. The operation was to be carried out as quickly as possible.

As our Range Rovers hurtled up the M4 at a steady 100 m.p.h., I noticed that the traffic seemed very light, and realised belatedly that this was Sunday.

In less than two hours we had reached a small warehouse in Notting Hill that had been taken over as a forward mounting base: the wagons drove straight in, out of sight, and the guys tumbled out to get their kit sorted.

By now the Firm had secured plans of the flat that Barrakuda was using. Markham Court was a small red-brick block, dating from the 1930s, in Seymour Place, north of Marble Arch. It belonged to West End Homes, a property company, and in June apartment No. 10 had been taken, fully furnished, on a three-year lease by a firm based in Malta. The area was up-market residential, central and convenient, and in recent years had been heavily infiltrated by Arabs.

The building had only five storeys, and No. 10 was on the top floor. A single lift went up from inside the front door of the building, with a staircase winding round the outside of the shaft. Lift and stairs both gave on to small landings, with two flats on each floor, to right and left. The only other access to each apartment was via a metal fire-escape, which served a back door leading out of the kitchen area.

Only five floors, I thought. The height's no problem. After our sixteen-floor epic in Moscow, this was money for jam in technical terms. The problem was going to be spectators: once explosions started cracking off, people would inevitably assemble to gawp. Still, that was a matter for the police.

The assault was easily planned. There was no need for anything elaborate like an abseil drop off the roof: all we needed was for our Red and Blue teams to arrive at front and back of the building simultaneously and secure the exits. Red would commandeer the lift and at the same time clear the front stairs. Blue would do the same at the back and go up the fire-escape. With the teams co-ordinated by covert radio, we'd blow both doors and storm the flat – the aim being, in the first instance, to overpower the people inside rather than kill anyone and possibly rob ourselves of vital intelligence. Only if we met armed resistance would we use our weapons, and only when the bomb had been found would we get rid of Barrakuda.

On the floor of the warehouse we laid out white mine tape to the exact dimensions of the rooms in the flat, and decided who would clear which. In the building across the street from the target, one startled family had to be evicted from their penthouse so that sniper observers could be installed and listening equipment brought to bear on the windows. Early indications suggested that the flat was occupied by two men.

Meanwhile, a Russian-speaking policeman – a young, dark guy called Michael, who looked more like a student than a police officer – was seconded to Red team, with orders to come up and join us as soon as the flat was secure. Two nuclear technicians from Porton Down were standing by to neutralise Orange, when or if we found it.

At 10.45 a.m. we were ready to roll. Our CO and ops officer were installed alongside the police in a control room set up in Marylebone police station. I knew that at the last minute, before we went in, the CO would take command of the operation by signing the formal order, but that didn't concern us at the sharp end.

The police team who had Markham Court under surveillance

confirmed that nobody had entered or left No. 10 since the arrival of Barrakuda, so we were reasonably confident that we'd find only two men inside.

Red team slipped into the building so easily that we might have been arriving for Sunday morning coffee.

Just as we were debussing a small, heavily veiled Arab woman came out of the block. Funny, I thought, she's just like us, dressed in black from head to foot. She did a big double-take at the sight of us. I thought she was going to dart back inside, but she kept going and walked off along the street.

One of our lads got a foot in the open door, saving us the need to pick or smash the security lock. Then it was three into the lift, two running up the stairs, and the sixth man staying down to guard the entrance.

Outside No 10. I paused till I heard from the commentary in my earpiece that Blue team were in position at the head of the fire-escape. Then I quietly said, 'Placing charge now.' The door had a peep-hole in the centre at head level, but as we'd arrived in total silence the chances that anyone was standing with his eye glued to it seemed exceedingly remote – so I ignored it and went forward to tape the det cord straight down the middle.

With that done, I stood back against the wall, the other guys lined up beyond me.

'Red, all set,' I reported.

'Blue, ready,' came the answer.

'OK then. Stand by . . . stand by . . . GO!'

I closed my clacker. The bang was very sharp and loud in the confines of the little landing, and the front door split in half and caved inwards. I lobbed a stun grenade through the opening, squinted sideways as it cracked off, and burst into the flat.

Two men in shirtsleeves were sitting at a table – or rather, they had been. By the time I entered the room they were half-way to their feet, staggering backwards in shock from the explosions.

'Stand still!' I yelled. 'Hands up!'

I saw immediately that the left-hand man was Barrakuda: a smaller version of Akula, with the same hollow cheeks, but younger, maybe in his late thirties, his features less haggard. He'd been taken completely by surprise. Before he could move two of our guys had him pinioned and cuffed with his hands behind his back. His companion was a big fellow, older and heavier, with stiff brown hair brushed up and back. He, too, was instantly overpowered.

Blue team, bursting through from the kitchen end of the flat, confirmed that there was nobody else in residence.

A rapid search proved that the device was not on the premises. We looked under beds, in cupboards, behind furniture: there was no recess large enough to conceal cases that size.

From out in the hallway I reported, 'Red leader. Flat secure. No casualties. Device not here. Repeat, device not here. Let's have the interpreter up soonest.'

Now I noticed two small suitcases standing by the wall inside the front door. I picked one up. The weight told me it was full. Back in the living room I saw that our prisoners' jackets were hanging on the backs of the chairs where they'd been sitting. On the table stood an open attaché case made of crocodile skin, which immediately reminded me of the Moscow apartment. This one contained only papers, but among them were two air tickets and two passports with green plastic covers.

The passports were issued by the Republic of Chechnya and made out in Cyrillic script, with Roman equivalents underneath the names. One belonged to Hussein Amadov, the other to Andrei Musayev. The photo showed that Barrakuda was using Musayev as a pseudonym. The Air Malta tickets were made out in the same names. The destination was Valetta, but the flight numbers and dates were so densely printed that I had to stare at them for a few seconds before I could make them out. Then I realised that the tickets were for 21 October – that very day – and that the departure was scheduled for 12.45 p.m. Eh, I said to myself. These guys were about to do a flit.

As I flicked through the documents, Barrakuda watched me without moving, but I could feel controlled hatred emanating from him. I was glad we had him cuffed. I still had my MP5 on its sling over my shoulder, so I moved in on him, jammed the muzzle into the front of his expensive-looking cream shirt and jerked it violently sideways, ripping off two buttons. Sure enough, under the hair on his scrawny chest was the tattoo of a long, slim fish.

'You speak English?'

He said nothing, but lifted both elbows outwards to mean, 'No.'

I gave him a crack on the right ear with the barrel of the weapon, and although the blow rocked his head sideways, he hardly flinched.

I turned to the big man and asked the same.

'A little.'

'Where's the bomb?'

He pretended not to understand. I repeated the question. Again it produced no answer. Then I heard a movement behind me, and there was Mike, the interpreter, in the doorway. Behind him I saw police officers moving in to evacuate the other flats.

'Tell this guy I know who he is.' I pointed at Barrakuda. 'His real name's Gaidar, Supyan Gaidar. Tell him I want to know where they've put the nuclear device.'

As I spoke the names, I saw a flicker of unease run through the prisoner.

Then Mike started in. His Russian was impressively fluent and fast, but it produced only a negative response.

'He doesn't know what you're talking about.'

'What's he doing here, then?'

This time the man did answer.

'He says he's here on business,' Mike translated. 'It's his first visit to London.'

'OK. Take a look at those papers on the table.'

Mike picked up a couple of sheets and scanned them briefly. 'They're about a shipment of goods from Valetta to Amsterdam.'

'Drugs, I bet.'

A telephone rang, right beside me.

'Pick it up,' I told Mike. 'Answer it in Russian.'

He lifted the receiver and said, '*Da?*' He listened briefly, went, '*Khorosho. Spasibo,*' and put the phone down. Barrakuda was glaring.

'What did they say?' I demanded.

' "Everything's in order. Precisely three hours from now." '

I checked my watch and said, 'Ten twenty-one. That gives us until thirteen twenty-one. Thirteen twenty.'

Immediately the phone rang again.

Again Mike said '*Da?*' and listened, but this time nobody spoke.

'Keep grilling him,' I told Mike. 'Back in a moment.'

I went through the shattered door on to the landing, out of earshot. I knew the telephone line had been tapped that morning so the spooks could trace the calls. Now that the flat was secure, the SAS ought by rights to hand control over to the police and get out; but I'd had another idea.

I jabbed my pressel and said, 'Red leader. I need to speak to the CO.'

'Here,' said the boss immediately.

I reported the calls and said, 'If they can trace the source, we need to hit it. But I've got another idea.'

'Carry on.'

'The Barrakuda guy's obviously trying to do a flit. He's got his flight out booked for this afternoon. But I'm sure he knows where the bomb is. He knows it's not far away, and that it's set to go off three hours from now. We could try beating hell out of him to get the information, but my hunch is that wouldn't work. On the other hand, if we just keep him on site, he's soon going to start shitting himself.'

'OK. I'll square it with the Director and the Police Commissioner that you remain on target. How many men do you need?'

'Red team will do fine.'

'All right. Blue can pull out, then. The QRF will remain on standby outside.'

'Roger.'

The six guys from Blue team disappeared down the stairs. I put two of our own lads to guard the back door of the flat, two outside the front door, on the landing, leaving myself, Darren Barnes and Mike the interpreter to harass the prisoners.

'Tell him he's not going to Malta,' I said. 'Tell him he's not going anywhere. He's staying here to enjoy his own little explosion.'

Mike translated. Barrakuda remained impassive but the big guy immediately began to look sick.

'Go through the briefcase,' I told Mike. 'Every bit of paper.' I turned to Darren and said, 'Get a brew on, for fuck's sake. See what you can find in the kitchen.'

He went out and rummaged in cupboards. 'There's tea,' he called, 'but no milk.'

'Black tea, then.'

The big guy started trying to say something to his partner. I waved at him to shut up and asked Mike, 'What was that?'

'Couldn't get it. Must have been Chechen.'

We hustled the two men to opposite ends of the room and sat them on chairs facing away from each other so that they couldn't communicate even with a look.

'Sugar?' shouted Darren from the kitchen.

'Three,' I called. 'Make it four.'

The scene had started to seem surreal. There were these two guys sitting handcuffed, back to back. Outside, London was enjoying a peaceful Sunday. Overhead, the cloud was breaking up, with occasional blue sky showing though. The odd jet went over on its way into Heathrow. Down in the street, cars accelerated as they headed north along Seymour Place.

Somewhere not far off, a nuclear device was ticking its way towards detonation.

I began to feel light-headed, almost as if I was floating.

Darren brought the tea. It was black as pitch and tasted like syrup, but it helped bring me back to reality. I got half the cup down my neck, then noticed some keys on the table beside the briefcase. One of them fitted the suitcase in the hall, but the luggage turned out innocent – spare suit and shirts, pyjamas, shaving kit.

Looking round the living room, I saw that it had old-fashioned mouldings, like fake panelling, on the walls, but that in an attempt to make it look more modern, somebody had put up large, abstract prints of geometrical designs, mostly black and white. The furniture was modern too, and expensive, the centrepiece a three-seat sofa covered in white hide.

Time crawled. After what seemed like an hour I found that only eighteen minutes had passed. I'd put my radio on listening watch, to conserve the battery.

Then, at 10.45, I got a double hiss and switched on again.

'Red leader,' I said.

'Your two calls.' It was Joe Darwent, the ops officer. 'The first was from a mobile. Sweeper vans are out, but it was too short for them to get a fix. The second call came from a house in St John's Wood, just north of you. Blue team are on their way there now.'

'Roger. What else is happening?'

'The top brass are meeting in the COBR. The Director's there, with the Home Secretary and a few others.'

'What about the police?'

'They've evacuated your block.'

'Is that all?'

'They're searching suspect houses, but they can't start mass evacuation unless they know where the device is. They might find they were moving people into a danger area.'

'Roger.'

For twenty minutes I sat on the window-sill and let silence go to work. With my covert radio switched on, I heard Blue leader reporting the arrival of his team at the location in Elm Tree Road, behind Lord's cricket ground. Quickly they deployed on both sides of the house and blasted their way in, only to find the place deserted. A search revealed no sign of the bomb.

At 12.10 the big guy began to get restless, shifting his arse around on his chair. At last he said something, which Mike translated. 'He wants to have a shit.'

'He can have a shit if he tells us where the bomb is.' It

288

sounded ridiculous, as though I was bargaining in an attempt to make some child behave well. 'Otherwise he can shit in his pants.'

The man was in obvious physical discomfort, which my answer only increased.

'Tell both of them there's only one way they're getting out of here,' I said to Mike. 'That's by giving us the information we want.'

Mike translated. Suddenly Barrakuda began to talk in Chechen at the top of his voice.

'Shut up!' I shouted – but he carried on regardless, even when I belted him across the side of the head. Soon he was yelling like a madman in a high, hoarse voice. The big guy began to bellow back, and all at once I felt glad, because I saw that stress was getting to the pair of them.

I left them to it, and from out on the landing I called Control. 'They've started arguing like lunatics,' I reported. 'Their nerve's going.'

'It had better break soon,' snapped Joe. 'Things are getting bloody fraught around here.'

'Same here,' I told him.

At 12.25 the big guy shat himself. The smell was repulsive, so I opened a window. Cold air blasted in, but it was better than the stink.

Barrakuda went quiet again. At 12.40, when I stood in front of him, his face looked white as flour, and his eyes seemed to have sunk into his head. After I'd watched him for a few seconds, he said something.

'He wants to make a deal,' Mike interpreted.

'Oh yes?'

'If he gives you the information, will you guarantee him free passage to Malta?'

'Fucking hell! Who does he think he is? Tell him not a chance. Not the remotest bloody chance.'

I waited while the information was conveyed. Then I ostentatiously ripped the lead out of the telephone and said, in a series of short sentences, waiting for Mike to translate each one. 'What's going to happen is this . . . The police have already evacuated the city . . . In ten minutes' time we're getting out too . . . We're not going to wait for the explosion . . . We're going to cuff you to your shitty friend, tie you up and leave you here . . . Talk now, or it'll be too late.'

That pushed him over the brink. He said something, and I saw Mike's eyes widen.

'What was that?' I snapped.

'He says the bomb is here.'

'Where?'

'In the garage below.'

'Jesus Christ! What garage? These flats don't have garages. We checked that.'

'In the small street behind.'

'What number?'

'Three.'

I hit my pressel. 'Red leader. What street is there immediately behind this block?'

'It's a mews,' said Joe instantly. 'Markham Mews. Why?'

'The bomb's there, in the garage.'

'Say that again.'

'Our prisoner says the bomb's there. In Number Three's garage. I'm coming down.'

I was already in the hall. 'Stay put!' I yelled to the rest of the team.' At the last moment I stuck my head back round the sitting-room door and said, 'Remember, nobody comes in here, and nobody's coming out of here alive.'

I couldn't wait for the lift. I took the stairs four or five at a time, heaving myself round the corners with the hand-rail. By the time I hit the street police sirens were screaming towards the block. A car nearly knocked me down as it swung into the mews. I was aware of a cordon in the distance, with a crowd behind it, and other figures running close to me.

There were the garages, built into little houses opposite the apartment block. One, two, three, numbering from the left. The third had bright blue wooden doors, freshly painted, with a white figure high on the right-hand side. The doors were secured with an old-fashioned hasp and padlock.

'Bolt-cutters!' I shouted. 'For fuck's sake, bolt-cutters!'

There was someone in black beside me, one of the QRF. Bolt-shears appeared in his hands. Two seconds later he had chopped through the soft metal guards around the padlock. I slid the bolt back, padlock and all, and dragged the doors open. The little garage was occupied by a beige-coloured van with the logo WEST END ANTIQUES painted in an elegant rainbow shape across its back doors.

Shit! I thought. Either Barrakuda was lying or he boobed on the number.

The guy from the QRF was more on the ball. He jumped forward, tried the doors, found they were locked, pushed his way between the right-hand side of the van and the brick wall, shone a torch through the driver's window and shouted, 'It's here!'

I was alongside him in an instant. There, in the back of the van, glinted a single, big, black object: Orange, with its two components united. From one corner, wires led to a red box just inside the rear doors.

My breath had gone. I hit my pressel and croaked, 'Red leader, we've found it. In Number Three garage. Locked inside a van.'

'DON'T TOUCH ANYTHING!' snapped a deep voice I didn't know. 'ATO here. We're on our way. Leave everything alone. Get clear of the site.'

We pushed back along the side of the van, trying not to rock it. In the doorway I looked up at the back of Markham Court, convinced that someone must have eyes on the site. More black-clad guys were hovering in the mews, hanging back from the target in uncharacteristic fashion. Their instincts were the same as mine – to go in and smash the timing device immediately. My watch said 1.13: we were within eight minutes of detonation. But they'd heard the ATO tell them to keep their distance, and they were wondering what the hell to do. It wasn't in our nature or training to run away – and in any case, there didn't seem much point. If the thing was about to go off, we'd never get far enough to make any difference.

What we did was to hustle back as far as the main road and tuck ourselves round the front of the apartment block, out of line of sight from the open garage doors. I tried to say something to the QRF guy, but words didn't come, my heart was pumping that fast.

This is fucking ridiculous! I thought. You get round the corner when you're cracking off an ordinary explosion. If *this* thing goes, we'll all be vapour and the building will simply vanish.

There wasn't long to wait or worry. Within seconds a van came screaming down the street. Its tyres squealed as it scorched round the corner into the mews and slid to a halt in front of the garage. Out jumped two men clad in white over-suits from head to toe, like astronauts. Each carried a heavy-looking hold-all full of kit.

'ATO on target,' the deep voice reported. 'Stand by.'

The lock on the van's rear doors held them up for all of five seconds. They flung the doors open and both leant in, on top of the live device, backs to us, reaching forward with their gloved hands. Fifty yards off, in full view, I stood transfixed, holding my breath. If it goes, I kept thinking, will I see the flash in the final split-second of life, or will the shock wave be too fast even for that?

The suspense was excruciating. I felt the whole world must be standing still, that everyone on earth had stopped breathing, like me. Mentally, I took off my hat to the two guys at the back of the van. By God they've got balls, I thought.

Then, after an incredibly short space of time, one of them stood up, turned round and raised both arms in triumph, as if he'd scored a goal. At the same moment I heard the deep voice say, 'Device made safe. Repeat: device made safe.'

I suppose I felt relief. I must have. But I don't remember it now. All I can recall is getting a sudden and intensely vivid mental image of the wretched sister device, Apple, sitting there in its hollowed-out niche beneath the Kremlin wall.

SEVENTEEN

On the plane to Moscow I had the unpleasant feeling that I'd gone back to the beginning and that the whole nightmare was about to start again. Flight number, departure time, type of aircraft, even the cabin crew – all were the same as on our recce trip.

Only I had changed. Instead of looking forward to a new experience and a bit of a lark, I was being driven by a personal compulsion at least as powerful as the jet engines thrusting us through the sky.

The morning papers carried no hint of the previous day's events: the media, thank God, had apparently not had a sniff of the drama in Markham Court and Mews. If they'd picked it up, they'd have had one hell of a story: LIVE NUCLEAR DEVICE DISCOVERED IN STOLEN VAN . . . GUN-BATTLE LEAVES TWO CHECHENS DEAD IN FLAT . . . SAS MAN LOSES FINGERS IN GROZNY TORTURE.

Wretched Toad! Word came up from the Services' hospital in London that surgeons had had to amputate the remains of both little fingers and the third finger on his left hand. When the Shark's men had realised that he was the one with knowledge of the bomb, they'd started in on him with bolt-shears, one joint at a time. But, tough little sod that he was, he'd given nothing away. Pavarotti, who wasn't seriously hurt, confirmed that he'd shown outstanding courage.

According to the headlines, international tension had eased. Even so, there were only about a dozen passengers on the 767. Feeling the need to relax, I got two miniatures of Haig off the drinks trolley, along with a can of soda water, and downed the

lot in a few minutes. The Scotch helped to lull my anxiety, and
when I stretched out across three seats with a blanket over my
head I soon fell asleep, and stayed unconscious for most of the
flight.

The arrival hall at Sheremetyevo was as dim and dire as ever,
but so few people were coming in that Immigration proved
relatively painless. Beyond the Customs, in contrast, the taxi
drivers swarmed even more voraciously than usual. Hardened to
their methods, I stood still until I spotted a short man waiting at
the back of the scrum. He had an open, friendly face, a neatly
trimmed red beard, and was wearing a peaked, dark-blue cap.
Instead of screaming at me, he was smiling.

I pushed through the mob and said, 'OK. Let's go.'

Outside, the cold bit, and I was surprised to see a dusting of
snow on the ground. My guide led the way to a clean-looking
grey Zhigudi and held one of the back doors open for me.

'Thanks,' I said. 'But I'll come in front.'

I settled in the passenger seat and asked, 'What's your name?'

'Sergei.'

'You speak English?'

'Some.' He gave a deprecating grin. 'City centre?'

'No. I want to go to Balashika.'

'Balashika!' He sounded amazed.

'Balashika first. Then city centre. Then back to Balashika.
How much will all that cost?'

'Dollars?'

I nodded. As he pulled out on to the highway, I could see his
mind ticking up figures. 'One hundred fifty.'

'I'll give you two hundred.'

'*Khorosho!*'

He drove fast but well, not taking risks, but watching all the
time for openings in the traffic, and taking short-cuts to avoid
the blocks at major intersections. When I praised his navigation,
he answered in quite fluent English. We chit-chatted about this
and that, and when I asked how old he was, he suddenly, with
a flourish and a big grin, whipped off his cap to reveal that he
was almost completely bald. 'Feefty!' he exclaimed. I refrained

from saying that without his hat he bore a strong resemblance to Lenin, but I felt that if I had, he wouldn't have given a damn.

He took the outer ring-road, round the north perimeter of the city. Out in the country there seemed to be more snow, and although the main road was clear, the ground was uniformly white.

As we approached Balashika I felt my anxiety building. I hadn't quite worked out how I was going to handle my re-entry into the camp. The time was 6.30 p.m., and the chances were that the team would be back indoors for the night.

Taxis weren't allowed inside the barracks, so I asked Sergei to wait outside the gate. Luckily the guy on the barrier recognised me, and even greeted me cheekily as *Starik* - Old Man.

I ran up the steps of the barrack block in some trepidation, but again I was in luck. The guys had eaten supper early and gone out again to run a night exercise. Only the two scalies were in residence. I had a word with them, and said I'd be back later. Then it was just a matter of collecting basic essentials from the caving kit: wire ladder, head-torch and bolt cutters, plus a towel, sweater and spare padlocks from my own locker.

In fifteen minutes we were heading back into town, down the all-too-familiar Shosse Entusiastov, past the scene of the fatal ambush. As we went by, I twisted to my left in an attempt to pinpoint the spot. Yes – there was the wooden hut the Mafia had used as a decoy GAI station.

Going against the flow of traffic, we reached the centre of Moscow in thirty-five minutes. Sergei must have been curious about what I was doing, but he had the sense or the good manners not to enquire. I asked him to head for Sofieskaya Quay, and got him to drop me a hundred metres short of the churchyard gateway, at a point where an alleyway ran back between two houses.

'Half an hour, back here,' I said.

'Is good.' He peered at his watch. 'Now seven-thirty. Back eight o'clock?'

'*Tochno.* See you then.'

I was confident he'd return, because so far I'd paid him

nothing, and I liked him the more for not having demanded the first instalment of his fee at half-time.

I walked a few steps down the alleyway and waited till I heard the car move off. Then I came back on to the embankment and hurried to the gateway.

Now, early in the evening, lights were on all over the convent building. Scarcely had I entered the yard when two women came walking towards me; but they passed without giving me a look, and a couple of seconds later I was safe in the pitch blackness of the old stable.

The bolt-cutters gave me sickening thoughts of Toad, but they did their work in a trice. I lifted the cover of the shaft, secured the top wires of the caving ladder round the hinges, and threw the rest of it down. Because of the wires, I couldn't close the cover while I was underground, but that was a risk I had to take.

Down in the tunnel the smell was exactly as I remembered it: damp, slime, decay. Of course I was scared – but in my experience the best way to hold fear at bay is to keep moving, so I hurried forward towards the river, anxious to discover if the water level was up or down. It was up. It was within three or four inches of the arched roof. Jesus! I should have brought a mask and dry-suit.

Too late now. At the top of the slope I stripped off my clothes and left them in a heap on top of my shoes. Then, with the head-lamp back on and the bolt-cutters in my right hand, I waded into the black flood.

The water was cold as ice. I gasped as it reached my crotch, but strode forward hard in an attempt to keep my blood moving. Quickly my whole body became submersed. I made paddling movements with my hands to speed my progress. Soon I was up to my neck, then up to my chin. Down came the roof, down, down. I reached the point at which, with the top of my head touching the bricks, my mouth was under water and my nose just entering it. From now on the only way I could breathe was by tilting my head back and turning my face upwards in the narrow airspace. To do that I had to push the headlamp on to the back of my head so that it didn't foul the roof.

I took a deep breath, ducked under and drove forward, five steps, ten. Desperate for oxygen, I came up in that peculiar attitude, hit the roof with the headlamp, pushed it back, gasped in a breath and inadvertently got half a mouthful of filthy liquid. When I choked explosively, all the grot flew upwards and came back down in my face. The setback left me gasping. For a few seconds I fought panic. Keep still! I told myself. Get yourself together.

With my mouth shut, I took in some air through my nose. Then to my dismay I realised that in going for the headlamp I'd dropped the shears. I felt around with my bare feet. No contact. Had I moved forward a short distance while struggling for air? I shuffled back a few inches and felt around again. Still nothing.

The cold was getting to me. I could feel my legs starting to go numb. If you piss about here any longer, you're going to get cramp and bloody drown yourself, I thought. Leave the damned things. You can manage without them.

I waded on. Then, after one more stop for air, the water level began to drop. My head came clear: once again I could walk and breathe normally.

I came out of the flood shuddering, adjusted the lamp with shaking hands, and ran naked the last few yards to the site. Everything was as we'd left it. Scrabbling with chilled fingers, I dug away some of the spoil under which we'd buried Apple, until I came to the co-ax cables leading down from the SCR. I remembered how carefully Toad had connected them up, tightening nuts with his special spanners. Now I took hold of one in both hands and gave a big wrench. The cable held. I cleared more of it, right down to its junction with the black case, and heaved again, so hard that the whole device shifted, and pieces of spoil tumbled down the front of the heap.

Again I was on the verge of panic. Nothing on earth would persuade me to go back and search for the bolt-cutters again. One last effort: a colossal jerk, and away the cable came, so suddenly that I hurtled back into the far wall of the tunnel, grazing my right shoulder.

297

I stood shaking, more from fright now than from cold. At least the effort of struggling with the cable had warmed me up.

'Right, you fucker,' I said out loud to the bomb. 'That's you knackered.'

Into the water again. This time the same breathing technique got me through without swallowing any sludge. By sod's law, I expected to tread on the bolt-cutters, now that I no longer needed them, but I missed them again. Back at my clothes, I looked at my watch and found I had ten minutes to make the rendezvous. I towelled off furiously, got dressed, stuffed the sodden towel into my day-sack and hauled myself up the ladder, pausing with my head out the top of the shaft to make sure that everything was clear. Finally I slipped two new padlocks into position, wrapped the old ones in the towel, and crept out of the courtyard into the street.

The wide embankment was clear of cars and pedestrians. I nipped across the road, threw the old locks into the river, and hurried back to the far pavement. I was still walking towards the mouth of the alleyway when Sergei's car came towards me; but by then I was a safe distance from the church.

All the way back to Balashika I was uncomfortably aware that I stank like a sewer rat. But Sergei made no comment, and when I paid him off at the barrack gate I gave him twenty dollars over the odds, so that he went off in high good humour.

My own schedule was tight, but possible. The lads were still out on their night exercise, so there was no need for explanations. My first date with Anna had gone down the tubes; but under our new arrangement she had agreed to pick me up at 8.45, so I just had time for a shower. One hell of a shower it had to be, too. I washed my hair twice to get rid of the smell, and as I scoured myself all over, I felt my spirits lifting.

The worst part of the evening was over. What lay ahead I wasn't sure, but at least there was a promise of some action and excitement.

Comfortable in clean clothes, I again left word with the scalies and headed for the guardroom. I'd asked Anna not to drive in, in case any of the lads saw her and started taking the piss, and I found her sitting outside at the wheel of her little blue Fiat. As I climbed into the passenger seat I got a kiss on the cheek and a waft of heady scent – not the cheap rubbish that the slappers at the hotel had been doused in, but something sophisticated and Western. In the dim light I couldn't see exactly what she was wearing, except that it was a trouser suit. She had a big fur coat thrown back off her shoulders, over the seat.

'Great to see you!' I went. 'Great of you to come. Where are we going?'

'A restaurant called the Taiga.' She turned and gave me a peculiar look, not quite mocking, but definitely amused. 'That's not your kind of tiger, by the way.' She spelled the word out and said, 'It means the forest in Siberia, the wild forest. The restaurant's only a small place. No tourists ever go there. But it has proper Russian food.'

'Sounds good,' I said. 'In fact, it sounds tremendous. I haven't eaten all day.'

'Well,' she said, as she zipped through the gears, 'tell me the story.'

'Sasha must have told you already.'

'He has. But I want to hear your version.'

'You will. But I won't bore you with it yet. Wait till we get there. I need a drink to get me going.'

'All right. It's not far.'

Once again we sped down that damned road, then cut away through the northern edge of the city. I complimented her on the car, on her driving, on her clothes (even though I couldn't see them) – anything to avoid plunging into the saga, because I was afraid that once I'd started, everything would come out.

My mind was whirling as Anna pulled up in a scruffy side-street.

'Here we are,' she announced.

A small, red sign proclaiming TAIGA glowed faintly above a battered wooden door. If you hadn't known what the place was you'd never have given it a second glance. But inside it was like a forest growing in a cave: real tree-trunks, some birch, some pine, divided up little cubicles from each other, and the ceiling was a riot of branches. The air was warm and full of a wonderfully rich, meaty smell.

The waiters were dressed in forest green. From the way one of them sprang forward to take Anna's coat, I saw that she was a star guest. Another man showed us straight to a table in a corner cubicle: he ushered Anna into her chair and held a brief conversation as he poured out two glasses of vodka from a bottle already sitting in an ice-bucket on the table. That was apparently all the ordering she needed to do: no question of menu or wine list.

She raised her glass and said, '*Poyekhali!*'

'What's that?'

'It means "Bottoms up" when you're drinking vodka. It's what Gagarin said when he was about to go into space – "Let's get moving."'

'*Poyekhali*, then.' I clinked my glass on hers, and we both drank. Now I saw that her suit was made of turquoise shot-silk, and that she was wearing a pearl necklace. For the first time since I'd met her, she'd put on visible make-up – not much, but enough to accentuate her good features. She had darkened her eyebrows slightly, which made her eyes look bigger, and a touch of lipstick made her mouth seem more generous. She'd washed her hair, too, and done it so that it stood up in a shiny black curve above her forehead.

'Have some caviar,' she said. 'It's the best thing with vodka.'

She took the lid off a white pot cradled in a bed of ice, revealing a nest of shiny black eggs underneath. At that moment a waiter arrived with a dish of hot toast wrapped in a napkin.

'Please!' she said. 'Dig in. Is that the right expression?'

'Spot on!' I dug deep with a teaspoon, and heaped caviar on to the toast – the best mouthful I'd ever eaten. More vodka, more caviar. She too seemed hungry, eating and drinking level with me. I don't usually pay much attention to food, but the salty fish eggs and ice-cold spirit were such a combination that for a few minutes I really had to concentrate on my taste buds.

'Don't overdo it,' Anna said presently, again with that amused glint in her eyes. 'There are other things coming – Siberian specialities.'

'Why all this Siberia suddenly?'

'That's where I come from.'

'Really!' I looked at her with new interest. 'Tell me.'

She began to talk, quite fast, about how she'd been born in a village called Charysh, three thousand kilometres east of Moscow, in the Altai mountains – a primitive community, without electricity in those days, and most of the houses made of wood. Her family had been dirt-poor, but her father was the local schoolmaster, and when Anna had showed intellectual promise at the age of nine, he'd sent her to live with an aunt and uncle in the capital so that she could get a better education.

The waiter brought us hot plates and a bowl from which steam rose in clouds, but Anna was so immersed in her narrative that she didn't immediately notice. Then, breaking out of her reverie, she said, 'Look! *Pilmeni* – dumplings with spiced meat. And this is special cabbage, cooked with walnuts.'

She helped herself and started to eat, but in a vague manner, not focusing on the delicious food. Her mind was out in the mountains and forests, and on she went, talking, talking, as she recalled how the River Charysh froze over in winter, so thick that army trucks could drive across it, and how, when the snow came, it would blanket the land a metre deep for four or five months on end.

Red wine had appeared on the table. I drank some, and kept eating. The little dumplings were irresistible. I lost count of the number I put away as I listened to her stories, fascinated to see a different, softer, more vulnerable person emerging from the tough chrysalis which was all I'd known so far.

Soothing taped music was playing, no more than a gentle background drone. But suddenly, as a new song started, Anna gave a twitch and cried, 'Oh! This one I love.' With a flick of the hand she bade one of the waiters turn up the volume, and the sound swelled into that of a male-voice choir, with a single, clear tenor reaching high above a groundswell of sonorous basses.

To my amazement, I saw her eyes fill with tears. For my benefit she began to translate the story, speaking low and fast as each haunting phrase of the song came to an end. 'A man is running through the taiga . . . He follows the tracks of wild animals . . . A storm is blowing . . . His way is long . . . Hide him in your breast, dark taiga . . . Far away he has left his native land, his mother, his wife and children . . . He will die in a foreign land and be buried there . . . His wife will find someone else . . . But his mother will never find another son.'

By the end, the tears were rolling down her cheeks. I reached over and covered her hand with mine. She looked up, smiled and gave a great shudder. Then she brought out a handkerchief and wiped her eyes.

'I'm sorry. The song is very sad.'

'I could hear that.'

'It reminds me of many things.'

'Anna,' I said instinctively. 'Why have you never married?'

The question seemed to jerk her back to the present. She raised her eyebrows and said, 'Married? I *am* married. My son is ten years old.'

I stared at her in amazement. 'You never told me.'

'Why should I?' She looked amused again. 'That's nothing to do with my professional career.'

'No, but . . . Where is your husband?'

'In Petersburg. He manages a bank there. We drifted apart years back.'

'And your son?'

'Mitya? He's at school here in Moscow. He lives mostly with his aunt, my sister.'

'Where's he tonight?'

'Who?'

'Mitya.'

'With his aunt.'

'And your husband?'

'In the north.'

She was looking at me steadily. 'Geordie,' she said. 'I've sent a message to your people at Balashika to say you'll be there in

302

the morning. You're coming back to my apartment, to spend the night with me.'

'Fantastic!' I took a deep breath. These revelations seemed to be the cue for me to open up. God knows what it was that made me decide to confess. Now that I'd disconnected Apple, there was no need or logical reason to reveal anything. Yet I knew in my heart that I had to do it. Otherwise, my conscience would never let me rest. It wasn't as if I'd reached this conclusion under the influence of alcohol: all this I'd worked out earlier, when I was stone-cold sober.

'Listen,' I said, looking round our little cubicle. 'I don't suppose the KGB have got this place bugged.'

'Of course not!' She grinned mischievously. 'You're probably the first foreigner that's ever come here. It wouldn't be worth their while.'

'Then I've got something to tell you.'

In the next few minutes I went overboard. I dived in headlong and told her all I knew about Apple and Orange. My mind was moving at incredible speed. I was vaguely aware of waiters removing plates and bringing tea, but I ignored them and rattled on, spilling secrets left and right. Even as I talked, I knew I was betraying my mates, the Regiment, my country, and that I was probably bringing my career in the army to a rapid end. But the accumulation of guilt had become too great to bear, and the act of freeing myself from it brought a feeling of fantastic liberation. I finished on a high, amazed at myself, but exhilarated.

Throughout my performance Anna had watched me as if half-hypnotised. She kept absolutely still, with her eyes fixed on me; yet after a while I realised that she was registering neither surprise nor anger. As before, her predominant expression was one of faint amusement.

When finally I came to a halt, she said, 'You need some cognac,' and signalled to the waiter, who brought two small glasses and a bottle.

'Armenian brandy,' Anna announced. 'Your famous Prime Minister used to say it was the best.'

'Tony Blair?'

'Don't be ridiculous! Winston Churchill. Cheers!'

We clinked glasses, and I drained mine straight down.

'Aren't you furious with me?' I asked.

'Why should I be?'

'For having double-crossed you all this time.'

'You weren't being very clever about it.'

'You mean you knew what we were doing?'

'Not exactly. But we knew you had some secret agenda.'

'How?'

'Every time you went to the Embassy you were followed.'

'Jesus! But not into the churchyard?'

She shook her head. 'We lost you there.'

'What about that time we went up to the university and we got chased?'

'Those were some of our people.'

'Were they hurt?'

'One was killed.'

'I'm sorry.'

I poured myself some more brandy.

'But when the bomb was lifted – that wasn't you?'

'No – that was the Mafia all right. But Geordie – the Americans will realise that Apple isn't responding to signals. In fact, they must already know something's wrong. What if you get an order tomorrow, telling you to go down and check the device?'

'I'll tell my people at home it's impossible. I'll say the churchyard's been compromised, that the head of the shaft is under guard.'

Her eyes were holding mine.

'Listen,' I said. 'What were you doing that day you came poking your nose into our lap-top?'

She threw back her head and laughed. '*That!* A throwback to my old habits, I suppose: a little private espionage. Of course I was curious to find out more about what you were all doing.'

'But you never got into the program?'

She shook her head.

'What'll you do now?' I asked. 'Now I've told you?'

'Nothing.' This time it was her hand that took hold of mine. 'We'll keep this between us. If you've killed the bomb, that's it. There's no point telling my bosses. They'd only go mad and stir everything up again on the international front. By the way – can I have some more of that?'

She pointed at the bottle. I started and apologised, filling her glass again.

'Besides,' she said, 'it's not as if our own consciences are all that clear.'

I stared at her. 'What the hell do you mean by that?'

'Compact nuclear devices,' she said teasingly. 'CNDs. They are not the exclusive property of the West.'

'You mean . . . you don't mean you've done this to us already?'

'That's rather a crude way of putting it.'

'Are you saying there are CNDs buried under London?'

'Not necessarily *buried*.'

'How many, for God's sake?'

'I'll have to check, but I think the last count was five. I acted as liaison officer on an operation in 1993, when two went in.'

Suddenly I felt punch-drunk – not intoxicated, but rather as though I'd taken too much punishment.

'I don't know what to say,' I began feebly.

'Don't say anything. That's enough talk for tonight.'